SHADES OF GREY

BY

CARON HARRISON

Published by

Caron Harrison
Ballabunt Croft
Cooil Road
BRADDAN
Isle of Man
IM4 2AQ

ISBN 0 9531155 0 X

Produced by
Axxent Ltd
The Old Council Offices, The Green,
DATCHET,
Berkshire, SL3 9EH

ACKNOWLEDGEMENTS

Thanks are due to my husband, Nigel, for his unfailing support and help with the word processor, to my family and friends who read the early versions, to Hildegard Becker for her hospitality and help with location research, to Mr Eric Hollowday of Aylesbury, and to the Hay-on-Wye bookshops for supplying exactly what I needed. Lastly I wish to express my gratitude to my late father, who finally made this all possible.

WHITE

CHAPTER ONE

The familiar shove between his shoulder blades woke him from the nightmare. Taking a deep, shuddering breath, Karl Driesler lay still for a moment, then leaned over the side of the bunk to peer into the darkness below.

"*Danke*," he whispered to the unseen form lying there.

"*Bitte*," came Döttinger's automatic reply.

Döttinger had tried unsuccessfully to change bunks, to escape from his duty as keeper of the peace at night. But only his ears were tuned in to the warning sounds, the grunts and muffled moans which were preliminaries to the full-blown yells that could wake the whole hut. At the first sounds of distress he would push his fist up between the slats of the upper bunk and give a mighty shove. It took a lot to wake Driesler from a nightmare, but it was worth the effort.

Rolling over onto his left side, Karl concentrated on breathing slowly and steadily, trying to dispel the awful images from his mind. Tonight it was the grinning faces, taunting him with knives. Döttinger had woken him just as one of them was about to slit his throat. He rubbed his neck where he could still feel the pressure of the knife. At least it had not been his worst nightmare, when the black walls closed in, slowly suffocating him with darkness until he woke up fighting for breath. It had all happened over three years ago, but still the nightmares returned remorselessly, night after night after night.

Licking his dry lips he stared at a model ketch suspended from the rafters out of harm's way. A fellow prisoner, formerly a Baltic fisherman, had been constructing it from used matches and other scrounged items since the end of the war. Eighteen months later it was now finished, complete with rigging, sails, anchor, and his wife's name – Katerina – proudly painted on the transom. Karl focused his thoughts on the moonlit ketch, blotting out the darker images threatening from his subconscious.

He had never been sailing; a troop-carrying ship to Norway and his passage as a prisoner of war across from Belgium were his sole experiences of the sea. Nevertheless he could imagine himself standing on the rolling deck, salt wind in his hair, the raucous shrieks of gulls circling overhead, the excited shrieks of a spray-soaked Ilse at his side.

Ilse. She had always promised to take him to her home in Hamburg and for a sail on her father's small yacht. He pictured her fine, silver-blonde hair matted with salt, her soft skin lightly dusted with salt crystals, her lips flavoured by them as he kissed her on that heaving sea. He surrendered his mind to the image; he was there, with her, free. For a few minutes he escaped from the hut at Upper Claydon, Herefordshire. From the guilt. Until the taste of salt became real as tears rolled down his hollow cheeks into his mouth. He licked them away, watching the *Katerina* sail off into the moonlight, taking his dreams of Ilse with her.

The news from home still had not sunk in. She had deserted him. Why hadn't she waited? Why had she gone and married someone else? Didn't she know it was her name he had called out so often when he thought he was going to die or lose his mind? She had kept him alive – kept him sane. Now she was gone.

A cloud covered the moon, plunging the hut into darkness, condemning him to the real world. The nightmare world.

The October morning broke dull and misty. Karl hunched his shoulders as he crossed the open ground from the tiny canteen which served the hostel at Upper Claydon. Oblivious to the morning chill, two grinning prisoners stood with their kitbags by the hostel gates. They were the first to be repatriated. Karl knew he would be one of the last. He strode briskly into the hut, made his bed and prepared himself for the day's work. He was just grabbing his overcoat when Döttinger rushed in from breakfast, late as usual.

The cocky Berliner noticed his bunk-mate's gloomy expression. "Cheer up, Driesler. It may never happen!"

Karl ignored him and stepped back out into the damp air, soon to be joined by the other eleven members of the work party. Döttinger excepted, they all seemed gloomy, all affected by the imminent departure of the two lucky men who were captured early in the war, had enjoyed a safe, cosy existance during it, and were now rewarded for their good fortune by an early release. The two were to share the same lorry as the work party for the start of their long journey home. Instead of the usual rousing Wagnerian chorus there was silence as the lorry careered down the narrow lanes. Karl looked down at the floor, not wanting to make eye-contact with the men gaining their freedom. He only raised his eyes when the lorry drew to a halt. Outside the canvas flaps he could see rows of neatly-pruned fruit-trees.

"Everybody out," he called, then remembered the pair with their kitbags. "Except you two lucky swine. Safe journey!"

"Thanks," they beamed. "Same to you when it's your turn."

Karl jumped down from the lorry. As it pulled away there were cries of "Good luck!" and "Give my love to Stuttgart!" from the men around him. Karl stood by, silently watching the lorry depart then suddenly stiffened, aware of being watched. Waiting for them by the gateway was a short, stocky man in his fifties, accompanied by a Border Collie. Karl approached cautiously, but the dog seemed friendly enough. The farmer too.

"You in charge?" he asked Karl.

Karl noticed a wheeziness in the farmer's breath. "Yes, sir. You must be Mr Carter. I am Karl Driesler. I speak some English – not well, but enough."

"Ah, right." David Carter nearly held out his hand, but realised in time such a greeting was not appropriate, probably not even allowed. Nevertheless, he could not help adding: "Welcome to Lane Head Farm ... Karl? Is that right?"

Karl smiled and nodded. "Yes, sir." He knew from experience these first few minutes were crucial. If they could establish a good rapport then the week would go smoothly. Otherwise their employer could make their lives hell.

7

David Carter returned the smile. "Right. Follow me and I'll show you what to do."

He led them into the orchard. By the hedge stood a large wagon stacked with crates. Beside it were ladders and sturdy baskets. "There should be enough to go round," he told Karl. "This lot should keep you busy for at least a day or two, then you can move on to the next orchard." He waved vaguely towards a distant gateway. "If you need me, I'll be somewhere in the meadows with the sheep or up at the house there." This time he pointed up the hillside to where Karl could see rooftops over the brow of a sheep-dotted meadow.

Whilst they were talking the other men had deposited their overcoats and crate of provisions on the wagon. David noticed the crate's meagre contents and frowned. "That won't keep you going all day. Look, I know I'm not supposed to, but I'll get my daughter to bring you down something extra. Can't have you not working properly, can I?"

Karl saw the twinkling eyes and warmed to this kindly man. "Thank you, Mr Carter. We will work hard for you."

It was not an idle boast and it seemed Mr Carter knew it. "Good. I'll leave you to it. I'll come and check on you later. See how you're doing."

He ambled off, closely followed by the black and white dog. Karl could hear the farmer's wheezing breath drifting through the grey mist until he was nearly out of sight. David Carter's state of health was none of his concern, however. Hoisting a ladder onto his shoulder, basket in hand, he went to join the others. He was happiest when working, when he could set his mind to a task. It was why he learned English so readily. Unable to speak any when first captured, he could now hold a reasonable conversation. It was good to work and think of other things. Try to forget the past. Try to forget Ilse.

Through the leaves of the apple tree, Karl could see the approaching horse. Its rider wore a faded green headscarf, but enough of her curls protruded to reveal they were the same chestnut colour as her horse. Balanced on the saddle in front of her was a cloth-covered basket. The horse turned in through the gateway, confirming Karl's deductions. Food! He clambered down the ladder, silently crossing the thick, damp grass as the farmer's daughter unloaded the basket onto the wagon then dismounted, unaware of his approach.

"Miss Carter?"

He saw her jump, look up anxiously and quickly step back a pace. It was a natural response, one he had seen many times, but it still hurt. He knew he looked rather skeletal with his hollow cheeks and dark-ringed eyes but it was not his appearance which frightened. No, it was the label, the yellow patch on his back and right thigh proclaiming him a monster, a German.

To her credit she rapidly conquered, or hid, her fear. "Yes, I'm Katherine Carter." Her voice was low but reasonably confident. "My father asked me to bring you these." She turned to the basket and pulled back the cloth covering a nest of freshly-baked potatoes.

"Thank you." Karl smiled reassuringly as he gave a brief formal bow, then turned on his heel to round up his men.

They were not slow to heed his summons. Katherine was soon serving potatoes and mugs of tea to the twelve ravenous men. Eighteen months ago these men were Britain's enemies. What were they now? She found herself studying their faces as they thanked her. It was difficult to put an age to many of them. Two were clearly boys of seventeen or eighteen. She wondered how old they could have been when they first became soldiers. The other men seemed considerably older, their world-weary expressions reminding her of Robert Murdoch, the village doctor's son. But these men could never have suffered like poor Robert at the hands of his captors. Poor Robert who suffered still.

Turning her back on the men to wipe the moistness from her eye, she noticed the filled crates stacked neatly on the wagon beside a heap of yellow-patched overcoats, reminding her of previous, Italian prisoners. Everybody said the Germans were far more industrious than the Italians had ever been. Katherine remembered what one of the guards once told her: "We work harder trying to make these Eytie buggers work than they do themselves!"

No guards now, Katherine remembered, trying to curb a flicker of apprehension.

Once they had their food and tea, the men politely ignored her, some lighting cigarettes. One young lad stroked Beth's nose with a familiarity which showed his love of horses. Forgetting all her previous fears, Katherine picked up an apple and held it out to the lad, indicating he should feed it to Beth. Youthful exuberance overcame him. He gabbled something to Katherine, grinning broadly at her.

The prisoner who had spoken to her earlier stepped closer. He reminded her of a scarecrow, with his bony hands hanging loosely from his battledress jacket, and his straw-like hair just visible under his cap. For a moment Katherine thought he would reprimand the boy; instead he translated his words.

"It is a beautiful horse. Ulrich wants to know how old it is."

"She's fifteen." Katherine returned Ulrich's smile. She felt perfectly relaxed and quite forgot the rule forbidding conversing with prisoners. "Have you any horses of your own?"

Karl translated her question, although Ulrich proudly answered for himself in English. "Two."

They chatted about farm life until the tea break was over, Karl acting as interpreter. Then, at a word from him, the men returned to work. He held Beth's head while Katherine mounted, then handed up the empty basket.

"Thank you for the food, Miss Carter."

Katherine was struck by the sadness in his troubled grey eyes. "You're welcome. I'm sorry it wasn't more." She was surprised how much she meant it.

During her ride back up to the farmhouse, Katherine found herself thinking about the men working in the orchards. For some strange reason she felt sorry for them, stranded here still, so far away from home.

David Carter stepped into Donald Murdoch's surgery and greeted his friend with a warm handshake. The doctor was

David's contemporary, but his pale, balding head contrasted markedly with David's thick, wavy hair and wind-scoured face. Originally from Edinburgh, Donald Murdoch had moved down to Herefordshire with Gertie his wife thirty years ago. His Scottish accent had mellowed over the years, but his origins were still noticeable in the lilt and burr of his speech.

"So how's your ticker today, David?" Donald knew full well why his friend had called. "Let's have a wee listen."

After his examination, Donald looked grave. "Sit down a moment, David. You know, you're not going to live to see your grandchildren if you don't get some more help on that farm. How'll you manage when young Captain Kellett returns from serving King and country to take Katherine as his bride? Have you given it any thought?"

David grimaced at the prospect. He buttoned his shirt clumsily with his heavy fingers. "Of course I have, Donald, but until Sarah finishes university I simply can't afford to pay anyone. She has only this year to go; Katherine won't be getting married until July. I'll find someone then."

Donald Murdoch shook his head firmly. "You need help *now*, David, not in ten months. You really ought to have found a replacement for Evan Hughes last year. I know shepherds are hard to come by these days, but in your condition you can't expect to keep working as hard as you do."

He sat back, his hands spread across his waistcoat, but seeing his friend's despondent face, decided some encouragement was necessary. He leaned forward abruptly, his hands slapping the desk.

"You'll find someone, I'm sure of it. It would be a great opportunity for a man who wanted to learn farming, without having to run any risks himself. There must be plenty leaving the Forces right now who would jump at such an opportunity."

"That's as maybe, Donald," David Carter replied cautiously. "I don't want anyone so wet behind the ears he doesn't know one end of a sheep from the other. I'd spend all my time hovering over him, making sure he didn't do anything foolish." David's fingers beat a tattoo on the desk top as he considered the problem. "I'd want to be able to trust the man implicitly to get on with the job. Only then could I allow myself to rest and not worry constantly. How can I attract a reliable man when I can't afford to pay a decent wage? A young man would expect more than I ever paid old Evan."

The doctor was suddenly almost dismissive. "Seek and ye shall find, David! I wish you good hunting."

On Tuesday morning rain fell solidly, forcing the Germans to shelter in the barn. David found them odd jobs: chopping logs, repairing sheep hurdles and the bottom panel of the stable door. Young Ulrich got to clean Beth's tack.

As soon as the rain stopped the men returned to the orchards and David had the chance to inspect their handiwork. He was pleased with their efforts; nothing shoddily done or botched. With a satisfied smile, he returned to the house and spent a large part of the afternoon on the telephone, but it was not until mid-morning the next day that he revealed his plans to Katherine.

He found her washing clothes in the outhouse. He perched himself on the edge of a small table covered in damson-filled Kilner-jars and studied the steaming wash-tub.

"I think I've found a temporary solution to our labour problem, Beauty. Subject to your agreement, of course. It should tide us over for at least a year, by which time Sarah should be standing on her own two feet."

Katherine looked up from the wash-tub, surprised her consent was required. "Oh? What is this great plan of yours?" She blew a stray lock of hair out of her eye. "I'm sure I'll agree to whatever you have in mind, Daddy."

Her father took a deep breath and prepared to drop his bombshell. "I've asked the Labour Officer at Kingshill Camp if we can employ a POW to help out here after the apple harvest. I've been impressed with their work, good sense and reliability." He finished in a rush, eager to hear her reaction. "I

12

would have a useful worker for the minimum rate of pay. What do you think?"

Katherine was dumbfounded. "My goodness!" was all she could find to say. She gave herself a moment to mull it over. It seemed to be such a simple solution to such a weighty problem. "Presumably your request was granted?"

"In principle, yes; but with one proviso."

"Oh yes? And what was that?"

"He would have to live here," David explained. "They can't spare the lorry to bring him over every day from the hostel at Upper Claydon."

Katherine nodded slowly. Soap suds slid gently down her hands into the tub. She voiced her immediate concern. "Sarah's not going to like it, is she?"

"Is that your only objection?"

"Well, I suppose so. But it's no small matter, is it? You know what Sarah's like! When she hears she's going to have to sleep under the same roof as a German, she'll go berserk!"

"Sarah is only home for a few weeks of the year. She'll leave home for good, come the summer." David stood up and went to look out of the window onto the yard. "Besides, he'll be sleeping in your old play room over the feed store. It's a bit draughty, but he won't expect the Ritz. He'll have his privacy and we'll have ours." He turned back to face his daughter. "I do want your approval on this, Beauty. You're the one who's going to have an extra mouth to feed."

Katherine picked up a shirt, spread a cuff on the wooden drainer and began to scrub. "If you'd asked me a week ago I would have said definitely not. But now, having met them, it seems sensible. As long as whoever comes is reliable."

"I don't think you need worry about that. You've already met him."

"Oh? Really?"

"Yes. I actually asked for one in particular. There was some delay while they checked his suitability or something. The call I had just now gave the go-ahead." David warmed to his subject. "Someone will be out tomorrow to look at our accommodation. We'll have to put a camp bed and a bit of furniture in there. He can wash here in the outhouse and use the bath once a week."

Katherine could not suppress a wry smile. So much for her agreement being sought. This was a *fait accompli*! And what about the German concerned? Did he have any say?

"Which one did you ask for? Scarecrow?"

Her father grinned at the description. "Yes. His name's Karl. He and I get on just fine. And he's keen." He remembered he was asking her opinion. "You're sure you won't mind?"

Katherine reflected for a moment. It was a big step to share their home with any stranger, let alone 'the enemy'; Sarah's reaction was certain to be stormy. She sighed. "I can't say I won't mind. We'll just have to get used to him though, won't we?"

"Indeed we will. I have a feeling there's more to Karl than meets the eye." He sensed her immediate anxiety and sought to reassure her. "Don't get me wrong, Beauty. I trust him completely. No, I ... I just feel there's something ..."

"Something troubling him?"

"So you've noticed it too."

CHAPTER TWO

On Monday 28th October Karl Driesler dropped his kit-bag onto the bare floorboards of his new room. He studied the plain but adequate furnishings with all the interest of a man who had not had a room to himself for far too long. Before the war he had shared with his younger brother, Rudi, but during it their spells of leave had never coincided. Now he relished his freedom once again from the noise, smells and habits of other men.

He took a good look around. He was surprised to find the room wired up to the electricity supply. Many farms he worked on had no electrical supply at all, yet here even an outhouse had modern lighting. David Carter struck Karl as a man who moved with the times, even if the farm did have a certain air of neglect.

He switched on the light. With its tiny window the room would always be dark. Karl felt a chill run through him at the thought of darkness. He quickly shook off the sensation. He must not fear the dark any more. It was all over. His hand went to the light switch, then fell back. He would leave the light on anyway so he could see the low beam in the middle of the room. Even David Carter, when showing him the room, was careful to avoid hitting both the beam and the sloping ceiling, and there was a good difference in height between the two men.

Karl began to unpack his meagre possessions: spare clothing, toothbrush, comb, shaving kit, all his letters from home. They barely filled the two drawers beside the bed. On top of the drawers he placed the photograph his family sent after the postal services resumed in the autumn of 1945. His thoughts turned to the photograph.

The summer of 1943. The birth of his nephew. Anna's little Uwe had never seen Uncle Karl and would never see his father, killed in Russia. Widows are two a penny now, Karl supposed. At least Rudi is home to help them all survive. Lucky sod, lasting out until the final surrender, then allowed home so soon.

He focused on his parents' happy faces. "You're lucky too, having both sons still alive," he told the photograph. "The miracle will be complete when I get home. Whenever that might be. Another year yet, maybe more, the way things are going. At least there'll be no more damned roll-calls here!"

It was a relief to get away from the petty restrictions of the camp. He had no real friends there, moving around between camps and hostels too often to make lasting friendships. When approached by the Labour Officer, he had jumped at the chance to come to this English farm; his first step towards freedom.

He looked out of the ill-fitting, draughty window. The room faced south over the stables and the lane leading up to the farm. Beyond lay the broad expanse of the valley. In the middle distance, over gold and crimson treetops, the square tower of the village church glowed rose-pale in the weak, morning sun. A pair of rooks flew up from the valley, cawing noisily towards their roost in the woods crowning the hill behind the black and white farmhouse. Already he felt halfway home.

Taking a last satisfied look around his room, Karl switched off the light and went down the steep stone steps on the outside of the feed store to the yard below, in search of David Carter. He strode across the yard and caught a glimpse through the kitchen window of Katherine Carter washing the breakfast dishes. He knocked on the back door and she beckoned him in.

She gave a welcoming smile. "Is your room all right?"

"Yes. Thank you, Miss Carter." He smiled briefly too. He appreciated the obvious effort she had taken in preparing the room for him. His experience of the English so far was very mixed: it ranged from outright hostility, to overt flirting from some of the Land Girls. The Carters seemed to strike a balance between these two extremes.

16

"My father is out in the sheepsheds," she said, pointing across the yard.

Karl looked past the woodshed and feed stores to the low, corrugated-iron roof. He saw where she meant, nodded, and left her. A sudden cool breeze prompted him to pull his forage cap from his pocket.

He found her father up a ladder by one of the sheds, securing a loose corner of the roof before the start of the autumn gales. David Carter descended as Karl approached.

"All settled in then?"

"Please?"

"You've unpacked already?"

"Yes, sir."

"Good." David handed Karl some nails, the hammer and hand-drill and briskly rubbed his numb hands together. His breath came in short gasps. "I hope your stay here with us will be a pleasant one, Karl. I'm sure we're all going to get on fine together."

Karl thought he detected the slightest misgivings in his employer's words, but brushed it aside and set to work. So far all his impressions had been highly favourable; he was as determined as the Carters seemed to be to make this arrangement work.

David left Karl to it and made his rounds of the flock with Joss, his Border Collie. While wandering the meadows he kept his eyes open and made a note of the numerous repairs which were needed to gates, fences and roofs about the farm. It was two years since his wife died; two years of neglecting the farm. Now he found himself looking at it all through Karl's eyes. Lane Head Farm at present would give the German a very bad impression of English standards. He drew up a long mental list of hedge-laying, ditch-clearing, fence-mending and numerous smaller tasks. All the tools could do with cleaning and sharpening when the weather was too bad for outdoor work. Just itemising the tasks seemed like the jobs were already begun, whereas before Karl's arrival the length of the list would simply have daunted him. Already David felt he had achieved something at last, instead of fearing the daily grind which nowadays left him weak and breathless.

His step was lighter as he returned to the sheepsheds; Karl was not there. A slow, rhythmic chopping directed him to the woodshed. Joss left his side momentarily to sniff once more at this man who had come to join them.

"That's a good job you're doing there. We always need more wood."

Karl acknowledged Joss with a pat on the head, then leaned on the axe. "Are those your trees, sir?" He tilted his head towards the crest of the hill at the back of the farm. "There are many old trees there that should only be firewood."

Was it a rebuke at his sloppy management, David wondered? If so then it was justified. "Yes, they're a part of the farm I've rather ignored in recent years."

Karl realised he had sounded critical when he heard the defensive ring to David Carter's voice. "I am sorry, sir. I did not want to ..."

He searched his memory for an appropriate English word but could find none. He gave up the attempt with an apologetic smile. "As you can hear, my English is not so good."

David returned the smile, no offence taken. "I know what you want to say. You didn't want to criticise. It's a valid point though. Do you know much about woodland? You handle that axe as though it's an old friend."

"Yes. It is my father's business."

"Really?"

"Yes. He is ... forest master and he owns a ..." Again Karl groped for the right word. "... a sawmill."

The word had cropped up during an English lesson at the camp; he was pleased he could remember it from so long ago. There was not only the sawmill; they organised hunting parties at weekends for visitors from the nearby Ruhr. His mother and sister ran the house as a guest house with the help of a girl from the nearby town. All this was before the war of course, but as Karl revealed more of his background, David

18

got the impression that the business prospered during the war and survived reasonably well now with the huge demand for timber.

At the kitchen table that evening, Karl's head buzzed with all the new words learned that day. He was content simply to listen to the conversation and to concentrate on the stew. He eagerly accepted a second helping, consciously trying to break the habit of gulping down food after years of interrupted eating.

The atmosphere in the kitchen was pleasant and relaxed. When, plate empty at last, Karl did join in the conversation, there was laughter at some of his more comical errors.

"Please, correct me when I say things false," he asked.

"We will," Katherine assured him, ignoring his first mistake. She began stacking dirty plates. "You go on through to the sitting room with my father, Karl. I'll join you in a few minutes."

David Carter took his customary seat in the fireside armchair. Karl chose the sofa and picked up a news magazine from a side table to occupy himself. When Katherine came in she switched on the wireless set, found her knitting and sat opposite her father, who was engrossed in the newspaper. The haunting, flowing sound of Welsh harp music filled the room, entrancing Karl with its novelty. The *Picture Post* slipped from his fingers and fell to the floor with a loud slap. Katherine jumped at the noise.

"I'm sorry." Karl felt suddenly intrusive. He should give the Carters some time alone together. He stood up. "I will go now. Goodnight."

David looked up in surprise from his paper. "Oh! Goodnight then, Karl."

As he was leaving the room, Karl paused by the bookshelf. "May I read one?"

"Go ahead," David said, his eyes back on his paper.

Karl bent down and found a well-thumbed book, suggesting it was probably a good read. As he stepped out through the back door, the wind nearly tore the book from his hand. He hurried up the steps to his room. As he opened the door, a fierce draught billowed the green curtains, making him jump. Hurriedly he switched on the light. He checked the window. Though shut fast it rattled in its frame. Karl shivered and tried to light the small oil stove.

The wick failed to catch the match flame. "*Verdammt!* It's empty." He thought of the Carters relaxing by the fire but shied away from disturbing them again to ask for oil. The kitchen seemed the best idea. The range was always lit there. He marched briskly back across the chilly yard, hoping the Carters would not mind this second intrusion. Once settled in the rocking chair he struggled bravely with *The Thirty-nine Steps*, but progress was painfully slow. He was not at all sure he understood properly what was going on. The exercise was not completely fruitless, as there were words he could hazard a good guess at from the context. English was intriguing, with its many nuances and shades of meaning. He had already discovered that for every one word in German there seemed to be half a dozen English possibilities.

His studies were interrupted at ten o'clock by Katherine coming to make some Ovaltine.

"I thought you'd gone to bed," she remarked, fetching a jug of milk from the larder.

"I hope you don't mind that I sit here."

"Good heavens, no! I expect it's jolly cold in your room."

"There is no oil for the fire."

"Oh golly, I'm sorry! I quite forgot to take some up there. But please! Feel free to sit with us in the evening – if you want to. Besides, it will save on fuel."

"Thank you. I will do that."

She poured milk into a saucepan then remembered Karl.

"Would you like some too?"

"Thank you."

"Is that yes or no?"

He corrected himself. "Yes. Please."

Katherine glanced at his book. "That's a good one. I think I've read it twice already. Are you enjoying it?"

He layed the book aside. "It is too difficult. Perhaps you know one that is easier for me."

"I'll look one out when I've made the drinks. You go on back to the sitting room," she suggested.

Karl did as he was told, replacing the abandoned John Buchan on the shelf. David Carter nodded at him over the top of his newspaper. Katherine returned with the Ovaltine and scanned the shelves for a likely book. Her parents' tastes ranged from Robert Louis Stevenson to Thomas Hardy. The latter was no easier to read than John Buchan. With a shrug of her shoulders she admitted defeat.

"All these are probably too difficult. If you don't mind children's stories I've some old favourites of mine in my bedroom. I'll look one out for you later."

"Thank you. That is very kind."

Half an hour later, warmed by the Ovaltine, Karl returned to his room. The silence there was blissful. As he lay in bed, Karl felt more relaxed than he had in years. Only the whistle of the wind in the rafters and the rustle of the curtains disturbed the peace.

"No nightmares tonight. Please," he told himself.

The wind died down next morning, but it prompted David to tackle another long-postponed job. A tall ash tree by the barn was battering at the roof. Karl was soon up a ladder against the tree. He tied a rope to the branch to secure it before sawing it off. While up the ladder, he noticed some tiles already dislodged from the barn roof. After removing the sawn branch to the woodshed, David and Karl went into the barn to check the roof from the inside.

Up in the rafters it was dark and dusty. A chink of light directed Karl to where tiles were missing immediately above a supporting beam. To Karl's dismay, the beam was already half rotted through and would need repairing. He climbed down the ladder to report the bad news just as Katherine entered the barn, looking for her father.

Karl stepped off the rickety ladder and turned to see a look of amused horror on her face as she stared at his left shoulder. His eyes followed her gaze. He grinned; a large spider was crawling rapidly towards his face. He scooped up the spider into the palm of his hand and held it out to her.

"You don't like her?" he asked, amused.

Katherine backed away. "No, I don't. I don't mind worms, mice, bats, beetles, moths or Daddy-long-legs, but the one thing I don't like is spiders." A sudden thought came to her. "How do you know it's a female?" she asked, intrigued by the possibilities of spider anatomy.

Karl looked nonplussed for a moment then realised his mistake. "*Ach! Eine Spinne* – a spider – is always she in German. I forget in English you call things it."

Katherine laughed. She watched as Karl gently placed the spider on the barn wall before brushing the cobwebs off his back. At least he had not teased her with it, as Andrew would have done.

"What are *you* frightened of then, Karl?" she asked him. She instantly regretted her familiarity as his eyes abruptly left hers. For a moment she thought he was not going to answer. When he did, his answer astonished her.

"The dark," he said. He walked away before she could question him further.

Later that morning, when the two men were coming indoors to clean up for lunch, Katherine detected a note of restored pride in her father's voice.

"Soon," he was saying, "I'd like to drain the lower meadow down by the river. It can get very waterlogged there at times and then there's always the danger of the sheep becoming infected with liver-fluke. They get it from snails, you know."

Katherine was not sure Karl understood all that, but her father rattled on, talking about his plans for the place, once all the wartime restrictions were finally lifted.

For his part, Karl very much enjoyed being spoken to as a person in his own right, not just another Fritz, as the guards referred to their prisoners. Even if he did not understand all David Carter said, he could usually follow enough to keep the conversation going. After only two days of speaking nothing but English, phrases sprang more readily to mind, and surely just now he even *thought* in English!

Over lunch he heard Sarah Carter's name mentioned several times and wanted to know more about her. He took advantage of a lull in the conversation.

"You speak of your daughter, Sarah. Where is she?"

David finished his mouthful of bread. "She's studying geography at Bristol University. You'll meet her at Christmas when she's back for the holidays."

He caught Katherine's worried eye. Was now the time to warn Karl about Sarah's deep hatred of Germans? Karl noticed their exchanged looks and David realised he might as well get the painful business over and explain the whole family situation to Karl, about Ethel's manner of death and Sarah's reaction to it.

He cleared his throat. "It's like this, you see, Karl. My wife was visiting relatives in London in July 1944. She was killed ... by one of those flying bombs."

He paused as his emotion threatened to break through. Karl sat silently, guessing what would come.

"We were all devastated, of course. Sarah took her death particularly badly." David's eyes slipped from Karl's. "I'm afraid she blames all Germans for the loss of her mother."

Karl made light of it. "Don't worry. I am used to it that people hate me. But I wonder why you and Katherine do not hate me also?"

Katherine spoke up. "It's not in our nature to hate people just because some label is applied to them."

Her remark stung him. No doubt she was referring to the Nazi doctrines he once believed in. Why did she have to mention such things now? Did she want him to defend himself?

Katherine saw Karl's frown and realised he must have taken her remark personally. She hurried to set things straight. "Sarah tends to see things differently from either of us. She doesn't allow another point of view."

Karl smiled at her efforts to be diplomatic. He would have to learn not to raise his hackles so readily. He accepted another slice of bread from Katherine as their talk turned to less treacherous ground.

When the men resumed work in the barn, Katherine sat down to write to Andrew while all was peace and quiet. She wanted to get the letter in the post that day. She found the letter easier to write than usual, with all the news about Karl's arrival and her father's increased cheerfulness. Usually she wrote the same things each time – how much she missed him, the hardships of rationing, enquiring what he had been up to. This latest effort would come as a breath of fresh air. With Andrew's letter safely out of the way, she had time to scribble quickly to Sarah before her trip to the village.

Hauling her bicycle out of the shed, she called out a "Goodbye" to the men in the barn, and flew off down the long, steep lane. Her reckless descent slowed once she joined the level valley road and she arrived sedately at the Post Office-cum-General Stores, propped her bicycle against the wall, popped the letters in the post box, and went inside the shop. As usual it smelled strongly of bacon and tea leaves. The tinkling doorbell alerted Mrs Tucker to her new customer, and she broke off her conversation with Mrs Collins, one of Penchurch's war widows.

Portly Mrs Tucker beamed. "Good afternoon, Miss Carter." Born in the village sixty-two years ago, she had a vast store of knowledge about all the locals. "We were just talking about you, wondering how you were coping with a German living in. I was saying to Mrs Collins here, you must be desperate to consider taking on one of that lot, after all your family's been through."

Pat Collins pitched in. "I don't know how you can bear to have one near you." The same age as Katherine, Pat Collins married a local boy after leaving school, and lost him almost immediately. This had left her bitter and resentful of the world in general and of Germans in particular. "If one of them came near me I'd spit in his face, I would!" Her expression betrayed her desire to inflict far worse retribution, if she could.

Mrs Tucker placed a tin of prunes on the counter. "I expect young Mr Murdoch feels the same about the Japs, after the terrible way they treated him and all."

Katherine let the pair of them ramble on. A trip to the village shop was always a trial of patience for her. If she ever got served before she had been in the shop ten minutes she considered herself lucky. She had left the shop and stowed her purchases safely in her bicycle basket before either Mrs Tucker or Pat Collins realised they had not elicited a single detail about the German from her to satisfy their curiosity.

The mention of Robert Murdoch prompted Katherine to pay a visit to the family who had become such close friends over the years. Since her mother's death, Katherine looked on Gertie Murdoch as a surrogate mother, and frequently called in after shopping for a cup of tea and a chat. She set off again through the village's narrow main street, and turned left up Cutbush Lane.

Yew Tree Lodge was a large, three-storey Victorian red-brick house, two hundred yards up the hill, set well back from the road behind a massive barricade of lilac trees, berberis, pyracantha and other ornamental shrubs. Gertie, as chief landscape gardener, contrived always to have some kind of blossom or colourful foliage between the house and the outside world as a demonstration, or so Katherine reckoned, of her eternal optimism.

Katherine ran up the stone steps to the imposing front door and lifted its heavy brass knocker. The sound of vacuuming in the hallway stopped, and Gertie's petite figure opened the door, her twinkling brown eyes lighting up at the sight of Katherine.

"Katherine, dear! Come on in. You've saved me from my Hoover! It's Megan's day off."

Gertie's passion for gardening did not extend to housework. Her involvement in numerous village and church social activities prevented her, so she claimed, from devoting as much time to housework as perhaps she ought, even with Megan's assistance. She led Katherine through to the kitchen. Like Mrs Tucker, she too was eager to hear Katherine's news, and after putting the kettle on for tea, settled down to find out. "So how are you finding your German? I hope David's leaving some work for him to do."

Katherine framed her answer carefully, knowing Gertie would pass it on to the rest of the village.

"Karl's doing wonders for Daddy. I haven't seen him so happy in a long time. They certainly get on well together."

"What's this `Karl' like then?"

"He's polite, helpful; seems to know what he's doing, which is what Daddy wanted most, I think. Good company for Daddy: he's enjoying having another man about the place."

She knew Gertie really wanted to hear more about Karl and tried to assess her own impressions so far.

"Karl's very serious," she said pensively, rubbing her lower lip. "Oh, he smiles and passes the time of day. He even jokes sometimes, but underneath the smile he seems very tense. Still, it's early days yet for him, after all."

"It must be rather a strain on him, having to work for his former enemy, and watch what he says and does all the time."

"Yes, I suppose he'll settle down soon enough. When you don't know the language all that well, or the customs, it must be difficult to fit in."

She began to tug thoughtfully at her earlobe. "There was something I said last night which he took the wrong way. I think I'll have to watch what I say in future."

"Perhaps with justification," Gertie said meaningfully, then noticing Katherine's shock at such an idea, she added: "But I doubt it. Your German was just an ordinary soldier, like Robert."

She left it at that. The comparison with Robert seemed to comfort Katherine, and she herself was keen to give this stranger the benefit of the doubt.

"Speaking of Robert," Katherine said, glad to change the subject, "where is he?"

"He's upstairs having a nap, poor dear. These nightmares take so much out of him. I do wish he could talk about it all, but he still refuses to speak about his experiences out there."

"I do so hope he'll be able to get over, if not forget, his ordeal. The pictures I've seen of those Japanese camps are horrifying. When I think Robert was actually in one ..." She looked questioningly at Gertie seated opposite her, safe and snug in her own kitchen. "Why do men treat each other so badly? How can they possibly do such dreadful things and still call themselves human beings?"

Gertie shrugged. "Men are made to do things in war that would be unspeakable in normal life; in a uniform, a gun in their hands, they seem capable of almost anything." She noticed the kettle boiling and stood up to make the tea.

"Sarah has no intention of forgiving the Germans for killing Mummy," Katherine said with a sigh.

"What about you, dear?"

Katherine was silent a moment. "I suppose I've come to terms now with her death. The bomb wasn't aimed at her – they weren't actually trying to kill my mother, she was just another victim of war. I think I might feel differently if she'd been whisked off to a concentration camp and deliberately gassed or whatever."

Gertie put the teapot on the table. "Sarah can only see things in black. You're right, she won't forgive your German so easily. I'm surprised David took him on."

"I must admit, I was too. Heaven knows how she's going to behave when she comes back at Christmas."

"She may surprise us all," Gertie commented. "She may have grown up at last."

"Let's hope so," Katherine agreed fervently.

It was nearly four o'clock by the time Katherine arrived back at the farm. There was no sign of her father or Karl in the barn. The ladder and tools were all cleared away. They must have gone off to start another job. She put her bicycle away and went into the house to change into her working clothes. She could have an hour in the kitchen garden before starting on the evening meal. Just as she came back in to scrub potatoes for dinner, her father appeared. He warmed himself by the range, looking pleased with himself.

"I reckon I made the right choice there with Karl," he said happily. "He certainly knows a thing or two about wood. I've left him in the toolshed making a new haft for one of my axes."

"I expect he's glad to be doing something constructive rather than destructive," Katherine said.

Her father looked at her tersely. "Let's have none of that now, Beauty. Don't let me catch you making any more comments like that! Or the one you made last night!"

Despite her father's warning, the question of how many men Karl might have killed troubled her. She forced herself to smile at him when he came in for dinner, then hurriedly turned her back so he would not see the question in her eyes, busying herself with setting the table.

Over dinner she recovered her composure, chastising herself for her silliness. After the meal, as on the previous night, Karl joined them in the sitting room, and began to study one of her father's farming journals. The wireless was on as usual, but Katherine found she was not listening to the play. Instead, her needles clicked automatically at the cardigan she was knitting, her eyes wandering to the face of the man she felt such curiosity about.

Despite his superficial friendliness, Katherine sensed an underlying unapproachability. He had a wariness, an alertness which made him seem permanently anticipating trouble. He was never completely relaxed. She tried to imagine his hands holding a gun, squeezing the trigger, but the image eluded her. All she saw were those same hands cradling the spider in the barn, or gently stroking Joss's ears. She was unable to imagine him in a war situation.

He noticed her staring at him. For a moment their eyes met, and her conscience pricked at her thoughts. She broke into an embarassed smile. He did not return it, but held her gaze long enough for her to realise he had not liked being stared at. He seemed even more on edge after that, flicking through the rest of the journal without the same interest as before. Suddenly he put the journal down on the table beside him and stood up.

"I will go now. Goodnight."

Oh dear! Katherine thought. I've offended him again. Why is he so touchy?

She tried to make amends. She remembered she had not yet looked out a suitable book for him. Dropping her knitting she ran after him, calling out to his retreating figure.

"Karl! Did you want a book to read?"

He turned round. There was a slight hesitation before he spoke. "Thank you."

His tone left her in some doubt as to whether he trusted her good intentions or not, but by the time she emerged from her bedroom clutching her cherished copy of *Heidi*, he seemed to have made up his mind about her. He smiled as he took the book from her.

Encouraged by this, she became bolder. "Please stay with us a while longer. It's still early."

Karl waved aside her plea. "I am tired. Last night I did not sleep so good – well, I mean."

Katherine immediately showed her concern. "Were you warm enough? I can find you another blanket."

"No. I was very ... comfortable." He said the word slowly, making sure he put in every syllable. "Sometimes I sleep bad, that is all," he explained.

"Badly," she corrected him.

"Badly," he repeated as he always did after a correction. "It also ... makes me tired to speak English all day, I think."

"Yes, I suppose it must do when you're not used to it. I'd better let you get to bed. Goodnight, Karl." She turned away.

He listened to her footsteps padding down the hall to the sitting room and shook his head in amusement at this English girl whose transparent face betrayed her every thought. So she was anxious not to offend him, was she? More likely she was one of those people who hated to be thought ill of by anyone ... even a German.

The following morning, David took Karl on a tour of inspection of the orchards to explain methods of pruning. Pointing out that cider apple trees were left unpruned, David led Karl on into a second orchard where trees had been planted shortly before the war. He pulled a small piece of bark off one of the trees.

"I'm looking for signs of weevil – that's like a kind of beetle. They overwinter in the bark here or the soil, then lay their eggs in the blossom buds – the flower buds."

He indicated a strip of folded sacking, about eight inches wide, tied around the tree trunk. Unfolding the top, he looked down inside the sacking and grunted with satisfaction. Karl peered in too and saw the long-nosed weevil lurking there.

"They like it better in the sacking, but they don't know we take it off and burn it before Spring," David said gleefully. "All the little blighters go up in flames."

Up in the house, Katherine was also thinking about flames. There was a distinct nip in the air that morning, and she was reminded to re-fill Karl's stove. As she tipped its chimney back she bumped the drawers by his bed and knocked over the little vase she had put there and a photograph leaning against it. She would never dream of reading the letter which lay alongside, but the picture drew her. She studied the faces on it, wondering who the young woman with the baby was. She turned the picture over and was rewarded by seeing writing there. The angular German script took a while to decipher, but eventually she made out *Dieter und Gisela, Anna und Uwe, September 1943, Medebach.* Turning it over again she studied it once more before carefully returning it to its place.

When the men returned for lunch she noticed a distinct sparkle in her father's eyes. His step was lighter, his back straighter: at last his period of mourning seemed over. Katherine found herself grateful to Karl for this change, thought of the little photograph, and wondered if he got on as well with his own father. There was a lot she didn't know about him.

CHAPTER THREE

Karl lay awake listening to the storm raging. The wind had picked up steadily during the afternoon. "Batten down the hatches" was a new phrase learned that day. He could hear the ash tree's branches creaking by the barn. Now at least the roof tiles were safe.

A stronger gust snapped twigs against the window, startling him. It was nothing compared with the splintering crash that followed. Leaping out of bed, he peered in vain through the rain-spattered window to see what had fallen. Hurriedly he pulled on his clothes and ran down the steps to the yard. He met David clutching a hurricane lantern, his coat billowing in the wind.

"I think it was the chestnut tree in the paddock," said David anxiously. "I hope to God it hasn't fallen on the stables!"

The moon was obscured by thick black clouds, rain lashed their faces. The feeble light of their lantern was hardly sufficient for them to avoid stumbling over wind-blown twigs and small branches on their way to the paddock. To their immense relief they could hear Beth's nervous whinnying as they neared the apparently undamaged stable. Sure enough, the ancient chestnut tree was down – not simply uprooted but actually snapped a few feet up its trunk. Fortunately the tree had fallen away from the stable and poultry house, but it had crushed the paddock fence, completely blocking the lane with its trunk and abundant branches.

David shouted against the blast. "There's nothing we can do now. We'll have to tackle it tomorrow. Let's get back inside!"

A sorry scene greeted them in the early light. The whole farm was littered with the storm's debris, the paddock and lane a tangled mass of crushed and shattered branches. The wind had died down considerably, but a stiff breeze still swirled great eddies of fallen leaves.

Karl went out first thing to check on the flock and the state of the orchards. He found the sheep all safely huddled in the lee of the hedges, with no sign of injury. In the orchards several trees were uprooted. Tidying these would take a few days, but priority would have to go to clearing the lane. He returned to the warmth of the kitchen to make his report.

"It could have been worse," Katherine commented, pouring tea for them all. "At least we'd harvested the apples."

Immediately after breakfast, David and Karl headed for the paddock armed with saws and axes. Katherine was to join them after seeing to the poultry. In the light of day it was clear why the old tree snapped. Its core was a spongy mess of rotted wood, offering little resistance to the force of the wind.

David eyed the trunk in self-condemnation. "I should have noticed how rotten that tree was. It was a danger to us all." He pulled a sliver of wood from the trunk, rolled it easily into a ball then tossed it angrily to the ground. "Now we're cut off from the village. It'll take us the whole day at least to clear the lane and paddock. I missed the tiles on the barn roof too. How much else is there on this farm that's falling to pieces and I haven't noticed?"

Karl said nothing. What David said was true but blaming himself would not get the job done. Hefting a large axe, Karl climbed over the smashed paddock fence into the lane and set about removing some of the smaller side branches to gain access to the main trunk. The narrow confines of the lane compacted the branches together, making the trunk's removal impossible without first stripping all its branches. As he swung the axe at an endless succession of branches, he was dimly aware of Katherine joining them, of her warning her father not to work too hard.

As the morning progressed David took more frequent rests; he sat on a log to regain his breath, his face pinched and pale.

Eventually Katherine intervened. "You look exhausted, Daddy. Why don't you go indoors and make us all coffee and sandwiches? Karl and I can carry on for a bit longer."

He acquiesced readily, and plodded back to the house.

"I'm worried about him," Katherine told Karl, once her father was out of earshot. "He won't stop working so hard and begin to take things easier. That's why you're here, to ease the load, but he still tries to do as much as he always has. He simply can't take it any more."

Karl watched the slowly retreating figure. "He is a proud man; he loves his farm too much." He decided they needed a short breather too and swung his axe into a log, then wiped his sweating palms down his thighs."What will he do when you are married and gone away? Will your sister stay here?"

Katherine sat on a log and picked a leaf from her hair. "Sarah won't stay. She wants her own career. You could never tie her down to a backwater like this now she's experienced the Bright Life. As for what Daddy will do once I leave here, I've no idea. I'll only be three miles away at Froxley Grange but he's certainly going to need a proper assistant once you've gone home." She plucked a grass stem and chewed it. "We've discussed it often enough together, but he seems blinkered; doesn't want to look beyond the time when I'm married. I put forward suggestions; he just ignores them, or finds arguments against."

"It is a pity that your ... the man you love has his own big farm."

Katherine looked wistful. "Yes it is, I suppose. Cattle and cereals are what Andrew's used to. He's not interested in taking this place on. He'd arrange a manager to run it for us, if we wanted, but Daddy isn't at all keen on that idea."

"He does not like your Andrew?"

Katherine looked sharply at Karl. "Of course he likes Andrew!" she snapped.

She stood up and brushed the sawdust off the seat of her corduroy trousers. "That's enough rest. We'd better get on and clear this road," she said stiffly, leaving Karl in no doubt of her displeasure.

Katherine picked up a saw and set to work on a large branch, but the seeds of doubt were sown. Did her father

33

really not like Andrew? She had never considered the possibility before. Andrew had always been there, throughout her childhood. They competed together at gymkhanas, danced together at church socials. Her father never said anything against Andrew all that time. What had made Karl say that just now?

She glanced curiously over at him as he worked. What had he, a virtual stranger, heard or seen to have induced him to make such a comment?

With a great creaking and splitting of wood the crown of the tree crashed into the ditch by the hedge, leaving the remainder of the trunk raised like a gun barrel across the lane. Karl leaned against the trunk a moment and Katherine saw that his hands were shaking noticeably.

"Hungry?" she asked him.

"Yes. Very." He held up one of his shaking hands in demonstration.

"Come on then. Let's go and find out what Daddy has made."

There were a few plates on the table and some bread, but no finished sandwiches to be seen as they entered the kitchen. Instead they saw David Carter in the rocking chair, his face contorted with fear, his chest shuddering.

Katherine rushed over to his side. "Daddy! What is it?"

Speechless, he held her hand on his chest. She felt the rapid, irregular rhythm of his heartbeat.

"I'll call Dr Murdoch," she said, trying to keep her voice calm, and ran to the telephone.

When she returned she barely noticed Karl's absence, she was so worried. Her father looked terrified, but all she could do was sit and hold his hand, promising him the ambulance and Donald Murdoch would soon be there. But it was another five minutes before she realised the lane was still blocked by the fallen chestnut tree. The ambulance would have to stop down the lane, where there was no turning space. It all meant more delay. She assumed Karl had gone down the lane to warn Donald Murdoch of the tree, otherwise there could be a terrible accident.

A few minutes later she heard the sound of a car engine labouring up the hill and the scrunch of tyres on the gravel outside. She rushed to the front door as the doctor walked in.

"He's in the kitchen."

"Well now, David," Dr Murdoch calmly greeted his old friend. "What have we here?" He pulled his stethoscope from his bag and listened intently to David's heart. He removed the stethoscope from his ears. "Have you any pain or tightness in your chest?"

"It feels tight," David gasped through his breathlessness.

"Well, the ambulance is on its way. They'll have you in the hospital in no time," the doctor reassured him.

"How did you get all the way up the lane?" Katherine asked in bewilderment. "Surely it was blocked?"

"No. That new chap of yours had hitched Beth to the trunk and managed to pull it sideways just enough for the car to get through. I told him he'd have to shift it further for the ambulance though."

"Perhaps I'd better go and see if he needs any help," Katherine suggested.

"Aye, perhaps you had."

Katherine scuttled out, back across the yard and through the paddock. As she climbed over the smashed fence she spotted Karl furiously sawing at the remains of the trunk in the lane. Obviously it refused to budge any further, despite Beth's best efforts, and still blocked the lane. Katherine could see that the weight of the trunk was opening the sawn gap and she grabbed another saw to battle from the other side of the trunk. It was fortunate now that the wood inside was rotten and the core hollow. Only the tough outer sapwood needed to be cut through. As sweat began to pour down her there came a final rending crack and the two halves of the trunk parted. Beth was still attached to the now freed trunk; it only took another minute to haul it to the side of the hedge, with Karl pushing and guiding from behind. Katherine just had time to unhitch Beth and lead her back into the paddock before the ambulance sped towards them up the hill, crunching over the twigs still strewn across the lane. She followed it at a run up to the house, leaving Karl slumped with fatigue on the trunk.

By the time a breathless Katherine arrived by the front door, her father was already being carried to the waiting ambulance.

"I'm going with him," she said to Dr Murdoch, grabbing her purse from the hall table before climbing up into the back of the ambulance. "Tell Karl where I've gone, please!"

Donald Murdoch watched the ambulance drive off then sat behind the wheel of his car and pondered the situation the Carters now found themselves in. David would no doubt be in hospital at least a week, leaving Katherine to cope alone on the farm. No, not alone. There was that German working for them. He posed another problem now. He could not possibly stay up here at night alone with Katherine. Donald shook his head wearily and started the engine. Something would have to be sorted out.

When he reached the site of the fallen tree he stopped and looked around for the man he had seen earlier. He caught sight of a blond head in the paddock, where the German was picking up discarded tools, and got out of his car to speak to him. Murdoch noticed that underneath the smears of dirt, green streaks and dried sweat, the man's face was ashen with fatigue. He passed on Katherine's message.

"You should take a rest," he added. "Go on up to the house and get some food in you. I'll be bringing Miss Carter back later on, then we'll have to sort out somewhere for you to stay the night. You can't stay up here now, that's for sure."

"No, Doctor."

Donald saw amusement in the man's eyes and took an immediate liking to the fellow. "I tell you what," he went on, "we have spare rooms at my house. You can stay with us at night, until Mr Carter is back home. It should only take you about half an hour to walk up here each morning. What do you say?"

"Thank you. That is kind. But first I must have the permission of the camp."

Donald brushed aside the technicality. "Yes, of course. I'll clear it with them." He added almost as an afterthought: "And with my wife!" So saying, he got into his car and drove off.

Karl returned the tools to the toolshed before washing his grimy hands in the outhouse at the corner of the yard. Wearily pulling off his boots at the back door he noticed Joss sitting watching him, bemused by the sudden disappearance of both his master and mistress.

"*Keine Sorge, Joss!*" he told the dog. "*Katherine wird bald zurück sein.*"

At his words the dog approached and sniffed Karl's outstretched hand, now smelling of soap. Karl gave the dog's head a comforting stroke, then moved to the kitchen table where the loaf of bread still lay, untouched. Grabbing a large hunk of it he crammed it into his mouth, before looking in the larder for something to go with the bread. He found some cheese, pickle and a pot of jam, and set about filling his empty stomach.

At last his hands stopped shaking. He sat back on the chair and closed his eyes for a moment. All was quiet, save for the gentle ticking of the kitchen clock. He had not been alone in the house before. On the two previous Sundays, when the Carters went off to church and on Wednesdays, when they went to market, Karl spent the time in his room or working outside. He had felt intensely gratified on the first occasion that they trusted him enough to leave him there all alone. His time in captivity had left him with the feeling he was considered a criminal, liable to make a dash with anything he could lay his hands on. This demonstration by the Carters that he was trustworthy gave a considerable boost to his flagging sense of pride. At the time of his capture and for some weeks afterwards, he felt no better than an animal. Only now was he beginning to haul his way slowly back up the ladder of acceptability.

He woke with a start. He had been dreaming again, but one of his less horrific dreams. No doubt the other men in his hut at the hostel were glad to see the back of him, having had their own sleep broken so often by his nightmares. He was anxious before he arrived at Lane Head Farm that he might also disturb the Carters, but stuck outside as he was, they did not seem to have heard him. Now he was to sleep at the doctor's house. He hoped his room would be similarly far removed from anyone else.

He looked at the clock. Ten to three. He ought to get himself properly cleaned up in the bath. He ran his fingers through his hair, pulling out bits of leaf and twig which were trapped there, just as he had seen in Katherine's hair.

He was careful to wipe away the prominent tide-mark around the bath, after rinsing his equally filthy clothes in the water. Dressed in his spare clothes he hung the dripping ones on the washing line. Katherine would have enough to occupy herself with over the next week or so without more of his mess to contend with.

As darkness began to fall, Karl made the rounds of the animals, housing the poultry, stabling Beth, feeding Joss. He was beginning to consider the need to feed himself again when he heard the doctor's car approaching at last, bringing Katherine back.

With heavy-lidded eyes Katherine stumbled wearily out of the car. Karl let them both get safely inside before enquiring after David's health.

"He's not too bad, thank God." She had come straight from the hospital. Although she had done her best to tidy herself up it was clear to both Karl and Dr Murdoch that what she needed most now was a bath, some food and a good sleep.

"You go and get your things together, Katherine, then we can go straight back for dinner," said Donald.

Katherine disappeared upstairs, while Donald explained what the plans were to Karl.

"Gertie – my wife – thought Katherine would be better off with us tonight. I've arranged everything with your commandant too. He's given permission for you to stay with us for the time being. Mind you, I had quite a job persuading him to let you stay on here, under the ... er ... changed circumstances."

He caught sight of Karl's kitbag packed and ready by the door. "Is that yours?"

"Yes, Doctor."

"Good. I'd just better give Joss his dinner and once Katherine's ready we can be off."

"Joss has eaten."

Donald smiled warmly. "David knew what he was doing when he took you on. You did a fine job clearing the lane today. Katherine was very grateful for your efforts, I know. She's going to be relying on you now, as I explained to Major Alderton."

Katherine did not keep them waiting long. "May I telephone Sarah from your house, Donald, to let her know what's happened?" She checked the range and found it damped down already.

"Of course you may. Come along now. Everything's been seen to here. Let's get to the house. I have evening surgery before dinner."

Gertie Murdoch heard their arrival and was waiting on the top door-step, holding wide the stained-glass front door. She gave Katherine a hug, and welcomed her other guest with a warmth that stilled any doubts in Karl's mind about his status there.

"Come on in, dears. My word! What a day you've had, Katherine. I expect you're quite worn out."

She led them into the spacious hall and took their coats. Donald deposited Katherine's bag and hurried to attend to the half dozen patients waiting in his surgery.

Gertie showed Katherine and Karl up to their rooms. Katherine had the proper guest room, overlooking the conservatory. Leaving her to have a relaxing bath and get changed, Gertie took Karl across the wide landing and on down to a smaller room at the front of the house.

"This was my elder son Michael's room," she told him. "I hope you'll find it comfortable during your stay here with us. There's a towel on the chair there, the bathroom is next door, and the toilet is on the turn of the stairs. We passed it on the way up here."

Karl found it difficult to say anything in the flow of words from Mrs Murdoch, only managing a quick "Thank you" while she paused to draw the heavy, navy-blue curtains. He noticed there was no evidence of the room's former occupant and wondered where the son was now, as well as the whereabouts of the younger son. He put his kitbag on the carpet by an old and scratched mahogany chest of drawers then followed Mrs Murdoch out of the room and back downstairs.

At the foot of the stairs they turned right, through the door of the room which lay directly below Katherine's. The living room was large; comfortable rather than elegant, with a battered leather three-piece suite, a baby grand piano and numerous bookshelves.

A young man was reading in one of the fireside chairs, toasting his slippered feet before the fire. A full ashtray and a tumbler of whisky stood on a table at his side.

Gertie Murdoch approached her son, who put down his newspaper as she made the introductions. "Karl, this is my son, Robert. He'll look after you while I pop out to the kitchen and finish getting dinner ready. Won't you, Robert?" She stroked his slicked-back raven hair affectionately as she left.

Robert Murdoch was slightly built like his mother, although he lacked her sprightliness. There was a lethargy to the way he stood reluctantly and took Karl's proffered hand.

"Sit down, please." Robert indicated the sofa in the centre of the room, before sinking back into his own chair and resuming reading. Clearly he was not bothered about further conversation.

Karl watched him. He was almost certain that Mrs Murdoch had deliberately left them alone together in the hope that her depressed son might feel obliged or tempted to speak to such an unusual visitor. If so, Robert needed some prompting. Karl tried the well-known English habit of talking about the weather.

"Has the wind broken anything here?"

Robert replied without looking up. "I don't know."

"I think you have seldom here such strong winds?"

"Mm."

This was getting nowhere. Shock tactics were called for.

"We had terrible storms in Russia."

Now there was some reaction: the newspaper was lowered.

"Oh, really?"

It was a start anyway. Karl was about to speak again but was pre-empted by Robert.

"With us it was rain and heat."

Steady, Karl told himself. Go slowly and gently. Like opening a bottle of champagne. Don't shake him too much. "Where was that?"

Robert Murdoch looked directly at the German for the first time. He recognised someone else who had personally suffered in that bloody war. A prisoner of war no less, admittedly under drastically different circumstances. Nevertheless he would recognise something of what Robert experienced.

"Burma," Robert replied. Emboldened by the German's attentive yet undemanding expression, Robert lit another cigarette and began his tale. "The rains started in May and ended in September – up to fifteen inches in a single day. At least it was a bit cooler when it rained. Afterwards we could hardly breathe in the sweltering humidity." He had to clear his throat as it became clogged with the memory of the suffocating air of Burma.

"I was captured in May 1944, just after the monsoon started. We were bogged down in thick mud, trying to get ourselves and our equipment over a flooding river. We could hardly see our hands in front of our faces for the rain." Once launched on his narrative, Robert did not pause to see if he was being understood, but kept his eyes on the flickering coals. "How the Japs spotted us I don't know. They must have heard our cursing and swearing even over the noise of the rain. They just appeared from nowhere out of the jungle, as was their way, shot half our men and captured the rest. We were marched for days through the jungle. Five men died on the way, two were washed away crossing flooded rivers and were shot and killed in the water."

Karl noticed the whisky glass trembling in Robert's hand.

"We were plagued by every biting creature you can imagine: leeches, mosquitoes, ants. We arrived at the prison camp smitten with dysentery, malaria and dengue fever."

Robert's eyes glazed. He was back in the steaming jungle. "There were no medical supplies at the camp to treat us. The Japs wouldn't listen to our doctor's demands for medicines."

Karl sat motionless, not wanting to interrupt.

"The doctor wouldn't give in. One day the Japs just handed over a box of medicines. It was a miracle! I owe my life to that man. I decided there and then I wanted to follow in my father's footsteps and study medicine – should I ever get home."

Karl felt he knew enough now to understand. "So now you are home. Will you study medicine?"

Robert slumped back in his chair. "When I'm well enough. When there's a place for me. Medical schools are full of all the chaps who got home before me."

"At least you are home. You should be grateful."

There was an awkward pause. Then Robert looked intently at Karl. "You're right. You're still a prisoner, aren't you?"

"Not so much now that I work for Mr Carter," Karl said lightly.

Robert's gaze rested on his slippers. He felt remarkably at ease with this stranger. He glanced up. "Thank you for listening."

"Perhaps you can one day do the same for me."

They sat a moment in contemplative silence. Robert suddenly stubbed out his cigarette and got to his feet. "Where is everyone? We must have been talking for ages. Surely Dad's finished surgery by now?"

He went down the passage to the kitchen. He found his mother and Katherine sitting at the table talking.

"Hasn't Dad finished yet?" Robert asked. All meal preparations seemed to be long since complete.

"He's in his study doing some paperwork. Now you're here, you can help carry some dishes through to the dining room, and give your father a call."

Gertie handed him a pile of plates from the stove, and bent down to remove the big casserole dish from inside the oven.

"Katherine, will you fetch Karl, while I bring this through?"

As Katherine entered the living room, she stopped with one hand on the doorknob. Karl thought she looked revitalised.

"You seem to be a success with Robert," she said quietly. "No one's been able to get him to talk since he came home."

"Have you listened through the door?"

His question sounded like a rebuke. "No, of course not. Gertie heard your voices and decided to leave you in peace rather than interrupt."

He held up his hands in mock surrender at her outburst. Evidently she misinterpreted his tone of voice, or his phrasing sounded aggressive to her ears. He could not yet use all the colloquial niceties of speech he heard the English use. He guessed his sentences might sound abrupt and curt sometimes.

He saw by the smile on her face that she had accepted his apology. "It is time to eat?"

"Yes. Through here. I'm starving!"

She led him across the hall to where the Murdochs were gathered round an elegant oval table.

Karl sat with Gertie on one side, Robert on the other. Like Katherine he was famished and tucked in to the casserole as Gertie led the conversation.

"Olive Thornton was telling me today the roof's leaking again in the church hall, Katherine. They'd better get it fixed before the Scouts' Jumble Sale next week."

She turned to Karl so he would not feel excluded from the conversation. "The church hall is far too small when we come to do our plays. There are no dressing rooms for a start. We have to park a delivery lorry by the rear door and use that to get dressed in, with only a curtain down the middle separating the men from the women!"

"That's half the fun for you of doing your plays, isn't it, Mum?" Robert joked.

There was a sudden hush. Karl wondered whether they were shocked by Robert's innocuous comment. Then he realised it was not the content of Robert's joke that stunned them all, but the very fact that he had made it.

Karl saw Donald Murdoch's raised eyebrows and Robert's embarrassment. He spoke up to fill the silence.

"It would be nice to see a play with women in it. At the camp we have men to act the women's roles. They are very good but all the time we know it is really a man there, and it ... er ..."

"Distracts you?" Katherine suggested.

"Maybe that is what I want to say. Sometimes I think you could make me say something bad."

They all laughed, even Robert.

"You never know, Karl," Donald said, "perhaps it won't be so long before you're allowed to come and see one of our village plays. The authorities seem to be gradually easing restrictions as time goes by."

Gertie chipped in. "You can't complain about the way you've been treated, can you?"

Karl shrugged awkwardly. Donald saw his hesitation.

"Come on, Karl. If you've got a complaint let's hear it!"

If Robert had not been there, Karl might have held his tongue. Their eyes met briefly. Karl sensed Robert urging him to open up to them all. As it happened, it was one part of his past Karl felt able to talk about.

"Except in February and March 1945 when I was first a prisoner," he began hesitantly, "I am well treated. The food is not so much, but we know you English also have little food because you feed our people in Germany. It is not our bodies which are ... troubled, but our minds."

Gertie looked at him in astonishment. "Whatever do you mean?"

Karl layed down his knife and fork. This was going to be difficult to explain.

"At first you think we are all bad Nazis. The camps have men who have not followed Hitler beside men who are still fanatic for him. These Nazis make much trouble for the others. Some Nazi prisoners killed other prisoners. So, at last, the British put the strong Nazis in special camps, away from the others. To do this they must find who the Nazis are, so they ask us questions to ... decide if we are Black, that means strong Nazi, or White, that is against the Nazis, or Grey, somewhere in the middle, like most of us. The White prisoners are sent home first. Of course we all think we are White, and are angry when they tell us different.

"These questions make us feel like bad criminals, and there is much argument about the colour they give us, especially because still we do not know when we can go home. Our families need us, yet we must stay here to work for you, to learn about your democracy and forget our Nazi ideas. They tell us we are guilty of the terrible things the Nazis did. We must learn to be better people."

Karl stopped suddenly, then smiled at them to break the sombre mood he had created. "But here I am away from all that anger and guilt. My life is much better outside the camp. Sometimes I can think I am free."

They all sat in silence, slightly embarrassed by Karl's criticism. Gertie sensed it was a good moment to clear away the dishes and bring in the stewed prunes and custard.

Later, when they retired to the living room, Robert brought up the topic of Karl's capture again, like a child picking at an irritant spot. "You said you were badly treated when you were taken prisoner, Karl. Is that right?"

Karl sighed. He did not want to have to explain all that to these kind people. "Think what it was like," he said simply. "Many of your soldiers had comrades or family killed by us. Naturally they did not like us. Also there were too many of us. They take us to camps in Belgium, but there were not enough ... tents, the weather was wet and cold and we had little food or water. It was better as soon as we come here to England. That time is nearly forgotten. There were worse times in the war."

"I wish Robert could forget," Gertie said with feeling. "You still have nightmares, don't you, darling?"

For the second time Robert felt embarrassed until he saw Karl's sympathetic face. Both knew what it was like to be stripped of all dignity and be made to feel the scum of the earth.

A yawn suddenly escaped Karl's lips. The conversation was threatening to become awkward. There was a limit to what he felt comfortable talking about, and that limit had been reached. He excused himself and made his way upstairs to the room which had belonged to Michael, whose bones now lay at the bottom of the Atlantic Ocean.

Katherine too was tired but she dallied a while, not wanting to lie awake worrying about her father. She also wanted to hear the Murdochs' opinion of Karl. Gertie promptly obliged.

"What a nice young man! I can quite see why David wanted Karl to work for him."

"He is certainly very candid," said Donald. "He obviously felt safe enough to level criticism at our methods."

Katherine frowned. "I was wondering what sort of questions they were asked. Do you think Karl still believes all that nonsense about the Master Race?"

There was silence. Donald spoke out first. "It's difficult to say. He was brought up under the Nazi doctrine after all. From what he implied he must have been classified Grey".

The telephone interrupted him. He hurried out to answer it.

"Well, after everything Karl did today, it doesn't make the slightest difference to me what he is," Katherine declared. "Though I have a horrible suspicion Sarah's going to judge him as Black, no matter what, when she's home for Christmas." She suddenly smiled. "That reminds me. Andrew said in his last letter he's reasonably sure he'll get leave to come home at Christmas."

"That will be nice for you, dear," Gertie said, eyeing the mantelpiece clock. Half past ten. She hoped Donald was not being called out now. "How long is it since you last saw him?"

"He was over in May for a week. Seems ages now. He says he's getting really fed up with administrative work and trying to create order out of chaos. I think the novelty of conquest has worn off at last, and he wants to leave it to the Germans to sort out their own mess, or so he says."

Donald heard her remark as he returned to the room. "Well you can hardly blame him when he's got such a pretty fiancée waiting for him at home."

Katherine pulled a face. "I think I'll go to bed, if that's all right," she said. "Must get up in good time tomorrow to get back to Lane Head."

"Don't worry, Katherine," Donald said. "I'll run you both back tomorrow before surgery."

Donald and Gertie followed Katherine upstairs, leaving Robert to contemplate the dying embers in the grate.

Katherine's plans for the following day very quickly came unstuck after a series of telephone calls put her behind schedule. First Sarah called from her lodgings in Bristol; she had just received the message Katherine left there the previous evening. Katherine spent a quarter of an hour reassuring her sister that their father was only under observation and not now in any danger. She eventually persuaded Sarah to stay where she was and not catch the first train home.

Then there was a telephone call from their supplier of winter fodder, wanting to deliver a load of mangolds that week. She then had to call the vet. Even by lunchtime she had scarcely touched any household chores. Lunch would have to be a simple affair of bread and cheese today; she had no time to make soup.

She trotted out to the paddock to call Karl for lunch. He had no watch, having lost his own as a spoil of war. She found him down by the broken fence with a hammer and a mouthful of nails, replacing the railing. Beth stood nearby, watching curiously, and Joss was scrabbling under a pile of stacked branches for a mouse.

"In five minutes I am finished," Karl said through his teeth.

47

"Shall I hold those for you?"

He removed the nails and handed them to her, swiftly completing the job, before tidying up the tools.

Joss followed them back to the house, waiting in the yard while they went in to eat their cold lunch. Katherine apologised for it, explaining her busy morning.

"One of my calls was from the feed-merchant. I'll need you to clear out the junk from the fodder store this afternoon, please, Karl." She flexed her shoulders, which were aching from yesterday's frantic sawing. "It's just as well this happened in a slack period. The sheep are tupped, the harvest's in, now apart from the pruning there's nothing major to do until lambing starts in March. That's a busy time, I can tell you!"

Karl knew little about the sheep. "Tupped? What is that?" he asked innocently.

Katherine smiled wickedly. "Oh dear, how do I explain this in words you'll understand?" she lamented. "We have about two hundred and fifty ewes, female sheep, and several rams or tups. At the beginning of October the tups were put in with the ewes. That's tupping. The lambs, baby sheep, come later. Clear?"

He grinned. "Clear."

"We only use the word tup for sheep," Katherine hastened to explain. She decided to enlighten Karl further. "We don't only rear our own lambs. We also buy in lambs from Wales to fatten up for market. We can graze more sheep on our pastures, you see, than they can on the rough grass of the mountains. Daddy also likes to keep a stock of purebreds in; at the moment we have the Clun Forests. He says it makes good sense to keep a pure bloodline available."

She was reminded suddenly by her last words of the conversation last night at the Murdochs', after Karl had left the room. Purity of bloodline. The Master Race. It struck her that Karl's appearance fitted well the Nordic ideal. The thought chilled her, and she tried to dismiss such an unpleasant notion. She was aware that Karl was watching her attentively. Heaven forbid he should guess what she was thinking! She felt her face redden, and immediately stood up to clear the table. A glance out of the west-facing kitchen window revealed the approach of a threatening black rain cloud.

"I'd better get those clothes in off the line," she said. "I don't think they'll dry now. At least you've got an inside job to do this afternoon."

Karl came over to the window beside her and looked across to the Welsh border; Hay Bluff was already concealed behind a sheet of driving rain. Taking the hint, he left for the fodder store.

It was still raining three days later, on 16th November, and for five days after that. Karl finished chopping all the branches of the chestnut tree, stacking them neatly in the woodshed. The fallen branches in the orchards could wait a while longer, as could the debris in the woodland. As rain continued to fall, he accompanied Katherine and the vet on their rounds of the sodden sheep, was shown how to inspect them for signs of footrot. As the lower ground became increasingly waterlogged, Katherine decided to move them all onto higher pasture. Karl was impressed at her control of Joss.

"You ought to see my father work Joss," Katherine said from under the brim of her dripping sou'wester. "Joss obeys my commands well enough, but when he's with Daddy they really work as a team."

"I have already seen them working together. Your father told me the different whistles and words he uses for Joss to go left or right, forwards and backwards," Karl replied. "Would Joss obey me, if I give the orders?"

Katherine looked doubtful. "He might, but it's not as easy as it looks. I suppose now he knows you a bit you might be lucky, but these dogs work best for one man. Mind you, I think Joss could do the job without a master, he's that clever!"

She stooped to fondle the dog's soft, black ears as he trotted beside her back to the house. Karl diverted to the toolshed, where he was going to sharpen and clean all the tools, while Katherine set herself to tackle the baking. She was not

49

planning to visit her father in hospital that evening; she had been the day before and he insisted she save the petrol for more useful purposes. That meant Karl would again have to walk into the village in the pouring rain.

These days his clothing was permanently damp, with one set always on the drying rack over the range. Every time he came into the kitchen he would stand in front of the range, his trousers steaming gently.

The telephone rang at four; with flour-covered hands she ran to answer it. It was Donald Murdoch. He had a patient to see soon further up the valley and would stop by to collect Karl afterwards. Katherine thanked him for the offer and returned to her baking, relieved she was not the one having to go out in this awful weather.

In a short while she called Karl to sample her scones with a cup of tea, before Donald arrived. Karl had only been with them a matter of weeks but already the hollows in his cheeks were beginning to fill out, although his dark-ringed, sunken eyes never seemed to change.

She remembered a half-finished letter she had left in the study. Karl would be able to pop it in the post box for her. Leaving him to finish drinking his tea, she disappeared to the study.

It was another three-quarters of an hour before Katherine heard Donald's car draw up outside. She popped back to the kitchen to see if Karl was still there. She found him fast asleep in the rocking chair, one hand flopped nearly to the floor. Not even the tinkle of the doorbell woke him. Katherine hurried back to the hall to let Donald in.

"My goodness! When's this rain going to stop?" Donald shuddered as Katherine opened the door to him.

"Dreadful, isn't it?" she replied, taking his dripping umbrella off him and standing it by the door, where a pool of water grew steadily by the doormat. "Karl seems to have fallen asleep in the kitchen," she continued. "I'll just go and wake him up."

"Asleep, is he?" Donald stalled her. "I'm not surprised really. I don't think he slept much last night. He seems to be troubled by nightmares, just like Robert. I was called out an hour or so after Karl had his nightmare and I could see his bedroom light was still on as I went out."

Katherine lowered her voice. "Did he wake you with his nightmare?"

"Yes. He was shouting something. I went in to see what the matter was and had to wake him up. He told me then he often has bad dreams."

What on earth could be going on in the minds of those two young men that disturbed them so much? Maybe with Robert she had a pretty good idea, but as for Karl ...? She suddenly remembered the words she thought he said in jest that day in the barn with the spider. He was frightened of the dark. It seemed now he had not been joking, but it was a strange thing for a grown man to fear.

She went on into the kitchen, sorry now to have to wake him to go into the torrent again. As her hand gently shook his shoulder and she spoke his name, his grey eyes flicked into instant alertness, his hand making a grab for hers.

Katherine stepped back in alarm. No matter how much she tried to ignore it, there was a violence in this man she could never understand. That or a fear.

"Dr Murdoch's here," she told him, satisfied he was fully awake. "I'm sorry I startled you."

He looked away, collected his thoughts, then allowed his eyes to meet hers. She thought he was about to speak, but instead he turned, picked up his sodden overcoat from the back of a chair, then headed for the hall.

Katherine slowly followed. What had he wanted to say?

CHAPTER FOUR

Upon David's return from hospital, Karl moved back into his draughty room at Lane Head Farm. It was the evening of Wednesday 20th November. For Katherine's sake he was glad that life was almost back to normal, but he would miss his evenings with Robert Murdoch. They had established a deep rapport, opening up with surprising frankness to each other, often until late in the evening. It was after one such session, his memories brought too closely to mind, that Karl suffered the nightmare observed by Donald Murdoch.

On his last evening at the Murdochs', Gertie spoke to Karl privately.

"Thank you, Karl, for all you've done for Robert; there's been a real change in him. He is even starting to talk about his future."

"I'm glad I could help." Karl had wished he felt better himself.

Unpacking his belongings once more, he put the photograph back in its place. He realised he had not written home for weeks. He was allowed two letters and four post-cards a month, post-free. With December approaching he ought to send his Christmas greetings and tell his parents of his change of address. Their letters would be at Upper Claydon hostel until someone brought them out or he returned there himself.

Katherine had said she would drive him over there on Saturday. Finding some paper and a pencil amongst his belongings, he went back to the warm sitting room, where David and Katherine were ensconced. He was surprised, both here and at the Murdochs', how quickly formalities were dispensed with, so that everyone was on first name terms.

The wireless was on quietly, David reading, and Katherine darning socks and the sleeve of a cardigan. Karl settled down on the sofa and began to compose his letter.

Dear All,

I am sorry it is so long since I last wrote. Much has happened since then. In fact it is strange to be using German again. You will see from the address that I am now working and living on a farm with an English family. David Carter and his daughter Katherine are wonderful people and I have made some good friends in the village. I speak English all the time now, as I seldom see a fellow German.

I still have no idea when I will be allowed home. I told you how depressed we all felt in October when the first men from our camp left for home. At least I am out of the camp now and quite enjoy life here. I'm trying to sort out David's woodland for him as he's let it get in rather a mess since his wife was killed in a bombing raid on London. He has another daughter, Sarah, who will be home at Christmas. I'm told she won't like me, understandably, because of what happened to her mother. I'll let you know how we get on!

I think of you all and would love to be in Medebach with you this Christmas. Perhaps next year I will be there to help light the candles on the tree.

Please don't let Uwe forget his Uncle Karl. I will be sending him a small present in a separate parcel. To all of you I send my love and best wishes for a festive Christmas.

Yours with affection, Karl.

He put the letter in its envelope and wrote the familiar address.

Home was a small town nestling in the forested folds of the Hochsauerland, its outlying villages and hamlets gathered like chicks to a hen, and the Aar and Orke, tributaries of the Eder, wriggling worms between them. It was a place where he was known and respected by everyone, where he joined in the singing and dancing in the *Bierstuben*, bowled in the *Kegelbahn* and drove on lamplit sleigh rides to potato roasts. A place where he did not have to hang his head in shame and avoid accusing eyes as he found himself doing in Penchurch. In Medebach the Driesler name was something to be proud of.

His thoughts turned to the woman he had once hoped would share that name. It would be a Medebach now without

53

Ilse, of course, and without many of his old friends too. It was not simply his home he yearned for, but the security of the familiar. He needed to belong somewhere again. Too much had happened over the past seven years, too much needed to be forgotten. Perhaps he would forget in Medebach amongst the people he loved.

Katherine was watching him again.

She finished her darning and was herself writing a letter. She noticed his eyes on her and spoke her thoughts.

"It's strange we both spend our time writing letters to Germany," she commented, seeing the wistfulness in his eyes. "Me to Andrew and you to ... your parents?"

"You need not write there much longer, no?" He shut out thoughts of home. Make the best of the present. The future will come, whatever it holds. That belief had kept him going through many dark hours.

"No, thank heavens. Andrew should be home for good in the Spring." Katherine smiled at thoughts of reunions and wedding plans.

Karl wondered what this Andrew was like, whether he would prove as amiable as Robert Murdoch. Somehow he doubted it. He rather trusted David Carter's instincts, and grew ever more convinced that David was secretly unhappy about the prospect of Andrew Kellett as a son-in-law. There was a notable lack of enthusiasm from David at the disclosure that Andrew would have nine days leave over Christmas. Maybe David was just tired. Karl would be able to judge for himself in another month.

Before that he would be judged. He awaited Sarah's arrival with interest. Forewarned was forearmed, so David said. Certainly he had plenty of time to put up his defences.

He listened to them both chuckling at the wireless. Karl found the rapid comic patter and innuendo impossible to understand, but he sat and watched his hosts' faces in the dim light as they laughed along with the jokes, safe and snug in their own little world. To his surprise he was beginning to look forward to spending a day at the hostel, refreshing a German identity whose essence seemed to be slipping away.

Karl picked up the magazine underneath his letter and flicked through it, trying to break the depression that was creeping upon him, but found no distraction in it. Quietly he put the magazine back down and slipped from the sitting room to the back door.

For the first time in a week the rain clouds were withdrawing, leaving dark holes of emptiness between their tattered banner edges. He picked his way carefully in the darkness across the cobbled yard and stood leaning on the gate to the meadow which looked out down the hill, across the valley and over to the black hulk of Hay Bluff beyond. Its outline was barely visible, emerging from the enveloping cloud to lie flat-topped, devoid of trees. To his homesick heart it was the Hochsauerland of home.

Night sounds infiltrated his consciousness as further prompts to his homesickness; the cough of a sheep became the grunt of a deer, the wind took on the whispering voices of the dark conifers which clad the surrounding slopes of his home. For a moment he even thought he could smell their resinous scent, until it resolved into the odour of creosoted gate posts.

He ignored his chattering teeth for as long as he could in order to enjoy this sense of communion with his home, then reluctantly turned and retraced his steps, soothing an alert Joss on the way.

The news was on as he entered the sitting room. There were reports of widespread flooding in Britain after eight days of nonstop rain. David and Katherine seemed not to have noticed his absence, and he felt even more of an intruder than before. He stayed only to pick up his letter and say goodnight, then made his way back to his silent room for an early night.

As the wireless news finished, David Carter folded his newspaper and stood up in preparation for making his evening rounds and locking up for the night. Katherine followed him out to the kitchen to make their Ovaltine.

"Karl was quiet tonight, did you notice?" David commented as she poured milk.

"No, I didn't notice. I thought he was writing a letter or something."

55

"He was at first but then he disappeared outside for quite a while after that." He rattled the grate of the range, dislodging the ashes, and set another log on to burn slowly overnight.

"I didn't really notice him go out, to tell the truth," she remarked, "but I did see him come in again. Now I think of it, you're right, he was a bit subdued. I hope he's not feeling too lonely up here. I gather he and Robert spent most evenings talking together."

"Perhaps we can get the Monopoly board out tomorrow evening, or something he can join in with."

"Why not?"

By half past ten Katherine could hear her father's familiar, resonant snores from his room along the landing. He seemed well enough now, although he had strict instructions from the hospital to rest completely for another week before he could even think about resuming light tasks.

She climbed into bed, wrapped her dressing gown around her shoulders and propped herself against the pillow to knit before going to sleep. She was suddenly aware of the grandfather clock in the hall striking twelve.

She put down the knitting reluctantly and switched off the bedside light. A dog fox barked away up in the woods and she hoped he was not bent on mischief in the poultry house, although she knew it was well secured for the night. An owl shrieked eerily, also from the woods, as Katherine tried to settle herself off to sleep, but her mind was too active.

She decided to put the time to good use, rather than waste it. It was seldom during the day that she had the chance to collect her thoughts and start to make plans for her wedding. She had some ideas but ought to start thinking seriously about it, now Andrew's final homecoming was not so very far off.

The dress would be a problem, with clothing coupons still the order of the day. She would consult Sarah on that; her sister had a far keener eye for fashion and materials. In the meantime she could draw up a mental list of guests to invite. Andrew would no doubt insist on inviting his brat of a cousin, Arthur Rowlands-Pickering, perhaps even ask him to be Best

Man. Arthur delighted in stirring up arguments to make a "lively debate" as he called it. Arthur usually chose the most contentious issues he could put his mind to – with Sarah it had been that women should stay at home and not expect to be as well educated as men – so he was not the most popular figure at social gatherings, which were fairly frequent at Froxley Grange.

What would her new life on the estate be like? There were always people milling about there, whether estate workers or guests of the house. It would certainly be very different from her isolated existence up here on the hill. She knew that once she was Andrew's wife these confines would be lifted and she would travel with him across the length and breadth of Britain, to all those towns and cities she had never visited, to London shows, house parties in Surrey or Suffolk. Andrew had a wealth of friends and contacts from school, and from army and riding circles. She would have to learn to fit in.

Her father's snores penetrated her thoughts, reminding her of her conflicting loyalties to him and to Andrew. The spectre of her father alone here on the farm haunted her future happiness. She knew he could well take care of himself as long as he was fit enough to do so, and he was a sociable man who enjoyed the company of his friends of an evening at the Walnut Tree or with the Murdochs. But the times when he was alone here would try him severely. And what if he should fall ill again, with no one around to help ...?

Katherine bit her knuckles to stop this train of thought. She would only work herself into a state of anxiety over ifs and maybes. She turned her light on to wash away the images conjured up in her mind and looked at her alarm clock. It showed a quarter to one already.

A distant sound caught her attention; someone crying out. Immediately she thought of her father, but his snores rumbled on. Again she heard it, a faint cry of fear from outside, repeated again more urgently. Hurriedly she jumped out of bed, tying her dressing gown tightly around her, pulled on her slippers and rushed downstairs, fumbling with the back door. Karl's terror-stricken voice was more audible now. She sped across the yard and up the uneven steps to his room, not pausing to knock first, and switched on the light.

He was lying face down on the bed, his pillow fallen to the floor. He was crying out repeatedly a word in German and seemed to be trying to push away or fend off something with his right hand.

Catching hold of his arm she shook him and called his name to wake him, but it was not like the time when he had dozed off in the kitchen and had woken with a start. Now she found it difficult to rouse him. The touch of her hand on his arm only increased his terror initially, until it became so great that he woke himself finally from his dream. As his eyes opened and he saw her face there was no recognition at first, only blind fear, but then she saw his tensed muscles gradually relax as consciousness took over. He dropped his gaze, ashamed for her to see him in such a state. The sweat on his face and body was rapidly cooling him; a reactive tremor began to shake him.

Katherine picked up the pillow, put it back on the bed and pulled the slipped and tumbled bedclothes back over him.

"All right now?" she asked him. She could see that he was not from the persistent trembling of the bedclothes. He would not look at her either. They both heard her father's slow tread up the steps and he entered, tousled and bleary-eyed to find out what the disturbance was all about.

"Karl has had a bad nightmare, Daddy. I think he's still feeling a bit shaky."

David Carter sat down on the single chair. Sarah had suffered nightmares for months after her mother's death and David used to get her to tell him about them. He tried this on Karl now.

"Do you want to tell me about it?"

Karl shook his head firmly, as though still trying to clear the terrors from his mind.

"How about a cup of tea?" Katherine suggested. "I must say, I could do with one!" She felt even less sleepy now than before the disturbance and was happy to stay up a while longer if necessary.

Karl agreed readily to her offer. He knew it would take him a long time to fall asleep again. David, however, declined the tea. He returned to his room, satisfied Katherine would look after Karl well enough without his help.

Katherine put the kettle on the range and took two cups down. She realised Karl was standing silently by the range, watching her prepare the tea. He had put his clothes on, for want of a dressing gown, but he still looked cold.

"You seemed quiet this evening," she said casually. "Is something troubling you?"

She hoped he would not think her question intrusive, but if she didn't ask then nobody else would, and she doubted whether Karl would ever say anything unless asked.

Her doubts were unfounded, however. He managed a smile in recognition of her concern. "I had ... *Heimweh*. I wanted to be home," he explained hesitantly.

Katherine knew it was a measure of his shattered nerves that he used a German word to her. Normally he tried to talk around a word he did not know, rather than resort to his own language in the hope there might be a similarity. The only German words she had heard him utter were that one just now – *Heimweh*, or whatever it was – the word for a spider, and some expletives when he had not known she was nearby. And the one in his nightmare of course. It was almost as though he was trying to deny his nationality, hide it even, and yet he complained of being homesick.

She automatically supplied his English word for him. "You're homesick? I'm not surprised. It must be awful for you all still being stuck over here. Do you want to talk about your home?"

She knew he did not want to talk about his nightmare, so this seemed the next best thing. Hopefully it would drive away the nightmare, which was evidently still lingering with him. She handed him his tea then sat in the rocking chair.

Karl drew up a kitchen chair close to the range next to her and sat down too. He studied the stone flagged floor for a moment then looked up at her. "It will only make me have ... no ... *be* more homesick, but I tell you. I come from the Sauerland, part of Westfalen, where there are mostly hills, forests and streams. Some valleys are made to fill with water – for the Ruhr industries."

She knew instantly he was referring to the dams bombed by the RAF. "I know where you mean," she said.

Satisfied, Karl continued with his guided tour of the Sauerland. "Many people from the Ruhr cities come to our area to walk, hunt and in winter to ski. Our hills are not like the *Alpen*, not so steep or high; a little bit perhaps like here but with many more trees – beech and pine. Also we have black and white houses, the same as you, but the roofs almost all are grey, not red, and often the walls have also these grey tiles."

He was beginning to relax now, warming to his subject.

"My family house is quite big. We have guest rooms for tourists or business friends. Rudi – he is my brother – he and I go with our father to hunt with our guests, or to ski. In the evenings we sing folk songs or drive in the ... like a wagon with skis ..."

"Sleigh," Katherine told him.

"In the sleigh," he continued with a nod of thanks, "to a forest house where we sing and dance – and drink of course!"

He sounded happier already, Katherine thought, as she listened to further tales of life in Medebach. She yawned abruptly.

"I'm sorry. I keep you out of bed," Karl apologised.

"That's all right," she assured him. "It was interesting for me to hear about your home. You must tell me more sometime." She yawned again and put the empty tea-cups in the sink.

"Sleep well, Karl," she whispered to him, her hand on the kitchen doorknob.

"Thank you. Sleep well too," he mouthed from the back door.

David Carter spent the following days in his study, sorting through various documents and keeping out of Katherine's way after her ever-watchful eye became too much for him. He was happy to leave the farm work to Karl.

He did not realise Karl often had nightmares until Katherine told him so, the day after their disturbed night. It made him even more dubious about Sarah's impending arrival, in case Sarah's intolerance sparked off more. Her latest letter expressed her opinion of Karl most acerbically, contrasting strikingly with the compassion he witnessed from Katherine for their exotic employee. He wondered how he and Karl would get along once Katherine left Lane Head to go and live at Froxley Grange with that ... He stopped himself from thinking the uncharitable word that had almost emerged.

Today was the day Katherine was going to take Karl over to the hostel, since he himself was forbidden to drive as yet. He looked at the date on his calendar. Saturday the 23rd November and still he hadn't received payment for the cider apples. He reached for some paper and began writing to the cider company.

Katherine popped her head around the door a short while later. "I'm just off with Karl now, Daddy, then I'm going on into Hereford to do some shopping. Is there anything you want from there?"

"No thanks, Beauty. Have you any idea what time you'll be back?"

"After I've collected Karl again, save me coming and going. I'll have lunch out. I've left you some sandwiches and soup in the larder."

Half an hour later Katherine stopped the Austin 10 at the gates of the hostel. "I'll be back here for you at five."

Karl climbed out of the car, his letter home tucked safely in his pocket.

"I'll be here."

She watched him walk over to the wooden hut by the gate to be checked in by a bored-looking guard. She had not been up to the hostel before, situated as it was in the middle of nowhere. It was no more than a couple of Nissen huts, a few brick-built blocks and the front gate the only sign of security. Of course the men were out working in the fields all day; it would be pointless to surround them with barbed wire just at night. She knew Kingshill still had a token barbed wire perimeter fence. It probably served only to keep out stray animals. There again, Kingshill was obviously designated as a Grey camp. She wondered what the really Black one was like, up in the north of Scotland.

She took a last look at the little German enclave then turned the car around and headed off for the city.

The day passed more quickly than Katherine expected. She browsed around the shops, getting ideas for Christmas presents as well as possible wedding presents, when the time came. At half past four she returned to the car with her shopping and set out for Upper Claydon, arriving with five minutes to spare.

She could see Karl already standing waiting outside. As she drew up, the gate-guard, a pasty-faced corporal, approached the car with deep suspicion when he saw its occupant was a woman.

"I've come to collect ..." She could not remember Karl's rank. What on earth should she call him? The corporal was eyeing her with even deeper suspicion, or was it even a leer? She felt herself growing impatient with him and her anger prompted her memory. "Sergeant Driesler is billeted with us. My father is unable to drive at the moment so I've come to collect him," she said coldly and distinctly.

The corporal did not seem impressed. "May I see your identification, miss?"

Katherine reached in her bag and showed him her card. "That's all right then, Miss Carter. We can't be having them going off with strange women, if you get my meaning, can we?"

The leer was definitely there, Katherine noticed crossly. She also noticed that Karl was looking as angry with the corporal as she was.

He slammed the car door as he got in and sat down heavily. "I'm sorry he spoke to you like that," he said.

She let out the clutch jerkily in her impatience to get away from the hostel.

"Don't worry about it. It was nothing really," she said but her driving gave away her anger, twice crunching the gears badly.

"I see you have some post," she said, indicating the parcel he had put on the back seat of the car. She also noticed his aggressively short hair cut, but she made no comment about that.

"Yes."

He seemed distracted. "Are you still angry with him too?" she asked.

He grimaced. "You noticed!" He looked sideways out of the window over the darkening countryside, to where the lights of a farm were twinkling in the gloom. "He searched me twice today. He does not like my freedom."

He continued to keep his head turned from her so she could not see the bitterness he felt. "To go back there," he continued, "is like I was back in the war. Today I was again a prisoner of war. Now I am free."

So the place was not as free as it looked, Katherine thought wryly. "You're glad to be back with us, then?"

He hit the dashboard with his fist. "I would be more glad to be home!" Immediately he regretted his outburst. "I am sorry. Yes, I am glad to be back with you. I am angry because they still call me prisoner of war. There is no war! Why am I still here?"

She knew there was no point trying to console him; they had discussed this issue before. She waited for him to speak again, sensing there was more to come, but he stayed silent.

They travelled a mile or more before Karl gave vent to his feelings once more.

"I saw today in our magazine, *Wochenpost*, that the British want prisoners who are forest workers to go immediately back to Germany. I could give my name, but I will not."

"Why ever not?" she demanded, incredulous that he should reject such an opportunity.

"Because I know that I would be sent to another part of Germany to work and must stay there a long time before I may go home. That is always the way they do things. I think, if I stay here, I will be home sooner, do you understand me?"

"Yes. Perfectly. You don't have much faith in bureaucracy, do you?" It was the sort of situation she could imagine Andrew having to handle, soothing irate Germans who found themselves in the wrong place because of some administrative ineptitude or lack of concern. She smiled at the picture it conjured up for her.

"I do not think it is funny," Karl snapped.

Katherine was taken aback. He *was* in a mood! He seemed to have been well and truly unsettled by his day at the hostel.

He eventually broke the silence as they drove into the yard at Lane Head. "Forgive me. I should not speak to you like that," he said stiffly.

"That's all right, Karl. It doesn't matter."

She pondered this change in him, while putting the car away. This brooding self-pity was simply a continuation of the conversations with fellow prisoners during the day. They were learning freedom of speech, trying it out amongst themselves without fear of the consequences. It seemed his initial pleasure at his newfound freedom was fast waning. The more freedom he was given, the more he wanted; the constraints that were still in force hung on him like lead. At least she would be prepared for such a mood next time he returned from the hostel at Christmas.

Having a POW about the place certainly gave her something else to think about rather than the usual village happenings. Every time she went into the Post Office, Mrs Tucker asked about "her" German, how he behaved, what he talked about. Until now Katherine did not have much to say, except to extol Karl's virtues. She knew she would not divulge the deeper side of his nature that she now saw: the homesickness and bitterness, let alone the nightmares. No wonder he always looked so tired. She had heard him cry out again last night, her ears sensitised now so that she woke up, wondering whether to go to him. But he seemed to have woken himself up and she decided to let him be.

She went through to the sitting room while dinner was cooking. Karl was showing her father a new photograph his family must have sent in the parcel. Karl's strange mood in the car seemed to have dissolved away entirely. He was back to his more normal self, pointing out who the people in the photograph were.

Katherine leaned over the back of her father's chair to get a good look at the photograph too. It was remarkably similar to the one he already had on his chest of drawers. Now, however, the baby was a serious little three-year-old boy, holding tightly on to his mother's hand. Anna had lost a lot of weight, although whether that was due to the natural slimming down after childbirth or a result of the serious food shortages in Germany, Katherine did not know. The main difference between the two photographs was the inclusion of Karl's brother, Rudi. He looked a good deal younger than Karl, almost as thin, but far more carefree, his jaunty smile at the camera showing a casual indifference to life's problems. Their parents seemed reasonably unscathed by the passage of time, and it was evident that Karl's mother was pleased to have her younger son back home.

"Is Rudi the youngest or is Anna?" Katherine asked, taking pains to pronounce the latter name in the German fashion. She would not attempt the magnificently rolled "r" Karl gave to Rudi's name.

Karl's reply astonished both Katherine and her father. "Rudi is in the middle. He is two years younger than I. Anna is a year younger than Rudi. She is twenty-two now, and already two years a widow."

It was David Carter who stated the obvious. "So you are twenty-five, Karl." And seem well over thirty, both he and Katherine added silently.

Karl nodded. "On Friday I will be twenty-six."

He was only too well aware of their surprise. He had spent much of the last six years fighting for his life, with very little break from the gruelling demands of warfare, only to become a member of a defeated army at the end of it all.

"I'll have to make you a birthday cake, shan't I?" Katherine said lightly, anxious to prevent Karl from slipping back into his earlier mood. "With twenty-six candles on it. Except I don't think we have that many. Will six do?"

Karl grinned, immediately lifting at least five years off his apparent age. "That would be nice. My mother said in her letter, she wishes she could send me a cake, but she keeps any special food for little Uwe, Anna's boy, as he has not been well."

"How are your family coping with all the shortages?" David asked in concern, looking again at the thin faces of the whole family.

"It is not so bad for them as for others," Karl said lightly. "They can even send a photograph to show it. My father's business was busy both before and during the war. We lived quite well then, so they have things they can give now for food. Also we have some land, two cows and some chickens. There is always food in the country. Naturally it is the people from the big towns and cities for whom the life is harder. There are many new people in my town who look for work. People who flee from the east, as well as from the cities. My sister Anna likes one of them who works for my father now. My parents hope she will marry him soon."

"How many men does your father employ?" David Carter's interest was purely that of a businessman.

"Now I do not know. Before there were usually five men in the forest, three in the sawmill, and a lorry driver, myself and Rudi too if not in the school or giving our guests skiing lessons. I think during the war he had more workers."

"Where would he get more men from in wartime?" Katherine asked, knowing only too well the difficulties of finding manpower at such a time.

Karl appeared uneasy. "From the same place as you."

Katherine's mouth dropped open. "You mean prisoners of war?"

David's face darkened. He did not think the comparison a valid one and could tell by Karl's rueful expression that neither did he. He imagined such prisoners would have been expected to work a good deal harder than Karl. Charitably he remembered how he himself baulked at the idea of using POW labour but ultimately gave in to expediency. Probably Karl's father had no choice in the matter. It was clear though, that the Driesler family was holding its head above water.

Katherine attempted to rectify her *faux pas*. "You gave skiing lessons? Gosh, I'd love to be able to ski. It must be almost as good as flying."

Karl was grateful for her diversion. "Yes it is," he confirmed enthusiastically. "Perhaps one day you will visit my home and I will teach you. We usually have enough snow in winter, but we can never be sure exactly when the snow will come. Not like in Norway."

It was the first time he had mentioned where he had fought, apart from his capture in Holland, but Katherine was so wrapped up by the thought of skiing that she missed the inference. David did not.

"When were you in Norway?"

Karl accepted his slip with easy grace. "From April 1940 until March 1941, so I was only one winter there, but what a winter!" His eyes sparkled at the memory. "It was very cold. We must be very careful of the frost, but what snow! I never skied so much before."

"Were you out on ski patrol then?" David thought the question innocent enough, but Karl's eyes narrowed.

"You want to know what kind of a soldier I was?"

David wondered at Karl's touchiness. "No. I just wanted to know whether you skied in your spare time or as part of your duties."

Karl decided he had nothing to lose. Tell them the bare facts and the rest could stay unspoken.

"I was in a mountain division in the north of Norway, near Narvik. We patrolled on skis. I was a ... sharpshooter?" He had translated the word directly from the German word *Scharfschütze*.

"A sniper!" Katherine gasped.

"Yes. As a boy I learned to shoot in the forest. In the Hitler Youth and in my home town I won shooting prizes. So, when the war came, my skill was used."

Katherine found Karl's revelations disturbing. A sniper aimed directly at a man, not just a tank or house or city. He saw his victim die. But, she told herself, she should have realised all this sort of thing was part and parcel of Karl's history. She just shut her mind to it. Now, hearing it from his own mouth, she thought she had some idea of Sarah's feelings.

Karl knew he shocked her, although why he was not so sure. He was a soldier. Such things were inevitable. But he resolved not to talk about himself again.

In an effort to defuse the awkwardness, David made reference to his own service in the Great War. "Yes, I'm afraid too many men of my generation and yours know what it is like to kill. We are all killers, even your Andrew," he reminded his daughter.

The ploy worked. Katherine was now too busy defending her fiancé to be unduly concerned about Karl.

"Andrew has never killed anyone," she retorted loudly.

Her father rebuked her quietly. "Only because of the nature of his duties. That doesn't mean to say he wouldn't kill if called upon to do so." He decided the topic had gone on long enough. "Is that dinner ready yet, Beauty?"

Katherine clapped her hand over her mouth in consternation. She had become so engrossed in the conversation she quite forgot the vegetables cooking.

The subject was dropped completely over dinner. Instead David and Katherine discussed the Christmas Bazaar in the church hall.

Karl found himself brooding upon Katherine's reaction. There was no doubt he was a killer, but he was a German killer, and that seemed to make a difference to her. Was he oversensitive to allegations of national guilt? In the Belgian camp he heard men blaming the poor conditions there on themselves. The victors were only getting even, was the lament. To what degree was he culpable? He could not answer

68

that question. Should he even have to? Only Robert Murdoch was privy to the details of his military career, and he wanted it to stay that way. There was no reason why anyone else should know anything.

David Carter noticed Karl hardly touched the pie he would normally have finished off in the space of two minutes. He guessed at the reason and thought of a possible antidote.

"We haven't had a good rabbit stew for a while, Beauty," he said with a covert wink at his daughter. "If Karl is such a good hunter, I suggest we send him out early with the shotgun tomorrow and see if he can bag us a rabbit or a pheasant or two. What do you say, Karl?"

It was the offer of absolution. He looked up eagerly, only to have Katherine once more drag him down into the mire.

"Is that allowed, Daddy?"

"Frankly I don't care whether it is or it isn't," David retorted. "As far as I'm concerned it's only a task I'll have given Karl to do as part of his general work on the farm. I can't see why anyone should complain."

Katherine was still uneasy about the legalities of such an activity for Karl. He was keen to hunt again, so did his best to put her at her ease. "When we had guards with us in the fields," he told her, "they often let us carry their rifles for them. There is no reason to worry."

"That's all right then. I just didn't want you to get into trouble, that's all."

She remembered an activity she was keen for him to try. "You could always come down to church with us afterwards," she suggested hopefully, "save being on your own all morning."

She had tried a different ploy each time she had asked him, and had received various excuses in reply. Churches were the one place where fraternisation of a kind was allowed. As so many POWs lived away from the larger camps, it was often difficult for their own padres to visit each hostel. POWs were thus permitted to make use of a local parish church, subject to the general consent of the congregation. The Rev. Thornton of St Michael and All Angels in Penchurch had extended his welcome already to the Carter's employee, via Katherine, but Karl's excuses had ranged from having been brought up a Catholic, to wanting to write a letter home. When she once suggested he might just like to go for a change of scene, he still declined. He gave her a ready answer now.

"I like to be on my own," he explained, hiding his amusement at her persistence to involve him in religion, which he knew was important to her. "I have only Sunday morning when I can do things for myself. Like the wooden shoes I made."

"Clogs," Katherine reminded him. He was right. He worked hard for them all week. She should not begrudge him his free time. His clogs had been masterpieces, saving his precious boots from perpetual wear. "Do you think you could possibly make me a pair?"

"Of course." He grinned. "On Sunday."

Upon their return from church and visit afterwards to the Walnut Tree, the Carters immediately noticed the two rabbits strung up and hanging from a nail in the wall by the back door. Karl had also finished making Katherine's clogs. He presented them to her after lunch and she tried them on for size.

"It's weird walking in them!" she said, taking some hesitant steps in the heavy, unyielding footwear. She found that by splaying her toes she managed better and did a trial circuit of the yard. "If we both wear our clogs out here Daddy will think Beth's got out!" she giggled. "You ought to make a pair for the Christmas Bazaar. I'm sure they'd be snapped up."

"Perhaps I will." He was going to have his work cut out to make everything he planned in time for Christmas.

CHAPTER FIVE

Sarah's Christmas homecoming coincided opportunely with a government announcement. Unable to offer the POWs a faster rate of repatriation or better food rations, more freedom was to be granted instead. Well-behaved prisoners would be allowed to walk unescorted within a five mile radius of their camp or billet until lighting-up time. Also, within the same radius, they would be allowed to accept invitations to private homes, subject to their camp commandant's approval.

David read these details with interest whilst waiting in the village for Sarah's bus to arrive. Not that the first allowance made much difference to Karl anyway, he thought, although he did tend to avoid the village in his wanderings. It was the second detail that was of more interest, as Karl would be able to visit the Murdochs now. Karl had not been back there since David's return from hospital, although Robert had called a couple of times on Sunday afternoons to go for a walk and chat with Karl.

David hoped such an official display of tolerance and compassion towards the POWs would rub off on Sarah. He was more worried than he cared to admit to Katherine about his younger daughter's prejudice. Her letters home remained vehemently opposed to Karl's presence. Now it would only be a few minutes more before she met him in person.

He folded up the newspaper so that the article of interest was uppermost, leaving it prominently displayed on the passenger seat of the car. The Hereford bus drew up in front of the school. Sarah was the last to dismount, a heavy suitcase hindering her progress. David hurried over to greet her.

"Hello, precious!" he called, giving her a peck on the cheek. Sarah hugged him warmly in return, giving him an extra squeeze in recognition of his illness.

71

"Hello, Daddy. You're looking well!" She stood back a step and took a longer look, nodding her head in confirmation of her initial impression. "You look better than you have for ages," she remarked with pleasure.

"And all the better for having you home again," was the response. "Let's get your suitcase into the car." He went to pick it up but she stopped him firmly.

"It's OK. I can manage, if you just get the boot open ready." She had been warned by Katherine not to be fooled by their father's eagerness to display how well he felt.

Sweeping aside the newspaper on the seat, she sat down and began to regale her father with tales of the term's happenings, in particular what a mess her friend Godfrey Wells made of his part in *Tartuffe*.

"You wouldn't have thought anybody could be such a complete ham. All he had to do was sit and be the King watching the play, but he fidgeted about so much that his wig kept catching on his coat and slipping off, much to the audience's delight."

David was only half listening to her as they approached the farm. He wondered if she sensed his increasing tension and this prattle was a reaction to it.

"Home Sweet Home," Sarah sighed with relief as David parked the car in the yard. "Or rather, not so sweet."

It was her first allusion to their new employee, and David decided there and then to take a firm hand, even though she had only just arrived home. He had to stamp on the sparks of her intolerance before they caught hold and burned out of control.

"I don't want to hear talk like that from you while you're here, do you understand?"

She made no reply, so he lectured her further. "Karl is a good worker, Sarah, and a great help to me on the farm. Katherine and I both like him and get on well with him. I don't want the efficient running of this farm jeopardised by any childish behaviour from you."

He saw her flinch at the word "childish". He was in danger of provoking a mulish reaction, but he hoped her new maturity might prevail.

His faith in her seemed to be partially rewarded. "Don't worry, Daddy. I'll try not to make too many waves."

It was not the promise he hoped for, but it would have to do. He stepped out of the car and opened the boot, noticing Karl lurking watchfully by the toolshed. David surreptitiously waved him back, to at least allow Sarah the chance to enter the house and greet Katherine while still in a reasonably good mood.

Karl's sense of foreboding was confirmed when David came over to speak to him, once Sarah was safely inside the house.

"Would you mind staying out here, just for a short while, so she can settle herself in and see her home is the same as it always was?"

"No swastikas here you mean?"

David was not sure whether Karl said this as a joke or not. If so, then it was in poor taste. He hoped Karl was not going to resent Sarah's attitude to the point where fireworks were inevitable. He knew from experience how trying Sarah could be. This Christmas would be a severe test of their mutual tolerance.

Sarah was always pleased to come home. Much as she enjoyed her university lifestyle, she always treasured the familiar house, unpacking her bags in her old bedroom where childhood toys and mementos stood as guardians of the past. She picked out the framed photograph of her parents from her suitcase and installed it on her dressing table. After unpacking the remainder of her luggage and text books, she changed into a navy woollen dress, repaired her make-up, then went downstairs to help Katherine in the kitchen.

Sarah noticed immediately that the dinner table was set for four. "Good God! Does he eat with us then?" she exclaimed.

Katherine was horrified, her eyes darting over to the larder. Karl emerged, holding the Worcester Sauce bottle.

"Yes, he does," Karl said neutrally, placing the bottle on the table, before approaching Sarah with his right hand outstretched in greeting. He hoped her innate manners would allow her to respond appropriately. "How do you do, Sarah? It is a pleasure to meet you at last."

From his English lessons at the camps, Karl knew that the phrase "How do you do?" demanded no specific answer, so he was not too surprised when he received none now, accepting without comment her refusal to shake his hand. She ignored him completely, flaring up at Katherine instead.

"I don't believe it, Katherine! You never said he looked so much like a flaming Nazi, all tall, blond and blue-eyed. But you've really got one of the Master Race here, haven't you!" She stormed out of the kitchen in a fury and crashed through into their father's study.

Slowly David put down his pen and listened to his daughter's outburst. The fireworks were starting sooner than expected.

"I'm not going to sit at the same table as him!" she protested. "I didn't realise you let him have the run of the house! I thought I'd be able to live here without having to see him. Instead he's made himself right at home, and you've gone and let him!"

"Of course we have," David answered her quietly, aware that Sarah's raised voice was carrying through to the kitchen. "He's not a dog like Joss to be kept outside. Of course we've given him the run of the house. This is his home for the time being." He took her hand. "Look, Sarah," he went on patiently. "Perhaps you don't fully understand or appreciate the circumstances here, but you must accept them as they are. I am not going to change anything just because you are home for a few weeks. Give Karl a chance and you'll find he's just like any other young man."

Sarah conceded defeat with ill grace. "Just don't expect me to talk to him, that's all!" She swept out of the room and crashed her way upstairs.

David watched her departure and sighed heavily. This was not a prestigious start. What a child she was still; headstrong and unreasonable. Why were his daughters so different in nature?

At the dinner table Sarah managed to put on a good act, apparently as unaware of Karl's presence as Macbeth's guests were of Banquo's ghost. If he said anything she cut in straight away with a comment to Katherine about some triviality or other. David watched the performance with growing anger, while Karl became steadily more aware of the rift he was causing in this otherwise closely knit family.

Abandoning any further attempts at conversation, Karl ate the rest of his meal in silence, listening to the sisters catching up on mutual gossip. Like David earlier, he wondered about the difference in their characters. In appearance they were not so dissimilar, sharing their mother's thick, wavy chestnut hair, hazel eyes and fine, oval face. Katherine's eyes reflected her mother's serenity, while Sarah's had a fire and determination he could not detect in either parent. He had studied the photograph in the sitting room of David and Ethel Carter, taken on their tenth wedding anniversary. From what he heard spoken of Ethel Carter, Katherine seemed to be a carbon copy. Sarah's different character was reflected in the harder lines of her face; or maybe it was the effect of the make-up. It was strange to see a woman wearing make-up as an everyday event. In Germany, women were discouraged from such displays of worldliness, and Katherine was not in the habit of using it regularly. But whatever the differences between the two sisters, the name "Beauty" could be applied equally well to either.

Karl slipped out to the toolshed to keep the peace after dinner. There was work out there which required his prolonged attention; the family would no doubt welcome a lessening of tension.

He reached up to a shelf stacked with half-used tins of paint and thinners and pulled out a sack hidden there. Sitting at the workbench, he unwrapped a piece of apple wood roughly carved into a form already recognisably Joss. Some weeks ago Karl decided to carve each of the Carters a present for

Christmas as a token of his appreciation of their friendship. Joss was to be for David. He had already finished the likeness of a girl feeding chickens for Katherine, and he had decided to carve Beth for Sarah. Having met her he thought that a fire-breathing dragon or maybe a cold and deadly polar bear might be more appropriate. Sunday mornings were his secret carving time, but now Christmas was rapidly approaching and he would have to spend a good few evenings shivering out here in order to finish in time.

By a quarter past ten his hands were too numb to hold the chisel. He tidied up and hid the carving in its sack up on the shelf behind the tins of paint, then strolled back to the kitchen. David appeared at the back door just as Karl approached.

"Ah, there you are, Karl. I was wondering where you'd got to." David lowered his voice. "Sarah has promised me she'll behave decently towards you; but it is difficult for her having a stranger in the house, so please be patient with her. I'm sure she'll come round to accepting you soon enough."

"Don't worry," Karl reassured him. "I can understand how she feels. I will try to stay out of her way. I don't expect all Britishers to be friendly."

As it turned out over the next few days, Sarah spent most of her time at her friend Audrey Patterson's house, or tucked away in her room revising or preparing an essay. Her cold-shouldering of Karl was tempered to a tolerable level, and David began to hope the storm had died. He even felt confident enough, after the new government directives, to suggest Karl came with them to the Christmas Bazaar. After a moment's hesitation Karl decided to take the opportunity to see an English village community in action. It would be an ordeal, he knew, but the more he mixed with them, now that it was allowed, the more used to him they would become, which he hoped might also be the case with Sarah. He realised his mistake in being too forward with her at first, and now held back.

On Saturday the 14th, the day of the Bazaar, Sarah set off early on her bicycle to visit Audrey, saying she would join them later at the church hall. The others left Lane Head Farm at a quarter to two riding in the dogcart since the day was fine. A crowd was assembled outside the hall. The Bazaar was a popular event. It seemed Karl would get to see most of the villagers today, as well as people from the outlying hamlets and further down the valley.

The church hall was a draughty, ramshackle affair with a corrugated iron roof and green weatherboarding, not unlike the cricket pavilion which stood in a corner of the meadow near the river. Gertie Murdoch stood at the door of the hall, welcoming visitors and collecting their entrance money. She was delighted when the Carter entourage turned up with Karl.

"It's about time the government's seen sense and let you out and about, Karl! I've managed to persuade Robert to help on the White Elephant stall. I'm sure he'll be very glad to see you."

Sarah had arrived at the Bazaar with Audrey a few minutes earlier and was astonished to see Gertie Murdoch chatting away to Karl and positively fawning over him like some long lost nephew, instead of a warmongering German whose countrymen killed one of her sons. She turned in irritation to Audrey.

"What's come over everybody? They're greeting that monster with open arms and cries of welcome! I can't believe it! Even Reverend Thornton's joining in now."

Apparently determined to set the standard for the rest of the village, John Thornton was giving Karl an enthusiastic handshake.

"Welcome to Penchurch, Karl! I'm so glad you're able to visit us here now."

John Thornton was of the same generation as David Carter and Donald Murdoch. He too experienced the Great War, but he always preached an open-mindedness which was absorbed and put into practice by many of his congregation. He did not want to be seen to fail in his policy now the severest test was put upon it.

The use of his first name by a total stranger quietly amused Karl. Such an honour is usually reserved for children and half-wits, he thought. It seems Germans come into the same category. Still it's better than being given the cold-shoulder.

Misinterpreting Karl's smile, the Rev. Thornton continued his welcoming speech. "I hope you will find something tempting to buy. Our ladies have been very busy making things for the cakes and preserves stall."

Karl disillusioned him. " I am sorry, I have no money."

The Rev. Thornton looked surprised, so David explained. "Karl can only spend his wages at the camp. It's not proper money he's given, you see, John."

"Oh, that's a shame. Never mind!" he said, turning back to Karl. "You can still enjoy the festive atmosphere we've spent all morning trying to achieve." He pointed to the holly and ivy fronds wound around the windows and roof supports, and the coloured streamers laced from corner to corner of the hall. "It's the nursery school Christmas party in here on Wednesday, so we thought the decorations would do for both events," he explained.

Karl held out the paper parcel he was carrying. "I cannot buy anything, but I can give something perhaps," he said, handing over the parcel.

John Thornton took the parcel and carefully unwrapped it to reveal a beautifully carved Clun Forest sheep, with its distinctive short, pricked ears and concave profile. David grinned broadly as he realised what Karl had been up to in the toolshed each evening since Sarah's arrival.

"May I?" he asked, once the Reverend had himself examined the carving.

"By all means." John Thornton turned to the tall young man beside him who was able to produce such a remarkable work of art. "You've got a great talent there. I'm sure it will fetch a nice price on our handicraft stall. If you ever have the time and feel like making any more, I'm sure we'll have a ready market for them."

"I'll see what I can do."

Karl was delighted to be able to use one of those stock English phrases to this amiable figure of village authority. He now had the approval of the doctor and the parson. He felt his battered pride and self-esteem begin to resume their former status.

He caught sight of Sarah glowering at him over on the other side of the hall. What would it take to earn her approval?

David paid the fourpence entry fee for each of them, which included a cup of tea and a biscuit later on. They moved on into the already crowded hall. Katherine began to feel embarrassed for Karl as heads turned whispering in their direction. Karl spotted Robert hard at work behind a table piled with old lampshades, vases, assorted crockery, even a wind-up gramophone prominently displayed complete with a stack of records, and made his way through the crowd.

Robert called across in mock despair. "Hey! Come and give me a hand would you?" Beads of sweat formed on his forehead in the stuffy air of the hall and the throng of people pressing for attention.

Karl pushed his way round to the back of the stall, whereupon Robert explained the pricing system. "Everything on this side sixpence, that side tuppence and those over there are individually priced. Got that?"

Karl found that most of the villagers were very patient with his ineptness with the unfamiliar British coins. One or two customers made it plain they would only be served by Robert, but the majority seemed to revel in the novelty of having a German serve them. When the initial rush began to die down Robert and Karl had more time to chat.

"My mother thought this would do me good and stop me brooding about the house," Robert said. Another satisfied customer walked away with a Victorian hallmarked silver toast rack for sixpence. "To my surprise I'm quite enjoying it. I suppose I have rather hidden myself away. I even volunteered for the cricket team for next summer."

Karl was pleased for him. So, he thought, Robert is regaining his lost confidence too. "That is wonderful! One day you must explain to me this cricket."

Robert laughed. "It would take more than a day to explain it, I fancy. There's a whole new language to learn – "bye", "leg-break", "silly mid-on", "maiden over" – and that's just for starters. I suppose I could explain the basic rules in a few minutes. The best thing though would be if you watched us play one Sunday afternoon when the season starts."

"When is that?"

"In May." Robert saw the light go out of Karl's eyes at the thought of still being in England then.

"Any news yet when your turn is for repatriation?"

"No. Could be another year or more," Karl answered despondently.

Katherine broke the gloom, bearing chipped white cups of tea and a biscuit each on a tray.

"Your stall seems very popular, especially with the younger women. Sorry about the spillage. I collided with Father Christmas on the way over."

Karl noticed another customer and went to take the money for a souvenir cruet set from Brighton. When he returned he found Robert and Katherine in the middle of a conversation.

"I was just saying you look as though you're enjoying yourself," Katherine repeated.

"Yes I am. But your money is mad. How can you work with it? Twelve pennies in a shilling, twenty shillings in a pound, and then also to make things worse, you have ha'pennies and farthings and eight half-crowns in a pound, not two." Karl shook his head in disbelief at such a crazy monetary system.

"It's what is called throwing you in at the deep end," Robert laughed.

The Rev. Thornton's voice broke into the babble of voices, calling for quiet and the crowd grew silent, except for some small children who still wanted to see Father Christmas.

"We're about to draw the raffle everybody, so may I ask Mrs Kellett if she would kindly draw the first ticket."

Karl leaned against a stack of chairs and watched the aristocratic mother of Katherine's fiancé begin the time-honoured proceedings. Each winner then drew the next ticket from the box. Karl felt a part of the event, a part of a community as he had not been for over seven years, excepting occasional home leaves when most of his time had been taken up with Ilse. He almost forgot what ordinary life was like, isolated as he was at Lane Head Farm. Hearing the shrieks of children, even speaking to elderly people, was a novelty. His presence was quite accepted there now; people were engrossed in the draw, snatching up the last few bargains. Not quite all though. He sensed someone watching him and turned towards the handicrafts stall where he spotted Sarah talking to an attractive blonde of about the same age. Sarah's friend Audrey perhaps. It was she who was staring at him intently.

Robert noticed the direction of his gaze. "A stunner, isn't she? But beware, she's a man-eater is young Audrey Patterson. She's broken many a heart already, including mine."

"I can see why." Even from across the room Karl was aware of the interest in her eyes. He deliberately turned his attention from her.

Robert had seen the danger. "She's out to hook you, Karl. I don't know how she intends to do it, but watch out. I mean it," he warned emphatically.

"She could make trouble for me," Karl agreed. "I know some men who have already spent time in solitary for seeing young women."

"Just seeing them?"

Karl shrugged evasively. "Some of the girls near the camps think German men are more interesting than the village boys they have always known. They will often talk to us when no one sees."

Robert had heard of such goings on and of the "fratties" as they were called. Karl nudged him in the ribs as Audrey, a reluctant Sarah in tow, was making her way over to the White Elephant stall.

Audrey's voice, calculatedly low-pitched and alluring, was directed at Robert first, while Sarah hung back awkwardly. "What a surprise to see you out of your shell at last, Robbie!"

She did not pause for a reply from Robert, but turned instead to the real purpose of her advance. She eyed him appraisingly, little daunted by the lack of response in his steely eyes.

"What a beautiful carving you made for the handicrafts stall," she greeted him warmly. "Sarah says it's the perfect image of one of her father's sheep, didn't you Sarah?"

Whether this was said innocently or deliberately to annoy Sarah, neither man was sure. They both saw the glare from Sarah as her favourable words about Karl's work were repeated.

"What carving is this, Karl?" Robert asked.

Audrey smugly produced the wooden sheep from inside her bag before Karl could speak. "This! I bought it earlier on. I couldn't resist it when I heard who made it."

The lure in her voice was unmistakeable. Robert's warning seemed well-founded.

"I'm glad you like it," Karl said. "Excuse me please."

Sarah quickly side-stepped as Karl abruptly made his way across the hall, taking their empty tea cups back to the stall where Katherine was helping out. She turned and hissed angrily at Audrey. "There was no need to make eyes quite so obviously at him!"

Audrey was not in the least perturbed. "Well you said he was handsome and that he is, no mistake. But his eyes are grey, not blue."

Robert, keeping well out of the argument, was amused at Audrey's irrepressibility with men, and Sarah's indignation that twice now she was known to be complimentary towards Karl. He watched the two of them move away, still at daggers drawn, but then the pair spent their entire lives falling in and out with each other. Karl now seemed to be one more stone cast into the pool.

Seeing the coast was clear again, Karl returned to say goodbye to Robert. The Carters had their fill of gossip and wanted to be off.

"Will you be down to church tomorrow? I believe my mother has asked you all for Sunday lunch," Robert asked him.

Now that he was spending the evenings carving, Karl's Sundays alone were no longer so important. "Yes, I will come. Mealtimes at Lane Head are a little difficult for me now Sarah is here. It will be good to have more people to talk with."

"Is she really that cold to you?" Robert asked, then was struck by a facetious thought. "Audrey is too hot, Sarah is too cold. Who is just right?"

The analogy with Goldilocks was lost on Karl, although he understood the implications.

"Are you ready, Karl?" Katherine's voice interrupted them. "We're off now, Robert. See you tomorrow."

Although Robert's question to Karl went unanswered, the eager tilt of Karl's head in Katherine's direction as she spoke was evidence enough of how Karl regarded her. No wonder Karl was keen to be repatriated, Robert thought. Here he was living amongst females for the first time in years, but strictly forbidden access to them, not to mention the fact that the one he liked best was already spoken for. It was enough to drive any red-blooded male wild. It occurred to Robert that he himself had taken no steps in that direction since his return home. Perhaps it was the smouldering look he saw Audrey give Karl that set his own thoughts on such matters, or maybe it was simply a general return to health and vitality. Whatever it was, Robert was grateful for the impetus Karl's presence seemed to have provided. The question now for Robert was upon which fortunate damsel he should turn his attentions.

Katherine lay in bed on the Saturday night before Christmas reading Andrew's latest letter for the sixth time, although she already knew every detail in it. He was coming home on a nine day pass, arriving sometime late in the afternoon of Christmas Eve, and would telephone her just as soon as he got home, hopefully managing to come up to the farm later that evening. A surge of excitement always ran through her at this point in Andrew's letter, but his next few lines quickly dampened her enthusiasm.

You can't imagine, darling, what you can buy here for a few cartons of cigarettes! I've found incredible Christmas presents for everybody, and can hardly wait to give you yours.

Visions of Karl's mother's fur coat or his father's camera impinged upon Katherine's mind, blotting out all the excitement such a promising gift might otherwise have created. His last line, in contrast, brought a smile to her lips.

How glad I will be to get away from these infernal Germans and relax with you in the heart of England once again.

He should read yesterday's newspapers, Katherine thought. Maybe they would reach him tomorrow. The government was encouraging Britons to invite a German to spend Christmas with them. Katherine was not too sure how many would be coming to Penchurch but Karl's presence at the Christmas Bazaar seemed to have inspired a fair few villagers to extend invitations to members of the hostel at Upper Claydon. Andrew was going to have a surprise when he arrived home to find the village teeming with Germans. Well, maybe not teeming. But she was looking forward to observing his reaction at church, when he noticed the extra members of the congregation.

The sound of a car door banging in the lane interrupted her cogitations. Sarah had been out to a dance with Robert that evening. He must have borrowed his father's car to bring her back home. It was good to see Robert socialising properly at last and out of his self-imposed exile. Sarah would know how to liven him up.

She heard the car turn around and head back down the lane, then listened to Sarah's footsteps creeping up the stairs. They paused by Katherine's door, then there was a muffled knock and Sarah's head appeared around the door.

"May I come in?" she whispered. "I saw your light was still on."

"Yes of course."

Sarah eased the door shut and her tight shoes off her aching feet. "Gosh, that's better." She wiggled her cramped toes.

"Well, how was it? Did you enjoy yourselves?" Katherine asked.

"Yes! It was great. Not a patch on a Uni. do of course, but pretty good for this valley. You should have come too, even without Andrew. I'm sure he must go out with his friends to bars and dances in Germany; I don't see why you should stay in all the time."

"Who would dance with me, except out of sympathy for a wallflower? All the young men round here know I'm engaged to Andrew."

"Why should that stop you dancing with them and having a bit of fun?" Sarah objected. "You ought to get out more, you know. You'll be turning into an old maid before he has the chance to marry you, if you don't watch out."

Katherine laughed quietly. "Maybe you're right. Still, Andrew will be here in three days time. I'll make the most of him then."

Sarah picked up her shoes. "I suppose if we're going to be traipsing round the woods tomorrow finding greenery to decorate the house, I'd better go and rest these weary feet of mine. Night night, sleep tight, and sweet dreams of Andrew."

"Will you be dreaming of Robert?" Katherine asked slyly.

"Who knows!" Sarah flashed her eyes before slipping quietly out once more.

Katherine switched off her light, suddenly stung by the memory of her sister's words. Was she becoming an old maid in Andrew's absence? She had spent the evening pleasantly enough playing Monopoly with her father and Karl, who took the opportunity in Sarah's absence to sit inside for once, instead of hidden away in the toolshed. She presumed he was busy carving more works of art, although he was rather evasive on the subject. He was as entitled to his privacy as much as anyone, but she was glad he had a friend in Robert. That must be the worst of being billeted out on a farm amongst comparative strangers. She knew he would not dream of confiding in her, and although he and her father discussed all manner of issues, some topics were definitely taboo. Only Robert seemed to have dug beneath the surface of Karl and he was not letting on what he had found there. She asked him once after church what Karl told him about himself. Robert sidetracked her so wonderfully she had only just realised that he never answered her.

Sarah did not appear for breakfast. Katherine seemed deep in thought as Karl downed his tea and toast. David was reading yesterday's newspaper which had gone unread because of playing Monopoly. Katherine eventually roused herself from her daydream.

"Do you intend coming to church with us today, after finally taking the plunge last week?"

"No. I will stay here," he replied. His work on Sarah's present was almost finished. He had found a piece of wood in the shed which would polish up just the right colour for Beth. He had asked David for permission to use the piece, as it was of good quality, but David was only too happy to see the wood used. Now it was transformed into a head-tossing Welsh Cob. All that remained to be done was the detail in the mane and tail, and for it to be given a good polish to bring out the rich red colour. Then he could wrap his three gifts in brown paper, label them, and forget about them for a few days.

Katherine expressed her disappointment that he did not want to go to church again. Her weekly visits meant a lot to her; she hoped Karl would find comfort there too.

"It wasn't so bad last week, was it? People are used to seeing you now."

Karl decided he had to disillusion her. "I went to church last week only because afterwards we went to the Murdochs' house."

"Is that the only reason?" Her voice reflected her disappointment.

"Leave the man alone, Beauty," her father said over his newspaper. "If he doesn't want to go, don't force him."

"I'm not forcing him, Daddy. Since he went last week I thought he might like to again. Since he doesn't, that's fine. I was only asking why, that's all."

"I don't go to church," Karl broke in to satisfy her curiosity and close the subject, "because I don't believe in God."

He said it without hesitation or guilt, unlike the very few English people Katherine had ever spoken to who professed to be atheists. No doubt in the circles Sarah moved in it was common enough, but here in the country, a non-acceptance of Christianity was not broadcast too widely. She felt shocked and could only stammer: "Oh! I'm sorry."

"Why are you sorry?" he asked, steadily meeting her eyes.

She thought carefully about her answer. "Because I think you need the comfort the church can offer," she answered eventually, no longer flustered.

Now it was Karl's turn to look uncomfortable, and Katherine rather regretted her pious words.

"Then you must say a prayer for me today."

He sounded serious, Katherine thought. Or was he just pulling her leg? You could never tell with Karl. She hoped he would say more but he excused himself and left the table to begin work outside.

"What did you make of that?" her father asked, when they were sure Karl was out of earshot.

"I wish I knew," she frowned.

Sarah was just getting dressed when her father and Katherine left for church. Farming hours were all very well for farmers; she had no intention of getting up at the crack of dawn if she did not have to. She made herself a quick breakfast, then brought all her text books and notes downstairs, spreading them over the entire kitchen table. Her little desk upstairs was too cramped to work on satisfactorily, especially when she was consulting maps and several text books at the same time. She would have to clear it all away before the churchgoers returned, but at least she could get on with her essay until then.

A roast was cooking in the oven, but there was nothing there that needed doing for the moment. Sarah immersed herself in her studies, sparing only a few brief moments to recollect the dance the previous evening.

Her eye was caught by something bright hanging by the door. It was the German's overcoat with its tell-tale yellow patch on the back. She thought it very fitting that a Nazi should now have to wear such an identifying mark, just as they made Jews wear the yellow Star of David on their clothes.

Blast! That meant he must be around somewhere and hadn't gone down to church with the others. He would have to wear his coat there. She realised she was alone on the farm with him, and he knew how much she disliked him. He might try anything while her father was away, she thought in horror. He was even allowed to use the shotgun. Her skin started to prickle as she imagined him somewhere outside, creeping about, gun in hand. Sarah had no trust in a man who could take orders from Hitler. No matter what her father felt, there was no way she was going to rest easy until she knew exactly where he was and what he was doing.

She put down her pen and went to search out the disconcertingly handsome man whom she feared so much.

She began her search in the stable, then moved on to the barn before stopping to think and realise that most probably he would be in the toolshed. There was a small window in the side of the shed but it was too grime-encrusted for her to see much through it, apart from a light patch which was Karl's hair. No doubt he was busy carving something, she decided with relief. Having eased her qualms, she turned to make her way back to her essay but the opening of the toolshed door suddenly made her heart pound with fright.

"Do you want me for something?" His voice had the polite but cautious tone he usually adopted when speaking to her.

"No." He must have seen me looking in through the window, she thought in annoyance. "I just wanted to know where you were, that's all."

He looked at her coldly. "I'm not making bombs in here, you know."

"I didn't think you were!" Sarah snapped. "I'm not an idiot, so don't you dare talk to me as though I were!"

To her surprise he apologised at once. "I'm sorry. I should not have said that. It is only that you always look at me as if you think I will kill you all in your beds."

"You killed my mother, didn't you? And Robert's brother. Not to mention Mrs Collins' husband and ..."

He turned his back and went back into the toolshed. Sarah wished he would deny her accusations. She knew what she said was ridiculous but she wanted to have a confrontation, wanted to hear him try to deny involvement in all the deaths, try to wriggle his way out of the guilt of his nationality. But he had not and she now felt hard done by.

"Coward!" she yelled at the closed door.

The door was flung open again and Karl strode out, fury blazing in his eyes. Sarah moved back, fearful she had overstepped the mark.

"Why do you call me that?" he shouted at her, fists clenched by his sides. "You know nothing about me! Why do you hate me so?"

He was standing threateningly close to her, within arm's reach, impaling her with the glare of his eyes. She reacted unthinkingly and instinctively, the way she always had, by means of attack. Her right hand flashed out to strike him on the face. She never made contact. Instead she found her wrist caught in an iron grip and herself being propelled firmly backwards towards the back door of the house.

"Leave me alone!" he ordered and thrust her inside. He shut the door on her.

Sarah stood staring at the closed door, rubbing her sore wrist where his fingers had held her. How dare he treat her like that! "I'll get you for this, you Nazi thug!" she shouted through the door.

On their return from church, both David and Katherine immediately sensed the strained atmosphere as they walked into the kitchen and were confronted by Sarah's black mood.

"Overslept most likely," her father whispered to Katherine as they hung up their coats. Katherine did not agree; Sarah was in no such mood when they left for church. When Karl appeared for lunch it was clear from his demeanour that something had happened.

"Right you two," David demanded, once they were all seated at the meal table. "What's been going on while we were out?"

Neither answered. David raised his eyes to the ceiling in despair. "I'm not sitting here while you both behave like a couple of sulky children. Let's find out what the problem is and clear the air."

Sarah pointed accusingly at Karl. "He's the problem!" she burst out. "I hate having him here. I thought I'd be able to cope with him. I did try at first but now I don't want to have to share my home with him. I'm going to stay at Audrey's for the rest of the holiday."

There was a moment of shocked silence before both David and Katherine began to speak at once, but they stopped in mid-flow as they heard the back door slam: Karl had gone.

Katherine rose to go after him but her father stopped her. "Leave him; for the moment. Let's hear what Sarah has to say first."

Sarah sat rigid and defiant in her chair, head held high in determination. "It's as I said. I've asked Mrs Patterson if it's all right for me to stay until I go back to Bristol, and she agreed, especially when she heard why."

"Oh really? Perhaps you would care to tell *me* why. Don't you think it would have been polite to discuss this with us first? What happened today to make up your mind so suddenly?"

For a moment Sarah seemed unsure of what to say, then decided the near truth was the simplest answer. "I made him angry and then he hurt me. Look." She held out her wrist where red weals still showed Karl's grasp.

"Karl did that to you?" Her father's voice held all the bitterness and anger of a trust betrayed.

Sarah nodded, her lower lip trembling with emotion. "Yes. What I said is the truth." She looked up at him with tears in her eyes as he stood poised to pursue the vanished Karl.

Katherine watched her father's reaction with alarm. He was really angry with Karl it seemed, yet she was sure they had not heard the whole story from Sarah. She simply could not believe Karl would do such a thing without great provocation.

"Just a minute, Daddy. I think we ought to hear from Sarah why he did it."

"He can explain it himself!" he barked, heading outside.

Katherine had not been deceived by Sarah's tears. She turned angrily on her sister. "You fool! Why do you have to go and cause so much trouble, not just for Karl, but for Daddy too? If he sends Karl away because of your stupidity we'll be back where we started with Daddy overworked and worried sick about coping with the farm. Why don't you think before you play your silly pranks?"

Sarah's tears instantly vanished. "I don't call being attacked by a German a silly prank."

"Knowing you, I bet you attacked first."

Katherine saw from the flicker of Sarah's eyes that she had hit the nail on the head. She flung back her chair and rushed for the door to find her father before he could say anything to Karl he would later regret.

Karl had retreated to the stable. His continued presence would only aggravate Sarah more, so he made for his usual sanctuary. Beth was there in her stall after her jaunt to the village, munching on hay. Its sweet smell reminded Karl of happy hours in Ilse's company. Today, the thought of Ilse and her baker husband only deepened his depression.

When he heard David's brisk footsteps crossing the yard, Karl did not move. David would stand by his daughter in such a situation. Karl knew he had been rough with Sarah. He should have let her hit him and expel her anger. With her victory she could have afforded to be more magnanimous. Instead, he won the battle; now she was set on revenge.

The stable door was pulled open.

"Karl?"

Karl came out and faced David. If he expected to see David angry, he was mistaken. The walk across the yard had given David time to compose himself. Now he looked serious but calm.

"I want to hear this from you, Karl. Everything, exactly as it was. I hope I'll get the whole truth from you."

Karl was reluctant to lay most of the blame at Sarah's feet, but he shrugged off his qualms and outlined the facts as plainly as possible.

David checked to make quite sure he had understood Karl correctly. "So she was going to hit you when you caught her hand?"

"Yes – but I could have let go sooner. I too was angry then. I pushed her into the house. I am very sorry I hurt her."

David grunted. "Huh. It sounds to me like you both need to apologise, but I don't suppose for one moment that Sarah would agree to that, so I'll do it on her behalf. I'm sorry she can't accept you for what you are, but I don't want her moving down to Audrey's house. No doubt you can well understand my feelings."

Karl nodded. "This is her home more than mine," he agreed.

"Yes, well, in future, Karl, please try to ignore her. Try not to take any notice, I mean; no matter what she says. Although she looks far more sophisticated than Katherine, she is by no means as sensible. She never has been; probably never will be." He paused a moment, reluctant to say what was coming next. "Just don't ever touch her again, or you will be in trouble!" he warned.

"I understand, sir."

David smiled generously. "You'd better stay out here a while, until we've sorted Sarah out and persuaded her to stay. Katherine can bring your dinner out to you." He turned as he heard running feet. "Speak of the devil, here she is."

It was immediately clear to Katherine that her fears were groundless. "I can see I'm not needed," she breathed in relief.

They all returned to the house but Karl waited outside the back door until Katherine emerged with his food on a plate. Karl could hear the sound of Sarah sobbing. Katherine shut the door behind her and gave Karl his plate and cutlery.

"I'm so sorry about all this, Karl. I hope Daddy wasn't too harsh on you. I know it was all Sarah's fault," she said in a low, troubled voice.

Karl shrugged, trying to make light of the situation. "I hope you can make Sarah stay."

"I hope so too. I suspect she arranged to go to Audrey's while still in a rage. She might think twice once she's calmed down." She remembered the plate in Karl's hand. "Better let you eat before it's cold," she said, and went back inside.

The toolshed seemed the best place to spend the rest of the day. After he had eaten, Karl picked up the figure of Beth, discarded since the morning, and ran his thumb over its smooth, glossy surface, almost satisfied with the finish.

At about half past two Karl noticed Sarah and Katherine setting off for the woods armed with secateurs and baskets to cut greenery. Sarah must have been persuaded to stay.

The dirty toolshed window acted like a net curtain, allowing him to see out but making it difficult for outsiders to see in. He deliberately left it dirty, rather than clean it as his instinct demanded, to ensure privacy for his task. Now all three presents were finished and wrapped. In Sarah's current mood he hardly believed she would accept hers, but it would be churlish to shun her now. He had learned much in England since his capture. Show kindness where hatred was expected and the results were astonishing. He supposed Katherine would approve such an apparently Christian act, but it made sense, if anything was to be gained from today's fiasco.

A knock on the door advised him of David's entry, but secrecy was no longer vital.

David pushed aside Karl's empty dinner plate and settled himself on the edge of the workbench.

"I know you're up to something in here so I don't like to disturb you, but while the girls are out I thought you'd better know the outcome of our talk with Sarah. We've managed to persuade her to stay. She admits she provoked you and that she can't really blame you for what you did, so I suppose that's some kind of progress. But she refuses to apologise in person, and she doesn't want you to apologise to her. I'm afraid she'd just rather not speak to you at all. Which is going to make Christmas rather deadly.

"Speaking of which," he continued, "Katherine has been invited to spend Christmas Day at the Kelletts', and we are all invited down for the day to the Murdochs'. They tell me they've invited one of your friends from Upper Claydon too, so we'll be quite a jolly party, I think. Sarah has agreed to come too, only because Robert will be expecting her to come, but she has absolutely promised me that she'll be on her best behaviour with you and the other fellow – Norbert Wennemann, I think. Do you know him?"

Karl smiled. "Yes. I know him. Katherine would like him. He always goes to church. But he speaks very little English."

"Donald asked for one who couldn't, knowing you would be there to translate for us."

David cast his eye over the empty workbench. "Finished whatever you were up to? I thought we might go shoot a pheasant to take to Gertie."

"As you see, I have finished for the moment." Karl now knew he had another gift to make – for the Murdochs – but it would have to wait until the evening. "Let's go."

They returned with a brace of pigeons and a solitary rabbit – the pheasants all seemed aware of the season and had hidden themselves well. Katherine and Sarah were busy making evergreen wreaths on the kitchen table. Sarah blanched when she saw Karl enter with the shotgun crooked over his arm, but held her tongue. She smiled to herself when, after returning the gun to its place in David's study, Karl disappeared outside again.

CHAPTER SIX

On Christmas Eve morning Katherine was in a state of high excitement. All day she flitted from chore to chore, singing her favourite Bing Crosby songs, unable to concentrate on anything except Andrew's imminent arrival. She was just putting the kettle on at four o'clock when the telephone finally rang, making her jump. Water spilled from the kettle onto the range, fizzing and spluttering in counterpoint with Katherine's excitement. She ran into the hall and, with trembling fingers, picked up the receiver.

From her room, Sarah could hear her sister's elated voice. She smiled to herself, happy that Katherine's long wait was nearly over. In another few months, thought Sarah, Andrew would be demobbed and become her brother-in-law. Trying to shut her mind to distracting thoughts of a large wedding party at Froxley Grange with all the personable young men of the neighbourhood present, Sarah returned to her studying.

A few minutes later, Katherine came upstairs with a cup of tea and a broad smile. "That was Andrew. He'll be coming up in about an hour," she chirped.

"Wonderful. Perhaps I'll get some peace and quiet at last."

Katherine's singing continued until Andrew's MG Midget drew up in the lane. He announced his arrival by several toots on the horn.

Hard at work on his next carving, Karl heard the hubbub, followed a quarter of an hour later by the sound of the sports car roaring down the lane at speed. Feeling hungry, and unsure of the time, Karl wrapped his new carving. At home in Germany Christmas Eve was the time for present-giving. Here he would have to hide them in his room until tomorrow, when he would leave them around the bottom of the Christmas tree he had recently cut from the woods.

David smiled as Karl entered the sitting room and warmed himself at the fire. "Just three of us for dinner tonight," he said. "Katherine's left something in the oven for us. I'd better call Sarah down to sort it out. If it was up to her we'd never get dinner."

Sarah was vexed at having to leave her books and came down grudgingly to serve up the food. Meals were served at set times at Lane Head; Sarah's late rising and sedentary lifestyle did not fit the general pattern.

An uneasy truce had existed between Sarah and Karl since the previous Sunday. David was beginning to hope it might prove an enjoyable Christmas after all, with Sarah diverted by Robert's attentions. She retreated to her bedroom immediately after she had washed up, content for once to allow Karl to stay inside. It was Christmas Eve after all.

The two men sat quietly reading in the sitting room, listening to festive music on the wireless, Karl's thoughts on his family's celebrations at home. David decided to wait up for Katherine. He had a touch of indigestion and knew he would not sleep. After Andrew's long journey and a busy day in store tomorrow he doubted they would be back very late.

They turned up at a quarter past eleven. Katherine invited Andrew for a nightcap and they both joined David in the sitting room.

Obviously there was no shortage of food for the Occupying Powers in Germany. Andrew looked as robust and hearty as ever, his face even fuller than David remembered. He began to regale them with tales of life "over there", of the places he had seen and the people he had met.

"Trying to flush out the remaining Nazis is quite a problem," he told them. "No one will admit to having been in the Nazi Party, of course, but it's painfully obvious when you talk to them they're all dyed-in-the-wool Nazis."

"*All* of them?" David asked doubtfully.

"Well, damned well nearly all of them. I've spoken to some of the repatriated "White" POWs, and I reckon they pulled a fast one on the person who screened them. Now all the civilians are wanting their precious "Persil Certificates". Makes me sick when I hear them try to deny all knowledge of what was going on. Then they complain about what we're doing to help them sort themselves out." He took a swig of coffee. "What about that Jerry working for you? Is he as bad as the rest of them? Have you asked him about the concentration camps?"

David and Katherine exchanged nervous glances.

"We don't talk about things like that," Katherine replied quietly.

Andrew's voice, boosted by a few glasses of wine, became louder as he laughed. "Why ever not? They've a lot of explaining to do, those Germans. It's no good pussyfooting around with them. Most likely if your man avoids the subject then he was somehow involved. That's my experience anyway."

David could see Katherine growing anxious, so he decided to end the evening. He stood up. "Well, Christmas Day already. I'm off to my bed so I can enjoy the rest of it. If you'll excuse me, Andrew?"

"Yes, of course. Best be away too, since I've been travelling the best part of a night and a day to get here."

David breathed a sigh of relief as they heard his car drive off. "Thank God Karl didn't hear any of that."

"A bit grim, wasn't it? Still, I suppose he does see more of them than we do. Perhaps it really is like that over there." She yawned, then kissed her father under the mistletoe. "Happy Christmas, Daddy."

Karl heard the car start up and drive off. More than usual he felt an intruder on this Christmas Eve. He read through his family's Christmas letter – they had all written something, even little Uwe had scribbled on the bottom of it – and decided now was the time to open the parcel which accompanied the letter.

His birthday parcel had contained his old woollen skiing hat. The Christmas one contained the gloves that went with it, as well as more photographs of his family and home taken from the family album. Amongst them was one of himself in uniform with his arm around Ilse, taken on his last leave in April 1943. He wondered why his parents sent it, since Ilse was not his any more: perhaps they simply thought he would like a reminder of happier times. It was one of several photographs of him taken then to show off his new rank and Iron Cross. On his right sleeve could be clearly seen the Edelweiss arm badge of the mountain divisions. He decided against showing that particular photograph to the Carters. It might prompt awkward questions.

Despite instructions to the contrary, his mother included food in the parcel: a small piece of sausage. When he unwrapped the grease-proof paper the deliciously heavy garlic smell promised him a real taste of home. Now was as good a time as any, he thought, and popped the piece into his mouth. The English seemed not to have heard of garlic. He had no idea what word they used for it even. His taste buds revelled in the flavour as he ate the sausage as slowly as possible.

He guessed the time must be around midnight when he heard the car drive off, and picked up the photograph of his family. "*Frohe Weihnachten!*" he wished them. Perhaps next year he would be able to say it in person.

Ilse's smiling face looked up at him from the bed. Karl fingered the photograph, then had a closer look at it. He would never forget Ilse, despite what she did to him. Her face had given him the courage to survive the Russian winter and what came after. The times he had called out her name and drawn strength from it. If she only knew how much he needed her, perhaps she would have waited for him to come home. But her needs had come first, naturally. Food and shelter. A companion. Someone to love.

The silence of his room enveloped Karl. He wondered whether the Carters were all asleep by now. Standing at his doorway he looked across the gulf separating him from the house. No lights there. He closed the door then drew back the curtains from the window. Down in Penchurch a few lights twinkled back up the valley at him. Late night revellers or participants of Midnight Mass; as remote from him as the distant stars.

He quickly undressed, turned out the stove then the light and got into bed. At least he had something to look forward to tomorrow.

Everyone was up in good time the following morning, even Sarah, who had never shaken off a childish enthusiasm for Christmas. Katherine packed her clothes for her stay at Froxley Grange. Karl went out to the sheep, doling out hay. David collected all the bits and pieces they were taking to the Murdochs': a bottle of pre-war elderberry wine, a game pie Katherine had made, the rabbit and pigeons, as well as the presents the Carters were giving to the Murdochs. At nine o'clock everyone assembled round the Christmas tree in the sitting room where, since breakfast, various parcels had mysteriously added themselves to the pile. Present-giving was to take place before church as Katherine would be absent after that.

David was in charge of handing out the presents, reading out what was written on each label. To each daughter he gave a gramophone record, Bing Crosby for Katherine, for Sarah, the Ink Spots. Next he read out a label which said: *To Karl. With our very best wishes for a Happy Christmas, from David, Katherine and Sarah.* The parcel was small and Katherine hoped he would not think them mean, but knowing he had no funds to buy them anything, she did not want him to feel awkward by too generous a gift. Karl opened the wrapping; it contained six large handkerchiefs with his initial in one corner. From their slight irregularity, Karl assumed Katherine had embroidered them herself.

"Thank you. All I need now is to have a cold," he said.

Next David pulled out a bulky parcel addressed to himself. He carefully unwrapped it to find a hand-knitted Fair Isle short-sleeved jumper, which he held against himself. "It's beautiful!" he exclaimed, admiringly. "How did you manage to keep that hidden?"

The girls smiled at his pleasure. "Katherine did the front in bed; I did the back in Bristol," Sarah explained. "It's a miracle the two halves fit together!"

After trying on the jumper, David turned once more to the remaining, plain brown paper presents. He knew these three were Karl's and deliberately left them until last, suspecting they would make an impressive climax to the proceedings. The first he picked bore his own name plus the words: *Christmas Greetings from Karl*, written in Karl's distinctive, angular handwriting. The parcel was heavy for its size. David hefted it appraisingly before pulling away the brown paper wrapping. A perfect likeness of Joss looked up, open-mouthed at his master, his feather-like tail almost seeming to wag. David was speechless at first as he admired the craftsmanship.

"Well! That's something special," he said at last, turning the piece over slowly in his hands. "Thank you very much, Karl. I know how long that must have taken you."

He put down the wooden Joss on the table beside him and picked up both remaining parcels, handing them simultaneously to his daughters. Katherine eagerly unwrapped hers to reveal a young woman, obviously herself, feeding chickens. As she too turned it over in her hands she saw Karl's initials, KDD, and the date carved on the base.

"It's beautiful," was all she could say, touched by his thoughtfulness. She noticed Sarah had not yet opened her own gift. "Come on Sarah. Let's see what yours is."

Reluctantly Sarah tore off the paper, unsure of her feelings. She stared at the figure of Beth on her lap. She was embarrassed that Karl should have made her such a present after the way she treated him, but she also felt angry because of her embarrassment.

"It's very nice. Thank you," she managed to say with a great effort.

Katherine felt more appreciation was required and asked to see the horse, admired it, then passed it over to her father, before collecting up all three figures and standing them on the mantelpiece.

"Better get going, if we're not going to be late." It occurred to her, as they waited for David to get the car out, that Karl might feel he was being forced to accompany them, as the arrangements stood. "Do you mind coming with us to church, Karl? You could go straight to the Murdochs' if you'd rather."

Feeling in festive mood already, Karl decided to indulge in a little leg-pulling. "No. I will come too. You have invited my gods into your house, so I will go with you to the house of your God."

Katherine frowned. Even Sarah looked nonplussed at his strange statement. "What do you mean by that?" Katherine asked in bewilderment.

"I mean the trees. You bring the woods into your house for the winter festival. You take part in my religion, so today I take part in yours."

Sarah actually laughed out loud, but Katherine did not appreciate the jest. "Please don't make jokes like that. I don't find them funny, even if Sarah does."

"How do you know he's joking, Katherine? He might really worship the trees. These Germans believe in strange things you know." For Sarah, the dig at Karl was a surprisingly mild one; he took it in good humour.

David finally managed to start the car and backed it out of the garage towards them. The two girls sat in the back; Karl joined David in the front. Karl felt decidedly shabby compared with the Carters, who all found something smart – if not very new – to wear. His one consolation was that today there would be other POWs at church.

Karl followed the Carters up the aisle, greeting some people he recognised from the Christmas Bazaar. Once seated, he looked round for the half-dozen men from Upper Claydon who might be attending church with their host families. He quickly spotted the diminutive Norbert Wennemann between Donald and Robert Murdoch, and a moment later the hostel's resident intellectual, Oskar Stritzel, sitting with a family Karl could only describe as coming from peasant stock. Someone had made a bad mistake, or had a good laugh matching those hosts to their guest. Stritzel spoke reasonable English but he doubted whether even Stritzel would find his way through the local dialect.

A light tap on his shoulder and whispered words in his ear drew Karl's attention to new arrivals in the pew behind.

"*Grüss Gott, Driesler!*" The words were spoken in the strong Bavarian accent of Georg Ochsenknecht. Karl turned to return the greeting; this time the authorities had it right. Both Ochsenknecht and his host family were from the same mould. A bull of a man, as befitted his name, Ochsenknecht's hosts were likewise swarthy folk, who seemed to have taken already to their guest, accepting him in a no-nonsense, down-to-earth way which evidently suited Georg, who spoke no English anyway, and could thus ease his conscience about entering a Protestant church.

The service was pleasant enough, the words of the lessons discernible to Karl even in English. He even joined in singing one or two of the carols.

Afterwards in the churchyard, the POWs had the chance to briefly discuss their initial impressions of their hosts with one another, and for those more acquainted with English ways to give some final words of advice to their fellows. As each pointed out his respective "family", Karl noticed for the first time that Katherine had been joined by a well-groomed young man, who stood with his arm possessively draped around her shoulders. He was half a head taller than Katherine, with that erect, confident manner of an army officer bred for the job, and the aristocratic arrogance Karl detected in Kellett's mother, whom he recognised from the Bazaar. Evidently Katherine had landed quite a catch in Captain Andrew Kellett.

There were signs of imminent departure from the Kellett party. Accompanied by Andrew, Katherine crossed the churchyard towards the huddle of POWs.

"Andrew, I want you to meet Karl, who works for us. I think I've mentioned him in my letters."

She certainly had, Andrew Kellett thought, looking up at yet another German face. Why Katherine had to drag him over here just to see a prisoner of war, he could not think. She had insisted, however, and so he humoured her. Now he found himself shocked by the reality of who this Jerry was, about whom Katherine wrote so warmly.

"I think we'd better be getting back to the car, darling," he said to Katherine. "My parents are waiting for us."

Katherine felt disappointed by Andrew's curt dismissal of Karl, but she tried not to show it. "Have a lovely day, Karl," she called over her shoulder.

"Thank you. You too."

As the pair receded into the distance there was a low whistle from Hans-Jürgen Fromm, a former shipping clerk from Hamburg. "You work for her, Driesler? *Mensch,* you're lucky!"

Karl looked witheringly at him. "As you can see, she is well spoken for. I would not try anything with her. She has a sister, though," he added provocatively, giving them something to speculate about in the long evenings at the hostel. "Over there." He noticed that the Carters and Murdochs were now preparing to leave. They waved him and Norbert Wennemann over.

Fromm could not resist a parting shot. "Even prettier than her sister. Give her a kiss from me, won't you?"

"Some hope!" Karl muttered to Wennemann as they joined the party for Yew Tree Lodge waiting by the lych-gate.

Once all were assembled in the Murdochs' living room, the hearth stoked and a sherry in everyone's hand, more presents were handed round. Norbert received a fountain pen from the Murdochs. Karl could not conceal his delight when he received a German-English dictionary. He sat and flicked through it as the other presents were distributed, including his own hastily carved pheasant for the Murdochs. He had used a piece of walnut whose shape and grain immediately suggested the bird to him. It had been a relatively simple task to complete the carving in the short time available.

Gertie and Sarah drifted off to the kitchen to finish preparations for dinner, leaving the men conversing in an awkward triangle, with Karl at the apex, acting as translator. He found the job difficult; Norbert would say things which Karl would normally avoid saying in English. He knew his translation was not always accurate but no one knew the difference.

As Gertie came in to announce that dinner was ready, Donald said to Karl: "I'm glad you're here. We'd have found conversation impossible."

Karl grinned. "I wonder how it is with other families all over your country who have German guests today. Difficult for some, I think."

There was a wonderful smell from the kitchen as the men trooped into the dining room. The table was laid in the grand manner for the occasion. During the meal Sarah proved excessively restrained and polite, even managing to fuss over Norbert to some extent, making sure he had everything he wanted, passing him second helpings of roast potatoes and chatting to him through Karl. Karl reckoned it was the most she had ever spoken to him, even though it was not to him directly she was talking. This served only to accentuate the hostility of her feelings towards himself. Norbert was forty-five and looked as though he would not hurt a mouse: maybe Sarah was able to accept him.

It was a much mellowed party which gathered in the living room again for coffee. By now Norbert was telling German jokes which Karl found untranslatable, even if he could be bothered to try. He knew if he sat in the over-hot living room much longer he would fall asleep, so he interrupted Norbert in full flow and suggested the pair of them tackle the mountain of washing-up, to show their appreciation to Mrs Murdoch.

Gertie came out to the kitchen with them, supposedly to sort out the chaos, then Sarah came with the coffee cups. By the time Robert joined them in the now crowded kitchen the party there was in full swing with a round of "London's Burning", which even Norbert managed to his surprise, with a resounding *"Feuer! Feuer!"*. Nobody noticed the deeper implications of the words to the round, or at least made any indication they had. Sarah was too busy impressing Robert with her fine soprano voice to connect the words to the two men in battledress by the sink.

Three-quarters of an hour after the last saucepan and knife were put away, tea was called for. The living room was cooler by now, and Gertie suggested to the more alert household they might like to sing a few songs around the piano.

"Do you read music, Karl?" she asked him. "You seem to have a good voice. I'm sure you could manage Stanford's *Songs of the Sea*. They're quite fun."

"Too much solo in those," her husband pointed out. "The *Just So Songs* would be better, don't you think, dear? We all know those quite well, Sarah too. Karl can sing bass, with Robert to help him along. I rather think Norbert will have to sit and be our audience, if he doesn't mind."

Norbert did not mind, and listened, sustained by tea and cake, as Gertie played the piano and sang alto. Sarah took soprano, David and Donald tenor. They sang several of the Kipling poems until it was time for Norbert to be taken back to the hostel. He was reluctant to leave his new friends, repeatedly thanking them for a wonderful day. David and Sarah also took their leave with Karl; the animals would be wanting attention.

On the drive back to the farm no one spoke, each wrapped in his or her own thoughts. The evening fell flat after the day's festivities. David switched on the wireless, Sarah brought out a jigsaw puzzle of Windsor Castle and set to work on a large board by the fire. The two of them concentrated on fitting in pieces of grey stonework and blue sky. Karl tackled a novel, armed with his new dictionary. He was tempted to help with the jigsaw to see if Sarah's spirit of Christmas was still in operation, but when he tentatively moved over to the fireside she looked up at him coldly, as if to warn him not to take any liberties just because it was Christmas.

When David opted for an early night, Karl caught hostile glances and felt obliged to leave the sitting room too, leaving Sarah to her puzzle. He picked up his book and dictionary and headed for the rocking chair by the kitchen range. Sarah came in an hour later to make herself a bedtime drink. She did not offer to make one for Karl.

"I see Christmas is over," Karl said, looking up from the vocabulary notes he was making.

"Our Christmas truce you mean?"

He guessed at the meaning of "truce". *Waffenruhe*, most probably. "Yes."

"Well, what did you expect?" she said brutally, and refused to be drawn into further conversation.

At Froxley Grange the night was still young. The Kelletts had relatives for Christmas, including the abominable Arthur Rowlands-Pickering. Every guest room would be occupied later, but for the moment dancing was in progress.

Katherine's suitcase had to contain an assortment of outfits for her brief stay. Now she was swirling over the parquet in her very best dress of green crêpe de chine, her hair piled up on her head, little ringlets falling by her ears. On her finger she wore Andrew's Christmas present to her: a gold ring, set with two diamonds and an emerald. It complemented her dress and hair colouring perfectly. It fitted reasonably well, but Katherine could not help wondering for what German lady it had been made originally. Andrew, on the pretext that an engagement ring could hardly count as a Christmas present, also presented her with an Arctic Fox stole.

Diamonds and furs. Andrew's family were not especially wealthy. She knew these presents were bought for a fraction of their true value in Germany. Nevertheless, they served to make a fine distinction between her old life at Lane Head and her new life here at Froxley Grange. In the drawing room, the rolled-up carpet was Chinese, a cabinet full of Chinese porcelain stood against one wall, while the other long wall held an impressive oil-painting in a heavy gilded frame, showing an early Victorian Hunt assembled on the driveway of Froxley Grange itself.

The gramophone record polka ended and dancers milled around a potent fruit punch on the sideboard, or sat down to chat. When Andrew went off to fetch her a glass of punch, Katherine was approached by the obnoxious Arthur.

"So Andrew caught you at last, eh, Katherine?" he drawled. "Must admit, I had an eye on you myself one time, you know. When's the great day?"

"We'll fix a date just as soon as Andrew's home for good," she answered haughtily, annoyed by his tone.

"Can't understand why Andrew's not staying in the army. Always thought he intended making a career of it, like Uncle James. Illusions shattered, no doubt, having to mollycoddle Jerry."

Arthur leaned against the wall, unwittingly spilling punch down Katherine's dress. Obviously he was more than half-way to being drunk. She dabbed surreptitiously at her dress with her hanky as Arthur droned on about the joys of army life, and following one's husband to exotic locations around the world.

"You would have loved the life, I'm sure. Instead you're stuck in this hell-hole."

Andrew returned with Katherine's punch. "What hell-hole's that, old boy?"

The music began again, this time with a military two-step. Katherine's attention wandered from their discussion. Arthur and Andrew stood entrenched by the wall for the next ten minutes, so Katherine was grateful when Andrew's Uncle Matthew, Arthur's father, noticed her bored expression and asked her to dance. Leaving her punch untouched on the window-sill, Katherine was led off round the room. When she returned to Andrew, he and Arthur were discussing race relations policies in Jan Smut's South Africa in loud, heated voices. Although it seemed they both agreed with Smuts on the subject, Arthur managed to make an argument out of it. They were joined in the debate by Andrew's father, Major James Kellett, and another local landowner, Tony Thomas. Stopping only to pick up her glass, Katherine moved on towards the chesterfield, where more of Andrew's cousins, Olivia and Hermione Holmes were sitting. All the relatives seemed to come from Mrs Kellett's side of the family; Major Kellett's close relatives had been killed in the Great War. Katherine knew it was Andrew's ambition to re-stock the nursery of Froxley Grange with plenty of new Kelletts. She pictured herself trying to keep raucous toddlers away from the treasures of the house, before concluding that was what nurseries and nannies were for.

Olivia and Hermione, twenty and eighteen years old respectively, were entirely different from their other relatives. Both were enthusiastic supporters of Mr Attlee's Labour Government. Their heretical views were frowned upon by one and all, especially their parents, but Katherine found it interesting to talk to such well-informed, politically-minded young ladies, and was sorry when the girls were claimed as dancing partners. Sarah would have enjoyed the conversation, she thought. She wondered what they were all up to at Lane Head and glanced at the ormolu mantle clock: midnight was approaching. No doubt they were all in bed. She wished suddenly she could retire too. Tomorrow was to be another hectic day of socialising and riding with the newly-revived Boxing Day Hunt.

A few minutes later she caught herself glancing at the clock again, and wondered if she might slip quietly to bed. But that was impossible. She would have to keep on politely chatting with Andrew's Aunt Beatrice, who had replaced the Holmes girls on the chesterfield twenty minutes ago. Sarah was right. She had become an old maid, tucked away at Lane Head all the time, and had lost the art of having fun.

She determined to tear Andrew away from Arthur Rowlands-Pickering, who was leaning at even more of an angle against the wall. She went over and, excusing herself, slipped her arm through Andrew's, pulling him out onto the dance floor, where a waltz was in progress.

"Sorry, darling."

Whether it was an apology for stepping on her dress or for neglecting her, Katherine was not sure, but at least she had his undivided attention again. When the dancers finally began to drift away to bed at one o'clock, Andrew accompanied her to her bedroom door, kissing her briefly on the lips to the accompanying roar of approval from Arthur, who happened to stagger by.

The sky cleared next morning; the weather bode fine, but chilly for the Hunt. Major Kellett as Master of Foxhounds was one of the few people in the area who still owned hunters. These days riders turned up on most unlikely mounts, some hardly fit to jump the hedges and fences. Sarah was borrowing one of Audrey's geldings for the occasion, while Katherine was honoured by the loan of one of the Major's hunters since Mrs Kellett no longer joined the Hunt.

Katherine changed into breeches and black jacket, her hair tied tightly back in a neat bun. She was chatting to other members of the Hunt when she saw her father's Austin 10 approach slowly up the long drive behind a pair of horses led by Audrey Patterson. Sarah sprang eagerly from the back of the car as soon as it stopped under the spreading boughs of an ancient cedar, and ran over to Audrey. David followed more sedately. Karl, persuaded that this was a sight he should not miss, remained discreetly by the car, leaning against its warm bonnet to ward off the shivers which seemed to grip him that morning. His throat felt sore too. He suspected he was going to need those new handkerchiefs. He should not have joked about catching a cold.

David went straight over to Katherine. "And how are you today, Beauty?" He greeted her as though she had been away a week rather than one night.

"Bit tired. We went to bed at one o'clock last night: I still woke up at the usual time, and had to wait around for ages before anyone else was up. Probably be later still tonight before I get to bed."

The Kelletts always hosted a ball on Boxing Day, to which the members of the Hunt were all invited, including former members such as David Carter.

"You're only young once. Enjoy yourself!" her father advised with a laugh.

Katherine suddenly remembered her new ring and took off her glove.

"Very nice, Beauty," was his only comment.

Karl watched the red, black and tweed coated riders mount up and enjoy a stirrup cup, surrounded by milling hounds. Katherine and Sarah looked totally at ease on their horses, even though Katherine's was frisky, and eager to be away.

So different from hunts at home: the town band would play, hunting was on foot with guns, and green was the huntsman's colour. A traditional song drifted through his head:

Grün, grün, grün sind alle meine Kleider,
Grün, grün, grün ist alles was ich hab'.
Darum lieb' ich alles was grün ist,
Weil mein Schatz ein Jäger ist.

He remembered Ilse singing it to him once, long ago, when the last line was appropriate – "Because my sweetheart is a huntsman". Now her husband was a baker. Karl imagined her singing the same song to different words.

A shrill blast from the hunting horn broke his reverie. The hounds were mustered and the Hunt set off down the drive and out of sight across the fields. David rejoined Karl by the car.

"How long away are they?" Karl asked.

"Depends on whether they get a kill or not. Some riders return early if they've had a fall, or can't keep up. My two will stick it out to the end, I'm sure. So we've a longish wait." He folded his arms across his chest as the cold began to bite. "I'm going inside for some refreshment. Mrs Kellett said you could go round to the kitchen if you want. You'll be given something there."

Karl shook his head. "I'll wait out here."

David understood Karl's pride. "Perhaps you would like to look around the stables and mews," he suggested. "They have some interesting equipment tucked away in there. I'm sure Major Kellett won't mind."

"I'll do that," Karl said, without enthusiasm.

He had a brief look at the old carriages and the well-equipped stables, before finding a nice warm pile of straw to sit in and await the hunters' return. Even so, the cold had begun to reach his bones by the time he finally heard clattering hooves on the cobbles. Brushing off stray wisps of straw, he went out to see if he could be of any help with the horses. He approached the mud-spattered Katherine and Andrew, who were pleased to hand over their mounts. The Kelletts' groom was already busy with the Major's horse.

"Trojan here has the first stall on the right," Andrew Kellett instructed, passing his reins to Karl. "Hector the second. I'll be out later to check you've attended to them properly," he added, brusquely.

"Thank you, Karl," Katherine added on Andrew's behalf.

Karl led the two steaming horses off to their appropriate stalls and unsaddled them. Hector's friskiness was now quite dissipated. He stood stock still while Karl rubbed him down and covered him with a blanket. Trojan, on the other hand, had life left in him and skittered about at this unfamiliar groom's touch, despite Karl's soothing words. Engrossed in his work and beginning to warm up at last, Karl did not hear soft approaching footsteps, but he recognised the sultry voice in his ear.

"That sounds nice. What are you saying to him?"

Karl straightened up to find himself face to face with Audrey.

"I was telling him to be still," Karl explained, feeling the full force of Audrey's provocative blue eyes from beneath her long lashes. He shifted uneasily. She was standing too close, her intent only too plain.

He edged away from her. "Why don't you be still too?" She laid her hand on his arm.

Karl could not back away any further, hemmed in as he was between Trojan and the sides of the stall. Her fingers slowly worked their way up his arm to his face, where they came to rest on his mouth. "Miss Patterson, I don't think you should ..."

Her lips met his. For a moment he gave way to the flattery of her seduction, enjoying the feel of a woman in his arms again. She pressed herself against him more urgently, her offer tempting, but far too risky. He broke away, pushing her carefully back from himself.

"No. It is not permitted, Miss Patterson," he told her.

"Not here perhaps," she smiled wickedly, "but we can always find somewhere a bit quieter. Tomorrow maybe?" she coaxed him, stroking his cheek.

He greatly needed the release she was offering, but his position at Lane Head was a precarious one, which he treasured too much to risk losing because of a moment's weakness.

"No," he repeated, "it is not permitted."

"Oh come now, Karl," she breathed, "no one will know."

He removed her hand gently but firmly from his face. "*You* will know, Miss Patterson, and you might tell someone else. Then I will be in great trouble."

Sensing defeat, Audrey redoubled her efforts. He had been close to succumbing. He would do so yet, she was sure of it. She moved in again. "I wouldn't tell a soul, I promise. Cross my heart." She ran her forefinger diagonally over her breasts as she spoke. His eyes followed her action.

Karl knew she would never keep such a promise. She would boast about it to somebody, most likely Sarah, and he was in no doubt Sarah would not hesitate to report him to the camp. His days of freedom at Lane Head would come to an abrupt and ignominious end.

"No, Miss Patterson."

Unused to having her favours refused, especially by such a catch as Karl, Audrey began to lose her temper.

"Don't tell me you're one of those Germans who will follow orders, no matter what!" she taunted him.

His reaction caught her completely off guard. He grasped hold of her arms, lifted her up and moved her bodily aside to let himself out of the narrow confines of the stall. He was halfway through this manoeuvre when an angry shout echoed through the stable.

"Hey! Put her down this instant!"

With his back to the stable entrance, Karl could not see Andrew Kellett running forwards. As Karl put Audrey down, a vicious blow caught him on the back of the head and he fell sideways against the nervous Trojan, who shied away causing Karl to lurch and fall under the horse's hooves. Frightened by the noise, Trojan kicked out at the body beneath him. Audrey screamed, serving to unsettle Trojan more as Karl extricated himself painfully from beneath the horse. While Kellett tried to calm Trojan, Audrey helped Karl to one side, sitting him on an upturned bucket, and began to mop at the blood running down his face from a gash on his forehead. He seemed dazed, and was clutching the left side of his rib-cage.

Kellett stood over Karl and cursed him freely.

"I'll report you to your commandant for this!" he bellowed, ignoring Audrey's feeble protests. But the sight of Audrey's blood-soaked handkerchief moderated his tone and his anger faded. "I suppose I'd better find Dr Murdoch."

The groom, busy with the other horses, had come running at the disturbance. He was sent to find David Carter, while Kellett hurried towards the house.

Audrey, still holding her handkerchief to Karl's head, whispered: "I'm sorry. I'm terribly sorry. I'll try to stop him reporting you. It was all my fault."

Karl did not answer. Already he saw himself back in the camp, all privileges withdrawn. He might even have his repatriation delayed. There were any number of ways of paying the penalty for disobeying.

Audrey was only too well aware of his anger. She sensed he did not want her near him and relinquished her handkerchief for him to hold against his head. She went to stand by the door to watch out for Dr Murdoch, who appeared very soon accompanied by all three of the Carters and Kellett. Donald went directly to Karl, while Kellett approached Audrey. He spoke in a low voice.

"I've decided to leave it up to you whether you report him. I know what you're like, Audrey; it's probably more your fault than his. Just keep me out of it."

Immediately denying her any choice in the matter, he raised his voice. "Tell them what happened, Audrey. How you startled Trojan and he kicked out at the ... German." He had intended to say "Kraut" but remembered in time that Katherine would object.

Audrey exchanged a quick glance with Sarah, then glibly corroborated Andrew's statement. "That's all there is to it," she told them. "Karl was bending over by Trojan, I came across to see if he needed any help. I must have startled Trojan."

Sarah's eyebrows were raised in disbelief. She knew exactly why Audrey had come in here. It was she who had told Audrey Karl was alone.

David turned to Karl for confirmation, much to Audrey's dismay.

"Is that right, Karl?"

Audrey held her breath.

"Yes. That's right." There was a clearly audible sharp intake of breath from Karl as Donald felt his ribs. Despite the pain he noticed disappointment on Sarah's face, as though she knew there should have been more to the story. Her complicity in Audrey's initial approach was now transparently obvious. She wanted him to get into trouble, and had used Audrey as a more than willing accomplice.

Donald finished his preliminary examination. "Can you walk to the car, Karl? Better get you back to my surgery; have a good look at you, and stitch that wound."

Karl stood up gingerly, his left arm across his stomach. "I can walk," he said.

Katherine watched Karl ease himself slowly into the car, and winced for him. "Doesn't look like he'll be fit for work for a while," she said to her father.

"No, poor chap. Still, not to worry. We're well up to date on the farm. He deserves a bit of time off, don't you agree?"

"Certainly. Will he have to go back to the camp though, while he recovers? He won't like that one little bit."

"Don't really know. I don't see why he should. I rather think it might be best if we keep this to ourselves and hang onto him."

Katherine looked sharply at her father. Kellett stood impatiently waiting for her on the front steps of the house. She waved to acknowledge she would not keep him much longer. Her father spoke again.

"I think I'll go straight to Donald's now, in case Karl's worse than he looks. I'll come back and fetch Sarah later."

"Fine. Let me know how he is, won't you?"

"Of course. See you later then, Beauty."

Gertie Murdoch did not support the Hunt, even though her husband attended the event in professional and social capacities. Robert also opted out. With no horse to ride, he was glad of the excuse to miss this particular social event.

Gertie heard the car drive up to the house and two doors slam. "Here's Dad back at last," she said over her knitting. "Sounds like he's got someone with him. I hope it's not a casualty."

She put down her knitting. She had been a young nurse when she first met Donald, and still assisted when required. She went to the waiting-room and was most surprised to see Karl, pale-faced and holding a bloody, lace-trimmed handkerchief to his head.

"Oh my goodness! What on earth has happened to you, poor dear?" Gertie exclaimed. She led Karl through to the consulting room. "Sit down, while Donald gets ready."

Her husband was washing his hands at the sink in the corner of the room. "Would you get silk and a needle ready, please Gertie."

Karl sat quite still and let them get on with cleaning up the gash, but when Donald picked up a hypodermic needle, Karl leaped up from the chair, heedless of the protest from his ribs, and backed away towards the door, his eyes fixed in terror on the syringe.

"No!" he cried. "Do it without, please!"

Hastily Donald hid the syringe from Karl's vision. Eventually Karl relaxed enough to be coaxed back to the chair by Gertie.

"You'd rather I stitched you without anaesthetic?" Donald asked.

"Yes. Without." Karl looked Donald more steadily in the eye now. "It's all right. I stay still."

Whatever was bothering Karl it was clear to the doctor it would be pointless trying to talk him out of it. The prick of an injection was nothing compared with what Karl was prepared to undergo in its place. Surely he must know that. Donald shrugged unhappily, but gave in. He was glad when he drew the last stitch taut and snipped the end. True to his word, Karl had kept tense but still throughout.

"Right! That's done." Donald tidied away the needle and remains of silk while his wife put a dressing over the wound. "I suppose you're not going to let me give you an injection against tetanus, are you now?" he sighed. "You really ought to have one, Karl, especially considering the muck in that wound. You understand what tetanus is, do you?"

"I understand. I had such an injection before," Karl told him.

"Really? When was that? Might need topping up."

"Three and a half years ago."

Donald hesitated. "I ought really to give you another one. If you had one then, why can't you have one now? Far less painful than having stitches," he reasoned.

"No injection please. It is not the pain I fear."

What was it then? Donald abandoned the idea and turned his attention instead to the next injury.

"Let's have a look at your ribs, then. Help Karl with his clothes please, would you, Gertie?"

He ran his fingers carefully over the badly contused area on the left side of Karl's chest, noticing an assortment of old scars, including an abdominal bullet wound.

"You've had a few close shaves in your time!" He felt for any misalignment or projections in the ribs. "Another one today. Nothing obviously broken. Going to be painful for some days, at least. I'll give you some strong painkillers. How does your head feel?"

"He ... it hurts."

"You've got a headache, you mean?"

"Yes, but I had that this morning. I think I have a cold."

Donald handed a bottle of tablets to Karl. "Take two every four hours, starting now."

Gertie fetched Karl a glass of water and helped him into his clothing.

116

"I'll need to see you in about a week to take out those stitches," Donald told him. "Best time would be New Year's Eve, when you come down for Hogmanay."

Karl stared in incomprehension. "What is that?"

"Scottish New Year," Gertie explained. "We always have open house here on New Year's Eve. You're welcome to come down with David and the girls." She gave him her arm to help him up off the chair. "Now. I expect you could do with a nice cup of tea. Come into the living room. I think David arrived while we were busy. I expect Robert's looking after him."

Karl followed her slowly into the living room where, sure enough, David was waiting with Robert. Karl sat himself down carefully.

"All patched up?" David asked cheerily.

"Mm." Karl closed his eyes a moment, wanting only to lie down in peace and quiet. As Donald came in the room he opened them again, reluctantly.

"David! You've come to fetch Karl? He's not in too bad shape, but he's going to have to rest up over the next week. Can you manage without him for that time? Or will you get someone else in? I don't want you overdoing things all of a sudden."

"Don't you worry," David smiled to reassure his friend. "The girls will keep an eye on me."

"Good. Because knowing you, David, you'll go and forget all the advice I've given you."

"How much do I owe you for patching him up?"

"Forget it – my way of repaying him for the help he's given Robert."

Gertie came in with tea. When she put Karl's down she noticed the colour had returned to his cheeks, although the bruise around the dressing on his forehead was more livid.

David quickly drained his cup and set it down carefully on the tray. "Best be getting back to collect Sarah. No doubt she'll want the rest of the day to get herself ready for tonight. You know what these young women are like. You three going this evening?"

117

"Yes," Gertie replied. "I may disapprove of hunts but not Hunt Balls. Young Sarah has persuaded Robert too, so we'll all be putting on our best bib and tucker."

"Good. I'll see you there." David called across the room to Karl, who was gazing absently into the fire. "Ready to go, Karl?"

"Mm?" He had nearly fallen asleep again. He felt rough, and was loath to leave the comfort of the chair. He leaned forwards to stand up then sank quickly back as pain shot through his ribs. With Robert's assistance he tried again, gritting his teeth. He had stiffened up while sitting there. Gertie went to fetch his overcoat from the hall and helped him on with it. He was lightheaded by now, and very hot. He waited impatiently through the thanks and goodbyes before he could sink down again onto the seat of the car.

"You look in a lot of pain," David remarked to a silent Karl as he drove back to Froxley Grange.

"I am ill." There was a distinct croakiness in his voice now.

"I thought you looked a bit peaky this morning. Better go straight to bed once we get back," David told him.

Katherine heard the car and came to meet them.

"How is Karl?" she asked her father as he stood by the car. She bent down and peered through the car window as she spoke. Karl seemed asleep.

"A bit rough I think, more from a cold coming on than his injuries. His ribs are badly bruised, but fortunately not broken."

"What a thing to happen! I don't know what Audrey can have done to have frightened Trojan and made him lash out like that." Katherine paused a moment. "I think I'll come back to the house with you Daddy, and get ready there. It's chaos here at the moment. I'll just go and tell Andrew, and fetch my bag."

She reappeared five minutes later; Sarah was in the car by then. Like Katherine, she was still wearing muddy riding breeches and boots. Sarah chatted the whole way back.

"I do wish we still had decent horses," she lamented.

"Perhaps we will again some day, but there's not much point really if neither you nor Katherine's here to ride them. Is there?"

"True!" Sarah laughed. "I'll have to come down to visit my dear sister and brother-in-law every time I want a ride, won't I?" She grabbed Katherine's hand suddenly. "Let's have another look at that ring, Katherine. I didn't get to see it properly before." She studied it closely. "Now you're well and truly engaged, aren't you?" There was a significant pause. "Are you going to ask *him* to the wedding?" she then asked, with a nod towards the front passenger seat.

Katherine glared at her. "He'd be very welcome to come to the church," she said, hoping Karl was fast asleep.

In fact he was not, but was trying to avoid being drawn into any conversation. When they arrived at the farm he felt worse than ever, and went straight to his room.

Some time later he was dimly aware of footsteps outside, followed by a gentle knock on the door.

Hearing no reply, Katherine lifted the latch and entered the room to leave a drink and plate of sandwiches she had made in case he was hungry.

She saw his eyes watching her over the edge of the blanket. "Oh! I thought you would be asleep." She put the plate on the floor next to the bottle of tablets. "Is there anything else I can get you?" She picked up his battledress jacket off the chair to clean the streaks of blood off it.

He cleared his throat carefully before huskily replying. "No, thank you."

"I'll come back before we all go out."

She drew the curtains, shutting out the draught and a greenish sky, then hurried back to the house. Sarah finally emerged from the bathroom, clad only in her dressing gown, and sat with her father eating sandwiches.

"Nice to be able to sit about in a state of undress again," Sarah said through a mouthful of bread. She watched Katherine put Karl's bloodstained clothing to soak in a bucket

119

of water. "Impossible with *him* around. I never know whether I'm going to bump into him coming out of the bathroom," she complained.

Her father snorted derisively. "I somehow don't think Karl would let on he'd even seen you. He always seems most proper in his dealings with you. Or is that only when I'm around?"

"No. You're right, but then he wouldn't try anything with me, would he? Might be different if I were Audrey though!" Sarah added mischievously.

"Why is that?" her father asked with a note of alarm.

Sarah giggled. "Well what do you think he and Audrey were really up to in the stable?"

She had easily persuaded Audrey to tell her the truth of the afternoon's events once the hue and cry died down, but Sarah decided to embroider in a few embellishments of her own.

Katherine was shocked. "How do you know that? Did Audrey tell you?"

Sarah nodded. With any luck Karl would be replaced by someone like Norbert. She could cope with him, despite his lack of English. He seemed less of a threat than Karl. She remembered the way Karl grabbed her wrist, lightning quick, and the barely controlled aggression when she taunted him. If she were a man, Sarah thought, she would not have escaped with just a bruised wrist.

"I don't believe it," Katherine whispered, horrified.

"I must say, I'm rather surprised myself," said David. "I would have thought he'd more sense than to roll in the hay with Audrey, especially with so many people milling around."

"Well that's what Audrey said," Sarah retorted. "Don't forget, he can't have had much contact with women for years. Audrey was a gift he simply couldn't refuse. I can't think what the government's playing at allowing such men to roam the countryside."

David remembered Karl's expression when Audrey explained what had happened. The memory left a niggling doubt in his mind. He recalled the incident between Karl and Sarah. Had there been more to it than he had been told? His faith in Karl suddenly cracked. He might have picked a ripe apple only to find a maggot inside. If there were any truth in either suspicion, then Karl would have to go. Yet he trusted his instincts when choosing Karl, and his instincts were seldom wrong. He hoped this was not the exception to the rule.

Katherine popped back up to Karl. The glass was empty, but the sandwiches untouched. He was asleep now, his breathing shallow. He looked flushed against the white of the pillowcase. She crept over to him and very gently laid a hand on his forehead. It was hot and clammy. He did not look at all well. She removed her hand; he stirred and half-opened his eyes.

"You feel as though you've a temperature. You ought to be inside the house where it's warm and we can keep a better eye on you. I'll go and have a word with my father."

She left him. Karl lay still, awaiting her return. He was all right as long as he did not move. Sitting up to drink was not a pleasant experience. It was a nuisance being ill. Now he would be a burden to the Carters. He wished it were not so far down the steps and across the yard. He closed his eyes again, until a slow, heavy tread on the steps caused him to open them.

"Katherine says you're not looking so good. I tend to agree. She's offered her room, for the time being. We've persuaded Sarah to let Katherine sleep on her bedroom floor."

Karl wanted to protest, but saw there was no sense in wasting energy. All was settled; he might as well comply. He raised himself cautiously on one elbow and swung his legs over the side of the camp bed. It was a long way up onto his feet. David helped him, picking up his tablets and holding a blanket to drape round his shoulders. They made slow progress down the steps and were glad to reach the warmth of the kitchen. It was then another painful haul up the stairs, before he could finally flop between the covers of Katherine's bed. He closed his eyes immediately; his head was swimming. Dimly he heard David shut the door behind him.

121

"I hope he'll be all right on his own," Katherine said anxiously to her father, as they donned their coats. "Perhaps one of us had better stay."

"If he's asleep, he'll stay that way until morning," he soothed her. "We won't be staying too late tonight, don't worry. You concentrate on enjoying yourself."

Kellett found his fiancée very distracted that evening. The sight of Audrey Patterson being twirled around the dance floor first on Arthur Rowlands-Pickering's arm, then by at least three more young men in turn, only served to remind Katherine how attractive Audrey was. Why should Karl be different from other men, given a willing Audrey? He was at liberty to take risks if he wanted to. As long as he was not caught. Or informed on.

Andrew spoke after a long interval. "I expect you're tired after a busy day,"

"What? Sorry, darling. Yes I am a bit. Woke up too early."

She tried to pay attention for the rest of the evening, but her mind would keep wandering. What must it be like to be a woman like Audrey? Not to care what people said. For Katherine to even contemplate sleeping with a man was impossible. Her experience with Andrew was kept very proper and would continue so until her wedding day. Even the prospect of giving herself to him then filled her with alarm. She knew Sarah felt differently. "If the right man presents himself," Sarah once said soon after starting at university, "I'll not wait until I'm married." Katherine blushed at her thoughts. She knew she was old-fashioned; the war seemed to have changed attitudes. But in Penchurch, at least for Katherine, traditional values remained.

By midnight, Katherine could tell her father wanted to leave. He was sitting by himself looking tired and bored. For most of the revellers, Sarah and Robert included, the night was young, but Katherine did not want her father to wait any longer.

"Andrew, I really ought to go home now. Daddy's tired, Karl's not well; I'd better be there to help out in the morning."

"You can't leave now! I can drive you both back later if you like. Your father can leave whenever he likes."

Katherine would really have liked to go too, but reluctantly she acquiesced. It was not until three in the morning that she and Sarah crammed into Andrew's small car to return to Lane Head, all three of them singing at the top of their voices as they roared up the lane. They quietened the instant the house came in sight, Andrew even making an effort to turn the car around as silently as possible.

Sarah giggled as they crept through the front door and up the stairs, but stopped as she reached her bedroom and listened intently. Katherine too heard the sound.

"Karl. He's having another nightmare," she whispered.

They listened to his growing cries of terror, uncertain whether to intervene. A particularly heart-rending cry spurred both to enter Katherine's room. Sarah turned on the light as Katherine leaned over the bed and patted Karl's cheek firmly to wake him from the terror which gripped him. She shouted his name as he began, just as before, to try to push her away. The violence of his movement pulled at his ribs. He gave a grunt of pain and his eyes opened to stare blankly at Katherine's cleavage. He looked up to encounter Sarah's amazed expression. She had heard one of his nightmares before, but not witnessed its effect.

Katherine sat beside him. "All right now, Karl?"

He managed a weak nod then turned his face away.

"Looks like he's still got a temperature," Sarah said, stating the obvious. "Shall I get the thermometer?" She was enjoying the drama immensely.

"Yes, all right."

Sarah went to the bathroom cabinet, Katherine took out her handkerchief to wipe the sweat from Karl's face. She noticed his tablets on the table. "Do you want some?"

"Please," he croaked.

"I'll get some water."

By the time she returned, Sarah had taken Karl's temperature.

"Hundred and three," Sarah reported with glee. "No wonder he's having nightmares."

"He doesn't need a temperature to have nightmares. He has them all the time. Like Robert."

Katherine set the glass on the table while she took out two tablets. Karl struggled into a sitting position. The cold water irritated his chest and made him cough unexpectedly. It was like being kicked once more. He gasped, hugging his ribs, then coughed again, before sinking under the bedclothes again. His eyes closed in pain.

"Ouch! Even I felt that." Sarah found herself sorry for the first time.

"Is there anything else you want, Karl?" Katherine asked.

His head shook almost imperceptibly.

"Come on then, Sarah. Off we go." Katherine was about to turn off the light at the door when she heard Karl's voice.

"Please. Leave it on."

True to her word, Katherine made the most of Andrew's leave and spent the day with him in Hereford. She felt reluctant to leave the farm with Karl ill. Sarah had her essay to finish, but her father insisted they would manage.

Karl was still asleep when she took up his breakfast. When she came back down Sarah assured Katherine she would keep an eye on him. Katherine realised with surprise that Sarah meant it. Her sister's attitude towards Karl seemed to have softened.

Sarah was busy preparing a tray for Karl when David came in for lunch.

"Poor old Karl's coughing and sneezing a lot now," she told him. "He's making good use of those handkerchiefs."

David could not hide his surprise at her new concern. "My word! I didn't think the day was ever going to come when I heard a word of pity from you!"

Sarah shrugged. "I can see he's not so bad after all. In fact he's pretty decent really."

She suddenly felt it was important to tell him what really happened in the stable with Audrey, as well as Andrew's part in the drama.

"I ... er ... I didn't tell the truth yesterday." She fiddled with the tray cloth. "Karl covered up for Audrey ... and Andrew. Audrey cornered him in the stable. Andrew saw them, jumped to the wrong conclusion and hit him, making him fall under Trojan."

"Well, I'm relieved to hear the truth at last. I was beginning to have some doubts about Karl, especially after your little fracas earlier."

"I hit a raw nerve that time. It seems Audrey found another one. I just hope there aren't too many more of them yet to be discovered. He quite frightened me. I did ask for it though."

She picked up the tray and went upstairs. Karl was less feverish but not at all comfortable. "Do you want to sit up more?" she asked him. "I'll fetch another pillow."

He seemed reluctant to accept her help when she came back with the pillow to prop behind him. She set the tray on the bedside table and sat on the bed. She waited for him to notice, but he ignored her.

"You blame me for what happened, don't you Karl?" Sarah said quietly.

Karl was not prepared to reply. He did not feel like an argument with Sarah now. He wished she would go away and leave him in peace. He was trying hard to fight back a cough which was threatening to overwhelm him.

Sarah knew that absolution required a full confession. She needed to make it now, while she had the courage and while Karl was lying incapacitated in bed, unable to walk away. She was about to speak when Karl succumbed to the cough brewing in his chest.

When the spasm subsided Karl opened his eyes to discover Sarah still watching him. Gloating over my pain, he thought. He eased himself onto his side, away from her, to show he did not care for her company.

Sarah felt the snub but launched into her confession in a rush of staccato sentences.

"You'd be right to blame me. I did encourage Audrey to seduce you. I went and told Andrew you were molesting Audrey. I wanted to get you into trouble. So you would have to leave. But now I'm truly sorry. I didn't intend you to get hurt. I'm not that vindictive." There was a pause. "I just felt you had become too much a part of the household."

Karl was silent. Unconvinced, she decided. She must continue her persuasion.

"Robert was telling me last night at the ball, how much you helped him find himself again, despite all your own problems. I thought he was laying it on a bit thick, but so many people at the ball said how much better he was."

She saw with relief he was paying attention, even though he still refused to look at her.

"I didn't know what Robert meant about your problems, but when I saw you having your nightmare last night, I finally realised."

She edged closer so she could turn his face towards her, to make him see the contrition in her face. She took a deep breath.

"I want to apologise for the way I've behaved towards you and for getting you hurt so badly. Please accept my offer of peace."

Her sudden surrender caught Karl by surprise. He suspected a new ploy.

Before he could interrupt she went on: "I just told my father the whole truth about yesterday."

It was enough. He nodded slightly. "All right."

Sarah's sense of relief overwhelmed her. She bent forward and kissed him on the cheek. He warded her off.

"Whoa!" he warned her. "Our countries are not yet so friendly."

She backed off quickly, then saw the corners of his mouth twitch. He paid for his efforts at speech with another bout of coughing. He was exhausted after that, and lay still with his eyes shut.

"Do you want these sandwiches?" Sarah asked him.

He shook his head. "Leave them there, please. I might want them later."

Sure enough, his appetite returned by the middle of the afternoon. He sat up gingerly and reached for the plate.

So Sarah had grown up at last, and discovered she was able to admit to a mistake. Having made her about turn, he hoped she was not in danger of going to the other extreme. That too would be most awkward for him. She was not worth getting into trouble for either, especially since she would be gone again soon.

He finished his sandwiches and lay back, letting his eyes wander round Katherine's room.

It was the room of a young woman who had inhabited it since childhood. There were rosettes from gymkhanas pinned to a ribbon across the pelmet. Perched precariously on a shelf, a doll with staring blue eyes and curly blonde hair reminded him unpleasantly of Audrey; all pouting lips and empty head. On the wall, a picture of a bluebell wood particularly held his attention. It reflected the natural beauty and tranquillity of the room's owner. He looked at the picture for a long time.

CHAPTER SEVEN

Katherine turned over the last page of her diary before putting it away in the kitchen drawer. Tomorrow would be a new year. The year she became Mrs Andrew Kellett.

That morning had seen the start of Andrew's long journey back to Germany. The next time she saw him he would be home for good. With that wistful thought she began energetically pounding the washing in the tub.

Her father popped his head round the back door, not wanting to come in with his muddy boots. "Where's Karl?

"He was going to mend the raspberry cage for me. Do you want him?"

"Yes. I thought I'd show him how to lay a hedge, now he's up and about."

"Don't forget he's taking it easy, Daddy. That 'flu really knocked a lot out of him."

"You'd wrap us all in cotton wool if you could!" he laughed. "Don't worry. He only needs to watch me. I'll be doing the work." Before she could comment, he quickly added: "And *I* won't overdo it either!"

He went out to the garden and found Karl amongst the raspberry canes, struggling with a roll of netting.

"Leave that for the moment, Karl. Plenty of time for that. It's about time you learned how to lay a hedge."

Arming themselves with billhook and strong gloves they ambled down through the meadows to the far boundary of the farm, where the lane joined the valley road. Here David began his lesson.

"Evan, my shepherd, used to do all my hedging. It must be a good six years since this was laid last. It's well in need. See. There's a gap here, where this thorn is dying back. We need to fill that with the healthy wood."

In demonstration, David cut some stakes from the hedgerow. Then he bent a hawthorn stem and partly cut through the base so the stem was nearly horizontal, its side branches effectively plugging the gap. He pushed the end of the stem under its neighbour to hold it in position, then drove the stake in at right angles to the trunk, interweaving it amongst the branches to secure it further.

"Got the idea now? We always lay stems uphill. You can do the rest of the hedge next week, if you feel up to it. There's fencing needs replacing too, down by the river. The posts have almost rotted through. They'll need to come out."

A sudden flurry of icy rain caught them by surprise.

"Katherine will tell me off if I keep you out in this," David muttered, and set off towards the house. "Sarah too. I notice she's changed her tune." He looked steadily at Karl, his expression that of wry amusement.

Did David suspect goings on between himself and Sarah? Karl sensed no opposition to such an idea but thought he should disillusion him. "Sarah is a clever girl. Her studies are important to her."

They paused at the gate to Long Meadow for David to catch his breath. The rain stopped as suddenly as it began.

"She's not interested in any of this," David said, encompassing the whole farm with a sweep of his arm. "Once she's finished at Bristol she'll find a good job somewhere, maybe even in London. Katherine's off to Froxley Grange in a few months. What am I to do then? I'll have nobody to run the farm for, except myself. Or any grandchildren that show an interest." He laid his hands dispiritedly on top of the gate and sighed wearily. "Your father is a lucky man, Karl, to have two sons to inherit his life's work."

"You have two clever and beautiful daughters. You should be very proud."

David smiled fondly. "They are treasures, aren't they?" He snapped himself out of his despondency. "What are your plans, when you get home?"

Karl shrugged. "I'm not sure. I don't allow myself to think about such a time. Now my brother is home, and my sister may marry her Stefan, there may be enough people to run the business without me. Father says Rudi tries to make new contacts with people in the wood industry. Now I speak English I may find buyers for our wood among the Occupying Powers. Some good must come from my time here."

"I hope so."

David had recovered his breath enough to proceed. They both took it slowly. Karl was still troubled by his cough, which in turn aggravated his healing ribs.

"You ought to mention that cough when Donald takes out your stitches. See if he can give you anything." David noticed tears in Karl's eyes, although they could be attributed to the icy wind. "Do you feel up to a knees up tonight? You don't have to come."

Karl wiped his eyes with the back of his hand. "I will come. I have to see Dr Murdoch and it is New Year's Eve. It is not a night to be alone."

"We won't be staying late. You and I can leave when we've had enough. The girls will find someone to bring them home, if they don't last out the whole night. I've known these Hogmanay shindigs to go on till morning. Somehow, though, I don't think Katherine will be staying, after all her late nights this week."

David stopped again, hands on hips, gulping down air. "Dear me! I am short of breath today," he gasped.

They continued the rest of the way in silence.

That evening both girls made a stunning appearance in their party frocks. These shimmering moths of the night were so different from the daytime creatures Karl was used to.

"What a pair of Beauties I've got, eh, Karl?" David beamed, remembering Karl's words that afternoon.

Karl smiled in agreement, but said nothing. The vibrant colour on Sarah's lips reminded him of another mouth. He wondered whether Audrey would be a guest this evening. He rather hoped to avoid meeting her again. Despite the events in the stable, he doubted she would give up her quest to snare a German. He had feared Sarah might pose a similar problem, but so far she was friendly but not over-familiar. The kiss on his cheek seemed to have been a symbolic gesture of peace, nothing more.

The party was already well attended by the time they pulled up in the driveway of Yew Tree Lodge. Robert had been given free rein to invite his friends, so there was a representative gathering in the hall and living room as the Carters arrived. To Karl's dismay he noticed Audrey immediately, chatting to a fresh-faced young man by the piano. Audrey's kiss had awoken sensations in himself which had been buried, firstly out of necessity, then out of obligation, ever since Ilse's last embrace. He did not want to be tempted again.

Sarah saw his anxious look. "Don't worry. I'll keep her away."

"Thank you. I would be grateful."

Katherine felt at a loss without Andrew after such an intensive week in his company. After accepting a glass of wine from Donald, she wandered over to join the younger people around Robert. A burst of laughter caught her attention. As she leaned forward to hear what was so funny, she noticed Donald take Karl off to his surgery.

David was in the hallway discussing the price of feedstuffs with Derek Patterson, Audrey's father, and was still there when Donald and Karl, now with stitches removed and a smaller, neater piece of sticking plaster on his forehead, came out of the surgery.

"Sorry to leave you like that," Donald apologised. "Had a small job to do on Karl."

They rejoined the party in the crowded living room. Gertie stood by the gramophone and announced they were about to start Scottish Country Dancing.

There was space for only one set at a time. Since everyone was game to have a go, each dance tune was played several times over. An experienced caller gave the steps. By the time he had seen the same dance three times and finished his whisky, Karl felt he had the measure of it. Sarah volunteered to be his partner, giving him a nudge at appropriate times and grabbing his hands in the correct cross-over position to swing him. His ribs protested and he had to restrain her enthusiasm. His various partners were generous in prompting him along, and as the evening progressed he discovered that the basic steps were often repeated. All in all he began to enjoy himself.

At ten o'clock everyone was ready for the food laid out on the dining room table. Each guest had brought something, including some traditional Scottish dishes. Robert teased Karl as to the animal origins of haggis and explained that "neeps" was only another name for swede. Donald kept the whisky, beer and wine flowing for the next traditional Murdoch event, the "Entertainments".

They flooded back into the living room, bringing chairs from dining room and kitchen. An area was left clear for Donald and Gertie, who sang a duet from *Ruddigore* – "The Pretty Little Flower and the Great Oak Tree" – accompanied on the piano by Olive Thornton. Having set the ball rolling, they then retired while other guests in turn stood to deliver their party pieces. John Thornton recited a comic poem, a magic trick followed, then more songs and poetry. A foursome of Robert's friends had brought along a flute, a violin and a clarinet to go with the piano, and gave a very respectable performance of chamber music.

No one had forewarned Karl of all this. During the second piece from the chamber group, he thought about what he might offer. It would have to be a song, even though his voice was not up to par. An unaccompanied song moreover, with a good tune to make up for the incomprehensible words. He had just decided upon *"Die Lorelei"*, as a well-known tune which might possibly be familiar to the British, when Sarah tapped him on the arm.

"How about joining us in *"Rolling Down to Rio"*? You know! One of the songs we sang here at Christmas."

He grinned. "Certainly."

The Murdochs were gathering round the piano with Katherine and David as Sarah stepped up, Karl behind her. There was a murmur of surprise from the audience, who seemed to think Karl would be exempt from making an exhibition of himself. With Katherine assisting Gertie in the alto part, the ensemble produced a rendition which filled the room.

Finding his voice not so husky as he feared and his ribs anaesthetised by the whisky, Karl had a quick word with Donald as the others resumed their seats.

Donald was clearly pleased at Karl's suggestion, and left the floor to him.

No stranger to singing in public, Karl sensed now the audience did not need cossetting with too simple a song. He decided upon a song about his home area he often sang with Rudi to houseguests: *Westfalenlied*. His voice swelled with emotion as he sang the last line – *"Du Land wo meine Wiege stand, o grüss dich Gott, Westfalenland!"* It was received with a moment of dead silence before thunderous applause broke out.

When midnight approached and everyone was intent on a full glass, Robert approached Karl. "We used to sing songs like that in the camp, supposedly to keep our spirits up. They always left us with a dreadful yearning for home. And a determination we would survive to get back there."

He glanced around to see if they could be overheard, then said in a low voice: "My mother asked me if I knew why you should be so frightened of injections – I know Dad's curious too. Do you want me to say anything? Perhaps it would be as well to tell my father at least?"

"No."

Robert shuffled his feet, disconcerted by Karl's abrupt refusal. "Why not? He would understand, I'm sure," he persisted. "I did."

"You are different, Robert. That is why I knew you would understand. But the others? How can they know? They do not need to know. Please. Say nothing."

Robert looked troubled. "I think you're making a mistake, Karl. They ..."

He was interrupted by a call for silence from Donald as the clock began to strike.

"Happy New Year!" came the general cry, and much kissing and hugging. Karl was made to join the circle as everyone linked arms and sang *Auld Lang Syne*. But he entered the New Year in melancholic mood, initiated perhaps by the whisky or the song about home, and he could not shake it off. Once again he felt on the periphery amongst the strange customs. The First-Foot arrived with his inexplicable lump of coal and much speculation by the guests as to whether it was a nationalised or privately-owned piece.

Shortly afterwards David sought him out to warn him they would be leaving soon. Katherine decided to return with them, but Sarah was set to last the night. They left her cavorting with Robert to the music of Glenn Miller.

"I don't know how she has the energy!" David said, struggling with the sleeve of his overcoat.

Katherine helped him with it, noticing how tired he looked. "I'll drive if you like. I'm quite sober."

"Thank you, Beauty."

As they set off in the starlight, Katherine noticed Karl seemed quiet too. She guessed the reason. For him, 1947 would mean yet another year of captivity, nothing more. Another year of homesickness and futility.

With a much later start than normal the following morning, David was itching to get on with some real work after Karl's illness and the extended Christmas break.

"I'm going to replace those fence posts today," he told Karl over breakfast. "I'll need your help to hold them while I knock them in, unless you feel up to doing the job yourself."

Karl saw a flash of annoyance cross Katherine's face. He knew she would not want her father attempting such heavy work.

"I can try," he said, "and see how I feel." A few hefty swings with a sledgehammer would soon prove whether he was fit yet.

They loaded up the wagon with posts, sledgehammer, staples and netting and made their way with Beth down to the river bank. Extracting the rotted posts was no easy task; the heavy red soil held on to them like teeth in their sockets. As the third post finally released its grip on the ground, David paused for a rest. He was still tired after the party, but he refused to waste yet another day. In a minute or two he would have his breath back. Karl was busy unloading the posts and laying one by each hole.

Not one for wasting a day either, David thought happily. What a bargain this arrangement is!

As David came over to hold the post steady, Karl lifted the sledgehammer over his head, grimaced slightly, then swung it down. As contact was made with the post, the shock waves jarred up Karl's arms, rattling him uncomfortably but not unbearably.

"All right?" David asked.

"Yes. I can do it."

He finished off the first post, and began on the second until each swing of the sledgehammer caused more and more discomfort. He put the tool down with relief as the second post finally held firm in the ground.

"I shouldn't have let you do a job like that yet. You're having trouble, aren't you?" David began to reach for the sledgehammer. "I'll do the last one."

"No, I'm fine, really."

Karl reached for the sledgehammer again, but David brushed aside his protests. Karl found it impossible to insist without being rude or using force against his employer. He understood the man's pride, and reluctantly held the next post in position. David had completed just four strokes when he suddenly let out a cry of pain, and dropped the sledgehammer with a heavy thud onto the mud. Karl saw with horror that David was clutching his chest, his face creased with agony. David stumbled and Karl caught him as he began to fall. For an instant their eyes met before pain, recognition, then life itself faded from the brown eyes and David's body hung limply in Karl's arms.

In disbelief Karl put his fingers on David's neck to find a pulse; there was none. Slowly he laid him down. He sat back on his heels and tenderly closed the eyes of the man who had taken an enemy into his home and given him friendship.

Joss, sitting nearby, sensed something was wrong and ran over, licking his master's still hand to yield a rewarding pat. He whined at the lack of response and barked nervously. Absently Karl pulled the dog to himself and patted him. After a long time he bent over, gathered David's body into his arms, then lifted it onto the wagon. Joss lay beside his master, his head in the crook of David's arm, while Beth drew them home.

The house was deserted. Sarah was not yet back from the party. Karl came back out into the yard and called Katherine's name. She was sweeping out the poultry house when she heard his call and wondered why on earth he sounded so agitated.

The instant she saw him she knew something was terribly wrong. He stood awkwardly, his arms half-raised, strangely reluctant to approach her. She put down her broom and walked towards him.

"What is it?" She feared an answer as she read his expression. His lack of urgency now told her to expect the worst.

Karl put a hand on her shoulder in a gesture of wordless consolation, then awkwardly withdrew it, as though he feared she would be offended. "Your father is dead," he said quietly. She closed her eyes a moment to let his words sink in. When she opened them again tears brimmed over her lashes but her voice was steady. "Was it quick? Was he in pain?"

Ever since her father's stay in hospital, Katherine had prepared herself for this eventuality. Now she found herself calm and able to accept Karl's news.

"It was quick. He had pain, but not for long," Karl told her honestly. "There was nothing I could do." He wanted to say more to ease her grief but felt at a loss for the right words. "I am ... very sorry."

She looked up at him. Her mouth tried to smile her thanks, but she began to lose the battle with her emotions and choked on a sob, which she hastily tried to swallow. "Where is he?" she asked through the lump in her throat.

"Joss is with him in the wagon."

She wanted to put off having to see him. In her mind he was still alive, until her eyes told her otherwise. At last she went to the wagon and saw her father lying there with Joss on guard. Katherine flung herself over him and laid her head on his chest, finally allowing the tears to flow freely. Karl left her like that for a long time, then gently pulled her down off the wagon. She clung to him then, her head against his shoulder, feeling the comfort of his arms around her. They seemed to stand like that for ever. At last, gulping hard, she looked up to see his silent tears.

"He was a good friend to me," he said.

She nodded too, vigorously, not trusting herself to speak.

"Come. We cannot leave him here." Karl felt Katherine's reluctance to move. "Can you help me lift him from the wagon?"

She swallowed her tears and nodded again, stepping out of his embrace. She took her father's feet and together they lifted him out and into the sitting room, where they laid him on the sofa. Katherine knelt to remove his muddy boots. Automatically she put them in their usual place by the back door. She realised her hands were shaking. To steady herself she put the kettle on the range.

It was Karl who made the call to Donald Murdoch. Katherine could not speak, her throat was so tight. Sarah had stayed the night with the Murdochs. At least she would be told the news now. He went back to the sitting room. Katherine was on the floor, her back to the wall, staring blankly at her father's body. He heard the kettle start to whistle in the kitchen and went to make the tea.

When Donald arrived he wasted no time in greetings. "Where is he?" he asked Karl.

Karl waved the doctor, still in hat and coat, into the sitting room. A quick examination revealed no further haste was required. Donald looked down at his old friend for some minutes before coming back to business. He went over to Katherine and took her hands, helping her up from the floor.

"My dear. If there's anything Gertie and I can do for you, you know we're always there."

Katherine shook herself out of her misery for a moment. "Where's Sarah? Does she know?"

"She was with us when Karl called. She's very distressed. Gertie insisted she stayed there, for the moment. I'll bring her up later, when she's recovered. In the meantime I'll organise everything, Katherine, but I'd just like to satisfy myself as to the cause of his death, so I can write the death certificate. Do you feel up to telling me what happened?"

"I wasn't with him. Karl was."

Karl braced himself. "We were putting in fence posts. I did two, but my ribs hurt. David took the sledgehammer, but very soon he cried out in pain and held his chest, like this." Karl put both fists clenched over his heart in demonstration. "I caught him as he fell, but he soon died. I felt his neck. There was no heart beat."

Katherine listened attentively. It was the first time she had heard the details.

"Were you holding him when he died, Karl?" she asked him.

"Yes. He knew I was there with him," he said, hoping it was of some comfort. The loneliness of death was something he understood only too well.

"Thank you. I'm glad he was not alone." Despite her own grief she realised Karl was anxious about something. She looked at him questioningly. "What is it?"

He began to speak, thought better of it, then decided to speak up anyway. "I should have tried harder to stop him to use the sledgehammer. It was because I could not finish the job that he must finish for me. It is my fault."

Katherine was shocked at his self-reproach. "No! You're not to blame, Karl. It could have happened any time, couldn't it, Donald?"

Donald agreed with her, his voice gentle. "That's true enough, Karl. No one's blaming you."

It was kind of them to say it, but Karl felt responsible. He had been made to feel guilty for all manner of events since the end of the war. The habit was hard to break now.

Donald cleared his throat gruffly. "I'd better be off to organise things, my dear," he said to Katherine. "Do you want to come down with me, or stay until I return with Sarah?"

"I'll stay here," she said firmly. "I don't want to leave him alone."

The remainder of the day passed in a flurry of comings and goings, as Gertie spread the word. The Rev. Thornton called by soon after Donald left. There was a telephone call of commiseration from Major and Mrs Kellett, more offers of help. Katherine made a few telephone calls herself to her father's relatives and to those of her mother still in close touch.

She was in the middle of such a call when Donald came back with Sarah, who wanted to see her father once more in the familiar surroundings of their home. She was very quiet and pale. Donald mentioned to Katherine she had been given a sedative. Robert came too, his arm around Sarah, and went with her to see her father. Karl made everyone a cup of tea as a distraction while they awaited the undertakers. He handed a cup to the flagging and barely composed Katherine, brooding on the precariousness of his position at Lane Head in the absence of David Carter.

A short while later the undertakers arrived. This proved to be most distressing as the car drove off down the lane. Donald too watched David's last departure with great sorrow, oblivious to the fact that although Robert was comforting Sarah, Katherine had no shoulder to cry on. It was left to Karl to provide that service for her, and she made good use of it.

With the hearse gone, Donald set about organising everybody once more. "Would you young ladies like to go and pack some things? Gertie's busy making up beds for you this very minute. We can't have you staying all alone up here tonight, can we?"

Katherine was immediately aware of his reasoning, but Sarah had not experienced this situation before. "We won't be alone. Karl will be here," she said listlessly.

"That's just the point, my dear," Donald said, trying to be tactful in front of Karl. "Karl had better stay up here to look after the animals. That's if you don't mind, Karl, just for a day or two? Until the girls are feeling more up to work."

Comprehension still did not dawn on the bemused Sarah. Katherine went upstairs to pack for both of them. Passing her father's room with the packed bags, she paused. She opened his door and looked in at a still rumpled bed, his pyjamas in a heap just as he had left them. She turned and made her way downstairs to the group sitting quietly in the kitchen. It was only then she began to think about Karl being left on his own. No one had eaten lunch and she had certainly not given a thought to dinner.

"There's some leftover apple pie and custard in the larder, Karl, as well as sausages, eggs, potatoes and bread." She hoped he knew how to cook; Andrew would not.

"I can manage. Don't worry," he told her, picking up her bags.

Joss sat at Karl's side watching the car's departure. Katherine turned in her seat and looked out of the rear window at the farm which was now her responsibility. Karl would manage perfectly well on his own for the next few days, and she could forget about the sheep until after the funeral, but the enormity of her new burden lay heavily. She envisaged a day when she and Sarah might have to hand over to sitting tenants or Froxley Grange. At the thought of losing her childhood home, her tears flowed anew.

She could only pick at dinner. She began to worry about Karl.

"May I phone home, just to make sure Karl's found everything?" she asked Gertie.

"Of course. Go ahead, dear. Tomorrow I'll send Robert with some provisions; you'll be staying here a day or two yet."

Katherine went out to the hall and picked up the receiver.

Karl had just given Joss his dinner outside the back door when he heard the sound of hooves in the lane. It was almost dark; late for a rider. He went to the front of the house to tell the visitor no one was at home. The rider, already dismounted, was almost invisible behind the bay horse, but the breeches-clad legs were female. Through the gloom Audrey's blonde curls appeared from around the tethered horse.

Did she know what had happened? Did she also know she would find him alone? He was suspicious but carefully polite.

"Good evening, Miss Patterson. Sarah is at Dr Murdoch's house."

Audrey walked up to him; her breeches emphasised her shapely hips. "I know," she said in her deep, husky voice. "I heard the dreadful news from Mrs Tucker. She said Sarah and Katherine had gone to the Murdochs."

"So why are you here?"

The answer was only too plain. She sidled close to him and looked up with startlingly blue eyes. "I thought you might be lonely, so I came to see if there was anything you ... needed." She gave an unambiguous stress to the word "needed".

He glared at her coldly. "I made my feelings clear in the stable. There is nothing I need."

He began to turn away, but she held onto his arm. "You made your feelings very clear, before you got cold feet. There's no one here now, is there?"

"Only David Carter's ghost."

Audrey shuddered, but her mission was not so easily abandoned. "After what I felt on Boxing Day, I know you need a woman, Karl. I give you my word I won't even tell Sarah. It wouldn't be very tactful at the moment, would it?"

"No, it would not be tactful, which is why I want you to leave now. I too am sad because David has died. This is not the time."

"You mean another time would be?"

Karl threw up his hands in despair. She was beginning to wear away his resistance. The need she described was certainly there, and Audrey was unquestionably an attractive proposition.

She saw him waver. "Let me come in and cook something. You haven't eaten, have you?"

"I can cook for myself." He felt himself being manipulated and thought of the risk he would be taking if he succumbed to her charms.

"Rubbish! Let me do it for you." She marched towards the house. He followed, not daring to lay a hand to prevent her.

She slipped off her riding jacket as she went into the kitchen, and dropping it over a chair, propped her elbows on the kitchen table, displaying her long haunches. She raised a foot backwards and drawled: "Take my boots off, there's a darling."

After a momentary hesitation, he turned and braced his rear against hers, tugging at each boot as it was offered. She pushed herself back against him shamelessly, so that his hands were shaking long before he was able to drop the boots by the range and sink into the rocking chair.

She smiled, knowing full well that she was now in total control. Easing off her long silk scarf, she removed her jumper and unfastened several buttons of her blouse. She watched him for a moment, gave a little laugh and walked to the larder.

A quarter of an hour later she sat opposite him as he hungrily devoured her hasty fry-up of sausage, egg and mash, his eyes flitting between her mouth and her breasts. When he finished she took his plate in one hand, leaned closer and brushed his mouth with hers.

She dropped the plate into the sink, and keeping her back to him, smoothed her hands over her hips and down the backs of her thighs. Languorously she released the side-fastenings of her breeches, then pulled her blouse slowly over her head. Stooping a little for maximum effect, she eased the breeches down, and stepped out of them. She turned slowly, thrusting forward her breasts through the silk camisole, a provocative smile tempting him to reveal them.

Karl stepped forward. Without futher hesitation he put his hands under her camisole and raised it over her head. Then he was upon her, kissing her breasts, tugging silk knickers over her hips, lifting her bodily onto the kitchen table. His urgency delighted her and she flung apart her thighs to receive him. When he had spent himself, she lay back on the table for a little while, his head on her breast. Then she ran her hands over his body, deftly removing his clothing, her sophisticated fingers rousing him again.

"That's better," she murmured. "Now it's my turn."

They enjoyed each other to the full until she at last broke away and settled with a naked giggle into the rocking chair.

"You needed that, didn't you? How long has it been, for heaven's sake?"

Karl said nothing, but the intensity of his gaze was enough; never had he experienced such open sensuality, in any woman.

She put out the tip of her tongue, her mouth spreading into a smile of huge delight.

"If I stay the night you can have some more."

He reached for his discarded clothing. "What about your parents? They will worry about you."

"No. I told them I was riding over to a friend's house and staying the night. They'll never bother to check up. They never do."

"So you knew you would stay?"

She smiled wickedly. "That's right. But if by chance you hadn't obliged, I had somewhere else in mind to go." She realised she had shocked him by this revelation and artfully tried to mollify him. "It wouldn't have been half so good as here." She raised her head and kissed him, before a shiver caught her and she too put on her clothes. "I hope your bed is warmer."

"I have only a camp bed," he told her. "Perhaps tonight we use a dead man's bed."

Audrey shuddered. "That's creepy. I couldn't possibly."

"The dead have no need of their belongings. They are there for the living. I have done it before; it does not worry me."

Karl went outside to stable Audrey's horse with Beth. Despite his own words, his conscience pricked him about making use of the Carters' home like this, but he felt Audrey, having achieved her ambition, would leave him alone in future. The thrill for her was the initial seduction. Once in her snare, men lost their attraction and she moved on to the next. He was perfectly happy to be her victim. He had buried his own desires so deeply, that it needed someone like Audrey to rekindle the flame. She had served her purpose. If she wanted to move on he did not mind, but it would be nice if her interest lasted a little longer than just one night.

While he was gone Audrey heard the telephone, but dared not answer it. Probably more tearful relatives she would not be able to cope with anyway. The ringing eventually stopped. She did not mention it to Karl when he came back.

She had not captured him as completely as she wanted. She liked men to worship her, to need her presence as much as her body. With Karl there was no emotional involvement. She felt he was using her as much as she him, and found the experience unpleasant. For the first time it dawned on her what her own actions may have felt like to the men she had abandoned. Perversely this only renewed her desire to win Karl's heart as well as his body. She needed a man's love; the only way she knew how to win that was to give her body. She was having to work hard for Karl. Perhaps he would be worth keeping.

When he came back she was lounging in the rocking chair, one leg draped indelicately over its arm, the other pushing rhythmically against the floor. She was smoking a cigarette. She offered him one but he refused, much to her surprise. She smiled coquettishly. "Don't they let you have these either?" she teased him.

A harshness in his reply warned her she was on dangerous ground. "I don't like to be ... dependent on something."

"I see." Catlike she changed her position, arching her back, thrusting out her breasts and pointing her toes in a sensual, full-bodied stretch. She fully intended making him dependent – on her.

The telephone rang again.

"Don't answer it! It will only be awkward for you," Audrey told him.

Karl felt obliged to go out to the hall and pick up the phone.

"Karl!" He recognised Katherine's voice with dismay. She sounded relieved. "I phoned earlier but there was no reply," she went on. "Were you outside?"

"Yes. Are you all right?" He could do without too many questions from her at the moment.

"Not too bad. Sarah's gone to bed with a sleeping tablet. I might do the same shortly. I just wanted to make sure you had everything you needed."

"Don't worry," he assured her guiltily. "I am fine."

"Good. I knew you would be, but we left in such a hurry -"

"You have a good sleep and let Gertie look after you. Stay as long as you want."

He hoped Audrey did not read too much into his words. He wanted Katherine to stay for her own benefit, not his.

After his conversation with Katherine, Audrey knew she had lost some ground. Karl was distracted. She spent the next hour on his lap gently reminding him of her presence. She talked lightly of herself and her job as a legal secretary in Hereford. When he kissed her again, she knew she had his full attention once more. When their lips parted she felt herself lifted and carried up to David's room. Audrey felt the thrill of renewed anticipation. He had a huge passion locked inside him, a barely restrained aggression; she almost feared what he might do to her. There had been triumph in his face after their first time. His motives were lost to her, but the power of his passion was not.

Straight after breakfast the next morning Robert Murdoch took his motorbike up to Lane Head Farm, carrying the provisions promised by his mother. As he turned up the lane to the farm, he passed Audrey Patterson out for an early ride. Katherine and Sarah were making a start on all the bureaucracy of death. He was glad to be out of the house and the atmosphere of mourning, even for a short while.

After putting away the food in the larder, Robert was directed by a noisy bleating to Steps Meadow, where Karl was filling a trough with chopped beet. Robert called out above the clamour of the sheep. "All well?"

Karl strode over, pushing his way through the heavy woolly bodies surging at the feed troughs. "Yes. Everything is fine. How are Katherine and Sarah?"

"Bearing up. They're over the worst of the shock, I think. Mum is keeping them busy with arrangements for the funeral; Monday, by the way. You will be coming, won't you?"

"Of course." Karl began to push the empty barrow back towards the fodder store.

"Can I give you a hand?" Robert asked him. Karl eyed Robert's neat tweed trousers doubtfully, but Robert was not to be dissuaded. "I might as well. Bit depressing at home at the moment. Some fresh air and work will do me good, anyway."

They reached the store and Robert began to feed whole beets into the chopping machine, turning the handle vigorously. "Didn't you find it depressing on your own here last night?"

Karl kept no secrets from Robert. It was an absolute necessity to have someone to confide in. It would be better if Robert were privy to this latest development.

"Audrey was here."

Robert assessed the significance of Karl's words. "All night?"

"Yes." He grinned at the expression on Robert's face, and held up his hands in mock surrender. "She made me forget the sadness," he explained. "Now she can forget me and find someone else to ..."

"Seduce is the word you want, I think."

Robert was intrigued by Karl's detached manner. Neither David's death nor Audrey's seduction seemed to touch him. Or else, like his shocking wartime experiences, he buried it all under a superficial veneer of nonchalance. Anything to keep sane.

Audrey's visit brought to mind a discussion between the Murdochs from the previous evening, once Sarah and Katherine were tucked up in bed.

"There's no way you're going to be allowed to live here now, once the girls return," he told Karl gravely. "Dad's not even sure you'll be allowed to work here. He said he was going to have a word with your commandant today; tell him

146

what the situation is, try to convince him you should carry on working for Katherine. This is just the time she needs you most. Dad says he's going to do his utmost to let you stay. Of course, you'll have to live with us, assuming Major Alderton agrees."

"I hope very much that he does agree. I like it here."

"Especially with Audrey around," Robert jibed, then grew more serious. "Katherine must never find out about that. She would be furious, especially since it was the very day her father died. I don't think she would understand your reasons."

"I do not intend she will find out. So long as Audrey keeps quiet. She promised she would."

"You never know with Audrey, that's the trouble."

The barrow was full once more with chopped beet, so the two men moved off to the next meadowful of hungry sheep.

"Is Audrey coming back tonight?" Robert asked uneasily. He did not want trouble ahead, for either Karl or Katherine.

"I think not. I told her she should not come. Someone is sure to find out if she stays here again."

"What will you do if she does come? Send her away?"

Karl shrugged. "You know Audrey. That is a difficult thing to do, is it not?"

Robert had to agree. When Audrey flashed her charms, men came running, himself included. Karl resisted her in the stable. It appeared he had been unable to resist her twice.

The following afternoon Katherine and Sarah returned, subdued and pale-faced but able to face their strangely empty home. Karl had left the kitchen and David's room tidy. He made up a fire in the sitting room to lessen the chill. The room had been unused since David's body was carried from it.

Donald brought the girls' bags from the car then called to Karl. He acquainted him with the negotiations with Major Alderton and the labour officer.

"Found this harder to arrange than I thought," he admitted. "I suppose we're so used to you being around we forget what restrictions still apply. I've had to give a personal guarantee to be responsible for you and make sure you do not abuse the privileges you are to be given."

Karl understood his meaning only too well. Definitely no more liaising with Audrey. She had turned up again the previous night; Karl feared Donald somehow may have got wind of it. A careful study of the doctor's face reassured him.

"Better pack up your belongings and I'll drive you back to the village. You'll be staying with us from now on."

Karl did as he was told, sorry to be leaving the room which had been his own. He looked out of the window, towards the valley and the village huddled against the hillside. As on his first day at the farm, a pair of rooks flew by from their roost towards the cluster of houses in the distance, like emissaries of his own relocation.

CHAPTER EIGHT

Sarah did not want to leave Katherine on her own, but with examinations to sit it was impossible to stay on. After another week she returned to Bristol, promising to telephone frequently. Sarah could immerse herself in her alternative life and hope to carry on as before; but each day Katherine saw empty chairs and rooms. It did not help that Karl had to move out, but at least he would be there during the day.

As she said goodbye, Sarah handed Karl a telephone number. "If you think Katherine needs a chat or cheering up, give me a call. Please, Karl. I'm relying on you to see she gets through the next few months until Andrew's back. Thank God she won't have to run this place alone."

She picked up her handbag from the kitchen table. Katherine was waiting to run her to the bus-stop. "One more thing, before I go." She stood on tiptoe an kissed him lightly on the cheek. "That's from Audrey. She said it was good while it lasted."

Sarah hurried out and climbed into the car before she could see Karl's reaction. He sat down slowly, listened to the car drive off, and drummed his fingers absently on the kitchen table. So. Audrey could not keep her mouth shut! Probably it would not matter. Since Christmas he had as much faith in Sarah's discretion as he had in Robert's.

Karl knew the route the car would follow, having walked it twice daily for the past week, as well as during his week with the Murdochs in November. On his second trek a group of schoolboys laid in wait behind the churchyard hedge, then jumped out, gave the Hitler salute and chanted: "Nazi pig, Nazi swine, hang by the neck with garden twine!" A clip round the ear from the sexton swiftly followed. They were

149

made to apologise to Karl – an agonising experience for them. He shrugged off the memory and set to work.

Those first weeks after David's death passed without event. The weather turned colder, frosts left the grass stiff until midday, and the pastures were cropped short. Katherine brought the sheep into the sheds to make feeding easier.

Karl was relieved that Katherine coped well with her new and solitary existence. On Sundays she made an excursion to the Murdochs and visited the most recent grave in the churchyard before attending church. During the week Gertie phoned frequently to check all was well.

With the first heavy snows, Karl's daily treks turned into expeditions. By the end of January the lane was blocked by deep drifts. He found it easier to take the longer route across the meadows. Here the wind scoured away some snow and ensuing frosts formed a crust on what remained, so that he sank over the tops of his boots less frequently. Before he could start work for the day or relax of an evening, Katherine and Gertie thawed him out with cups of tea or bowls of hot porridge. Gertie found a large pair of gumboots and more pairs of socks to keep his feet warm and dry. But after a slight thaw conditions worsened, and both women became increasingly concerned. The weight he had put on over the last few months was falling off him at an alarming rate.

Katherine almost persuaded the Murdochs that Karl should stay in the village until conditions improved: there was little work to be done in such weather other than to feed the stock and the kitchen stove. But one morning in early February she discovered the water in the pipes, and the old pump in the yard were frozen solid. When Karl arrived, bundled in ski hat, scarf and overcoat, his trousers stiff with snow, she was almost in despair.

"Look!" she wailed, even before he took off his hat. She turned on the kitchen tap. The pipes clanked and banged, a trickle of water emerged, then dripped to a halt. "How on earth are we to water the sheep? The tap and pump in the yard are just the same!"

Karl set down a rucksack containing bread, milk and a tin of corned beef from Mrs Tucker's shop, pulled off his gloves, and breathed hard on his frozen fingers.

"So. We will have to melt snow," he said lightly, in truth realising what an undertaking that might be.

"We'll be at it all day, with all the sheep troughs to fill," she said despondently.

"Then we must begin now," he told her calmly, sensing her growing panic.

"No. You must have your porridge first." She knew he ate breakfast at the Murdochs' before he left, but the difficult walk now took forty-five minutes. She did not like to send him out to work straight away. She rummaged in the rucksack.

"Did Mrs Tucker have any oats?"

Katherine had arranged with Mrs Tucker that while she was stranded, Karl should bring supplies and she would settle her account once the weather improved. Under the circumstances it seemed ridiculous for her to even bother saddling Beth to make the journey, when Karl passed that way each day. Mrs Tucker also gave him Katherine's post, since the postwoman had not reached Lane Head Farm in over a week.

Karl replied to her question. "No. But she thinks she will have some later today, if the road to the village is cleared. It was blocked again last night."

He could feel life tingling back into his numb fingers, while drops of water trickled off his eyebrows. He hung his hat and gloves over the drying rack while he ate his porridge.

He was always hungry at the moment, even more so than usual with the cold and the additional calories he burned struggling to and from work. He thought of the other POWs who had to work without the benefit of one of Mrs Murdoch's breakfasts inside them, or the extra rations Katherine gave him. Even Mrs Tucker slipped him a biscuit or two, or a slice of bread and jam, when she filled the rucksack.

While he was eating, Katherine assembled a collection of pots and pans, old tin bath, preserving pans and the like. Then they donned their outdoor clothing and proceeded to fill the containers with clean snow from the garden, and stood them on or around the range to melt. Katherine was horrified to see the tiny amount of melted water a whole bucketful of snow produced.

"Oh, Karl, " she sighed, shaking her head wearily, "however are we going to keep this up?"

"It is only so much trouble because we filled all the buckets at once. In a few hours we will have only to fill a bucket or two at a time. I will do that when necessary. Now I will clear a path to the sheepsheds and the feed store. It will get easier. You will see. Perhaps soon the pump will work."

She tried to believe him, as she helped carry the first buckets to the sheep troughs. At least it was warmer in the sheds, where the animals' body heat kept water from freezing in the troughs. On leaving the dark, pungent sheepsheds, the raw air caught her throat and she coughed. Karl looked at her in concern.

"Are you all right?" Heaven help us if she were to become ill now, he thought.

"Yes. It's just the cold air."

They continued all morning topping up the troughs in all the sheds, then Katherine filled toilet cisterns while Karl packed more buckets with snow. The whole day was taken up with this cyclical process. The pump remained obstinately frozen. Karl found time at the end of the day to bring in a stack of logs for the range, so Katherine would not need to go to the woodshed. He made a neat pile in the outhouse, making a mental note to increase the size of the pile tomorrow in case of a further blizzard.

Katherine glanced anxiously at the kitchen clock and at the steadily darkening sky when he returned to the kitchen. She noticed how tired he looked. "Time you left, Karl."

He looked out at the sky. "More snow, I think."

"I hope you get down before it starts. Would you telephone me to say you're back safely?"

He was touched by her concern. "Yes, I will do that. Shall I take those eggs?"

On reduced rations few hens were laying. Even so, Katherine had more eggs than she could use herself, and supplied Mrs Tucker with her surplus. "I'll put them in a box."

While he waited, Karl looked out at the glistening slopes he would soon be struggling across. "So easy to ski down," he said wistfully, as Katherine put the eggs into his rucksack.

"Michael Murdoch had a pair of skis," she said. "I wonder if they're still around. You could ask."

Karl grinned. "Yes. I will."

It did not matter he would have to carry them all the way uphill in the morning. He would be fresh then. It was at the end of the day he needed them. He picked up the rucksack. "So. If there is nothing more, I will say goodbye."

She watched him disappear into the gloom, a hunched figure leaning against the wind. She did not envy him his walk, yet he did not complain. Without him she would never have got through today. This morning she was on the verge of giving up, of leaving the sheep to die, abandoning the farm in favour of Froxley Grange or Yew Tree Lodge. She now found herself alone, the power supply off, no water for a bath; yet despite all this, with Karl's help, she would survive. His assistance was far beyond what could be expected of any paid hand. He seemed as keen as she not to let her father's efforts come to nothing. He had done the brunt of the heavy outdoor work that day and he now had the long walk to the village. What if he were prevented from coming tomorrow by a blizzard?

She cast an eye over the various containers of half-melted snow by the range, at the basketful of logs to hand. She was well provided for tonight. His quiet, careful concern moved her. The house seemd all the emptier for his absence.

The power came on at four o'clock. Katherine switched on the light and the wireless set which she had brought from the icy sitting room. The only rooms she used were the kitchen and her bedroom. The rest of the house was as cold, silent and unwelcoming as a tomb.

She decided to do some ironing before preparing a dinner of corned beef hash. Joss would have to be fed shortly. His supply of rabbits and pigeons might be at risk if this weather persisted too long. Perhaps Gertie had some scraps she could send up with Karl.

A gust of wind hurled icy flakes against the window and screeched around the chimney pots. Katherine shuddered. Was Karl still out in this? In answer to her query, the telephone jangled behind the closed kitchen door. Katherine slipped on her coat before entering the freezing hall to pick up the receiver, expecting to hear Karl's voice. It was Gertie who spoke.

"Hello, dear. Karl said you wanted him to call you when he got in, but his teeth were chattering so much I sent him straight off to have a hot bath. Really, he looked like the abominable snowman, he was so covered in snow. He mentioned Michael's skis. I'm sure they're in the loft. I'll send Robert to have a look. I don't suppose the ski boots will fit though. Michael's feet were smaller. I do hope this weather doesn't last much longer. I was worried about Karl in this blizzard. And I worry about you, dear, all alone up there."

"Oh, I'm all right," Katherine said lightly. "Just wish I had enough water for a bath."

"Why don't you try to come down with Karl on Sunday afternoon and stay the night? Come and rejoin civilisation!"

The prospect delighted Katherine. "That would be lovely, as long as I don't get stranded. Maybe I'll go to Evensong too."

"We'll expect you on Sunday, assuming it's not snowing. Perhaps you might set off a little earlier than Karl normally does, so you get here before dark."

Katherine had another call that evening, from Sarah, who wanted to make sure Katherine was still coping. She was distraught when she heard about the water.

"You poor thing! What a nightmare. Are the feed stocks lasting out?"

Katherine managed to reassure Sarah she was not in imminent danger, thanks mainly to Karl. "I feel almost as though Daddy is keeping an eye on me through Karl. You know how it was when we were little. Nothing could go

154

wrong when Daddy was around. Well I feel the same way with Karl. He gets on with the job without any fuss, and suddenly the problem is halved, if not solved."

Sarah detected an over-enthusiastic tone in Katherine's voice. Bearing in mind what she knew about Audrey, she began to wonder about her sister being alone all day with a man who could charm even such an embittered case as herself. She felt like probing deeper. "Have you heard from Andrew recently?" she asked casually.

"Yes. Had a letter from him just the other day. I was going to write tonight, but I feel too tired after lugging all that snow about. I was about to make my hot-water bottle and go to bed."

"I'd better let you get on with it then. Take care. I'll be in touch again soon."

Before jumping into bed, Katherine rubbed a clear patch on her frosted window. Snow was still falling, although the wind had died. Karl would have a difficult walk tomorrow, and there were no oats to make porridge. She could hardly give him Beth's.

Karl arrived late but triumphant next morning, a pair of skis over his shoulder. Katherine had been watching out for him and stepped into the chill air to greet him.

"I was beginning to think you were stuck in a snowdrift," she chided him, relieving him of the rucksack. She pointed to the skis. "Had a go yet?"

"Yes. That's why I'm late. Robert found the skis last night, but the boots were too small. We had to make two wooden blocks which I could strap over my ordinary boots, so the bindings would fasten on them. You see?" He showed her two pieces of wood which protruded from his pocket. Each had a square toe section and a groove cut into the heel to fit the ski bindings, and two wide leather straps with buckles to fasten them over the boot. They looked like ice skates, but much wider. Karl demonstrated how they fitted onto the ski bindings.

"I wanted to try them this morning to make sure they were safe. Robert came with me to the top of their road and I skied

155

down it. They do not hold my feet so well as I would like, but they are better than nothing. I must be careful at first until I am used to them."

He looked longingly at the steep slopes of the meadows, but there was work to be done. He stuck the skis and poles upright in a pile of snow by the back door then hurried Katherine inside out of the cold.

She unpacked the rucksack and found another letter from Andrew alongside an already opened one for Karl. She popped Andrew's letter on the mantelpiece to read later. That made two that needed answering now. She poured tea for Karl.

"I see you had a letter from home. How is your family?"

"They are all well. They told me how much Uwe enjoyed Christmas, though it was difficult to find special food. I think the weather is as bad over there, but like you they have enough wood to keep them warm. I must write soon."

"I have a letter to write. We ought to sit and write them while we have lunch, then you could take them to the post office on your way back."

They spent the day as before, refilling containers with snow. It was not until mid-afternoon that Karl could afford the time to clear snow from a gate to open it. He had no intention of interrupting his ski run to vault it. Katherine helped him with the task as the light was beginning to fade. In overcoat and scarf with Joss beside her, she watched him set off down the slope in a series of graceful curves, before skidding to a halt on the crest of the next meadow. He turned and waved up the hill to her, then set off again, leaving only two shadowy tracks in the snow to show his passing. She caught sight of him once more when he reached the gate to the road, where he had to negotiate piles of hard packed snow.

She envied his skill. What would have taken a quarter of an hour to flounder through, took less than a minute to ski. It looked an effortless flight; she wondered whether he could be persuaded to let her try on the way to the Murdochs' on Sunday.

She put this to him the next morning; he looked doubtful.

"First I would have to make some blocks to fit your feet. To ski is not so easy as it looks, even with proper boots to hold the feet secure. If you fall you could break a leg."

She pleaded with him. "I'll only have a go on the very gentle slope at the bottom, right by the road."

She kept up her pleading all day and the next too, apparently with little effect. But on Sunday afternoon as they made to leave, Karl produced from nowhere a pair of wooden "ski clogs", as Katherine called them, and presented them to her.

"I hope they fit," he smiled.

With her overnight things in the rucksack on Karl's back they set off, Katherine struggling through the snow, Karl making a series of long, gentle traverses back and forth across the slope. Even so he reached the first gateway before her, and waited for her to join him, her cheeks flushed pink with exertion. He continued right down to the lowest meadow where he finally stopped at one end and removed the skis. Before him stretched the entire length of the meadow, sloping very gently all the way down, parallel to the road.

Katherine was breathless with haste to get on skis at last. She stepped nervously onto the wooden blocks which Karl had already exchanged with his own. He bent down to fasten them securely for her. She slid her feet experimentally, finding the skis heavier and more cumbersome than she expected. The blocks fitted exactly around her boots, like an overshoe, so that any tilt of her feet was transferred to the skis. Karl showed her how to hold the poles properly, the strap around her wrist and under her thumb, then indicated the slope ahead.

"This slope is not too bad for a learner. You see it is quite flat at the end there, even a little bit uphill by the gate, so you can easily stop. If you fall over, try to fall on here," he slapped his rear in demonstration, "not on your hands."

Katherine felt her confidence draining away, but Karl had more words of advice before he let her loose. "Now remember. Keep your body forward, don't sit back, and bend your knees – not too much."

He corrected her posture then stood to one side. He could see she was anxious to have a go. He would not delay matters further by telling her how to stop. She would probably fall over before she needed to do that. "You will not go fast here. Just turn your skis so they point down the hill and push a little with the sticks."

She did as he said but stayed stuck where she was. The slope certainly was gentle and she felt a little happier again.

"Push more with the sticks," he commanded.

She began to move and found her feet sliding out from underneath her. She wobbled, frantically tried to regain her balance, but sat down suddenly and unceremoniously. She laughed in embarrassment, then tried to stand up but could not keep her feet underneath her

"You must sit above, up the hill from your skis," Karl told her helpfully, not laughing.

She shuffled her bottom over so that both skis were to one side.

"Now you must have the skis across the slope so they do not slide away." Karl helped her by moving the skis for her into the right position. "Now. Sticks behind you, and push up."

She felt a complete idiot. No matter how hard she tried she could not stand up. Suddenly she found the right angle of push and was on her feet again, sliding straight away. Karl jammed his boot against the skis to stop her until she was ready.

"So. Try again. Lean forwards more." He moved his boot away and she pushed tentatively with the sticks, once more feeling that sliding lurch as she began to move. This time she was more prepared and kept her balance longer until she felt speed building up and she fell over again, more in fear than loss of balance.

"That felt a bit fast," she gasped as he helped her sort her legs out. "Although I'm sure it couldn't have been." She could not be bothered to push herself upright again with the sticks, so held out her hand to Karl instead. She came up in a rush.

"Now you know how it feels, you can start to learn how to ski slowly. And how to stop."

Karl carefully explained the elements of the "snowplough" position to her. While staying still she pushed her heels out as he told her. Her knees felt as though they were about to break with the strain, but Karl gently pushed apart and down on her knees and she felt the strain ease.

"Be careful the fronts of the skis don't cross," he warned.

Once more Katherine pushed off, finding the speed miraculously reduced, but now she veered off to the left. She managed to come to a halt, then swivelled at the waist to speak to Karl. "What happened then?"

"You are pushing more with your right knee. Use your left more."

She tried again. By varying the weight on each knee she found she could steer herself better until she grew over-confident, crossed her ski tips and took a tumble. She had left Karl behind up the slope, so had to get herself onto her feet. It took a few attempts and Karl caught up with her by the time she was upright.

"I think I'm getting the hang of this!" she beamed at him. "Can I have another go? I seem to have run out of slope now."

He helped her off with the skis and carried them back up the length of the meadow for her, this time starting a little higher than previously. By the end of three-quarters of an hour she felt tired, soaking wet, cold. And very happy.

"You've had enough?" Karl asked.

"Yes, I think so. It was fantastic! I can't wait to have another go!"

He smiled indulgently at her childlike enthusiasm.

The brisk walk to the village warmed her. It was deserted. The children, long since grown tired of building snowmen, were safe inside their homes. Darkness was beginning to fall. John Thornton saw the pair go by as he glanced out of the vicarage window to check the time on the church clock.

Robert was so impressed by Katherine's account of skiing he came back with them next day. While Katherine went to prepare lunch, Karl took Robert to the paddock for his first lesson. It was not so suitable as the lower meadow, but saved them from traipsing all the way back up the hill for lunch. Robert, wearing his brother's boots, soon got used to the feel of the skis and was negotiating gentle snowplough turns by the time Katherine called them in. He stayed inside while Katherine took her turn after lunch, but curiosity got the better of him. He wrapped himself up well to face the elements, picked up the camera he had secretly brought with him, and pottered off to find the skiers.

They had moved on from the paddock to a meadow with more of a slope. Robert located them by Katherine's shriek of glee as she successfully reached the hedge at the bottom after a reasonably controlled descent. He stayed where he was by the sheepsheds, sheltered from the wind, and watched as Katherine took off the skis, and Karl carried them back to the top of the meadow. Her next descent was not so graceful; she ended up in a heap only yards from her starting point. Katherine's carefree laughter rang over the snow as Robert took a photograph.

It was good to see her enjoying herself. Come to that, it was good to see Karl happy. Robert grinned. He had never heard Karl laugh out loud before. He realised he was spying on a couple in the early stages of discovering each other. Katherine took off her tam-o'-shanter and shook her curls in the wind as she paused for a breather.

An intriguing thought struck him. Katherine was flirting with Karl, subconsciously maybe. Even from this distance the signs were clear: the smiles, the tilt of the head, the desire for physical contact. She could stand up by herself after a fall, yet persisted in getting Karl to help her whenever she could. Karl could not possibly fail to read these signs too.

Robert was keenly aware, as was Sarah, of how much time these two spent in each other's company. Surely it was inevitable nature would take its course? They seemed so right for each other. They would make a fine team. Lane Head Farm would have a secure future. Pity such an outcome was unlikely, given Karl's circumstances. In Karl's place he would have thrown caution to the wind for such a prize as Katherine.

He watched them a while longer until he felt the cold air seeping into him and returned indoors to consider the dilemma. Although Karl freely told him about Audrey, he never breathed a word about his feelings towards Katherine. No doubt he liked her. He would never have agreed to devote so much effort into seeing her through the Big Freeze unless he really wanted to. But as for Katherine? She had a fiancé who would be home in a matter of a month or two to claim her. Her flirting with Karl was probably no more than an expression of her need for a man's attention.

He was still sitting pondering when they came in to warm up.

"You're looking very serious, Robert," Katherine commented, shaking impacted snow from her coat. "Anything the matter?"

He shrugged. "I was just considering the future."

Katherine assumed he meant his own. "How are the applications for medical school going?"

"Slowly. I'm still waiting to hear from a couple."

Karl went outside again with two empty buckets to fill with yet more snow.

"Here, let me give you a hand," Robert offered, picking up the tin bath. He tipped the meagre amount of water into another container, then followed Karl outside.

As they shovelled snow together Robert could not help commenting: "She likes you, you know."

Karl answered noncomitally. "Yes, I can see that. It is only because Captain Kellett is away she laughs so with me. It will be different when he is home. Then her eyes will be for him."

These last words of Karl's did not seem to ring true during the remainder of the afternoon. To Robert's probing eye, Katherine's attitude towards Karl had subtly changed since the death of her father. She looked to Karl for companionship and found in him a good friend. Was that all it amounted to?

Robert wondered whether he was letting his imagination run away with him.

By the time Robert and Karl left the farm it was already dark, although there was sufficient moonlight on the snow for Karl to ski to the road, where he waited for Robert to catch up. Robert's legs were aching from the unaccustomed exercise by the time he fell into step beside Karl.

"Can't imagine how you manage this journey every day," Robert groaned, stumbling over a frozen block of snow.

"I must for Katherine's sake. She needs me."

It was an enigmatic reply, revealing little except a sense of duty. Robert wanted to know more about Karl's feelings for Katherine. "Do you need her?"

Karl stopped dead in his tracks and glared at Robert. "What are you asking me?" Robert's words were too reminiscent of Audrey for Karl's liking.

Robert saw he had ruffled Karl's feathers and tried to rectify the situation. "I was only wondering how you felt about her. She seemed to be flirting with you today."

Karl grunted and skied on. It was a moment or two before he replied with an almost set piece quotation from the rule book. "I am not allowed to feel anything for an English girl."

"What about Audrey?" Robert persisted, refusing to let Karl off the hook.

"I felt nothing for Audrey. I needed her. Katherine is different."

"In other words, you do feel something for Katherine?"

Karl scowled. "Why do you ask me these questions?" he said defensively. "She is different because already she has a man. Is that answer good enough?"

Robert thought he seemed unnecessarily angry. "If I wasn't planning on studying medicine and leaving the village, I would have made a play for Katherine. Watching her with Andrew I'm not convinced she loves him. She never seems relaxed with him; is always on her best behaviour. That's no way to go into marriage. Yet with you, she's totally at ease. It's obvious she cares for you."

A van approached. They both stood against the hedge to avoid the slush thrown up by its wheels. Its tail lights winked around the bend ahead, towards the lights of Penchurch.

Karl's eyes were cast to the ground as they continued, concentrating on the treacherous surface. It was clear he was brooding on what had just been said. The urge to intervene in Katherine and Karl's lives proved irresistible. Robert knew he was doing the right thing. He went on before he got cold feet.

"I don't think she realises she doesn't love him. She's never considered anyone else. She doesn't deserve to be landed with a stuffed shirt like Andrew. She needs someone like you, Karl."

Robert was watching Karl's face intently, fearful of going too far and incurring his wrath. Even though Karl had told him all his recent history, he never felt the German had let all his barricades down.

Karl avoided Robert's gaze, his face giving nothing away. "This conversation has no point. In my position I can do nothing more than work for her."

"Come off it, Karl! They'll do away with these ridiculous "no fraternisation" laws eventually. They're bound to after all the contacts that were made over Christmas."

"Then I must wait until they change the law."

Robert smiled triumphantly. "So you do like her!"

"Of course I like her. Everybody likes her. But that is enough of this talk. We are in the village."

"All right. Just don't wait too long, or it'll be too late."

Karl was worried by Robert's comments. Had anyone else noticed his feelings for Katherine? Certainly since coming to work at Lane Head he was gradually shedding the protective casing he had wrapped himself in during the latter stages of the war; was slowly learning to let go, and feel again those emotions buried deep inside himself. He had cried in Katherine's presence when her father died, for the first time allowing himself that small freedom. Audrey was a continuation of that freedom, a purging of the past, a new foundation for the future. She had helped him refocus his sense of purpose away from self-preservation, to start taking

163

risks again. She, of course, knew what she was doing. Katherine, however, was an innocent in this world. Karl was loath to come between her and the law.

"Thinking over what I said?" Robert asked him.

They were sitting in the living room at Yew Tree Lodge after dinner. Gertie was at a rehearsal of the Penchurch Players, Donald was out on call.

"Yes," Karl admitted. "You seem very sure Katherine does not love Kellett; that she would have me if I showed interest. How can you be so sure?"

Robert stretched his stiff legs out towards the glowing fire. "I've seen the way she looks at him sometimes; impatient, frustrated by his boorishness. Even when he's being amorous she seems to hold back. In contrast I've seen the way she looks at you. I watched her when you sang that song about your homeland at New Year. She looked really proud of you."

"You spend a lot of time watching people."

Now it was Robert's turn to feel frustrated. Why did Karl always deflect observations away from himself? Was he still trying to hide in the background? His reluctance to show his feelings for Katherine seemed a manifestation of the same desire not to draw attention to himself.

"And you spend a lot of time hiding," he countered. "Bugger what people might think! The war is over. Start living again, Karl!"

If anyone other than Robert had said that, Karl would have dismissed the suggestion. But Robert himself had done just that; crawled out of his hole and started living again. Karl knew there were some folks in the village who were not so tolerant as the Carters and Murdochs. Katherine lived amongst these people. Her relationship with Kellett was congratulated and welcomed. How would she cope with the derision and rejection if the villagers ever became aware she had turned down Kellett, and all that he offered, in favour of a German? He could not bear to subject her to that scorn, assuming she would even do such a thing,

All night long Karl's thoughts swayed back and forth. The more he thought about Katherine, the more he realised he loved her. Yet loving her was not enough. She must love him too. Did she? How could he find that out without jeopardising his new life at Lane Head? He remembered Robert's final words to him that evening: "Nothing ventured, nothing gained." He would have to choose his moment very carefully, to be sure of victory over Kellett. He had lost Ilse to another man in his absence. He had no qualms about letting Kellett suffer the same fate.

CHAPTER NINE

Next day the sky was heavy with snow. Sickly yellow clouds built up during the morning. The first soft flakes began to fall soon after lunch, gently at first, as though limbering up, then with an increasing determination to obscure the last traces of form from the landscape. At three o'clock Katherine looked out of the kitchen window, unable to see six feet beyond the pane. She turned to Karl, who was sitting at the kitchen table rebinding the string around the handle of the kettle.

"There's no chance of you skiing down in this. Or even walking down. Can't see a thing." The wind was picking up again too and hurled the snowflakes against the window with a rattle like thrown gravel. "It would be suicidal to go out in that."

Karl came over and stood by her, looking into the swirling white emptiness. "Suicidal?" he asked.

"Killing yourself," she explained.

"I was out in worse in Russia." But she was right. He knew better than to underestimate the results of being disorientated in a blizzard.

In Yew Tree Lodge the same conversation was taking place.

"He can't come back down tonight, surely, Mum?" Robert said from his position by the window.

By way of answer, Gertie turned a troubled face to her husband, who was likewise concerned about the weather, but for reasons of his own. A call out now would be impossible.

"Robert's right, dear," Donald said. "We can't expect Karl to set out in this. He'd never find his way. I don't want to have to report to his commandant we found him dead of exposure. I suggest we telephone Katherine and make sure he stays there. This weather looks set for the night."

Gertie wrung her hands in despair. She knew this would happen sooner or later. The inevitability of it was no comfort to her sense of propriety, but she could see no way out of her dilemma. "Very well, dear. I'll give her a ring. I just hope the village doesn't hear about this."

"You can bet Mrs Tucker will be the first to know, when Karl doesn't pop in to her shop as usual this afternoon," Robert said wickedly, ignoring his father's frown.

Gertie too was frowning as she went to the telephone. As usual the power was off at this time of day, but at least the telephone was still working. The lines were bearing up despite the weight of snow and she got through to Katherine without any trouble.

Katherine sounded very relieved at her suggestion, and Gertie returned to the living room feeling a little happier. It would be good for Katherine to have company for once, especially in conditions like this.

Katherine stirred a handful of oats into the corned beef to make it go further. This evening would make a very welcome change from her past weeks of loneliness. Having Karl at the dinner table reminded her of happier times when her father was alive.

They chatted amiably throughout the meal, Katherine frequently glancing at the chair where her father used to sit, as though expecting to see him there. She caught Karl doing the same and smiled.

"Here am I, with both of my parents dead now and yet your family has survived the war more or less intact," she said without a trace of bitterness. "Apart from your sister's husband you're all still alive and well. Isn't that remarkable?"

Karl pushed aside his empty plate and eyed hers, still with half the food to be eaten. Apart from the fact that his mother's relatives in Berlin and East Prussia had been wiped out by war, tuberculosis or hunger-induced diseases, and the majority of his friends in Medebach had been lost or were prisoners in Russia, what she said was basically true.

"Yes. Remarkable."

He watched as she put a forkful of food in her mouth, his eyes caught by the flash and sparkle of the diamonds and emerald on the ring she wore. Kellett's ring.

"But you will have a new family soon," he said, his eyes still on the ring.

She looked at the ring, then put her hands on her lap as though to hide the confirmation of her betrothal. "I suppose I shall. To tell the truth, I can't stand most of them. Andrew's father is just about bearable, and two of his cousins are quite fun, but his mother and all those dreadful other cousins, uncles and aunts are unbearable. It's pretty grim there when there's a family gathering, I can tell you."

Karl smiled. "Does Andrew know you don't like his family?"

She looked horrified. "Of course not. I wouldn't dream of being rude about them. Besides, *he* gets on well with them."

"Because he is like them, perhaps?"

The inference of this question took a moment to dawn, then she reacted.

"Are you saying I shouldn't like Andrew either?"

He was on delicate ground. He was attacking her fiancé and she could very well take an appropriately strong defensive position. Somehow he must make her realise how little she did feel for Kellett, assuming Robert was correct in his observations.

"I think he is a habit for you – maybe."

He waited anxiously for her wrath to fall upon him, but she was silent, head hung low, studying her ring. She stayed like that for a long time before slowly, silently lifting her hands onto the table. She looked at them with a deep frown, then began to turn the ring slowly around, watching the jewels appear and disappear behind her finger. Six times the diamonds and emerald came into view and on the seventh she carefully took off the ring.

"I think you're right," she said at last. "I've probably known it for a long time and never had the courage to do anything about it. I don't think I should fool him or myself any longer."

She put the ring between them on the table. There was silence save for the crackling of a log in the range, as she summoned the courage to express what she really wanted to say. "I've discovered recently what love really is."

She looked at him now, intently, trying to gauge from his expression the extent to which she should reveal her thoughts. What she saw gave her courage.

"At first I thought I was confusing love with mere physical attraction, but my feelings are far more than that." She searched his face. "Saying goodbye to Andrew at New Year for the next three months seemed bad enough at the time, but saying goodbye to you every evening, just for the night, is even worse."

He had not expected this, that she would make the running. He reached across the table for her hands, held them in his, caressing them with his thumbs as he sought words to say to her. He leaned forwards and kissed her hands before murmuring in his mother tongue: "*Schatz, ich liebe dich.*"

It was a deliberate reminder of his nationality. She must be in no doubt of what she was entering into by declaring her love.

She smiled at his words, glad to have understood them and the implication. "I love you too, Karl. I know this is going to be difficult for us. Don't imagine I haven't thought about it. But the relief! To have told you at last and to know you feel the same way is indescribable!"

They both smiled, all barriers down now, joy written in their faces. Their mutual declaration took both by surprise and they seemed for a moment unsure what to do next. Karl remembered Katherine had not finished her meal. He took his hands from hers and tapped her plate. "You must finish this, Schatz, before it is cold."

She laughed at his soldier's concern for her stomach and picked up her knife and fork. "What was that you called me just then? Schatz?"

He nodded, reached for the dictionary he always carried in his pocket and passed it to her. "Look for yourself what it means," he told her.

169

She opened the well-thumbed book and leafed through until she found the word. There was a selection of meanings but the ones she wanted were evident. "Treasure, darling, love," she read out with a smile of delight. She repeated the word to hear how it sounded. "Schatz. I rather like it. It's heaps nicer than "darling", that's for sure. I always think that sounds like a second-rate Hollywood film, for some reason."

She put the dictionary down on the table, nearly knocking her engagement ring to the floor. She picked it up, holding it in the palm of her hand and looked troubled once more.

"It's going to be awfully difficult telling Andrew, especially as I daren't tell him why. I think he's going to take it very badly."

"Have courage, Schatz," Karl said gently. "It must be done."

"Yes." She stood up and put the ring carefully on the mantelpiece above the range. She heard the scrape of his chair on the floor as he too stood up. The hairs on the back of her neck tingled as they sensed his approach and she turned slowly to face him.

His arms encircled her; she felt again the comfort and security they offered, just as on the day her father died, drawing her towards him until she felt the warmth of his body against hers. She tilted her head up to receive the kiss she knew was coming, a kiss she had awaited for so long – a kiss of passion. This was what a kiss should be. Nothing in her experience of Andrew prepared her for this. She felt his hand caress the back of her neck. A shiver ran down her spine and deep within. When their lips parted he remained close to her, his nose touching hers in intimate proximity, the air from his nostrils mingling with her own breath. His fingers ran lightly through her hair, smoothing it back off her temple, then cupped her jaw, lifting it for another long kiss.

"If I were a cat you would hear me purring now," she told him once her mouth was free. "You're making me feel things I never felt before. I've never talked like this before either."

Karl backed away slightly. He suddenly felt events were moving too rapidly. Both needed time to get used to their new relationship.

"I like to hear you talk. Say some more while I help you with the dishes."

He had brought her back to earth gently and she appreciated it. He certainly knew far more than Andrew about women. How many women had Karl known? The thought disturbed her, but she brushed it aside. The past was gone. The future was what was important now.

They tidied the kitchen before Karl dashed out to fill empty buckets with more snow to melt overnight, and to give Joss his dinner, safe and snug in his straw-lined outhouse. Joss had never been inside the house and did not intend to avail himself of it now, just because of a blizzard. The sheep were secure in the sheds, their breath swirling mistily in the lamplight. Beth had sufficient hay for the night, while Katherine had seen to the poultry before dinner. Satisfied all was well, Karl searched for the lights of the house through the blanket of falling snow and stumbled through a thick drift by the back door. When he entered the kitchen Katherine helped beat snow off his coat then she stood on tiptoe and wiped the snowflakes from his eyelashes.

"I feel as though I've known you all my life," she said, flinching as the icy tip of his nose brushed her cheek. "Because you've lived here with us these months, I feel so at home with you. Almost like we've been married for years."

She stopped herself from saying any more, fearful suddenly she was being too forward. Her emotions were overtaking her ability to cope with them. They had been bottled up behind the dam of her engagement to Andrew; now they overflowed in a rushing torrent she felt powerless to contain.

She turned her mind to more practical considerations.

"We'd better get some bedding aired for you. It'll be best if you sleep in here. You can't possibly use your old room. We can bring cushions from the sitting room and warm them up for you to lie on. You should be warm enough, I hope."

How different from Audrey, Karl thought. It had not occurred to her he should sleep anywhere other than by himself. She was setting ground rules of behaviour without realising. There was no need. He would not dream of letting Katherine betray her high moral standards. From what she had intimated, Andrew Kellett had been kept at bay, despite being her fiancé.

While Katherine draped blankets to air over the drying rack, he fetched the sofa cushions from the frozen sitting room and laid them against the wall near the range, then turned two of the kitchen chairs to face the range and sat on one of them. He indicated the other chair for Katherine.

She settled herself with her head on his shoulder. He put his arm around her.

"Tell me about yourself, Schatz."

She snuggled into him. "There's not much to tell, really," she said, into his chest. "You know most things already. I've even seen you looking at the photos of Sarah and me when we were little. Yet I know almost nothing about you. For a start," she said, remembering his Christmas presents, "your initials are KDD, but I've no idea what the second D stands for."

"Dieter, like my father. I was born on the 29th November 1920 in a house a short distance outside the town of Medebach. I became a soldier in 1939 and a prisoner of war in 1945. What more do you want to know?"

There was a short pause.

"When did you first realise you loved me?" she asked shyly.

She could not see his whole face, only the underside of his jaw, or else she would have seen his relief that she had not asked him for details of the war years. He had deliberately led her questions to the present day; his tactics seemed to have worked.

"I think ... I began to love you almost as soon as I first came with the other men to pick apples. You rode down on Beth to bring us food. You looked so beautiful. Then you spoke to us as people, not just Germans, or as men like the other girls. When I spoke to you, I felt I was speaking as Karl Driesler and not just another POW. The other men there, they all liked you. And we respected you. I saw the love you had for your father, and his love for you. I saw how hard you worked. How fair you were with us. So when I came here on my own, already I was a little in love, but I could not allow myself to know that."

"You certainly never let it show," she touched the scar on his forehead lightly. He laid his cheek on the top of her head, her soap-scented hair tickling his nose.

"You know why I could not show my love." He stroked her hair, rubbed his cheek against it. "So. When did you first love me?"

Katherine pursed her lips, thinking hard. "I can't really say. It was only this evening I realised I loved you, or rather acknowledged that I loved you, but I must have started to love you long before. I kept finding myself comparing Andrew with you and he never seemed to come out favourably. I think my feelings for Andrew began to fade with your arrival, but like you, I never considered it possible I could have a relationship with you. It left a sort of emptiness in me, so I didn't quite know where I was going, or what the future held."

"Do you know now?" he asked almost casually.

He felt her go tense, as she realised her thoughts might have gone far beyond anything Karl had in mind. She began to stall.

"I know that one day you will be going home."

Karl was silent. Katherine had put her finger on a point not yet fully considered; his return home. Until this moment his only future had been at home with his family. Now he had Katherine to consider. How would she fit in with that plan? Could he ask her to leave her comfortable home to live in a country where her own people were conquerors? He was uncertain now how to procede. One of them would have to pay a high price for a union between them. Whether she came to Germany or he stayed in England, there would be many occasions when the wisdom of such a union would be questioned. And there was the unpleasant prospect of having to tell her all about his past eventually. But she must know him a great deal better before he could risk that.

His silence made Katherine stir uneasily, lifting her head from his shoulder. She knew she must not rush him, yet she was convinced he felt as she did; that their future lay together despite his present predicament. So what was it that was bothering him? She moved away from the minefield she was treading, not wanting to risk spoiling the evening.

"You just told me your middle name. Do you know what mine is?" she asked him.

He turned his head to look directly at her. "No. What is it?"

"May. It's the month I was born in."

His face was perfectly solemn as he spoke the next words. "Katherine May Carter, I love you."

Katherine looked long into his eyes. The way he spoke was like a promise, a vow made in church, but open ended. She knew she must be content with that. She made the appropriate response. "Karl Dieter Driesler, I love you." Then she giggled with suppressed relief and unaccustomed happiness.

They sat in each other's arms the remainder of the evening, on safe and neutral ground, talking of inconsequential matters, revelling in their newfound discovery of each other. Karl yawned suddenly, making Katherine yawn too. She helped him make up his bed of cushions and blankets on the floor, moving some of the containers away from the range. Karl stuffed newspaper under the draughty back door, then Katherine filled her hot-water bottle.

"Goodnight, Schatz. Sleep well," he said, kissing her. The hot-water bottle gurgled between them.

"Goodnight, Liebling," she replied, pleased to show off one of the few German words she knew.

Before getting into bed, Katherine looked at the photograph of her father on her dressing table. "Thank you for finding him for me, Daddy," she said to the cherished features.

The freezing cold of her room invigorated her and sleep evaded her. Her body was tense with excitement. An inner glow warmed her as Andrew's company never had. Her relationship with Andrew had been superficially romantic, but restrained. She never encouraged more than his kisses; he had never attempted to make greater demands. But tonight a fire had been lit deep within her. She felt it smouldering even now, ready to burst into flame. Even though Karl had only kissed her that evening, she had become aware, for the first time in her life, that she could want more from a man.

Now she knew something of what Audrey sought in men; felt for herself what desire meant. This combination of spiritual love and physical desire was a potent force, untapped by Andrew. She felt she was drowning in her own emotions, sucked under by the strength of her feelings now they were released by the man who lay asleep in the kitchen below. She wondered whether he felt the same, but quickly dismissed the thought. He had loved before. It was no novelty for him. She could tell Ilse had meant much to him by the way he spoke of her.

She wondered what Ilse was like, what colour her hair was, whether she was pretty. She found herself envious of this other woman who had possibly already ... She blocked the thought. Karl's past was nothing to do with her. Ilse was safely married to someone else; Katherine had taken her place.

She tried to picture his face; his sad, grey eyes. Why were they always so sad? Even when he laughed, which he had only just started to do, a sadness was still there. It gave him a vulnerability she found irresistible. She wanted to comfort him, be close to him, feel his body pressed to hers ....

She sighed and rolled over into a cold patch. She pulled her legs up under her and placed the hot-water bottle on her stomach, but then her feet were two ice-bound extremities. She tried putting them on the bottle, but then her body was cold. She began to shiver and got out of bed to put her cardigan on over her nightdress. Between the sheets again her feet were still cold. The curtains billowed in the draught from the window. She got up to find some woollen socks for her feet. It really was a bitterly cold night.

Her feet slightly warmer, she might at last fall asleep. It was a vain hope. Gooseflesh ran down her arms and legs; she remembered the same effect had been achieved by Karl's hand on her neck. She lay there, remembering every touch of his hands and lips and the electrical effect they had on her. She would gladly give up Lane Head Farm to follow him, should he want her. He had been evasive on that issue. Why? Because he thought she would not want to leave England? She would have to persuade him otherwise. Perhaps show an interest in learning German.

The hot-water bottle had cooled and still she was not asleep. If she were alone in the house, she would go downstairs to refill the bottle, but she would wake Karl if she did that. Having thought of the idea, it would not leave her. She shivered again and knew she would not sleep unless she were warmer. Reluctantly she stepped out of bed, wrapped her dressing gown tightly round her, found her slippers and set off downstairs clutching the cool bottle.

She hesitated outside the closed kitchen door, then cautiously turned the handle and opened it. The kitchen was dark, no moon filtered through the curtains. She listened, heard Karl's regular, deep breathing. She thought she might be able to reheat the bottle without waking him, using the light from the hall. Her eyes grew more accustomed to the dark; she could now make out his motionless figure on the floor by the range.

She crept across the flagged stone floor to the kettle on the hearth. She stooped to pick it up and was suddenly aware his breathing had stopped. He was watching her, the whites of his eyes showing dimly near her slippered feet.

He raised himself onto one elbow. "I was wondering why you were here," he said softly.

"I ... I was cold," she stammered, embarrassed by the strange tone of his voice. "I wanted to refill my bottle. I'm sorry I woke you." She felt him watching her in the dim light as she set the kettle on the range.

"You will be even colder while you wait for the water to boil."

He reached forward and put another log on the glowing embers in the range, the blankets slipping from his bare shoulders. Satisfied the log had caught, Karl held the blankets wide, gesturing that she should share them with him. She hesitated, then stepped back towards the door.

Disappointment surged through Karl until he saw she was only shutting out the draught. The closed door left the kitchen in darkness, but Katherine refrained from turning on the light. She did not want Karl to see her bundled up in her faded old dressing gown and bedsocks, like somebody's granny. She felt her way towards him, her fingers brushing his hair. Dropping her hand to his shoulder, she let it linger on his warm skin. His hand came up to meet hers, intertwining with her fingers, then pulling her gently down to sit beside him. He put his arm and the blankets around her, drawing her in towards his body. Enveloped by him, she slipped her arm round his waist as she tried to relax against him. But the touch and scent of his skin aroused such primaeval urges in her, she nervously drew back her arm. What was she doing here? She should never have come down!

Karl felt the retreat of her hand. He could not let her go now! He drew her even closer, his hand advancing from her arm to her breast. His fingers eased through the layers of clothing. "You were cold, weren't you," he whispered. "Perhaps you should sleep here in the warm with me."

Katherine could not reply, or even move. Her upbringing told her to push him away, her instinct urged his fingers on. They reached her nightdress. Slowly Karl unfastened the tiny pearl buttons at the neck and on down. Katherine held her breath as his fingers paused. She ached for his touch.

The kettle began to whistle in a bubbling crescendo. Karl leaned across and took it off the range. The interruption gave them both time to reflect. He had not meant this to happen, but Katherine clearly wanted it too. He could feel her trembling with anticipation as his fingers found her mouth in the darkness and he put his lips on hers. Her mouth opened, accepting him. He moved his fingers down, through the opening of her nightdress. Through their kiss he felt her gasp as his hand moved over her breast. Such an innocent! He was grateful he could take his time, caressing and soothing her body, so she could enjoy what he wanted to give.

"Not so cold now?" His lips were nuzzling her ear; she squirmed. Her dressing gown fell from her shoulders, then her cardigan. She hugged him close as gooseflesh once more rose at his touch. She ran her fingers now down his back, exploring his body as he explored hers. They truly belonged to each other. There was none of the awkwardness or embarrassment she had anticipated with Andrew. She was Karl's and only Karl's.

She felt her nightdress raised, then removed. Her last defence was gone. He pressed her down to lie full length on the cushions, his muscular body poised over her. This was the moment. She did not care if it hurt. She wanted him so much.

She felt him inside her. She had thought it would be an intrusion, but he belonged there. His breath was hot on her neck, the hair on the nape of his neck damp. She held him, urged him on, marvelling at the sense of union and the joy she felt at his pleasure, until he lay still once more, the firelight flickering over his skin.

Tenderly she kissed his neck, stroking his fine hair. "I have just done something I vowed I would not do until I was married, and I have broken the law for the first time in my life at the same time," she told him. "And it was wonderful!"

She saw his teeth glisten as he grinned. "Next time I hope it will be more wonderful for you."

"How could it be?" she asked him.

He shifted off her to lie on the narrow space beside her. "You don't know?" He could not believe she was so innocent. Ilse had needed no explanations. Katherine was shaking her head.

"Let me show you."

In a little while she learned something of what he had meant; what it was he experienced that left him breathless and spent. Afterwards she looked at him with fresh eyes, overwhelmed by the power he had over her body.

"Are you warm enough now, Liebchen?"

"Mmm," she replied sleepily.

Karl stirred from his sleep and shivered. He was lying wrapped in a blanket on a stone floor. For one awful moment he thought he was back in the land of his nightmares, but when he opened his eyes and saw Katherine's tousled hair and peaceful face in front of him, he smiled at the beauty of the woman who had become his. There was no going back now. He could not doubt what lay ahead for them both, nor how treacherous that way might be. He was well aware of what Katherine had given to him last night – a commitment to him that he must reciprocate.

He brushed a lock of her hair from her eyes and kissed her lightly on the lips. She stirred in her sleep but did not waken, so he kissed her again, harder this time. He felt her mouth open followed by her eyes. He saw with relief they held no regret or remorse.

"Morning, Schatz! I'm cold. Let me in."

He nudged her gently to the far side of the cushions. As he lifted the blankets higher for himself to slide under, Katherine remembered that she was as naked as he. It had not seemed to matter in the darkness last night, but now she felt shy of his gaze.

"I'm sorry you ended up on the floor," she said, shivering as his cold body nestled close to hers.

"No matter. There was not room for us both on the cushions." Her warmth seeped into him, arousing him. He ran his fingers down her spine, over her thigh and inwards.

"You need a shave," she murmured as his face rasped over her breasts.

This time he could look into her beautiful green eyes, see her unspoken love, her wonder, her shyness. Daylight would bring a new perspective. He rose to his knees, the blankets falling aside. She could see him clearly now and he was not ashamed of his body. Taking courage from his boldness, Katherine knelt too. With hands on each other's hips, they admired what they saw.

Karl raised his hands to her breasts. "You're so beautiful. It is an honour to love you."

His mouth found hers. As they kissed he leaned against her, gently urging her to lie down. Now she knew what to expect, Katherine could allow herself total surrender. When she felt he was ready, she let him take her with him, until they both lay gasping on the rumpled sheets.

He lay there with her a few moments longer, kissed her, then sat up to put more wood on the range. She could see now what her fingers had felt before: long blister-like scars across the whole of his back, down to his thighs. She wondered how he had acquired them. When he turned to face her again she noticed the puckered round scar on his lower abdomen – a bullet hole, she guessed.

"Golly, you have been in the wars, haven't you, Liebling?" she said, then bit her lip. "I'm sorry. That was a stupid thing to say."

He knelt beside her. "You can never forget that you will marry a soldier. If you want to."

"If that's a proposal," she said, flinging her arms round his neck, "then I accept."

They both hoped for another blizzard so he would have to stay again, but the sky, although overcast, was not threatening. When it was time for Karl to go, Katherine helped him on with the rucksack containing a few eggs for Gertie and Mrs Tucker, then passed him the ski sticks. She felt ridiculous that she should have tears in her eyes when he would be back the next day. With his gloved hand he wiped away her tears.

"What we did we must not do again," he warned her. "There is too much risk for you and for me. It is best that I don't stay another night."

His words were no comfort. She felt reckless in her love for him, but of course he was right. If she found herself pregnant then it would be a disaster worthy of the national press.

Reluctantly she nodded her agreement. How long would she have to wait before she could enjoy the comfort of his body again?

"Take care, Karl. I'll miss you tonight," she told him.

"And I'll miss you. Until tomorrow, Liebchen."

He blew her a kiss then set off across the yard. All trace of his previous tracks had been obliterated by the fresh snow which hung on the hedges and gates like grotesque fungus, devouring the countryside beneath it.

He went carefully, aware of the precious eggs on his back, and as he arrived at the gate by the road, he found himself whistling Katherine's favourite Bing Crosby song, *Accentuate the Positive*. She had explained what the words meant; he agreed wholeheartedly, especially with eliminating the negative. The way he felt today had almost achieved that aim. He fairly bounced along the road to the village. When he called at Mrs Tucker's to drop off the eggs, she noticed his happy mood at once.

"Well, you're a touch of Spring in here, I must say," she said. The glint in her eye warned Karl to be careful. "I wondered where you'd got to, you know, when you didn't show up yesterday as usual."

"Travel problems," was all he said, making a speedy exit before she could probe further.

The Murdochs were glad to have him back safely in the fold again. Gertie kept justifying his staying up at the farm with comments about the blizzard. "Really, I was quite glad to know you were up there with Katherine on such a night."

Robert gave a slow grin and caught Karl's eye. Could he suspect already?

After dinner Donald and Gertie braved the elements to attend a Parish Council meeting. Robert tackled Karl on the subject of the previous night.

"Well?"

"Well what?" Karl said apprehensively.

"You look like the cat that got the cream. I just wondered why," Robert speculated.

Karl cleared his throat. Since it was Robert who persuaded him to try his luck, he might as well tell him.

"You were right. Katherine doesn't love Kellett. She's not going to marry him." He paused then dropped his bombshell. "Instead she will marry me!"

Robert's mouth gaped open in astonishment. "My God, Karl! You don't waste any time, do you?"

Karl laughed. "Naturally no one else must know. Not even your parents. Until the law allows it," he warned Robert.

"No, of course not. I won't breathe a word to anyone. But you'll have to hide your feelings a bit better than you are at the moment, or everyone will suspect something's going on between you and Katherine."

Karl acknowledged Robert's warning. "Yes, I know. Mrs Tucker has already noticed."

Reaching forward in his chair Robert shook Karl's hand, pleased his attempts at matchmaking had met with such instant success. "Well, congratulations anyway, Karl. You've got yourself the best girl in the neighbourhood."

"I know."

"We'll miss her when you both go back to Germany."

Robert remembered his first thoughts on this subject were that Lane Head Farm would have a bright future with Karl and Katherine running it, but of course Karl had a home and a business of his own to inherit. It was too easy to forget about Karl's other life sometimes.

"When are you going to start teaching her German?"

"Why should I teach her?"

Robert was puzzled. "But surely it's best if she can speak at least a few words to your family when she meets them?"

"That would be true if we live in Germany. I think though that it might be better to stay here. If that is permitted."

The idea was formulating in Karl's mind as he spoke, and he used Robert as a sounding board.

"Much as I love my family and my homeland, I have not lived there – been a part of the town, that is, rather than home on leave – for over seven years. So much has changed. My brother, and my sister's friend, Stefan, help my father with the business now. My life would not be the same as it was before, especially without Ilse. I have little to lose if I stay here, where I already have friends and where I know Katherine is happy. There is much that needs to be done at the farm."

"But I thought you were desperate to get home!" Robert exclaimed.

Karl looked pensive. "I was; until I found a good reason to stay here. It still might not be possible. That depends on your government. They may tell me I can't stay here and that I must go home without Katherine as my wife."

Robert sympathised with his friend's predicament. "You don't make life easy for yourself, do you Karl?"

Karl was able to smile at the thought. "For the moment we can only wait."

And hope, he thought, that the gods did not decide to bless Katherine with the fruit of their loving. It was going to be very difficult to abstain indefinitely. They had tasted paradise. Would they both be tempted to take the risk again?

He and Ilse never bothered with precautions. Under the Nazis it was a girl's duty to provide a soldier with a baby. Anyway, on that last leave, they had been planning on getting married, before ...

Eliminate the negative! Forget! He marshalled his thoughts back onto their former track. With Katherine such a risk was impossible to contemplate. Katherine's reputation would be in ruins; he would be punished, imprisoned even.

Robert noticed his abstraction. "Is anything the matter?"

Karl shook his head quickly. "Not at the moment." He had not intended to give any clues; Robert intuitively understood.

"Let's hope it stays that way. For both your sakes."

Once more Katherine ate her dinner alone, composing in her head the letter she would have to write to Andrew. She was sure he had not noticed any change in her attitude over Christmas, so her letter would come like a bolt out of the blue. She cleared the table, got out pen and paper, then sat staring at a blank sheet. What on earth was she going to tell him? Only that she was sorry she had not realised earlier that she did not love him, and could not marry him? Would he suspect there was somebody else? Perhaps he would think Robert had stolen her from him. They had been rivals once, long before Robert went out to Burma.

Ill-satisfied with what she had written, but unable to think of anything better, she sealed the envelope and addressed it to

Andrew's unit in Germany. It was ironic that Karl would post it for her tomorrow.

She went to the bookcase in the living room, found the home medicine book she wanted and brought it back into the warm kitchen. She checked her dates with her diary. "I should be all right," she thought. "Please God."

Her whole world had been turned upside down overnight. Nothing was the same. Froxley Grange and its inhabitants no longer loomed on the horizon, which had now broadened beyond anything she ever imagined. She took the book back to the bookcase and exchanged it for an atlas. Karl had shown her once where his home lay. As she sought the area again her eye was caught by a familiar name: Hereford. She looked again in disbelief. She had been wrong. The name was Herford, a town to the north of the hilly region where Karl lived. Land of a Thousand Hills, he called it. Karl's home town was called Medebach, and not so very far from where she sat was a hamlet called Merbach. Perhaps Germany would not seem so foreign. She had never been abroad and had little idea what to expect. She had only once visited London, and that had seemed a foreign country. A village in Germany could not be so different from a village in England, surely? Katherine was determined to make the best of whatever was to come.

It was eight weeks since her father had died. Eight weeks which could have been the most miserable of her life. Instead his dying brought her a new life. Yesterday would never have been possible if her father were alive. She knew now he had not cared for Andrew as a prospective son-in-law. No doubt he would have approved of Karl. He could rest easy in his grave now. Whether her mother would have approved was a different matter. She would like his personality, but his lack of religious belief would disturb her, even worry her. A man with no God has no guidelines for life, she said once. Perhaps that accounted for Karl's reluctance to discuss his past. He fought on the side of evil, now he had no means of cleansing himself. Was that why he looked so sad? Was he searching for peace of mind? His nightmares spoke of continued turmoil within. She must do what she could to help him find God, forgiveness and tranquillity of soul.

Katherine was rinsing her blouse and listening to Housewives' Choice when the stamping of boots on hard-packed snow warned her of Karl's arrival at the back door. She dropped the blouse and threw the door wide, throwing herself at him in enthusiastic greeting. Karl stepped hurriedly in through the door, then picked her up in his arms, lifting her mouth to his.

"Did I see a ray of sunshine out there through the fog?" she asked when he put her down.

"Yes, it looks like it will be a nice day today."

"Do you think the weather's on the turn?"

Karl shrugged. "I have no idea what to expect from your weather. At home when we have a north wind we say: *Der Nordwind ist ein rauher Vetter, aber er bringt beständig Wetter.* That means a north wind brings weather that does not change. I don't know if that is the same here."

Apart from his song at New Year, it was the most she had ever heard him speak in German; she felt keen to hear more. It seemed to provide access to that other Karl, who had lived a life of his own, long before she ever set eyes on him.

"Do you have any more sayings like that?" She was unpacking the rucksack and found her newspaper. She would read it tonight.

Karl thought a moment. "Of course. Here's one we can use now. *Der Februar muss stürmen und blasen, soll im Mai das Vieh schon grasen.* Bad weather is necessary in February, so the cattle can graze in May," he translated for her before continuing in full flow. "*Januar hart und rauh, nutzt dem Getreidebau. Gibt's im Februar weisse Wälder, freuen sich Wiesen und Felder.*"

He would have gone on but Katherine put a finger to his lips. "Enough!" she giggled. "I can't understand a word you're saying. It sounds so strange, hearing you speak in German."

"You will have to get used to it when we visit my country," he told her.

185

Katherine stood back a step to look up at his face in surprise. "Visit? Don't you mean *live* in your country?"

Karl put his hands on her cheeks, cradling her head and caressing the soft strands of her hair. "I thought about it all last night. I think you would like it better if we lived here, where you are not a stranger and know the ways of people."

Katherine felt slighted by his assumption she would not be able to find her feet in Germany. She took his hands from her face.

"How do you know that, Karl? What about you, your family? They're waiting for you. They would be terribly hurt if you stayed here, wouldn't they?"

"Yes, but they are not so important now as you are. Also ..."

He looked away, unable to say what he really felt – that his past might stay buried here. Instead he gave a positive reason for wanting to stay. "Also I like it here."

Katherine could understand that. His words brought a deep sense of relief to her. She would follow him to Germany willingly, but she preferred by far to stay here. Certainly they would visit Germany once it was possible, but to know her home, and Sarah's too of course, would be safe, was an unexpected bonus.

The Big Freeze continued, with more blizzards and snowstorms, until the Giant Thaw began in early March, coinciding with the start of lambing at Lane Head Farm. Katherine was up half the night, keeping an eye on the ewes. During the day Robert helped Karl while Katherine took herself off to bed for a few hours sleep. They called her only if a ewe was showing signs of distress. David Carter had taught Katherine how to turn or disentangle a lamb presenting incorrectly, or, if twins were presenting together, how to push one back until the first was voided. She in turn showed Karl. Robert looked on, taking a medical interest in events. The first warm, slippery lamb Karl helped deliver himself, pulling only when the ewe pushed, was one of a set of twins. Katherine promptly took it to a ewe whose lamb was stillborn, wrapped it in the dead lamb's skin, and let the foster mother accustom herself to her new offspring in a pen by themselves.

"You seemed to manage that remarkably well," Robert said to Karl.

"You forget, I've done this sort of thing before," Karl reminded him, to Katherine's bewilderment. Neither of them chose to enlighten her.

Despite Robert's presence, Katherine felt able to relax and show her affection for Karl. Just as she informed Sarah of the less intimate details of her new relationship with Karl, so she knew Karl told Robert. When Karl first suggested telling the whole story, she refused, embarrassed at the thought, but Robert was so pleased at the success of his matchmaking, that Katherine was soon tempted to agree to Karl's suggestion.

Since the beginning of her love affair, she was aware of a growing recklessness in herself. It was a time of self-discovery; she detected a rebellious side never expressed before. She was brought up to respect the law, to conform to her position in society. Now she almost wanted to have Karl's child, to become the centre of gossip, to say to the world: "Look at me! I am not the tame creature you thought I was. I want this man, and who are you to tell me I can't have him?"

The time they had alone together was limited. Sarah would return home for Easter, and daylight hours passed only too quickly before it was time for Karl to kiss Katherine goodbye and return to Yew Tree Lodge. Their love remained a closely guarded secret. Not even his family knew. When Karl had a letter from home telling him that Anna was to marry Stefan Lipinski in the summer, it seemed his decision to stay in England was right. His family home was already crowded with displaced relatives.

A glimmer of hope for them came with the latest news from the camp. Clothing restrictions on POWs were to be lifted soon; the tell-tale patch could be done away with. Robert helped Karl celebrate this news by handing over a packet of contraceptives with a sly: "There's more where they came from!"

The future was fast looking brighter for Karl. Katherine had given him back his self-respect. Her calm, quiet ways, her gentle eyes which he found so enchanting, erased the horrors of the past. The nightmares persisted, but interspersed with pleasanter dreams in which Katherine often featured. And now he could make love to her again.

Conditions on the farm eased too. Burst pipes were repaired, the last lambs were born, the meadows began to dry as Spring tried to catch up. The sheep were still penned while the pastures were sodden, but feeding them was no hardship now the snow was all but gone and more fodder could be delivered.

Katherine had time to think about Andrew. He would have received her letter by now; as yet there was no reply. He probably wanted to wait until he came home before trying to get any answers out of her. No doubt he would arrive on the doorstep in a couple of weeks wanting a full explanation. She would have great difficulty protecting Karl's position and not giving Andrew the slightest clue to her true reason. The enormity of the problem was only becoming apparent now that Andrew's arrival was imminent.

Sarah was expected on Maundy Thursday. Katherine found Karl tinkering with the engine of the Austin that morning, making sure it was running properly after its long hibernation.

"How's she doing?" she asked, peering over his shoulder into the oily workings.

"Not too bad. I am just cleaning the ends of these." He held up a sparking-plug. "The contact was not good. I think it will be better when I have finished."

"Sparking-plug," she said automatically, then said what was on her mind. "Andrew will be home soon. He's sure to come up here to see me. Whatever happens, Karl, I don't want you involved. The less he sees of you the better."

"I understand perfectly, Schatz, but what if he will not leave you alone? In his position, I would try everything to win you back. He could make trouble."

188

"I'm prepared for that. But he mustn't suspect you. Knowing him, he'd march straight off to the camp and tell them about us. Then they'd take you away from here, wouldn't they?"

Karl replaced the last sparking-plug and wiped the grease from his hands. "Yes. Your Andrew would do that." He shut the bonnet with a bang as if to close the discussion on his predecessor. "I will wash my hands and try the car. Do you want to come?"

She smiled indulgently. It was typical of Karl, she realised, not to have asked her permission to drive it. Now that they were to be married one day, he had ceased behaving like an employee and begun to treat the farm and its contents as his own. She remembered hearing her father once say that sometimes he felt as though Karl were the boss on the farm. She did not mind in the least and was glad that he felt free to behave in such a way at last.

"Yes, I'll come to see how you manage driving on the wrong side, as you call it. But you'd better not go beyond the lane. I don't think the police would approve."

When he returned from the washroom, Karl held the passenger door open for her and bowed politely. "Where to, madam?"

"London please, James," she replied with magnificent hauteur.

He started the engine. It now ran smoothly, but the fuel gauge showed almost empty. "We can't reach London, madam. Will the end of the lane be far enough?"

"Very well." Katherine looked across at Karl and grinned, unable to keep up the play-acting any longer. "I'll be watching to see if you try to open the door instead of changing gear," she warned him.

In fact he found it easier than expected to drive sitting on the right of the car. When they arrived at the bottom of the lane, he turned the car round and drove back to the farm, without once having used the wrong hand to change gear.

Katherine got out of the car and congratulated her chauffeur. "Brilliant. You're almost as good as I am!"

Mock indignation crossed his face. "Before I worked for you, madam, I was driver to the King himself!"

Katherine squealed with delight as Karl made a grab for her. He whispered in her ear: "But I never used to do *this* for the King!" and began to unbutton her coat.

As Sarah climbed from the bus she was reminded of Christmas when her father had been waiting by the car. This time it was Katherine.

"What have you been up to, since I last saw you?" Sarah asked mischievously in the car.

Katherine pretended to concentrate on driving as she pulled out onto the valley road, keeping her face straight ahead. But Sarah saw a blush creep over Katherine's cheeks and her suspicions were aroused.

"Just as I said in my letter," Katherine told her. "It gradually dawned on me how much better I liked Karl than Andrew. Once he saw the way was open, Karl told me how he felt."

"And he proposed to you straight away?" Sarah asked incredulously. "Come on, Katherine, I want to hear the whole story, before we get home!"

Katherine found herself blushing again. She could not possibly tell Sarah the whole truth, even though she knew Sarah was far more broad-minded than she. It was bad enough Robert knowing. She had never kept any secrets from her sister before, but this was going to have to be the first. She told the partial truth.

"We were in the kitchen at the time. He was actually on his knees when he proposed, now I come to think of it." She smiled to herself. She knew she was painting a rather different picture from how it really was.

"On his knees! How romantic. What did he say?" Sarah demanded.

Katherine thought hard, but Karl's exact words eluded her. "I'm not sure. Something about marrying a soldier. I was so excited at the time I can't remember much about it, only how happy I felt and how much I loved him."

Sarah sighed. "You lucky devil. I despair of ever meeting anyone I like enough to marry, who also wants to marry me. I'm quite a handful. Robert would be a good catch, now that he's come out of his shell, but he's set on studying medicine and won't be available for six years or so."

Katherine was surprised at such talk from Sarah. "You're young still; you've your career to start. You don't want to get tied down, surely?"

Sarah shrugged. "No. I suppose you're right. It's just that your romantic involvements always seem to rub off on me. I'm fine as soon as I get back to Bristol. I've got other things to think about there, like finding myself a job at the end of it all."

They were approaching the farm now. Sarah looked artfully over at Katherine. "Do you mind if I give my future brother-in-law a congratulatory kiss?"

Katherine laughed in delight. "My word! You have changed your tune since Christmas. I'm so glad you grew to like him."

The car drew to a halt in the yard and Katherine saw Karl approach from the woods above the farm, accompanied as usual by Joss. "I don't mind you kissing him, just as long as you remember he's mine," she warned Sarah good-naturedly.

"Don't worry, I won't make eyes at him. You'd better just keep Audrey away, that's all," Sarah replied pointedly.

They were still sitting in the car, but Katherine could not move until Sarah had explained her curious statement. "Why?"

Sarah realised she had said too much. It was probably best Katherine never learned about Audrey. She was convinced Karl would have nothing more to do with Audrey, now he had Katherine to keep him happy.

"Oh, you must have seen the way she looked at him at Christmas," she remarked, trying to sound offhand.

Katherine seemed satisfied that Sarah meant nothing sinister by her comment. She got out of the car as Karl opened the door. Sarah came round the car and stepped straight up to Karl, planting a warm, sisterly kiss on his cheek.

"Congratulations, Karl! You've saved me from being that beastly Andrew's sister-in-law!"

Didn't anyone like Andrew, Katherine wondered? Then, as much for Sarah's benefit as her own, she gave Karl a possessive kiss on the mouth.

"It must be very lonely for you in the evenings now without Daddy or Karl," Sarah said over dinner.

"Certainly was, at first," Katherine agreed, "but now the days are longer, Karl stays later. I think I'm beginning to get used to being on my own."

"How long do you think it will be before you and Karl are allowed to get married?" Sarah paused then laughed. "Gosh, that sounds so strange, when I say it out loud like that. Who would have believed it possible you would end up marrying a German? Presumably you'll have to wait until he's set free before you marry, then he'll take you back to Germany."

"That's just the strange thing," Katherine said. "He doesn't want to go back to Germany. He wants us to stay here."

Sarah frowned. "That's odd! He used to be so homesick, didn't he? It's not as if he comes from the Russian Occupied Zone, and was frightened of going back. What's changed his mind, apart from you?"

"Well, he had no choice in the matter before we got together, did he?" Katherine pointed out. "But I must admit I was as surprised as you are when he first proposed staying here. I would have willingly gone to Germany."

"Ah well, Daddy obviously knew what he was doing when he picked him for your husband."

"Don't be daft, Sarah. Although to tell you the truth, the same thought occurred to me. I never realised *none* of you liked Andrew, until Karl mentioned something Daddy said."

For the first time since Sarah's arrival home some of the exuberance left Katherine. She continued, more subdued now. "I'm dreading Andrew's return," she said. "I can't give him a proper explanation of why I don't want to marry him. He's just going to think I'm being fickle and will try to win me round."

Sarah tried to think of some means to ease matters. "I see your problem. I'd offer to flirt with him myself to distract him, but I don't think I could keep up the pretence for long. I tell you what! We could always ask Audrey to oblige."

Katherine was appalled. "Really, Sarah! I'm sure Audrey isn't half as bad as you make her out. Don't you dare suggest anything of the sort."

Sarah's eyes twinkled. "You're too generous. You're the one who doesn't know the half of what she gets up to!"

Katherine was reminded of Sarah's earlier comment. "Is she *still* after Karl, do you know?"

The thought left her cold. She felt an overpowering possessiveness towards Karl now, particularly since she was unable to make that possession known.

"No, I don't think so," Sarah lied. A recent letter from Audrey revealed she found herself drawn back to him, attracted to him physically, by the appeal of his nationality, and the added spice it gave to such an adventure. She wanted Sarah's help in arranging another clandestine meeting. Sarah would have to explain to Audrey this was out of the question, without revealing exactly why. Audrey would never keep her mouth shut about such an exciting piece of gossip.

"I'll give her a gentle nudge in Andrew's direction. I'll tell her you're having second thoughts and want him to have a soft cushion to land on, so to speak!" Sarah said, beginning to clear away the dishes. "That way she shouldn't suspect anything and it'll keep her hands off Karl."

Katherine reluctantly decided she could not waste such a chance to get both Andrew and Audrey safely out of the way. "All right, but promise me you'll be very discreet."

"Don't worry. It will all work out in the end. You wait and see."

BLACK

CHAPTER TEN

Karl was tempted to join everyone at church on Good Friday. Appearing at such an occasion was a useful way of integrating himself into the village community. He had attended three services now, including David's funeral, but each time was acutely aware of hostile glances from a few members of the congregation, notably young Mrs Collins. Even now she would cross the road if she saw him walking towards her. He understood her feelings and tried to avoid her whenever possible. On one occasion he turned the corner out of Cutbush Lane into the main street of Penchurch and almost collided with her. Her look of hatred served as a bitter reminder of the recent past. Knowing she would be safely out of the way in church, Karl decided to decline Katherine's request to accompany them, in favour of a stroll around the village. The Christmas service was one he could tolerate, but Easter was more serious in its devotions. He did not want to hear about suffering.

A mild breeze from the river brought with it the smell of the earth's rebirth. Karl set off from Yew Tree Lodge with the Murdochs; when they turned right towards the church, he turned left, crossed the valley road and wandered down the track which led to the cricket green by the river. Leaves were bursting rapidly from their buds, the flowers of Spring – daffodils, grape hyacinths, primroses and violets – greeted him from garden and hedgerow. A pair of sparrows fluttered by in a confusion of wings, chasing each other through the tangled branches of a hawthorn. On the path ahead a brimstone butterfly sat sunning itself, its wings camouflaged against a cluster of primroses. Karl watched it a moment then moved on towards the river meadow which served as a cricket green. It was still strewn with debris from the recent floods, but the tidemark stopped just short of the pavilion, built on higher ground. Flooding had been more extensive across the river. Pools of water still lay on sodden fields. Karl remembered potato-picking there the previous summer, before his work party moved on to fruit-picking and Lane Head Farm.

Retracing his steps up the track to the village he wandered the back streets, although the village did not spread much beyond the valley road, confined as it was by river and hills. Glancing at the watch which used to be David's he found he had another twenty minutes to while away. He stood by the village notice-board, reading posters. One requested jumble for a sale the week before, another advertised a forthcoming production of the Penchurch Players: *Hay Fever* by Noel Coward. Karl was looking forward to seeing Gertie Murdoch as Judith Bliss.

The church clock showed ten-thirty; still time to waste. Entering the churchyard by the lych gate he read those headstones whose inscriptions were not obliterated by time and lichen. His feet carried him to a corner where the most recent grave contained the remains of David Carter. Katherine's mother had been buried in the South London cemetery of her childhood home. It seemed a pity she could not lie here, next to her husband. Karl stood a while contemplating the two people who had produced such a fine daughter as Katherine; he found himself silently thanking them and promising he would take good care of her, then smiled at his own superstition. Katherine would get him into church yet if he carried on like this, talking to dead people! No doubt she would want to be married in this church, if that day ever came. She would never agree to a civil wedding. The question was, would Thornton agree to perform the ceremony when one of the "happy couple" was a lapsed Roman Catholic atheist? It seemed likely he would have to become a regular church-goer after all, if Katherine were to have her church wedding – and Mrs Collins be damned.

The first few worshippers began to move into the churchyard. Karl hung back until he saw the Murdochs and

Carters leaving together. Mrs Kellett stepped up to Katherine and exchanged a few words, unaware yet of the changed circumstances. Karl waited until she had gone, then joined the small group whose lives he now shared, making sure not to stand too close to Katherine.

"Did you have a pleasant walk, Karl?" Donald asked him, nodding courteously at the same time to a passing patient.

"Yes. Thank you. But I haven't walked far. I stood out here for a while." He indicated the recent grave in the corner of the churchyard. "I decided I should go with you next time to church. Mrs Collins must accept me there."

"Good for you!" Gertie said warmly. "You mustn't let the few people who still have grievances put you off. I'm sure she'll come round to accepting you in the end. Most people have."

So it was that on Easter Sunday Karl once again entered the heavily scented church, bursting with golden daffodils, and followed the Murdochs up the aisle, passing the eagle-eyed Mrs Collins on the way. Robert saw the look she gave Karl, and himself felt chilled by the venom in her eyes.

Karl hastily passed her by and sat studying the stained-glass windows. It had occurred to him on his first visit there that the window depicting a ploughman and his horse had soil of exactly the same colour as that which now stained his own hands. It was as though the church itself accepted his presence, even if certain of its congregation did not.

During the service he listened intently to what John Thornton said, to the music and words of the hymns, to the readings. Some of the sermon seemed applicable to himself, but nothing reached any deeper part of him. He could discern the individual notes but not the melody; everyone else seemed to appreciate the music but him. Even Robert seemed to gain something from being there, but then he had always held on to his religious upbringing, even in the prison camp, whereas Karl had been deliberately severed from such influences in his youth. He had all too readily abandoned the church in favour of the pageantry and rituals, activity camps and combat

197

training supplied by the Hitler Youth, had never thought to question what he was told, had accepted it all as easily as he had abandoned religion. "Trust in the Lord" became "Trust in the Leader". The difference seemed negligible at the time. In those heady days of the Hitler Youth he had learned to obey orders without question. When he had finally started to ask questions, he found no answers. Nor was he finding any here.

He was glad when the service finally ended. The two families made their way back to Yew Tree Lodge for one of Gertie's famous Sunday lunches. Katherine and Sarah helped Gertie in the kitchen, leaving the men to read the Sunday newspapers or talk in the living room.

While she was stirring the gravy Gertie brought up a subject which she had wanted to raise with Katherine for days.

"Katherine, dear," she said over her shoulder to where Katherine stood washing the first round of pots and pans. "Excuse me for asking, but why don't you wear that lovely engagement ring any more?"

Sarah and Katherine exchanged worried glances. Katherine had put off telling anyone and thus avoided having to answer the inevitable questions for as long as possible, but it seemed the time for explanations had come. She thought of saying the ring had been loose, that she was frightened to wear it lest it should fall off and be lost, but there would be no point in lying.

She took a deep breath and committed herself. "I've decided I don't want to marry him. I've broken off the engagement."

Gertie was not unduly astonished. She quietly took the gravy pan off the stove to give herself time.

"Is there any particular reason, dear? I hope you'll trust me as much as you would have trusted your mother."

Katherine stumbled over her reply. "I just ... What I mean is ..."

Gertie thought she knew what the problem was. "You've found someone else, have you, dear?"

Sarah smirked. Katherine looked intensely relieved to have the truth out at last. She put a greasy pan back in the water and turned to Gertie. "You've hit the nail on the head! Perhaps you can guess who the someone else is, then you'll know what a problem I've landed myself in."

Gertie's face became grave. "Well, I can certainly guess who it is. You've both kept it a good secret from us all, although come to think of it, I'm sure Robert is in on this. Am I right?"

Katherine nodded. "It was Robert who set the ball rolling, convincing Karl I didn't love Andrew. How he saw that when I didn't know myself, I'll never know. But he was right, and I'll be eternally grateful." She could see Gertie was not. She tackled the greasy pan rather than face her.

"Robert should know better than to encourage this," Gertie protested. "Much as I like Karl, he is not at liberty to ..."

"To what? To love? I thought you would understand better than that." Katherine slammed the pan onto the draining board.

Gertie lowered her voice. "Look, dear, I'm only trying to protect you. If it were up to me I would be thrilled. But not only is this against the law, it also flies in the face of good sense."

"Love has nothing to do with good sense. Karl and I are well aware of the problems. It would be helpful if we had support rather than criticism."

There was a hiss of surprise from Sarah at Katherine's unaccustomed bluntness. Her determination astonished Gertie too. She decided that Katherine was probably right. Support was needed if the pair were to survive the testing years ahead. "Very well, dear. I will help you all I can. Even if it comes to sticking up for you in any confrontation with the authorities. Heaven forbid that should happen."

All the tension left Katherine. She hugged Gertie, her wet hands leaving damp patches on her blouse. "Thank you. I can't tell you what a relief it is that you know. We'll have to tell Donald, but apart from him, no one else must know."

Gertie looked dubious. "What about Andrew? What have you told him? If I can guess the reason, others may do the same. There's going to be a storm over this, sooner or later."

Katherine had all the optimism of youth. "We'll survive, you'll see."

At the dinner table, Katherine tried to warn Karl with her eyes that the cat was out of the bag. Gertie caught the signal too and after serving out their sparing portions of meat and the plates were loaded with vegetables, she turned to her husband.

"Donald, dear. Katherine has something she wants to tell you which is rather important."

Donald put down his knife and fork and gave Katherine his full attention.

All other eyes were on Katherine. She sought momentary strength from the grey pair. "I ... told Gertie something in the kitchen that both Robert and Sarah already know," she began.

Donald waited expectantly, his benign face set in a pleasant smile. When Katherine told him her news his lips pursed but the expression remained unruffled. His eyes cast towards Gertie to ascertain her stand and saw that her blessing had been given. He made up his own mind and delivered his opinion.

"Well, I'm sure your father would have been very pleased. He was always telling me what a fine chap Karl is. My warmest congratulations to you both. I think this deserves a proper celebration!"

Karl looked across at Katherine and grinned. He could not have felt happier than he did at this moment.

Donald fetched a bottle of wine and proposed a toast. "To Katherine and Karl!" He paused and added wryly: "And to the Government, in the hope they see fit to change the law as soon as possible!"

As Andrew's return approached, Katherine's optimism began to falter. She sought company and comfort with Karl, working with him outside in the winter-neglected kitchen-garden, leaving much of the housework for Sarah. Sarah made a discreet visit to Audrey's home the Saturday following Easter, partly to prime Audrey for her seduction of Andrew, partly to give Katherine time with Karl. She guessed how far their relationship had progressed without Katherine having to tell her.

Audrey turned out to be putty in Sarah's hands. She latched on to the bait dangled in front of her, forgetting her intended quarry. Andrew had always been Katherine's. Audrey, to give credit where it was due, had never attempted to come between them. Now the way seemed clear. Andrew would be vulnerable; Audrey was only too keen to pick up the pieces. If Katherine had no need of Froxley Grange, Audrey certainly had. She had no intention of working as a secretary all her life.

Sarah returned to Lane Head, confidently able to report success. If only they might be so sure about Andrew.

Katherine had received no reply to her last letter. She was uncertain what to make of his silence. Had he accepted the situation? Was he simply forgetting about her? It seemed hardly likely.

The day of his return passed without a word. Karl saw the tension on Katherine's face as he prepared to leave at the end of the day. Kellett might call that evening and he sensed her fear. He held her close for longer than usual.

"Have faith in yourself, Schatz," he told her. "I wish I could help you."

She put on a brave face. "I expect I'm making a mountain out of a molehill. Andrew will act the proper gentleman and accept my wishes gracefully. I hope he does come this evening, so I can apologise to him properly, face to face, for treating him so badly."

Her bold words were only for Karl's benefit. Inside she knew Andrew was used to getting his own way. His delay in contacting her was probably a ploy on his part to unsettle her, weaken her defences for a renewed attack on her affections. Reluctantly she broke away from Karl. "Come early tomorrow. Please, Liebling!" she begged.

His hand lingered on her cheek. "Of course."

Sarah shared Katherine's tension, unable to settle to her books, but there was no visitor to disturb the peace of Lane Head Farm that night.

Next morning, true to his word, Karl arrived early. He could tell at once Kellett had not made contact; Katherine was dark-eyed with worry and lack of sleep.

"Perhaps I ought to call him today," she suggested.

Sarah disagreed. "That's just what he wants you to do. Come crawling to him for forgiveness. Leave him be."

Katherine looked at Karl.

"I think the same," he said.

Karl decided to work near the house, rather than clear undergrowth in the woods as intended. Katherine's fear troubled him. He had experienced Kellett's aggressive side at first hand and had no desire to see it manifest itself on Katherine. From the kitchen-garden he would be within earshot but safely hidden from view.

The broad beans Katherine planted the previous autumn had been flattened and shrivelled by the snow. He cut off their blackened shoots and began to dig over the soil, leaving the roots in the ground as Katherine had told him. He was busy raking the area to a fine tilth for new seed when he recognised the sound of Kellett's MG.

Katherine and Sarah also heard the car. Sarah quickly collected her books from the kitchen table. "I'll be upstairs out of your way. Call me if you need me."

There was a long, challenging ring on the front doorbell. Katherine's heart skipped a beat. She walked steadily to the hall and opened the door to a stony-faced Andrew Kellett.

"Oh, hello, Andrew," Katherine said, dry-mouthed, a stupid, ingratiating smile on her face. She remembered Karl's words. Have faith in yourself. She wiped the smile from her face. "Please come in."

She waited while he took off his hat and coat, then led him through to the sitting room. "Please sit down, Andrew," she said coolly. "Can I get you a coffee or something?"

He did not sit. "Stop playing games, Katherine. You know why I'm here. I want some answers. You didn't explain yourself very well in your letter. I came here to ..." His brusque facade crumbled as his true emotions began to show through.

He continued, more gently. "I love you, Katherine. I thought you loved me. How could you write me such a letter, completely out of the blue like that? You don't seem to realise how hurt I was. Please tell me you don't really mean what you wrote. I'm prepared to forget all about it if we can only carry on where we left off."

He stepped nearer to her, his hands reaching out imploringly towards her. Katherine felt herself weakening. He really was hurt. It was the first time she had ever seen him display his emotions like this. She had to harden her heart as she moved away and sat on an armchair, forcing him to take a seat opposite.

"I admit my letter was very awkward, Andrew. I just didn't know how to tell you. I'm afraid I did mean it. I don't want to marry you." As she spoke she sat back further into the chair in a subconscious distancing. "After you left at New Year I began to think over our time together and suddenly felt ... I was not ... right for you. I don't fit in with your family. I would never be right as the lady of Froxley Grange."

Andrew's composure vanished. "Damn it!" he shouted, leaning forward aggressively. "I'm not asking you to be "The Lady of Froxley Grange"! I'm asking you to be my wife. Can't you see that? I want a better reason from you than that, Katherine."

Katherine bit her lip, retreating still further back into the armchair. "I'm afraid there isn't one. I don't love you and I don't want to marry you. Please leave it at that." She stood up. "I'll return your ring of course."

She made as if to go out of the door but Andrew sprang from his chair and grabbed her by the shoulder. "Don't turn your back on me! I haven't finished this conversation yet. I don't want the bloody ring. I want you!"

His fingers were digging into her shoulder and she winced. "Let go of me please. You're hurting me."

He drew her face closer to his. "I think there's more to this than you're letting on," he said through gritted teeth. "You're not telling me the truth, Katherine."

She tried to look him in the eye and deny his accusation, but she could not. She knew he would detect the lie. Her silence, however, was just as much a confirmation of the truth of his accusation, and his fingers dug harder behind her collar bone.

"I want to hear the truth!" he shouted angrily at her.

"Ow! Let go!" Katherine cried out, desperation high in her voice. She heard the door to the hall open abruptly and saw Andrew's eyes flick across to see who was there. The grasp of his fingers eased and Katherine stepped hurriedly back out of reach, then turned to face the door. Karl was there, motionless but watchful.

"What's he doing here?" Andrew growled. He confronted Karl. "Get out of here! This is none of your business!"

Karl did not move. He looked at Katherine, awaiting her instructions. He had no intention of leaving whilst Kellett was like this.

"It's all right, Karl," Katherine said quietly. "Please go back outside." She could see Karl's presence unsettled Andrew. He was unlikely to hurt her again. More disconcertingly, she could also see comprehension dawning on his face. He was looking from Karl back to her and putting two and two together.

"Don't worry, Katherine. I can see I'm not welcome here any more. I'm going." He strode towards Karl, who was still blocking the doorway. Karl sidestepped to allow Kellett by. As he reached the front door, hat and coat in hand, he turned and made a last threatening retort. "Just don't think you've heard the last of me!"

As his car drove away Katherine flung herself at Karl, tears pouring down her cheeks. "I think he's guessed," she wailed. "You shouldn't have come in."

Karl wiped the tears from her cheeks. "He was hurting you. I couldn't stand and listen. I had to stop him." For a moment images from the past flashed across his mind. A similar incident, with disastrous results for himself. He warned himself to concentrate on the present.

Katherine did not notice his momentary disquiet. She heard Sarah coming downstairs and hurriedly wiped away her remaining tears.

Sarah burst into the room. She relaxed as she saw Karl. "What happened? I heard Andrew shouting, then he suddenly left."

Katherine quickly told her the details. "I think he's guessed about Karl," she added woefully.

Sarah grimaced. "Oh crikey. That's bad news."

Karl looked down at Katherine. Whatever happened next would prove to be a testing time for her. Public knowledge would condemn her, not himself. He would be removed from the area and she left to face the music; they had always known that was the risk.

"Schatz," he whispered, "don't forget, whatever happens, I love you. We must be patient. Our time will come."

They were all on edge for the remainder of the day, but again Kellett kept them waiting. No one came from the camp to haul Karl away. The silence was ominous.

For a second night Katherine slept badly, trying to convince herself that Andrew had not in fact made the connection between herself and Karl.

When Karl arrived in the morning she told him to work well away from the house, in case Andrew returned. Karl protested briefly but acquiesced. He could not hang around indefinitely; there was too much work to be done. The orchards needed spraying, but were too far from the house. He decided to compromise and set off for the woods above the house to continue the scrub clearance he had already begun.

The woods had been badly neglected over the years. Too many saplings had been allowed to grow and compete for light and space. Now the undergrowth was encroaching from the woodland edge, needing clearing before its luxuriant Spring growth became established. Alder trees were growing like weeds amongst the more useful ash, chestnut, sycamore and oak. There was an area of ash which looked as though it had been coppiced in the past, but now the woodland presented itself as an unruly tangle which offended his forester's eye.

Fine for nature lovers, he thought as he wielded the axe to a young alder, but economic folly on a farm. The wood could earn its keep and still provide a home for pheasants, rooks and owls.

Happy at work in the Spring sunshine, Karl could almost forget Kellett, although the problem never quite escaped from the back of his mind. All morning he listened for the sound of the MG; he stiffened when he eventually heard it roaring up the lane. Lodging the axe in a tree stump, he went to the edge of the wood to look down at the house. He could see the car parked on the turning area by the front door. There was no sign of Kellett. He must already be inside.

Karl deliberated what to do. Katherine was emphatic he should stay out of the way. Warned by yesterday's episode, Sarah said she would remain with Katherine if Andrew returned. Reluctantly, Karl stepped back into the woods and retrieved the axe. At least Kellett had not brought the authorities with him. Perhaps he had not guessed after all.

A bare five minutes later Joss jumped up from his sunny pile of leaves and wagged his tail. Karl noticed the dog's welcome and straightened up. Involuntarily his grip tightened on the axe when he saw Kellett following a white-faced Katherine. Why was she bringing him up here?

Katherine came to a halt five feet away from Karl. She ignored Joss's welcoming sniff. It took her a moment to bring herself to speak, such was her anger.

"Why did you lie to us?" Her voice chilled the warm woodland.

Karl stared at her in bewilderment, then switched his gaze to the smug-faced Kellett, who was clearly enjoying himself immensely. What had the man told Katherine?

"Lie? About what?" Karl asked, trying to sound calm when his heart was beginning to thud with the shock of seeing such anger directed at himself by Katherine. It seemed, even before he heard her words, that she would allow him no defence.

Katherine drew herself erect to deliver the accusation. She could barely bring herself to say the ghastly words. "You always said you were in the army. Andrew saw your camp record card yesterday. He has just told me you were really in the SS. Is he right?" She watched Karl intently as she spoke.

"I have never lied to you!" He had to choose his words carefully. Katherine was like an overwound spring, ready to snap. "I was ..."

"Were you or were you not in the SS?" she demanded. "Yes or no?" She knew what his answer had to be, yet she did not want to hear it.

They would not understand. He had kept his past a secret for that very reason. His eyes darted over the trees, desperately searching for a way to avoid her condemnation. Reluctantly he met her harsh stare. She was still awaiting an answer. He stepped towards her, left hand outstretched in supplication to her to remember what they both meant to each other. The admission was not easy to make.

"I was in the Waffen SS, but only ..."

"Don't touch me!" she screamed. She felt an irrational fear growing inside her as Karl approached, still clutching the axe. The SS were the embodiment of evil, and Karl was one of them. She felt physically sick at the thought of what she had let him do to her. "I don't want your murdering hands to touch me! Ever again! If you lied to us you must have something to hide. I bet you lied when you told me you loved me, just so that you could ..." She stopped short, realising she was about to tell more than Andrew ought to know.

Karl felt his own anger now. "I didn't lie to you, Katherine," he shouted back. "Please listen to me and let me explain."

"I don't want your excuses. I don't want to see you again. Leave this farm. At once! Do you hear?" She was in tears, despite her anger.

Karl could not believe what he heard. "Please, don't do this to me!" he begged. "I need you, Schatz. My God, how I need you! Think, Katherine. Think what you're doing! The future is what is important."

He was close to her now, about to reach out to her. She was his lifeline. Kellett intervened.

"You heard her! Don't touch her!"

Karl swung around, the axe raised towards Kellett. They stood in open confrontation, poised like two rams about to charge. Katherine was in no doubt Karl was capable of killing Andrew with that axe. She stepped quickly between them, her earlier fear gone, replaced by a furious rage that Karl dared to threaten an unarmed man.

She looked up and saw the murder in his eyes. "Put that axe down, Karl! If I ever meant anything at all to you, then put it down."

To her intense relief the message got through. His stare switched to her face. He lowered his arm. The axe fell from his grasp onto the leaf litter. Katherine picked it up herself to prevent Andrew from taking it. She spoke without taking her eyes off Karl's.

"Back away please, Andrew. Let him pass. He is going now. I will tell the camp I no longer require Karl's services."

The two men eyed each other carefully, but the situation was defused. Andrew stepped back off the path, hands by his sides. Katherine picked up Karl's jacket and held it at arm's length. He snatched it from her, then paused, head down, eyes closed. When they met hers again, his eyes had lost their ferocity. Instead they appealed for clemency. She stonily ignored his plea. Turning dejectedly on his heel, he pushed through the scrub to the edge of the wood.

Katherine and Andrew followed. They watched him walk slowly down the track towards the lane. He turned once and saw them watching, like judges who have condemned a man to execution. Angrily he turned his back again and strode off down the lane.

Once Karl disappeared from view, Kellett turned to Katherine. "Well now. Aren't you grateful to me for exposing such a monster?" He laid his arm over her shoulders. She shrugged it off.

"Don't think because I've sent him packing, you can step back in his place. I've told you once I don't love you, Andrew. I loved Karl, or at least, the Karl I thought he was."

208

Andrew looked bitter. "You loved him enough to sleep with him? I ought to report you both for what he did. You never let me take any kind of liberty with you."

Fear crossed her face. His threat gave him a lever. "But I won't, out of consideration for your feelings. I still love you. You were taken in. Even if you have been defiled I'm willing to have you back."

"Defiled? How dare you! I expect you've had your share of German girls."

"That's different altogether."

"Why? Why can I be ... defiled, as you put it, by a German, and you can't?"

He laughed and shook his head. "They were just women trying to keep themselves from starvation. He's a murderer. You saw the way he looked at me. He was using you: to establish a nice safe lifestyle, where his past would not catch up with him."

His words had a dreadful ring of truth. Was that why Karl did not want to go home? Because people there knew what he had done? "What did his record say," she asked.

"Only that he's SS. Despite that, he was classified "grey", if you know what that means?" She nodded. "Well it goes to show how clever these Germans are at lying, doesn't it?"

Her anger was directed back at Karl now. He would give her time to adjust. "I'll find someone on the estate to give you a hand here," he offered.

She had no choice but to accept. "Thank you."

Kellett climbed into his car a happier man. With gentle persuasion she might come round, eventually. He meant what he said about her being defiled. God help that German if he showed up again!

He had driven no more than a couple of hundred yards before he spotted Karl leaning against a gate at the side of the lane. Kellett's anger resurfaced. Was the man planning on going back up to the house once the coast was clear? He stopped the car by the gate and got out, bristling at the German's antagonistic glare.

"You were told to clear off. Go down to Dr Murdoch's house and wait for someone from Kingshill to fetch you."

Karl looked at him coldly. "You are not in the army any more Mr Kellett. Also you are not my employer. I will not take orders from you."

"You impudent bastard! How dare you talk to me like that? They were Miss Carter's orders, not mine!"

Karl was not impressed. "She is no longer my employer. I will go to Dr Murdoch when I am ready."

"And I say you go now!" Andrew Kellett yelled. He grabbed Karl by the arm and pushed him out into the road.

Something snapped inside Karl. He had been pushed and ordered around for too long. He threw himself at Kellett's stocky, red-faced figure, sending him crashing to the ground. Kellett was well built, but had been behind a desk for too long. Karl's leanness belied his strength, and he was skilled in the art of combat. He grabbed his opponent by the ears and smashed his head against the road, oblivious at first to the sound of pounding feet.

Katherine and Sarah watched Andrew drive off. They were surprised to hear the car come to a halt a short way down the lane. Katherine set off down the lane to see why he had stopped; Sarah followed. She had sensed something dreadful had happened as soon as she saw Katherine and Andrew return from the woods. Katherine had said nothing and seemed to be in a state of shock.

They had not walked far before they heard raised voices. Katherine rounded the corner and let out a shriek of horror. Karl looked up to see the women hurtling towards him. Dropping Kellett's head he stood up, then made off down the lane.

Sarah bent over Andrew and saw blood trickling from the back of his head. His eyes were closed. Katherine crouched at his side; he groaned and moved his head.

"Andrew? Are you all right?" Katherine asked.

His eyelids fluttered open. He seemed dazed, incoherent. After a minute he sat up shakily and gingerly felt the back of his head.

"Good thing I'm thick-skulled," he quipped feebly. "I believe that bastard meant to kill me."

Sarah sprang to Karl's defence. "No! He was about to leave you, when he saw us coming."

Andrew looked around anxiously. "Where is he?"

Katherine answered. "He ran off." She was puzzling over what Sarah had said. It had not looked to her as though Karl intended to leave Andrew alive. "We'd better get you down to Donald, and hope we don't bump into Karl."

The two girls helped Andrew into the car.

"I'll drive him there, Sarah," Katherine said. "I don't want to be here on my own if Karl's still around. You'll be safe enough I should think. He's got nothing against you."

Sarah could not fathom her sister's strange attitude. "I think you've got him wrong, Katherine. You're not being fair. We didn't see who started this fight."

"He did," Andrew groaned through his aching head.

"You would say that, wouldn't you," Sarah retorted. "Have you forgotten how he kept quiet about your part in the incident on Boxing Day?"

Andrew ignored her. "Come on Katherine. Get me away from here."

Katherine glared at her sister. "How could you side with a Nazi?"

As Katherine drove off, Sarah stared after the car, wondering what on earth was going on. Katherine had called Karl a Nazi. She had just seen him with her own eyes assaulting Andrew. It all seemed so impossible. She was to return to Bristol in a few days, leaving behind another catastrophe. It was not Katherine she feared for this time, but Karl.

Robert was in the front garden, mowing the lawn, when he saw Kellett's red MG turn in at the gateway with Katherine at the wheel. He realised that Andrew Kellett was hurt, left the mower and ran across to the car.

Andrew forestalled his question. "That Nazi friend of yours just tried to kill me," he said as he got out of the car.

Robert looked incredulously at Katherine.

"It's true. Karl was in the SS. Andrew told me. Karl didn't like his little secret being made known."

Robert was horrified. Katherine seemed totally against Karl. "I already knew he was in the SS," he told her, "and it didn't worry me."

Katherine looked at him aghast. "You knew?"

"Yes. He told me. Ages ago."

"Why on earth didn't you tell me?"

Robert scowled. "Karl didn't want anyone else to know. For the very reason you're demonstrating now."

Andrew was growing impatient. "Shut up about him and let's get my head seen to! Is your father around?"

"No. He's on his rounds. He should be back for lunch. My mother can patch you up."

While Gertie Murdoch fussed over Andrew in the surgery, Robert got Megan, the maid, to make Katherine a mug of tea.

"So the last thing you saw of Karl was him running down the lane. You didn't pass him on the road?"

Katherine was slumped in an armchair. "No. No sign of him. I hope he doesn't turn up while we're here. I don't want to see him ever again. He lied to me ... and Daddy. That's what hurts. If we'd known from the start it might have been different."

"Katherine, he never lied to you. He was an ordinary soldier, like all the others."

"Then why didn't his record say he was just an ordinary soldier? Why did he have to be SS? If it's nothing to be ashamed about, why did he lie? I've heard dreadful stories about the SS; shooting prisoners of war, destroying whole villages." She swigged her tea. "You've been hoodwinked like the rest of us. You didn't see the look in his eyes when he threatened Andrew with an axe. Nor the way he smashed poor Andrew's head against the ground."

"Katherine, just accept what I tell you. You don't know the whole story. Don't judge him on what you think he is." His voice dropped. "I'm worried about him now."

212

"Worried? Why, for heaven's sake?"

"You don't know what he's been through, Katherine. I do. That's why I'm worried."

"Pah! You're just sticking up for him because you've both been prisoners of war. I've had enough of your lame excuses. I'm going to see how Andrew is."

Her sleepless nights were taking their toll. She was short-tempered, as well as being emotionally drained. She did not know what to think any more. The person she trusted most turned out to be a monster. Robert and her own sister sided with him. Andrew seemed to be the only one who saw sense.

She left Robert and went to the surgery. Donald had returned and was ministering to Andrew, who was lying on the couch, looking pale.

"How is he?" she asked Gertie.

"A bit concussed, but he'll survive."

Donald led her by the arm into the waiting room. He lowered his voice.

"What's all this about, Katherine? Andrew says Karl tried to kill him!"

Katherine hesitated. "I'm not sure. He looked as if he would. Sarah says he let go of Andrew before he saw us. I expect only Karl knows the truth."

Donald was worried. He was responsible to the camp for Karl. There was going to be one almighty stink. "Where is he now?"

"No idea. And I don't want to know." Katherine sniffed hard. "Did you know Karl was in the SS?"

Donald's eyebrows shot up. "Good heavens! No. When did you find that out?"

"Today. Andrew told me. He made use of an army contact in the prison camp. That's why Karl tried to kill him."

"Karl can't have done anything too dreadful, Katherine. The authorities would never allow him out if they suspected him of war crimes. He was only a sergeant after all."

By now Katherine was only prepared to believe the worst. "How do you know? Andrew has told me about SS officers putting on other uniforms. Besides, I seem to remember it wasn't only officers on trial for atrocities."

Donald could see arguing was useless. "Don't make accusations Karl's not here to answer. I tend to trust your father's judgement. You must give Karl the chance to speak for himself."

Katherine burst into a flood of pent-up tears. "It's too late now!"

CHAPTER ELEVEN

Before he allowed Robert to drive him home, Kellett insisted on telephoning the commandant. He made Katherine corroborate his story and Donald confirm the extent of his injuries. Donald took Katherine back. She was hardly through the door when Sarah pressed for news.

"What's going on? For heaven's sake, Katherine, tell me what happened!"

Katherine was tired. She sat down at the kitchen table feeling in need of an ally. Perhaps Sarah's initial anti-German sentiments would help her see Katherine's point of view?

"Has Karl been back?" she asked as Sarah pulled up a chair opposite.

"No. I haven't seen him since he ran off down the lane." Sarah's eyes bored accusingly into her sister's. "What did you mean when you called him a Nazi?"

"That lying swine was not the simple soldier he made himself out to be, Sarah. You were right to hate him. He was actually in the SS!" To her intense relief, Katherine noticed her own horror now reflected in Sarah's face.

"How on earth did you find that out? Didn't the camp know?"

"They already knew about him. That's how Andrew found out."

This last revelation altered Sarah's whole perspective. "You mean to say, Andrew deliberately set out to discredit Karl in your eyes? I think that's despicable! I really do! No wonder Karl was furious."

Katherine cried out in vexation. "What's the matter with you, Sarah? Can't you understand? Andrew put it very neatly. He said I'd been defiled. And he's right. It's partly my fault, I suppose, allowing Karl to go so far. It was a sin; now I'm being paid for it."

215

"Oh, don't be ridiculous!" Sarah stormed. "You're always complaining at me for seeing things in black and white. You're the culprit now. At first Karl was the poor, defeated and homesick prisoner of war. Now, suddenly, he's an evil Nazi, who deceived and used you. Come off it, Katherine! Even if he were in the SS, everyone deserves a second chance, especially Karl. I like him. He's never said or done anything that has made me the least bit suspicious. Or rather, only once," she added, remembering the bruised wrist. "How can you forget everything he did for you over the winter?"

Katherine was not listening. "What about his nightmares? We don't know what those are all about, do we? He would never tell us anything. Why was that, do you think?" She did not wait for an answer. "His guilty conscience! That's why!"

"At least he has a conscience!" Sarah was becoming infuriated by her sister's obtuseness. She stood up. "I'm going to phone Gertie, to see if Karl's turned up yet. If not, I'm going out to look for him on Beth. What must *he* be feeling at the moment, eh, Katherine?"

While Sarah was on the telephone, Katherine reflected on what Sarah had said. She could not forgive Karl. He had deceived her badly; that was what hurt most. She saw his clogs standing by the back door, as hollow as his love.

Sarah reported back. "He's still not there. Robert's getting very worried. He said he would search along the valley road, if I look around nearer here. You coming?"

"No. I told Karl I didn't want to see him again. I'm still of the same opinion."

By nightfall Donald had the unpleasant task of confirming that Sgt Driesler had indeed gone missing. Major Alderton had already alerted the local police.

After his call Donald summoned a dejected Robert into his study for a quiet word.

"I always respected the confidence between you and Karl. I never enquired what he told you. Now I learn you knew he was in the SS. I want you to reassure me of my assessment of Karl; that I'm doing the right thing taking his side."

Robert gave a weak smile. "You needn't worry, Dad. Apart from the fact he was fighting for the wrong side, I'm proud to call Karl my friend. What he told me was in strictest confidence, partly because he *does* have a guilty conscience, mostly because what happened was so terrible. He didn't want to be an object of pity. He had to bury it. He needed a lot of courage to tell me."

Donald thought for a moment. "Presumably his nightmares and his fear of injections are all part of it?" Robert nodded, not intending to elaborate further. His father tapped his teeth with his pipe as he tried to understand what could have caused such terror as he had heard and seen for himself. "Why are you so worried about him now?"

"I don't really know. All his hopes and dreams have been shattered; he's back where he started. Now he's disappeared. You see where that leads?"

"You think he may try to kill himself?"

"Or Kellett."

Donald was horrified. "We should warn Andrew. You're sure that's what Karl might do?"

"No, of course not. It's only a guess. It's probably not worth worrying Andrew, although we ought to warn the police. If Karl were all right, he would have come back here, I'm sure."

Donald went out to the telephone. Gertie hovered by the kitchen door, wanting to be told what was going on. Her husband's conversation with the police came as a terrible shock. His request to be summoned as soon as they found Karl demanded an explanation.

"Gertie, dear, all I'm able to say at the moment is that Karl may need my help. We shall just have to sit and wait, and hope they find him soon."

Robert sat helplessly by the telephone for the rest of the evening. Why had Karl not come back? At eleven o'clock Gertie insisted he went to bed. Reluctantly Robert followed her upstairs. The police were hardly likely to find Karl at this time of night.

The telephone rang first thing next morning. Robert rushed to answer it; it was Sarah checking for news.

"Have you heard anything?"

"Not a thing. How is Katherine? Is she still angry with Karl?"

"Yes, I'm ashamed to say. She won't even let me talk about him. Wants to forget him, she says."

"Damn! Excuse me, Sarah, but she's going about this all wrong. Can't you do anything to persuade her to be more charitable?"

"Don't you think I've tried? She won't budge. She's being as obstinate as I used to be."

Robert was anxious not to have the line engaged for too long. "I promise I'll let you know the instant I hear anything. In the meantime, keep working on Katherine, will you?"

"I will."

It was a fine morning on Hay Bluff. The weather was settled and the boggy ground had dried out a bit. Edith Powell, the middle-aged wife of a local schoolmaster, had ridden her horse up the escarpment the previous evening. She had been surprised to see a man sitting on the top at that time of day, gazing out over the Wye valley and beyond. When she saw him again the following morning she suspected he had been there all night. She debated whether to approach him, alone as she was. Her curiosity and concern got the better of her. She turned her horse along the path towards the most easterly point of the Bluff, where the man was sitting.

He seemed to be wearing an army uniform. She found comfort in that observation. He had not yet heard her approach; the sound of her horse's hooves was muffled by soft ground. When she was within thirty yards she noticed the POW patch on his battledress. She reined in her horse, which snorted and alerted the man to her presence.

More cautiously now she continued. The man stayed where he was. Remaining on her horse, she greeted him politely. "Good morning."

The man looked coldly up at her. His unshaven face confirmed her suspicions. He acknowledged her greeting with a nod.

"I noticed you here yesterday. Are you all right?" She had to assume he spoke English. Most POWs knew some by now.

"Yes," the man replied curtly.

Mrs Powell felt bold enough to speak further, even though the man had a strange look about him. After all, she was safe on horseback, she told herself. "What are you doing up here? Surely you shouldn't be up here all this time?"

In reply the man simply turned his back on her, drew up his knees and rested his chin on folded arms. Edith Powell sniffed in disgust. Arrogant Hun. "I'll report you to the police," she told his back. "I'm sure you shouldn't be here." She wheeled her horse and set off back to carry out her threat.

Karl watched her figure until she disappeared over the brow of the hill. He saw her again ten minutes later, trotting down the road leading to the isolated farms around Hay-on-Wye. He calculated he had an hour at the most.

It was a little less than an hour when two police cars drove fast up the single-track road, scattering sheep as they went.

He knew it would take them some time. They would have to walk over the Bluff. He spent this time looking again towards the hill where Katherine lived, but where he would no longer. He supposed he ought to be able to see the farmhouse, since the Bluff was visible from there, but found it difficult to be certain which white blob on the distant hillside was Lane Head Farm.

When he saw six policemen reach the summit of the Bluff, Karl stood up. They had yet to walk its length to reach him, but he felt he might as well show them where he was. He was cold and very hungry by now.

As he rose one of the policemen shouted a warning. "Stay where you are!"

They began to run towards him and were quite out of breath when they surrounded him, puffing noisily.

"Search him," the sergeant ordered one of his men.

Slowly Karl reached inside his jacket for his pocketknife and gave it to the young constable, but he was searched nonetheless. His eyes fixed on the distant hillside, he scarecely seemed to notice.

The policemen began to relax. They were led to believe he would resist; clearly his night out on the exposed Bluff had quietened him. The last thing they had wanted after a rapid ascent of the Bluff was to overpower a crazy Jerry.

Karl allowed himself to be escorted down to the waiting cars. He took one last backward glance at the brooding mass of rock, before he was pushed into the back of a car.

The telephone call came at midday. Robert rushed back into the kitchen to tell his mother.

"They've found him! He's all right."

Gertie sank onto a chair in relief. "Thank God for that," she exclaimed. "Where was he?"

"On Hay Bluff, would you believe. They've already taken him back to Kingshill. They said Dad could go over there, since he had asked to see Karl. Wish I could go with him, but they said only Dad was to go."

"Well he'll have to have his lunch," Gertie said. "He's out seeing Mr Bridges at the moment."

Robert went back to the telephone to let Sarah know. "Apparently he came without any trouble," he told a delighted Sarah. "He must have known the police were coming, yet he didn't try to run. That's a good sign. I hope. We'll have to see what Dad says."

"You really thought he would try to kill himself, didn't you?"

"Yes. Then again, at this time of year, a night in the open on Hay Bluff could do the trick. We don't know how long he intended sitting there, do we? He'd been there all night."

"Well at least he's safe now. I'll go and tell Katherine the good news. Let me know what your father says."

Donald did not wait for lunch. He took sandwiches and drove straight to Kingshill, fifteen miles away. He had never been there before, and was surprised how different it was from the small hostel at Upper Claydon. Kingshill Camp was not only large, but bore the hallmark of its intended function: security. Barbed wire and gates separated the inmates' breeze-block huts from wooden administration huts, although most of the perimeter fencing had been removed. The place retained a grim air of internment.

He was checked through the gates and led to a nearby office where Major Alderton awaited him.

Alderton shook his hand. "Good afternoon, Doctor. We've spoken by phone, of course. It's a pleasure to meet you at last. Do sit down!"

His genial voice did not fit the straight-backed, impeccable figure who faced Donald. The Major was a career soldier who ran his camp on well-defined lines. He aimed to be scrupulously fair with the prisoners in his charge, but demanded a strict adherence to discipline. Driesler's recent exploits were a notable digression. Fights between prisoners were not uncommon, but for a prisoner to attack a local civilian was a grievous crime. Not content with that, Driesler had then caused local police forces to be alerted to find him. Major Alderton was not a happy man. To cap it all, this doctor insisted on seeing the prisoner.

"Thank you for allowing me to come here, Major," Donald was saying. "I hope you agree that this behaviour is very out of character. That's why I'd like to see Sgt Driesler now, to make sure there's no underlying problem that needs attention."

"Medical attention, presumably."

"Quite so. My son has come to know Sgt Driesler well. Knows his background, which you may not. Robert is convinced Driesler was trying to kill himself."

Alderton looked shrewdly at the doctor. "That's quite a claim. Could your son be trying to protect his friend from the consequences of his attack on Captain Kellett?"

Donald contained his irritation. "I very much doubt it. I know Sgt Driesler quite well enough myself to feel uneasy. A talk with him would be very much appreciated."

"Very well. If you think it necessary, doctor. I always bow to medical opinion. I'll send for him." He paused. "There will be a guard on the door. I don't want him absconding again."

Donald was shown to the Adjutant's room, a small office nearby, where he sat and waited. When Karl arrived he was

221

dark-eyed and sullen. Donald waited for the guard to close the door behind him.

"Good to see you're safe, Karl. We were worried."

Karl sat in silence, his eyes downcast.

"Why didn't you come back to us? Why did you stay out all night?"

Karl raised his head and looked at him defiantly. "You would not want me in your house. I went to Hay Bluff to have some freedom, before they lock me up."

"What do you mean, "wouldn't want you in my house"? Why ever not?"

"For the same reason Katherine wanted me to leave and never come back. You must know by now!"

The bitterness was unmistakeable. Donald was amazed at the change. He spoke quietly and gently. "I know you were in the SS, but Robert assured me there is no significance in that. Karl, you are always welcome in my house, for what you are, not what you were. I knew you to be a considerate, well-meaning and good person. My opinion has not changed."

"I want to hear Katherine say that," Karl muttered.

"Yes. It's unfortunate she's taken it so badly." At least Karl was talking, getting it out of his system.

"Kellett did not tell them about Katherine and me."

"How do you know that?"

"I have been told there will be a court-martial, but only because I hurt Kellett. Already I have solitary confinement for twenty-eight days because I was away from the permitted area. They said nothing about Katherine."

It was the maximum permissible time in solitary. Donald knew how hard that would hit Karl. "You've grown used to your freedom, haven't you? Solitary's not going to be easy for you."

Karl did not answer. Donald had no idea how he felt being locked away even for the short time since returning to the camp.

"Is there anything I can do for you? Any way I can help?"

"Only Katherine can help me."

222

Donald sighed. "I just wish there were something I could do, Karl. I don't like seeing you like this." He stood up to leave. "Don't forget about us. We'll do our best to keep in touch." Karl scarcely seemed to hear him. "I'll be off then. Goodbye, Karl. Chin up."

Donald reported back to the commandant.

"Well, doctor. What did you make of him?" asked Alderton.

"To tell you the truth, Major, I'm still worried. I'm afraid I can't say anything more definite. I don't think solitary confinement is a good idea; especially for that length of time."

"Serious breaches of discipline warrant such punishment. The Senior German Officer here agreed with the sentence." Alderton began to tire of this doctor trying to interfere in camp business. "We have a doctor here, whom I will appraise of your fears. That's as far as I'm prepared to go. Now, if you will excuse me, Doctor, I have a great deal to do."

Donald returned to his car, glad to be outside the gates. He knew most prisoners wandered freely in and out now, yet the feeling of being penned was all-pervasive. Twenty-eight days in solitary then whatever punishment was decided by the court-martial! Donald shuddered.

Robert and Gertie were waiting. When Robert heard about Karl's punishment he groaned. "I don't think Karl can take it, Dad. It's the worst thing possible at the moment, to be shut away to brood, with nobody to talk to. It'll make his nightmares worse, I'm certain."

Donald was sympathetic but unable to offer consolation. "Alderton made it perfectly plain he considered I was overstepping the mark. There was nothing I could do."

"He's been on his own too long."

Donald wished Robert would explain. "I don't suppose we'll hear anything more for at least a month. Might as well get used to the fact that he's not going to be living here any more. Gertie, you'd better get Megan to pack his belongings and have them sent over."

Katherine stood at the five-barred gate of Steps Meadow and looked out at Hay Bluff. Why on earth had he gone there? She watched lambs frolicking in the meadow, butting their mother's udders to release the milk. They were free now from the darkness of the lambing sheds; free to run in the warm sunshine and breathe fresh air. Freedom. That was what Karl had wanted on Hay Bluff. She felt remorse for her part in his confinement, but would not allow herself more than that. She was determined to ignore the emptiness within her. When Sarah left she would be alone. Andrew had sent two farmhands to help out, but she refrained from having him back. Audrey had a job to do there. Katherine wished she would get on with it.

She was about to return to the orchards to check on the two new hands, when she heard a horse clatter across the cobbles behind her. She turned to see Andrew astride Trojan, watching her.

"There you are, Katherine!" Andrew called out. "Such a fine day I thought I'd take a bit of fresh air and come to see how my two men were faring." He clicked his tongue. Trojan stepped towards Katherine. She held his bridle while Andrew dismounted.

"Admiring your flock, were you?" he asked. "You did well to have so many lambs survive, considering you had to cope all by yourself. That must have been a terrible time for you, cut off by the snow. But you've come through with flying colours – an admirable achievement."

Katherine realised he was dismissing Karl's part in everything, almost as though Karl, and their time together, had never existed; an aberration on Katherine's part, nothing more.

"I wondered if you felt like coming into Hereford with me, at the weekend," he said suddenly, laying his hand over hers on the gate. "We could go dancing, see a film. Have a meal. Whatever you like."

Katherine was tempted. She had not been out for so long. None of those things had been possible with Karl, though at the time she had not missed them. "I'm sorry Andrew. I've a ticket to see the Penchurch Players on Saturday. Gertie Murdoch's in it; I promised I would go." She realised there would be a spare ticket – Karl's. "Perhaps you'd like to come too."

Andrew beamed. "I'd love to!"

When she saw them together in the village hall, Audrey Patterson wondered why it was that Katherine was still with Andrew Kellett. She went up to Sarah during the interval.

"I thought you said she'd finished with him," she whispered behind her hand.

"She has," Sarah replied in similarly hushed tones. "He's proving harder to shake than she'd anticipated, that's all. She wants you to do your bit, if you're still willing."

Sarah hoped her sister would forgive her scheming. She was doing it for Katherine's own good – and Karl's too. She had to get those two back together somehow. Katherine would never be happy with Andrew as second best. It was Katherine's rigid sense of moral duty which caused the problem now. Karl was in the wrong, there was no doubt about it. Yet somehow he did not fit the image she had of the SS. She just had to make Katherine see it too.

"Shall I do that then?" Audrey's voice broke in on Sarah's self-debate.

"What? Sorry, my mind was wandering. Do what?"

Audrey rolled her eyes in frustration. "Follow him out riding one day and ... well ... see how it goes," she repeated.

Sarah shrugged. "You know best about these things. I'll leave it to you; I won't be here anyway. Write to me at Bristol and keep me informed of progress, won't you?"

The lights dipped as a warning to the audience to return to their seats. Sarah rejoined Robert and Donald Murdoch. Katherine was standing with Andrew near the stage. They returned to their seats just as the curtains opened. Sarah sighed to herself. Audrey might have a tough time luring Andrew away.

Summer weather coincided with the onset of Double Summer Time on 13th April. Spring had been all too brief an interlude.

Down in the orchards Katherine was examining the blossom buds. The James Grieves were ready for spraying. The last thing she needed now was a late frost. The day was quite hot, as she instructed the two new hands, Les Whitelock and Dick Davies, which trees to spray.

Lambing had been successful, the orchards were coming on apace. Katherine breathed in sweetly scented air and lifted her face to feel the sun. But Karl cast a shadow on her happiness. If only she could forget him. Completely.

It was stuffy inside his cell. The barred window did not open. Karl waited impatiently for his half-hour exercise period. He could see blue sky over the roof of the administration block opposite. Yesterday he had looked at it for endless hours, seeing the occasional bird, measuring the progress of the clouds, following one another sheep-like, always in the same direction.

He dozed a lot during the day too. He slept better then. If he did have a bad dream, at least it was light in the cell, and he could more easily wipe the dream from his vision. At night the dream would linger. He would have to count the stars to distract himself, but as soon as he faced the darkness it would return once more.

He heard shuffling feet outside his door, then the turning of a key. The door swung open.

On the first day the guard had made some attempt at being friendly. Now, six days later, he knew better than to try to make conversation. Scarcely a word was exchanged. Even the German who brought food from the kitchens fared no better.

"Out!"

Karl walked down the short corridor to an outer door. There were no other occupants in the cells which these days were only very rarely used. Karl stepped into a small, fenced-off exercise yard. "Tommy" would stand and watch, check his wristwatch every so often, until the allotted time was up. Karl made slow circuits of the yard. He had no inclination to attempt anything more energetic. Even so time passed quickly and he found himself back in his confining cell, with his small patch of sky. He was allowed out each morning, to use the small washroom in the cell-block; then again in the afternoon for exercise. His days revolved around this pattern for another week, but Karl did not keep a track of days. What difference whether it was twelve or thirteen days to go? He couldn't care less. He couldn't care about anything, except trying to escape from the nightmares.

When he tried to stay awake at night, he could hear a pair of owls in the woods on the other side of the perimeter fence; a sound he had been used to in his room at Lane Head. When dawn broke, the hooting was replaced by the rattling squawk-cluck of a pheasant. A pair of sparrows were nest-building under the eaves of the cell-block; their noisy twittering told him that the security of daylight had arrived. He could close his eyes at last, until breakfast.

A brief interlude came with his court-martial. Kellett was there to give evidence, but refrained from mentioning Katherine. Karl was sentenced to six months in camp for assaulting Kellett, then returned to his cell to finish his solitary confinement.

On the sixteenth day he was particularly slow to wake himself from a bad dream. He was fighting for breath as he opened his eyes. He went to the window wishing he could throw it wide open to dry the sweat from his face. The desire for fresh air grew stronger and suddenly he put his hand through the bars and banged his fist against the glass. There was not enough room between the bars and the pane, however, for him to exert sufficient force on the glass to break it. He tried pushing with the palm of his hand as hard as could. With a splintering crack, his hand went right through the pane, ripping his flesh against the shards of glass as it went. Heedless of the blood, he pulled away more glass to enlarge the hole he had made. The air was still. No breeze came in to refresh him. Angrily he withdrew his hand, catching his wrist on a sharp edge as he did so. The blood was really flowing now. He hurled himself at the door, battering at it with his hands and shoulders. He had to get out into the fresh air.

His hand left a lurid smear down the door which transferred itself to his face as he leaned against the door, crying now in his rage to get out. Footsteps came running down the corridor. As the door opened, Karl burst out through it, sending the guard crashing against the corridor wall. The man gave a warning shout and jumped to his feet to give chase. As he reached the outer door, Karl was dimly aware of more feet running from the administration block. He hesitated briefly, unsure which direction to run, long enough for the guard to tackle him and bring him down. He struggled under the weight of the man, almost shoving him aside in his desperate attempts to be free. Three other men reached them and joined the fray. They hauled Karl back to his cell, where they noticed the blood-spattered door and the state of the prisoner.

"Christ! Fetch the doctor!" one of them yelled, as they struggled to restrain Karl, who was pinned to the floor by their combined weight. Eventually he stopped struggling, but the men did not loosen their hold on him until the German doctor arrived, accompanied by a British officer. As soon as he felt the weight on him lift, Karl began to move again, kicking out at whoever came near. He dimly heard some discussion going on in his own language, then orders were barked in English.

"Hold him still!"

Karl felt his arms and legs securely held. The British officer bent down and began to roll up Karl's left sleeve. The doctor approached, hypodermic needle at the ready.

Karl arched his back and let out a yell of terror. "*Nein!*" The hands on him increased their grip as he fought to escape their grasp. "*Bitte! Nein!*" he shouted again, over and over. "*Bitte, NEIN! NEIN!*" Then blackness began to creep in, shutting out the doctor's anxious face.

He opened his eyes slowly. A metal lampshade hung from the ceiling above his head, the bulb in it glowing brightly, so that his eyes watered to look at it. He felt tired and made no effort to move until he became aware of the ache in his right hand. He looked down towards it on top of the blankets, bound up with bandage. A small spot of blood had seeped through to the outer layer. Karl's eyes fixed on the spot.

Later he began to wonder where he was. The bulb was out, the room was light. Day. He still felt tired. Thirsty too. He turned his head slowly. There was another bed nearby, empty, and beyond that another. He was in a long room, with a partitioned-off area at the end, like an office. The doctor's office, it dawned on him. He was in hospital. He turned his head the other way and saw a small chest. On top stood a glass of water. He lifted his left arm and reached for the glass. His fingers would not grasp it. He dropped it, heard it smash. Wearily he lay back on his pillow and watched the lampshade sway above him in a gentle breeze.

When next he opened his eyes he was no longer thirsty. Nor hungry. He could not account for that. There was another glass of water beside his bed. Even though he was not thirsty, he thought he would try to pick it up. He was not feeling so tired as before. He flexed his fingers a few times, then reached for the glass. This time he got it to his mouth, and took a few careful sips before replacing it. He looked round the ward. All the beds were still empty. He seemed to be the only patient. No wonder it was quiet.

The ward was really a hut, a temporary construction. He tried to work out where he might be. Through the window he could see another hut, like this one. Beyond that some woods. Some of the trees were well in leaf, others had still to emerge from their winter sleep. At least he knew the time of year. He heard voices in the distance, cheering, like at a football match. The door at the end of the hut opened.

It was dark again. He was still not hungry. He could not remember eating. Also his bladder seemed empty, yet to his certain knowledge he had not relieved himself since he first woke in the hospital. He knew there were times he missed, times things happened he was not aware of. The dressing on his right hand had been changed. The red spot was no longer there.

He felt uneasy. He realised he had no idea what had happened to his hand, even though his mind seemed more alert, his body more under control. He sat up. Where was everybody? Why was no one there to tend to him? Perhaps they were all outside. Holding his right hand clear of the blankets, he pushed them aside and swivelled on the bed to put his feet on the floor. Carefully he stood up and began to walk down between the rows of beds towards the end door. As he neared the office he became aware there was someone in it.

He was back in bed again. A different bed this time. A room to himself. The building was different too. Lampshade white, not green. Cream-coloured walls, floor linoleum. Flowery curtains. By the window an upright chair with a pile of clothing. A washstand with toothbrush, toothpaste, soap. And a towel. No razor. He felt his chin. It was smooth.

Beside the bed was a small table. On it a wristwatch and some magazines. The wristwatch was not his. He glanced at the top magazine, then looked again, more closely. He picked it up. To his immense surprise it was foreign. English, he thought. Yes, there was a picture of London. Why had they given him an English magazine? He closed it again. The date on the cover caught his eye. April 1947.

Karl dropped the magazine in shock. 1947! Was it a trick? What were they playing at? This was 194.... He tried to think what year it was. He cast his mind back for some kind of a reference point. Home. When was he last home? He could not even picture his home. Suddenly an image of the black and white half-timbered house came to mind. Memories came flooding back. His return, wounded from that terrible winter in Russia, leave in the early Spring of 1943. His thoughts dwelt briefly on an idyllic time at home with Ilse. That was not what he was trying to remember. Yugoslavia. Early summer in Serbia. What came next? Nothing. A blank. It was Spring now. He knew that from the trees with their bright green leaves. The magazine confirmed April – but the year!

Karl felt lost. He turned to the magazine to try to find answers. One thing was certain from the photographs.

England was still in English hands. No German signs or uniforms in the streets. Was the war over? The pictures showed rebuilding, plans of new towns, smiling faces. No account of warfare. Perhaps it was not that kind of magazine.

He went to the window and looked into a small quadrangle, enclosed by the brick walls of the building. In it were some wickerwork chairs, all unoccupied, although abandoned books and magazines were evidence of recent use. The place had the look of a hospital. He looked again at his own right hand. He saw purple scars where cuts were healing. Around the base of his thumb and on the back of his wrist were dressings covering deeper wounds.

He decided to get dressed. It was something real to do in this otherwise unreal world. He had been provided with a uniform of sorts; plain chocolate brown, British-style battle dress. It fitted reasonably well, even the slip-on shoes. There was no belt for the trousers. He folded his pyjamas and placed them neatly on the chair, his right hand stiff and awkward, but useable.

As he turned he noticed that the door to his room was ajar. It had not been like that before. He went to it and stood for a moment, listening. He pulled the door open and looked into the corridor. It was deserted. All the other doors were either wide open or securely shut. None was ajar.

He turned left and wandered slowly down the corridor. He remembered doing a similar thing in that other hospital, but could not remember the outcome of his expedition. At the end of the corridor was a pair of swing doors with frosted glass windows. He pushed against one door and stepped out into a hallway.

He was back in his room again.

Where was everybody? Why would no one tell him what was going on? There were people around. He could hear footsteps in the distance. He sat on the end of the bed and put his head in his hands. He felt so alone ... and afraid.

He began to make use of the wristwatch. He kept a close track of time. There were large chunks of the day which he could not account for. Some meals he found placed on a tray on the table beside his bed. Other meals were experienced only by the after-taste of food in his mouth. He never shaved yet he had no beard. After a few days he noticed the wristwatch left a white stripe on his skin when he took it off. He must have been out in the sunshine.

He was sitting in the courtyard. As usual he was alone. It was pleasant to be outside at last. He felt he was being watched. By whom or from where he could not tell. He checked his watch at five minute intervals. He did not move from the seat. Time disappeared when he tried to explore.

He picked up a magazine. To his great relief it was in German. It was called "*Wochenpost*" and answered many questions. He was a prisoner of war in Britain and the war was over. Too many questions remained unanswered. What had happened in Germany to end the war? Were his family still alive? Did they know where he was? What about Ilse? Was she still waiting for him?

He felt lonelier than ever. Where *was* everyone?

He looked at his English watch. Ten past two. Pleasant as it was out here in the sun, he felt restless. He stood up and looked for a door. There was one behind him. It was locked. He could easily climb through an open window. Why had they locked him out?

He was back in his room. He noted the time. Twenty minutes gone. He tried the door. It opened. He shut it again. He felt safer with it shut. The fear was almost gone, but he could not shake it off entirely. If only he had someone to talk to.

CHAPTER TWELVE

Weeding the rockery was a task Katherine enjoyed when she needed to think. She needed to now. She had to decide exactly what she felt for Andrew. It was three weeks since that dreadful day when she had learned the truth about Karl and had to turn back to Andrew for help and companionship. She was in danger of letting old habits of association with Andrew take over again, yet knew she would never feel about him as she had about Karl. She felt her anger rise at that name. At first she had felt pain with her anger; now she had managed to harden her heart.

But how did she feel about Andrew? Should she tell Audrey she still wanted Andrew? He was impatient for some kind of commitment. She had been to a couple of dances with him since the play, but there was no sparkle in their relationship. If she dallied too long, he might indeed give up and notice Audrey.

She pulled up the last piece of groundsel, tipped the basket of weeds on the compost heap, then called to Joss. The evening sun was still warm as they set off up the track to the woods. She had not been up there, except to retrieve the tools Karl had left, including the axe. She shuddered at the thought of what might have happened. No, she could never have Karl back. But Andrew ..?

She sat on a tree stump in a glade Karl had cleared. He had left a stack of ash poles, useful for sheep hurdles, to one side of the glade, and a pile of kindling beside it. There was a peacefulness in the quiet wood, like a church. She almost felt the presence of Karl's gods. She almost sensed Karl himself, as though at any moment she would feel his fingers on her hair, smell the warm earthiness of his skin. He had an animal attraction which she found irresistible. It was why she had so easily given herself to him. She felt that need now, here in the stillness of the warm wood.

Abruptly she made her decision. She did not want Andrew. She needed time. And a fresh start. She would arrange a friendly picnic after church on Sunday and tell him then.

Katherine saw Audrey at church. She gave Andrew the slip for a moment, taking Audrey to one side of the churchyard. "The way's clear for you, Audrey. I've finally decided to cast off all claims to Andrew this afternoon."

Audrey was pleased. "I wish you luck. Your loss is my gain. I've already got my foot in the door!"

That settled it for Katherine. If Andrew had already started looking in Audrey's direction, he could jolly well have her. She left Audrey daydreaming, and rejoined Andrew.

"You look very fetching under that hat," he said. "A real peach, waiting to be plucked! Come on, darling, let's be off away from all these people. Where did you have in mind?"

He had started calling her "darling" again after the play. To Katherine's ears it sounded even more hollow and meaningless than before. She fingered the neckline of her dress.

"I thought we might sit by the river. There's a nice grassy bank, not too far from the road, next to the orchards. No point driving far and wasting petrol."

"Fine. I got Cook to pack us something nice, and there's a bottle of a rather fine wine too." He led the way to where his car was parked on the verge and helped her into the narrow bucket seat. They drove up the valley road towards Lane Head, past the orchards, until Katherine told him to pull in by a gate to the meadow.

"Don't want to be too close to the road," Andrew said, lifting a blanket and hamper from the car. They walked on along the river bank, out of sight of the road. Katherine spread the blanket over the long grass.

It was too early to eat. Andrew lit a cigarette, lay back propped on his elbows, and patted the blanket for Katherine.

She sat beside him, legs tucked under, and idly plucked buttercups. She wondered how to tell him this was to be their last time together, and thought it best to wait until after they had eaten.

"How's life without Sarah again?" Andrew flicked away a troublesome midge which seemed tolerant of cigarette smoke.

"I'm growing used to it. I quite like being on my own really, now the weather is fine. Last night I went for a walk with Joss up to the woods. It was so peaceful up there and I ..."

"Should have been over at Fairley's on Thursday," he interrupted. "Had a cracking game of bridge. Audrey was there, as it happened, so she was my partner. Why won't you come out during the week?"

"I've told you before. I have the farm to run; housework to do. I don't have cooks and maids and gardeners like you."

"That can easily be rectified. Just need to wear that ring. You still have it, don't you?"

"Yes, I still have it," she said wearily.

Andrew stubbed out his cigarette and sat up. "You work too hard, darling. Now you're on your own, why don't you give yourself a break? My men can manage the farm. Come and live at the Grange. My parents are happy to have you stay there until we get married. It's pointless trying to keep this place going by yourself!"

He had brought up the subject. It would have to be settled. "I don't want to marry you, Andrew," she told him quietly. "I decided last night this would be our last time together."

"Why, for heaven's sake? That Kraut's gone in disgrace. What's holding you back? I want you to be my wife, Katherine!" He gripped her by both arms, and pulled her towards him, kissing her hard to emphasise his love for her. She pulled away, her lips bruised by his onslaught.

"I don't love you, can't you realise that? I loved him. I know he loved me!" It was true, she realised. Karl had not lied about that, despite what she had told herself. "You could never love me like he did."

She could have kicked herself the moment she said that.

His grip on her arms tightened. "I'll show you I can love you! Better even! I'll give you a reason to marry me!" He pushed her over, her feet trapped awkwardly beneath her. She tried to kick them free, but was pinned down by his weight. To her horror she felt it was not only his fury which was aroused. She tried to throw him off, but he held her still.

"You let *him* do this," he hissed.

Katherine felt his fingers on her neck. He would get his way whether she consented or not. She decided it was better not to fight him. She lay still and felt his hands leave her throat and pass over her body, pulling the straps of her dress, exposing her slip, then her breasts. She did not move or cry out until it was all over. When he was finished he sat up to light a cigarette. She calmly readjusted her clothing, smoothed down her hair, picked up her hat and bag and walked off up the meadow.

She heard him call out after her. "Think I'll stick with Audrey! She's a hell of a lot more fun! Mind you, she let slip your Kraut got in there before me too!" His laughter taunted her all the way up the hill.

Defiled was not the word for it. Violated. She lay in the bath, trying to control the shivers which had begun as soon as she reached home. She was not sure which she was more angry about; Andrew's behaviour or his parting shot about Karl and Audrey. She had been naïve to think a friendly picnic and chat would solve everything.

That evening she telephoned Sarah in her lodgings. "Sarah! Thank goodness you're in. I simply had to speak to someone."

Sarah could hear that something was very wrong. "What's the matter?"

Now it had come to it, Katherine found it difficult as usual to express herself. "I've finally seen the last of Andrew. Only after he raped me. That's not all. He told me that German had ... had ... with Audrey! And I believe him. That's the only thing the brute wanted all along."

"I believe it's Karl you're talking about," Sarah said coldly. "And you're wrong. Audrey had great trouble seducing Karl. The only reason she succeeded was because he was upset when Daddy died."

"You knew about it?" Katherine gasped. "Why is it that people always hide the facts from me? First Karl. Now you. Why didn't you mention it?"

"There was no point. It happened before you and Karl got together."

"Well how come both you and Andrew knew about it? That's something else Karl hid from me."

Sarah was incensed. "Katherine, why did you phone me? Did you want sympathy or something? Because if you keep on denigrating Karl like that, you'll not get it from me. What's all this about Andrew raping you? Did he?"

Katherine pulled herself together. She was alienating Sarah. "I had to ... let him. I was frightened what he might do if I didn't."

"Well then! He did rape you! Are you going to tell the police?"

"No! Of course not! The whole thing's such a mess. And partly my fault. It would cause trouble for everyone. Anyway, how could I possibly prove it? Audrey's got him now, and good luck to her!"

Sarah had not envisaged her plan working out quite like this, but nevertheless, one thing had now been resolved. Katherine was free of Andrew.

"Pop down and tell Gertie all about it. She can be perfectly discreet when she has to. I think you could do with someone nearer home to talk to."

"That means I'll have to tell her everything, even about Karl and me. I don't want anyone else to know what I let that Nazi do to me."

"Katherine! Stop *calling* him that. Anyway, I'm sure Gertie has some idea of what went on. You had it written all over your face."

"Did I? Perhaps I ought to tell her." Then, rather grudgingly, she added: "Thanks."

237

It was two weeks before Katherine finally decided not to mention to Gertie what had happened. She wanted to be sure first there were no unpleasant consequences from Andrew's assault. With the onset of her period she had no further cause for worry, especially since Andrew was now very obviously going around with Audrey. For Andrew's sake, Katherine kept quiet.

Andrew did not keep quiet. His family was told that the engagement between himself and Katherine was definitely over. As the news filtered around the village, it became connected in people's minds with Karl's sudden disappearance. That such a respectable and upright girl as Katherine Carter should have been lured by the charms of a German was the talk of the village. Those who were amongst the last to accept Karl's presence in the village were first to condemn Katherine.

Mrs Collins was most voluble. "It was immoral and illegal", she told everyone.

Mrs Tucker did her best to shield Katherine, reminding her customers how Lane Head Farm had survived the winter because of Karl's valiant efforts. Housewives waiting for the market day bus to Hereford talked of little else and speculated interminably about whether "Miss Katherine" had slept with the German. Some even dared to admit they could see why she had fallen for him.

Although the villagers were divided, the county was not. Katherine knew she was no longer welcome at Froxley Grange. That attitude was mirrored by other landowners influenced by Froxley Grange. Friends of the Kelletts no longer dared entertain or speak favourably of Katherine. The Murdochs were, of course, steadfast friends throughout, and she spent Sundays with them as before. She was determined to face the whole business with dignity, remembering, rather ruefully, her ideas of defying public opinion should she have become pregnant by Karl. So on Sunday afternoons she watched Robert playing in the village cricket match and helped Gertie and the other stalwart village ladies serve tea.

Robert was a strong member of the cricket team now, fully fit at last and raring to start his medical studies in London in October.

One Sunday he sat with her on the stone wall of the rose garden at Yew Tree Lodge. "I really miss Karl," he confided. "I've not managed to contact him since his return to Kingshill."

"I suppose it's all part of his punishment," she commented.

"Yes, but surely he could get somebody to post a letter? Even if they won't give him mine, he must know someone who walks past a letter box," Robert complained. "He must be well out of solitary by now. So why hasn't he been in touch?"

Katherine shrugged. She was really not that interested in Karl, but she let Robert talk about him, knowing what good friends they had been.

"I think I'll ask Dad if he can find out," Robert said pensively. "They let him in once. They might again."

"You're still worried about him, aren't you?"

"Yes I am. And I wish I could tell you why, so you'd understand the whole story. But I promised Karl I wouldn't tell anyone, and I haven't."

"Well I wouldn't want to hear it. The more I hear about him, the less I like him." Katherine mentioned what Andrew had told her about Karl and Audrey, and that Sarah seemed to have known about it too.

"I hate to tell you this, Katherine, but I knew too. Karl told me."

Gertie watched the two of them out of the kitchen window, where she was finishing the trifle, prior to pouring sherries before lunch. She had refused Katherine's offer of help, insisting that Katherine had a good rest one day a week. She knew that with haymaking and sheepshearing in the offing, Katherine would have her work cut out to feed herself adequately. Robert had offered to help with haymaking, tired as he was now of reading through the same old medical books. He needed more outdoor activity to toughen him up before medical school.

Gertie spread a thin layer of whipped cream over the custard, arranged glacé cherries on top, and put the trifle in the larder. She glanced out of the window again. Katherine seemed to be cross about something. She had never been the same since Karl. Such a shame Karl had never mentioned he was in the SS, and more to the point, that Robert had not told them.

After Katherine had gone home Robert brought up the subject again. He was jubilant after the cricket team's success that day. "I only wish Karl had been there to see it. Wish I knew how he was. I was only saying to Katherine today, I was surprised we hadn't heard anything. I did think he might be able to write to us, at least. You couldn't have a word with the commandant, could you, Dad? Just to make sure he's all right."

Donald remembered his last meeting with Major Alderton and grimaced. "To tell the truth, I was wondering myself what had become of him. I don't fancy trying to get round Alderton again. I suppose I could ask to speak to someone else."

Donald contacted the camp the following morning. He was put through to Lieutenant Smart, who was more helpful. Afterwards Donald went straight to Robert in the garden. Gertie was there too, deadheading tulips. Donald called them over to the deckchairs on the lawn.

"I've just telephoned Kingshill Camp. Rather bad news. You were right to be anxious, Robert."

Robert shifted uneasily.

"About two weeks after he started solitary he had some kind of breakdown; tried to break out of the cell. Supposedly went berserk. He put his hand through a window, cutting himself badly. So they fetched the camp doctor who sedated Karl." Donald caught his son's eye.

"He was given an injection, you mean?" Robert asked in horror.

"Yes. That was enough to send him over the edge. After that a shutter came down. He won't acknowledge anyone's presence. Has completely shut his mind to other people. On his own, he behaves normally, feeds himself and the like; but

240

the instant somebody comes near, he withdraws into his shell, unaware of anyone."

Gertie was appalled. "Oh, Donald, how dreadful! Can they do anything?"

Donald shook his head. "Not at the camp. They've sent Karl to a POW hospital near Gloucester. If we want more information we'll have to phone there."

Robert was silent, then seemed to make up his mind. "I've got to have a word with the doctors there. They'll have to know all about Karl, if they're going to be able to help him."

Gloucester was an hour by road. It was another hot day in the middle of May, when Robert wheeled his motorbike from the garage and set off for his meeting with a Dr Goldberg.

It astonished him that a Jewish doctor worked in a POW hospital, but he quickly reasoned that Christians could not hold the monopoly on forgiveness and reconciliation. It just seemed an immensely harder task for a Jew.

The road as far as Ross-on-Wye was reasonably good, but he had to keep his speed down on the winding route over the hills. Then the graceful pinnacles of Gloucester Cathedral's tower appeared above the plain of the Severn valley, and Robert referred to his map.

He found the place at last, and was uneasily reminded of his own stay in a military hospital. What had happened to Karl could so easily have happened to himself. He had seen it happen to fellow prisoners: the moment came when they gave up all hope and collapsed in on themselves, waiting only to die.

Yet with Karl it was not quite the same. They said Karl was able to look after himself, so long as he was alone. There must be some other factor at work here.

Robert reported to the main entrance, and was led down a series of corridors, through several sets of swing doors, to an office marked "Dr S.A.Goldberg". In a middle-European accent, the orderly told him to wait on a chair outside.

Many of the staff here would have to be German-speakers, Robert reasoned. Especially a psychiatrist like Goldberg. If this were wartime, Karl might have been repatriated, but now facilities for treatment were probably better here. If he could be treated. Robert felt a growing pessimism. Karl was still confined, deprived of the freedom he craved, and of the love he had found and lost.

Robert sat on a hard-backed chair and waited. Some magazines were scattered on a small table by him, some English, some German. He picked up a German one, out of interest, and tried to make sense of it, but soon put it down, exchanging it for an English one.

He waited about ten minutes without seeing another soul. Then swing doors at the end of the corridor opened and a solid man hurried down the corridor. Mid-thirties, Robert guessed from the sprinkling of grey hairs amongst the dark brown mat.

Dr Goldberg held out his hand. "Mr Murdoch?" Robert nodded and stood to shake the doctor's hand. "I hope I haven't kept you waiting too long. Do come in." His English was good, with only a slight trace of an accent. His voice was deep and pleasant, matching a friendly exterior. He sat behind a desk, clear of all paperwork, and reached for a file from a desk drawer. Robert sat opposite.

"I'm very grateful to you for contacting me," Goldberg said, putting on a pair of reading glasses. "The camp omitted to tell me that Karl had a good friend outside camp. I asked Lt Smart there for names of any comrades of Karl's, but he said there weren't any. A reason for Karl to find himself here for a start, I thought. A man with no friends is a man in trouble." He put down the thin file and peered at Robert. "But you are his friend?"

"Yes. Karl stayed at our house, and worked on a farm in the same valley. I got to know him quite well. He told me things I know he told no one else, which I'm sure the camp wasn't aware of. If that's all of his file," he nodded at the document on the desk, "it's likely you don't know either."

"I know very little. The report said he'd been dismissed by his employer, a Miss Carter, for attacking a friend, a Mr

242

Kellett," he read from the file. "He went missing, was found the following day on top of a hill some miles away. Punished with four weeks solitary confinement, managed two before his breakdown. Not much to go on."

"I can tell you a great deal more than that. But first I'd like to know how he is, if you don't mind. Has there been any improvement?"

"None I can detect. It's very difficult to assess his state of mind when any kind of communication is impossible. At first he was in better spirits than we would expect. Recently, he has shown more overt signs of depression. It means keeping a careful eye on him, yet allowing him sufficient time by himself for his more "conscious" moments." He saw Robert's puzzled look. "Perhaps you would like a chance to see him, before you tell me about him."

Robert jumped at the chance.

Dr Goldberg reached for the telephone. "George, can you tell me the whereabouts of Karl Driesler at the moment?"

Robert faintly heard an answering voice.

"Is he alone? Can you move the others away for me please? I've someone here who wants to observe Karl, on his own. We'll be along in a few minutes. Thank you." He put down the receiver. "We're all on first name terms in this part of the hospital. Makes a friendlier atmosphere. Now, while George is sorting that out for us, perhaps you can start to fill me in."

Dr Goldberg produced a pencil and notepaper from a drawer and settled himself to listen. He interrupted only once. "Are you saying there was a physical relationship between Karl and Miss Carter?" He saw Robert's hesitation. "I need to know."

Reluctantly Robert replied. "Yes. There was. They wanted to get married as soon as it became possible. Once Miss Carter was told that Karl was in the SS, she wanted nothing more to do with him."

Dr Goldberg nodded. "So, now I know what made him depressed, but not why his depression has taken this form. We'll leave that until later. I expect George is ready for us

243

now." He put Karl's file in his drawer, and stood up. "If you would care to follow me please?"

He led Robert down the corridor and along another at right angles. An alert young man in a short white coat stood near a closed door.

"All ready, George?" Dr Goldberg asked him.

"Yes, sir. He's been on his own for about five minutes now. He's started to read his book."

"Thank you, George. I'll give you a call."

George headed for an open area where Robert could see a small group of men sitting in armchairs, some talking, others doing nothing.

Goldberg stood to one side of a nearby window and looked through it carefully. He appeared satisfied with what he saw. "Now, Mr Murdoch, I want you to look through this window, but try not to let yourself be seen. Karl has his back turned to us, more or less, but I think you can see he's reading and turning the pages."

Goldberg stepped aside to let Robert look. Sure enough, there was Karl sitting in a sunny courtyard, calmly reading. Robert saw him slowly turn a page, as though sick to death of reading, then absently brush aside a fly from his face. He turned back to Goldberg. "What happens if we go in?"

Goldberg sighed. "Let's find out, shall we?" He unlocked the door they were standing by. "To keep people from going out and disturbing him," the doctor explained. They stepped into the courtyard.

Karl made no outward sign that he heard the key turn in the lock, or their voices. He sat still, looking at his book. Goldberg drew up a couple of wickerwork chairs opposite Karl and sat down. Robert, his eyes fixed on Karl, also sat. Karl still did not move or look up.

"He must be aware of our presence to shut himself off like that, and then on again once we have gone," Goldberg said. "All the while we are here it is as though time has stopped for him. He will do nothing spontaneously until we leave. I can touch him; turn his head. He will hold it where I leave it." He reached out, took Karl's chin and turned his head towards

Robert. The eyes were unfocused, the face without expression. "We can feed him with a spoon, or get him to drink. He will co-operate with us in getting him undressed, stand up, sit down or whatever. He is not entirely switched off, you see. At a certain level he wants to survive. His mind allows him to behave appropriately to do that. We don't think he ever contemplated suicide, although we're not taking any chances."

Robert was dumbfounded: Karl was an automaton, who responded only to touch. Tentatively he spoke Karl's name, thinking that perhaps a familiar voice would be recognised. Karl's head did not move, his eyes remained unfocused.

"I'll show you something else."

Goldberg took out a pencil, picked up Karl's hand and wrapped his fingers around the pencil. The pencil stayed in Karl's grasp. When Dr Goldberg came to take back the pencil, Karl let it go. "You see, there is awareness. If only we could find a way to reach him."

Robert looked despondently at the immobile Karl. "Are there no drugs you could give him?"

"To begin with we gave him sedatives, then stimulants; neither seems to affect the main problem. I have yet to try some other tricks, but when you contacted me the other day, I thought it best not to start with those. I wanted to hear what you had to say." He stood up. "Have you seen enough? Shall we return to my office?"

Robert was reluctant to leave Karl so soon, but it seemed he needed to be left alone.

Back in the corridor they again stood and peered through the window. It took a full two minutes before Robert knew for certain that Karl was aware of his surroundings again, then his head moved and he seemed to be reading once more.

Goldberg called down the corridor. "Thank you, George! We've finished." George acknowledged the call; Robert was led back to the office.

"Would you like a cup of coffee before you begin?"

Robert knew he was about to embark upon a long story. "Yes please."

CHAPTER THIRTEEN

A column of starving and freezing Wehrmacht soldiers was pinned down in retreat by a Red Army machine-gun position at the only crossing point of an ice-bound river. With no more ammunition or shells for their artillery or mortars, the exhausted troops radioed headquarters requesting relief from their hopeless position.

Visibility was too poor for an air strike, there was a shortage of fuel for tanks. Leutnant Karl Driesler, newly promoted in the field from the ranks, was sent to take out the Soviet position with his unit of mountain troops. His mission was a success. The Wehrmacht crossed the river, rejoined the supply teams and survived another day. One of the mountain troops was killed, two were wounded. A dying Russian soldier by the machine-gun singled out the officer as the target for his last effort. The bullet hit Karl low in the abdomen even as he was ordering his men to check the bodies for survivors.

At the field hospital, Karl was awarded the Iron Cross, First Class, for a successful mission which saved the lives of over fifty men. His convalescence was followed by a preliminary officers' training course back in Germany, after which he was granted a week's home leave prior to rejoining his unit.

The people of Medebach gave their local hero a warm reception, the warmest from his long-standing girl-friend, Ilse Brünninghaus. His proud parents took several photographs of Karl in his new officer's uniform, alone and with Ilse. It was Ilse who enjoyed the greater part of Karl's company. Her duties as Kindergarten assistant took up part of her day, but the rest of the time was spent with Karl. His latest near miss with death was a warning to them both that their time together was precious. As he prepared to leave her again, Karl decided that if he survived until his next leave then they

246

would marry, not wait for the war to end. The idea of getting married by proxy, while he was away at the Front, did not appeal to either. Ilse had no qualms about waiting. But her expectation of a decisive and imminent end to the war was not matched by Karl, who had seen what the Red Army was really like. It was no rabble of Stalin's hordes, as the Propaganda Ministry maintained.

That the war would be protracted was confirmed when he received travel orders, not back to Russia, but to Yugoslavia, a country which refused to be tamed. Not content with fighting invaders, the whole country was also in a turmoil of civil war: royalist Chetniks fought communist Partisans fighting Catholic, Nazi-backed Ustashi. Serb fought Croat. In all this carnage whole villages were razed to the ground, the inhabitants shot or hanged by Germans, butchered or burned by Chetniks and Ustashi. Revenge for attacks on Axis troops was swift and brutal.

Four major Axis offensives were mounted against the Partisan guerrillas, who moved by night, ambushing German patrols and sabotaging the vital rail links and bridges. Villages suspected of supplying or harbouring Partisans were wiped out ruthlessly as the Partisan threat grew. The 1st Mountain Division was pulled back from the Eastern Front, to be rejoined in Yugoslavia by a new second lieutenant, recently arrived from Germany.

After a month of continuous heavy fighting, four Partisan divisions once again managed to break through the German encirclement, aided by the rugged terrain, and fled north to the mountains.

On a blisteringly hot day in July, Karl halted his foot patrol at the mouth of a thickly wooded gorge, in a remote part of western Serbia. The stream flowing down the gorge eventually fed the River Ibar, itself a tributary of the Western Morava River. An important road bridge across the Ibar had been blown up the previous night by Partisans, who fled westwards into the wild, rugged hills. Spotted by a scout plane at dawn, the Partisans were sighted by the dozen men under Karl's command disappearing into the depths of the gorge.

Karl ordered the radio operator to pass their position back to base. Radio reception in these mountains was poor; once within the gorge, impossible. It was bold to raid so close to a garrison town, but the Partisans were like goats on the mountains, climbing up hidden trails at a pace even battle-seasoned mountain troops found taxing. Karl watched for movement on the precipitous flanks of the gorge. It was an ideal location for ambush by the Partisans, if they were aware of their pursuers.

Using high-powered binoculars, Karl followed the trail winding along the gorge's left rim until it disappeared into dense woodland which obscured its upper reaches. Karl referred to his map. The trail led to a remote, ruined monastery hidden behind a spur. There was no sign of the Partisans. Either they had already crossed the spur or were hidden by foliage.

According to the scout plane there were half a dozen, lightly armed men. Karl had a dozen fresh troops at his disposal, who, unlike the Partisans, had not been out all night. He elected to climb straight up the hill through the woods, avoiding the winding gorge trail, and make directly for the monastery. If an ambush had been laid, the Partisans would eventually give up waiting and go to the monastery, where they would find a reception party. If the Partisans had not stopped, the manoeuvre would shorten the distance between the mountain troops and their quarry.

Making swift, silent progress up the steep hillside, Karl and his men reached the top of the spur overlooking the trail below. The twin cupolae of the monastery church could be seen five hundred metres to their left. Between there and the crest of the spur were the Partisans.

They saw a file of six men, in the khaki uniform and red stars of the Communists, walk briskly from the spur. Sure enough, the men carried only rifles and stolen German MP4O machine-pistols. They seemed unaware of being pursued.

Cover was less plentiful up here. The woods began to peter out, with only craggy rocks to offer hiding places. They would need to attack from where they stood, at the edge of the woods. The range was long, but not impossible. The element of surprise should enable them to overwhelm the Partisans.

The six men were on open ground approaching the monastery when Karl gave the order to fire. Three men fell immediately, the others a few seconds later, before they could return a single shot. Wary from his experience in Russia, Karl ordered a burst of fire into the bodies until he was satisfied there were no survivors. It occurred to him the Partisans may have weapons or a supply cache at the monastery, and decided to take a look. Caution still prevailed. They back-tracked into the woods, hiding their whereabouts from possible observers in the monastery who would by now be alerted. Although the trail near the monastery was clear of the woods, the flanks of the gorge below were thickly wooded, enabling the Germans to approach still hidden.

From behind a tree Karl scanned the walls for signs of life. His men lay dispersed and well hidden in the undergrowth.

There was a smell of fresh manure. Donkeys had been up this way very recently. Their droppings lay in the gateway to the ruins. The monastery was not as empty as it seemed.

One of his men spotted a crouching figure dart across the roof of the church, between the towers. The first was followed by a second. Karl's troops opened fire, revealing their position. Grenades were thrown onto them from a high window. They fell short but allowed the men on the roof to return fire as the Germans ducked away from showers of shrapnel and rock. More grenades followed, on target this time. The two men on the roof were silenced, but more grenades were hurled from several different locations on the monastery walls, accompanied by machine-gunfire.

A change of tactics was urgently required. They were pinned down. Karl was about to signal a retreat into the woods when a boulder, loosened by an exploding grenade, caught him on the elbow and spun him off his feet. He began to slide down the steep scree of the gorge until a tree trunk knocked the wind out of him. As he lay gasping, more gunfire followed. Another grenade exploded a short way up the hillside. Rock fragments showered down; a large stone hit the back of his head. He lost consciousness.

Karl heard sporadic gunfire close by, then silence. He opened his eyes. He could see a rifle lodged against a boulder. As he stretched out his right hand, a large boot came into view. His head was yanked up by the hair, exposing his neck to a knife already thick with blood.

Karl had been theoretically prepared to die for the Fatherland when he joined the Hitler Youth. The reality was terrifying. The owner of the knife wanted him to know what was coming. There was a sudden shout. The knife stopped, and Karl breathed again, but the knife came to rest on his throat. Held like a pig about to be slaughtered, Karl could hear a heated debate between the Partisan with the knife and another, a short distance away. "Knife" let go of Karl's head and kicked him onto his back. He began to slide down the side of the gorge. He tried to grab a branch with his left hand and let out a yell of pain as the broken ends of his collar bone dug into his flesh, and a further searing pain shot through his elbow. This time a thorny scrub caught him. He lay on his back, head downhill, until his vision was filled by the silhouette of a Partisan aiming his machine-pistol directly at him. For some reason the man did not fire but indicated with his looted gun that Karl was to stand up.

This proved extraordinarily difficult, in his upside down position and one-handed. Thorns clung to him, he felt sick and giddy. Eventually a hand pulled him upright, steadying him until he found his balance. He surveyed a scene of devastation around him. Karl's heart sank. The bodies of his men lay all around, some dismembered or disembowelled by the grenades, others shot. Two had their throats slit. The slaughter was complete. Why had he been spared? The Partisans were not noted for taking prisoners, especially officers, who were normally shot as a matter of course.

A gun muzzle jabbed his back. He was made to climb the gorge behind several of the Partisans, retrieving his cap on the way. He tucked his left arm into his tunic to support it as best he could. By the time he reached the top and stood on flat ground once more, his head was pounding like a steam hammer. A large group of Partisans, which had been hiding in the monastery, did not wait, but set off at a brisk pace with the laden donkeys across the hillside towards a distant forest. They were right out in the open now. Any spotter plane could not fail to find them, but there were not even birds in that searing blue sky.

As he stumbled along, he assessed his chances of escape. Zero. Unless he could grab a weapon. The smallest member of the group was in front. It gradually dawned on Karl that a female was within the battledress, her sex given away by long wisps of dark hair escaping from her forage cap and by the sway of her hips. He knew women Partisans were not uncommon but found it difficult to contemplate attacking her. At home, women were strictly noncombatant. Even in Russia he had not personally come across fighting women. Yet she was the easiest target.

He had no chance on the open hillside. They had taken all his equipment, including water bottle and knife. Despite the fast pace, there was always the muzzle of a gun in his back. The Partisans were anxious to reach the cover of the forest as quickly as possible. He was not sure how many were behind him. When he tried to look he was clubbed by a rifle butt.

Once they reached the forest the pace slowed fractionally. A brief halt was called for water, although none was given to Karl. He had a chance now to count his captors. Nineteen. Impossible odds, yet no doubt he would be killed eventually. What they wanted of him now he could only guess, but it would be better to attempt to escape than risk being made to divulge information. The forest offered a better chance than the open ground.

He saw the woman watching him. She looked no more than twenty. Her expression left him in no doubt she would kill him with her bare hands. She seemed to have read his mind. She spoke to the leader of the group, a man with a bristling moustache. At a word from him, two men of gigantic proportions thrust Karl's hands behind his back and tied them tightly. His left elbow and collar bone screamed in protest at this new strain. Then they were back on the march.

When night fell the group stopped for a longer rest in a sheltered gully, protected by an overhang. Exhaustion hung on every face, but they refused to lie down in case they fell asleep. Abandoning thoughts of escape when he saw the two giants stationed to watch him, Karl alone took the opportunity to rest properly. It was clear they were not going to feed him, although they had, at last, given him some water. Within an hour he was hoisted back onto his feet. They progressed down forest paths to the end of the trees. In the distance, beyond a broad expanse of open, undulating farmland, Karl could see the mountains of their hideout. They wanted to cross this open space under cover of darkness.

A tiny hamlet lay ahead in the moonlight. Fresh supplies were waiting for them in a derelict barn. An old man, baggy peasant breeches tucked into embroidered socks, awaited with a message for the Partisans. He scowled when he saw the prisoner, and spat in Karl's face.

By dawn they reached the mountains, and forced their weary legs to climb the sheep track to a pass between two peaks. At the top the group paused again, their profiles low against the sky. They scanned the area behind and ahead for signs of pursuit. Satisfied they were alone they began the descent to a sheltered bowl nestling within the security of the mountains. A small collection of ramshackle wooden huts, bleached grey by the sun, spoke of former herdsmen's shelters. It was to these that the group now headed. Any pursuers would have to come up the sheep track; they would make easy targets from the top of the pass.

The huts were already occupied. As the returning party approached a cry went out and several women ran to greet them, followed by two toddlers, no more than two years old.

One mother sternly rebuked her child when he fearlessly strode up to the man in the uniform with the badges on. Uniforms were part and parcel of his life; even stolen German uniforms were a familiar sight. How was he to know this one still had a German in it?

The women bustled about, relieving the donkeys and the raiding party of their considerable burden of supplies and weaponry. Most of the men soon disappeared into the huts to rest and recuperate. The young woman stayed with the two giants to deal with their prisoner. Karl found out she was the only one who spoke German.

"Take off your boots!"

His hands were untied by one of the giants using the knife Karl recognised only too well. He sank onto the ground and did as he was told. Once he handed over his boots he was dismayed to realise she wanted all of his clothes and his wristwatch. Without his clothes he could now see his wounded elbow – badly bruised but no longer bleeding.

Satisfied at last he had nothing concealed on him, the two men frogmarched him to a metal ring stuck deep into the ground to which a lone goat was tethered. Tying his hands behind him to the ring, they left him out in the hot sun while they retreated, along with the goat on its long tether, to sit in the shade of a hut.

Within minutes Karl could feel his unprotected skin start to burn. He shifted to present as small an area of himself as possible to the sun. He was deathly tired; the pain in his arm and head was relentless. Eventually he compromised and lay on his right side, feet towards the sun, and closed his eyes, hoping sleep would deliver him from pain.

It did, but not for long. The goat wandered across to sniff at his straw-coloured hair, then relieved itself nearby, before ambling back to the shade. Flies made their presence felt, drinking the sweat off his body, the blood from his arm and cracked lips. He was tormented by them, powerless to flick them away. The sun hammered down until he could feel every pulse beat in his skull. All thought evaded him, pushed out by the clamouring protest of his entire body. He tried to concentrate on a buzzard circling high over his head.

He was woken by a stream of hot liquid on his face and a burst of laughter. Not the goat urinating this time, but one of the men. The salt water stung Karl's lips, but he refrained from shaking his aching head to rid himself of the stinking urine.

The Partisans looked refreshed after their rest. The sun was lower in the sky, about to dip behind the highest peak, and they were ready now to begin their fun. Life in their mountain stronghold could be boring between raids. This German officer would ease that boredom and satisfy, in part, their thirst for revenge. The woman explained this to Karl as his hands were released. He had been burned, now he would learn what else her people had suffered.

She held her nose as demonstration of the stink emanating from him. The men laughed again, although they stank as much as he did.

Karl wished he was already lying dead with his men in the gorge. These people were going to play with him like a cat with a mouse. His would not be a glorious death in battle, glibly extolled in song. He would die slowly, in agony, among hostile, mocking faces.

They discussed something. Rough hands grabbed his red and blistered skin, pulled him towards an animal trough. It contained water thick with scum.

"You want a drink, German?" the young woman laughed.

He was pitched forward, head first into the stagnant water and held by eager hands. There was a roaring in his ears, a redness behind his eyes. His lungs gave up the fight to hold out the water. He struggled fiercely against their restraining grasp. He began to choke on the filthy liquid. They dragged him out coughing and retching before he inhaled too much. They gave him a few seconds then plunged him in again. This time he had no time to draw breath. His struggles began almost immediately. His chest constricted and heaved for air. He almost passed out that time. He was given a little longer to restore some air to his lungs before they repeated the exercise, delighting each time in his frantic struggling, his gasping for breath.

He came to draped face down over a trestle table, inside a hut where the donkeys were stabled. There was no sign of the woman, or any of the women who were witnesses at the water trough. Only the men were there. Two coarse hands grasped his hips, bracing him firmly against the table. It dug into the burned skin on his thighs and chest, chafing rhythmically once the assault began. He did not bother to count the number of men who used his body. His senses were dulled. He could no longer summon the energy to protest. To make matters worse, he could not shake a growing conviction that their actions were justified. For the first time he began to doubt the worth of everything he had fought for in the name of Hitler and the Third Reich. What was the point of dying so ignominiously in a distant land? Whatever the answer, he would welcome death when it came.

After that they left him alone. He was in no state to provide entertainment for the time being. The fun would be resumed in the morning. Once again he was tied to the goat's ring outside, where he lay and watched the stars come out, feeling the heat radiating from his roasted body. He coughed a few times, his throat as raw as his skin, pain coursing through his entire body. The young woman brought him a cup of clean water.

"We don't want you to die yet," she said. "Unfortunately I must leave tonight, so I will not see you die tomorrow, but I have asked Joze and Vjeko to give you my share in your death."

He presumed she meant the two giants. So tonight was to be his last. Through half-closed eyes he looked up at her face, searching for some show of compassion. There was none. She grinned instead at his pitiful condition. He heard her walk away and longed for her to return to share the time with him, enemy as she was. Instead the lonely heavens gaped at him.

After an interminable night, shivering with cold, he watched the first morning grey outline the mountain peaks. All too quickly rosy hues overwhelmed the grey, followed by the blue of daylight. Sounds of activity from the huts reached Karl's ears. One of the toddlers was crying. For most people it was an ordinary start to an ordinary day. It was to be his last. He wondered what his parents were doing now. Of course it would still be dark in Germany, although further north the night would be shorter ... What was he doing thinking such thoughts? Simple. Trying to distract himself from the fear which gripped him. Fear of death, no. It was eternal sleep, no more than that. Fear of dying, yes. If he had a God to pray to he would at least have that to take his mind off his near future. But there was no God.

He was no longer alone. People were gathering around him. His hands were untied. A kick in the back got him to his feet. Satisfied he was fit to make their entertainment worthwhile they formed a ring around him. Each one, women included, held a stick. Even the toddlers had sticks, although their mothers kept them out of the circle. To shouts of encouragement from the men, the four women stepped forwards. The men had their chance yesterday, now the women were being given first crack. They dealt a frenzy of blows across Karl's back. Some sticks held nails, which ripped his flesh. Shielding his head with his right arm, he collapsed under the onslaught, only to be hauled to his feet by Joze and Vjeko. They dragged him to one side, against a fence, so each man could be assured of a go at him. His arms were secured over the top rail, leaving him arched backwards, his entire body exposed to the impatient crowd.

A spatter of dust crossed the earth. Several onlookers fell. Only then did Karl hear the guns' ceaseless cacophony. One of the toddlers was split in two within its mother's arms, as she grabbed it and ran for cover. The other toddler fell open-eyed, blood pouring from its mouth. Panic broke out amongst the Partisans; bullets flew from all sides, mowing them down resolutely, unsparingly, until only the dust moved, settling over the silent bodies, to be followed by the flies.

Karl hung from the fence, unable to drag his eyes from the scene in front of him. Gradually he became aware of figures in camouflage jackets running forwards, guns at the ready. They had done their job well. No one shot back at them. They fired bursts into any body which still twitched. The first SS trooper reached Karl, who, without his uniform, could have easily been included in the slaughter. It seemed they were looking for him. The remains of his patrol must have been found.

"Leutnant Driesler?"

Karl managed to nod once before his head dropped forward and he blacked out.

They had to carry him down the sheep track on a door ripped from one of the huts. On the way they passed the bodies of Partisan lookouts, who had been looking the wrong way, watching the scene by the huts, rather than the pass. Karl's uniform was retrieved, but they did not put it on him, covered as he was in blood and peeling skin, but laid it over to keep the flies and the sun off.

He remembered little of his journey. He grew delirious with fever and pain. The heat was suffocating. He had difficulty breathing, and choked when given water. The bumpy track of a road jolted him. It was a blessed relief when he was given a shot of morphine.

The hospital, a requisitioned villa, was cool. A pleasant breeze wafted through an open window above him. Karl lay still, eyes shut, his cheek against the clean sheet, listening to a clattering trolley being pushed past his bed. He decided he felt better. His back no longer felt like he had been skinned alive; it was beginning to itch abominably. His breathing was easier. He was aware he had been in hospital for some days; he had no idea how many. His left arm was a problem. Finding a comfortable position for it lying face down was impossible. He wished he could turn over.

Tentatively he drew up his legs to lever himself onto his side. That was an improvement.

An orderly saw his movement and came over to the bed. "I see you're feeling a bit better, sir," he said to Karl in the accent of Pomerania .

"Yes." The effort of talking made him wheeze slightly, but he had a question. "How long have I been here?"

"Over a week now, sir. You were in a terrible state when they brought you in. Dehydration, sunstroke, then pneumonia on top. You're lucky to have come through."

A young Wehrmacht doctor came and asked him for details. Karl told him.

The doctor raged. "It's a good thing that SS unit got the whole damned lot of them."

"They didn't," Karl informed him. "There was a woman who left the previous night."

"Really? I'll mention that to Riedel. He was in command of the unit that found you. He wants a word with you anyway."

Karl managed a smile. "I'd like the chance to thank him. How on earth did they find me?"

"You'll have to ask him. Now, let's have a listen to that chest."

Once the doctor had gone, Karl regretted mentioning the woman. He felt no desire for vengeance. Their country had been overrun, they were simply defending it. His own life had cost the lives of over twenty Yugoslavs, including two small children. The memory of their deaths came back to him. He was no stranger to carnage, had seen plenty, and worse in Russia. Why did he feel so sickened when he thought of those children? Their lives were enough recompense for the loss of his men. Now he had sent the SS after that woman.

A voice from the next bed interrupted his questioning conscience. "Looks like we'll get some peace around here at last, eh?"

Karl turned his eyes across the narrow gap between the beds. His neighbour, a lad of about twenty, was propped up on his pillows, his right arm bandaged down to the elbow, after which came empty space. "Why's that?"

His neighbour grinned. "You've kept us all awake with your shouting, you know?"

"No, I didn't. I'm sorry."

The lad grinned again. "Don't worry. It's the only excitement we get in here. I couldn't help hearing what you said to the doctor. I'm not surprised you were shouting. Those filthy swine." He glanced down at his missing hand.

It was not Obersturmführer Riedel who came to interview Karl later on that day, but the higher ranking Sturmbannführer Goslar. He asked Karl for details of the attack at the monastery, and why Karl's life had been spared. Karl had an uncomfortable feeling he had to justify himself. He readily answered questions concerning the young Partisan woman.

"You're sure she made no mention of where she was going?"

"Yes, quite sure, Herr Sturmbannführer."

Karl breathed a sigh of relief when Goslar left. He felt intimidated beyond belief by the man.

"I wouldn't like to get on the wrong side of him!" Karl's neighbour, Hans Kowatsch, muttered.

Karl shot him a warning glance. One of the orderlies was nearby.

Several days later Karl was able to sit in a chair and play cards with other patients. Kowatsch had left the hospital the previous day, bound for a convalescence hospital in the Fatherland. Karl was told he could go home at the end of the week. He would not be deemed fit for active duty for another four weeks, at least.

The game of *Skat* was going well when an orderly came up to Karl.

"Excuse me, Herr Leutnant. Sturmbannführer Goslar's orders. You are to dress and go escorted to SS headquarters."

Karl frowned. "What has Stabsarzt Doktor Eckhardt got to say about that?"

The orderly shrugged his shoulders; the matter was out of the doctor's hands. It was clear who took precedence. Reluctantly Karl put down his cards. The orderly helped him with his uniform, adjusting the sling for his left arm. He followed the orderly out of the hospital. A car was waiting.

He was driven to a solid-looking building on the other side of the town and led, at a painfully brisk march, to a plainly furnished office where Goslar was waiting. Karl saluted and stood stiffly to attention, trying to ignore his uniform catching on the skin of his back. A groan from the corner of the room drew his attention to a pile of bloody rags.

Goslar smiled. "As you see, Driesler, we think we've caught your Partisan for you. Trouble is, she's not letting on. I thought you might be able to save us some trouble and identify her, and have the chance to see her punished."

Goslar nodded to the two men who stood guard over the woman. "Hold her up and let Leutnant Driesler see her face."

Karl looked at the woman's bloody, battered features. She appeared near dead. For a moment he was tempted not to recognise her. Surely she had suffered enough already. He would sign her death warrant if he said he knew her.

Goslar did not give him the opportunity to lie.

"I see you recognise her. Good. That gives us more to work on. I know you're not fit yet, Leutnant, but I thought you might enjoy a chance to show the little bitch what you think of her and the rest of her kind." Goslar strode to the door. "Take her back down."

Karl stepped aside to let the guards drag the limp body out. Not so long ago he had been in the same condition.

Goslar picked up his gloves. "Follow me."

They went down into the cellars, to a room whose purpose was plain. The woman groaned again when she realised where she was. She was strapped to a table, her full peasant skirt hitched over her thighs. She wore trousers before, Karl remembered. He tried to keep his face expressionless.

Goslar went to one side of the room, where a stove burned. In its hot coals was a poker. "I've heard what those pigs did to you, Driesler. You can give her some of her own medicine." He put on his gloves, grasped the wooden-handled poker, it's tip glowing red hot, and waved it near the woman's face. "You know what I want from you." He spoke soothingly, bringing the poker between her thighs to lightly touch the soft skin. She jerked and let out a gasp. "Names!" he barked.

Goslar spun round and held out the poker to Karl. "Here. You should be doing this, not me." He smiled challengingly.

Karl flinched. He knew exactly what Goslar had in mind. It was obscene, a vile form of torture, barbarian and unworthy of the Third Reich. Yet he knew he could not refuse to obey Goslar's order, for such it had been, despite its apparent casualness. He took the poker from Goslar, and slowly approached the woman. The longer he hesitated, the more heat would be lost from the poker.

But Goslar sensed his ploy. He stared coldly at Karl. For him the woman had lost importance. It had become an exercise to test the loyalty of this young Wehrmacht officer, who was showing signs of weakness. He turned his suggestion into a direct order.

"In!"

Karl stood stock still, terribly aware of what he was doing. This was not a soldier's work. He could not possibly do such a thing.

There was still no forward movement from Karl. If anything Goslar noticed his hand drawing further away from the woman's body.

"If you don't obey at once, Leutnant Driesler, you'll be taken out and shot. Put it in her. Now!"

Karl shut his mind and let his years of training take over. He obeyed. A short piercing scream came from the woman. The sound and smell of sizzling flesh filled his consciousness. White-faced he released the poker. He had to prop himself up against the wall. After a moment he lifted his head; to his relief he saw the woman was unconscious, or dead.

Goslar paced slowly over and stood with his face close to Karl's. "That was not very impressive, Leutnant. The Führer expects his army to obey orders instantly, without question. You took an oath of loyalty when you became a soldier. You have shown that loyalty to be wanting!"

"I am a soldier, Herr Sturmbannführer," Karl protested, "not a torturer. Naturally I obey orders, but this ..."

"This is warfare!" Goslar hissed. "These people are killing our troops, as you well know. Orders are orders, no matter who gives them. I question your suitability as an officer of the

Wehrmacht. However," his voice softened slightly, "in view of your recent ... unfortunate experiences, I am prepared to consider this a temporary weakness on your part. I will give you another chance to prove your unquestioning loyalty to the Führer."

The atmosphere in the cellar was icy. Karl waited, full of apprehension. The young woman moaned faintly. He could not help glancing across at her. He would not hurt her again. Even though she was as good as dead. If this was what the Third Reich demanded of him, then it would have to do without him. He wished he had made that decision earlier, and not succumbed to his cowardice. A bullet was a quick and easy way to die. He did not fear dying like that. Not now. Not any more.

Goslar returned the poker to the stove. He stood by it, hands on hips, watching it become red once more. He turned abruptly. "You've had long enough to consider your position, Driesler. Do you still object to my methods?"

Karl did not hesitate this time. "Yes, Herr Sturmbannführer. I do."

"That's a pity, Leutnant. The Wehrmacht needs men of your calibre. The Reich, however, does not need disloyalty or sentimentality. Such behaviour poses a threat to security." Goslar turned his back dismissively. "Lock him up," he told the guards.

From a neighbouring cell, Karl heard the woman's agonised screams begin again. He heard her beg for mercy. Finally she began to talk. Later there was a single shot. Another soul would haunt his dreams that night.

He expected to be taken before a firing squad. To his surprise he was taken back to Goslar's office the following afternoon, where to his immense relief he saw his own commanding officer, Major Pietsch, seated at the side of Goslar's desk. The Major seemed ill at ease in Goslar's company, even though their ranks were equal, but he had come for a purpose and he intended to return with Leutnant Driesler, alive. When the hospital reported the Leutnant's prolonged absence to his company commander, Pietsch instantly contacted SS headquarters and demanded to know where he was, only to be told he was being held on a charge of treachery. Such a charge was preposterous, considering Driesler's record. Pietsch came personally to speak on his behalf.

Acknowledging Karl's salute, Pietsch studied the young officer who stood wearily before him. He had not seen Leutnant Driesler since his patrol was annihilated and was shocked at the change he saw. Apart from physical deterioration in him, there was now a grimness, a determined set to his jaw which tended to confirm Goslar's accusation of rebellion. Gone was the happy-go-lucky demeanour which had survived all that the Russians could throw at it. Pietsch sensed uneasily that gone too was faith in the rightness of the cause. He had to make sure.

"At ease. I'm sorry to see you here under such awkward circumstances, Driesler." Pietsch spoke reassuringly. "I can see you ought really to be back in hospital." He paused for a moment, glanced at Goslar uneasily. "There seems to have been some misunderstanding between you and Sturmbannführer Goslar. I'm sure we can sort this all out."

Karl spoke out. "No misunderstanding, Herr Major. I did not consider the orders of the SS worthy of the attention of a Wehrmacht officer. As I told the Sturmbannführer, I am a soldier, not a torturer."

There was silence. Pietsch digested his subordinate's words. Goslar had a self-satisfied smile on his lips. Driesler had condemned himself.

Pietsch finally spoke. "What if I had given you that same order, Driesler?"

"I don't believe you ever would, Herr Major. But if you had, then ... I think I would have refused to obey it. We are not allowed to treat our prisoners of war like that. Questioning for military information is permissible, but torture definitely not. Don't you agree, Herr Major?"

Goslar had had enough. Pietsch was being asked to take the Leutnant's side. "These scum aren't prisoners of war! They

263

are bandits to be dealt with appropriately. Orders are orders, Major! You can't have your officers questioning your commands. He has just admitted he would refuse to obey an order. You must be convinced of his treachery!"

Pietsch was unhappy. He felt great sympathy for Driesler's case, but Goslar could be a problem in future. A report sent by Goslar to higher quarters could result in unpleasant consequences.

"I will arrange for a court-martial," Pietsch said. "We must have jurisdiction over our own officers."

Goslar nodded. "If you insist. I expect to be informed of the outcome, naturally."

"Naturally," Pietsch replied coldly.

Karl felt himself a pawn in the game of Wehrmacht-v-SS politics. To keep Goslar sweet, Karl was sacrificed. After a dishonourable discharge he returned to Germany under guard. In Munich his Wehrmacht guards were exchanged for SS ones. No explanation was given. Karl and his new escort waited some hours for their train connection, before travelling on. Nine other men, all in civilian clothes, were also under guard in the carriage. Karl had no idea where they were from. He saw their eyes dwell on his uniform where his various insignia and Iron Cross, First Class had once been proudly worn. His fall from grace was only too clear.

As night fell the train drew up at a large compound. The massive outer gates boldly proclaimed *"Arbeit Macht Frei"*. They were marched towards an imposing building, separated from long rows of identical huts, into a large room where their names were checked off. The others were led through a doorway to one side, leaving Karl on his own with a bored SS sergeant. A flicker of surprise crossed his face when he read what was written next to Karl's name.

"Medical wing for this one," the sergeant muttered.

Karl assumed he was going to be given the once over by a doctor. He was taken out through a different door, down long corridors. The atmosphere suddenly changed. It felt cold, smelled clinical. Karl was taken to a shower room. His uniform, even his sling disappeared while he was in the shower. In its place was a loose-fitting, pyjama-like outfit. No shoes or socks. It looked as though he would be staying in the medical wing.

More suspiciously his room was obviously a cell: no window, an electric lightbulb covered by protective mesh, a narrow bed with palliasse, a single blanket. Nothing else, not even a bucket. A grill in the door spoke of unseen eyes.

Karl sat down uneasily on the bed. He remembered the rows of huts and the *Totenkopf* Division insignia on the SS uniforms. Was he in a concentration camp? If so, he had no idea how long he might be held. He had been told nothing. He could not easily measure the passage of time. The light stayed on constantly. Hunger and anxiety kept him awake. In the morning, he assumed it was morning, he was taken to a washroom and allowed to shave. He found a tray with water, bread and a small slice of sausage in his cell when he returned. It was his first food in two days.

It must have been the middle of the morning when his cell door was unlocked again. He was taken to the washroom and allowed to use the toilet, then led through a set of locked doors into another corridor. Here there were more people: two Luftwaffe doctors talking to an SS doctor, an orderly wheeling an uncovered corpse down the corridor on a trolley.

With intense foreboding Karl looked for signs of a ward or other patients. The place did not have the atmosphere of a hospital. He was led through a doorway into a clinical room containing only a small table and chair fitted with restraining straps next to a trolley of medical instruments. Karl knew his real punishment had not yet begun.

The SS doctor followed Karl into the room. "Sit there," he said, with hardly a glance. Karl had no choice but to obey. The orderly entered and rolled up Karl's right sleeve in a procedure that spoke of a well-followed routine. The guards fastened straps tightly over his arms and legs then left the room. The doctor wrote in details on a chart, selected a small phial from a box on the trolley and filled a hypodermic needle from it.

Fear gave Karl a voice. "What are you doing?"

The doctor looked at him at last. "Research," he replied. "I've been waiting for someone like you to turn up. A certain SS officer in Yugoslavia heard of my request for a pure-blooded Aryan hero of the Reich as a test comparison. Former hero, I should say, eh?"

Karl tried to keep his voice steady. "Comparison with what?"

"Jews, gypsies, Slavs, whatever filth I can find. I seek scientific proof such people are truly inferior. They are, of course. But I'd like to provide facts and figures." The doctor approached Karl and inserted the point of the needle. "Don't worry, you won't come to any harm. Just some slight inconvenience."

The doctor started a stop-clock. Karl watched apprehensively as the second hand ticked around. Before a minute passed he began to feel dizzy. The dizziness quickly became akin to motion sickness; a cold sweat broke out on his forehead. Karl was first sick in a bowl held by the orderly, then continued to retch violently and exhaustingly, his empty stomach aching from the strain. It was like the worst kind of seasickness. All he wanted to do was die. For an hour he sat shivering and retching until the nausea passed and the shivering ceased.

The doctor, who sat impassively at a small table writing notes, stopped the clock and recorded the time on the chart. He gave no indication as to whether he was impressed with Karl's performance.

Karl felt cold and weak. He wished they would give him a drink of water to take the metallic taste from his mouth. Instead he saw the doctor return to the trolley with the phials and select another.

This time Karl felt the effects as soon as the injection was given. A cramping pain in his arm spread quickly all round his body. Its most frightening effects were in his chest. It felt as though a tight band had been tied round him; so tight he could hardly breathe. His limbs began to burn, his muscles locked tight. He felt paralysed, each breath became harder to take. His ribs would not move, he laboured for every breath. He tried to speak, to warn the doctor that he could not take much more. The effort was too great. His head dropped forward onto his chest.

An aeroplane droned overhead. Karl opened his eyes. He sat up stiffly to rub his aching limbs. He spotted a tray of food by the door and stood to fetch it. His legs refused to bear his weight and he toppled over. He sat down again with the feeling that eyes were watching through the door grill. He rubbed his legs again with his weak right arm and decided he did not feel hungry.

He began to think about this place he was in, what purpose it served. It was a concentration camp. The doctor spoke of Jews, gypsies and Slavs. No doubt he gleaned his research victims from the other side of the wire. Karl was aware that thousands of Jews and other undesirables had been sent to camps like this. He had always accepted the doctrine of racial inferiority, drummed into him from his school days. He never gave it a second thought. Now he was confronted by the fact.

The doctor's experiments were a comparison of racial fitness, and pre-supposed a man of Aryan blood would be stronger and more resistant to stress than others of inferior blood. But why should that be so? Karl thought seriously about the matter for the first time in his life. He had seen for himself what Russians could suffer and survive to fight back, likewise Yugoslavs. No hint of inequality there. His own race had fallen as easily as anyone else, when faced with appalling winter conditions in Russia. Why then had he always been taught that Aryans were the Master Race? Easy to accept such glib statements when he himself was a shining example of the race, excelling in outdoor activities, always admired for his looks. Now he knew such details were irrelevant. The Partisans sought revenge and entertainment, Goslar sought information and entertainment. Which was the purer motive? This SS doctor subjected human beings to degrading and painful experiments in the name of research. He assured Karl he would not be harmed. What if there were other doctors who had not given their subjects the same promise?

267

The brutality he had witnessed on all sides filled his mind. He mentally transferred some of that to his present, clinical environment and was sickened. He remembered the corpse on the trolley. The size of this medical wing was evidence there were others, doing other cold, calculatedly cruel research, sanctioned and financed by the Third Reich.

He felt a deep sense of shock as the significance of his deductions sank in. He was a part of all this. By swearing allegiance to Hitler and his doctrines he gave tacit assent. He felt betrayed by the man he had worshipped as a god, and by his country. Most of all he had betrayed himself, his own humanitarian principles, by not seeing through the charade until his own nose was rubbed in the dirt.

He knew there had been people undeceived by Hitler, who had always seen the evil of his policies. What had become of them? Were they all dead, or incarcerated? Were there still people out there who could put a stop to all this? If he ever got out he would try to find them.

He was still not hungry, but knew now he must survive, not give in to fear. He tried his legs and was able to stagger to the door and back with the tray. Some kind of thin soup, now stone cold, and a piece of bread. He forced it down, hoping he would be allowed to digest it this time.

He lay back down on the bed and stared at the ceiling. He must learn to hide his anger, if he was going to be able to use it.

He soon discovered fear was worse than pain. Fear of the unknown. Each time the injection was given he dreaded what would happen. When the pain, the hallucinations, the depression came, he found it harder and harder to cope, to remind himself of his purpose while his mind walked in hell. Fear compounded pain. There was never a mark on his body other than the needle prick, or bitten lips, but he could feel his mind being battered, his recent resolve to fight slipping away down cobweb-festooned corridors.

Then suddenly the pattern changed.

Instead of fearing the next injection, he began to crave it. Gone was the pain, instead the days passed in a glorious golden haze, an intense sensation of well-being. The doctors were not so bad after all. This was wonderful. He did not want anything else. Sometimes on his bed at night, he could still feel the after effects of his last injection. The light in its wire mesh was warm sunshine. He could look at it and smell the sweet, resinous scent of the forest, hear the splash of a waterfall. He could float through the forest and see everything with a crystal clarity.

When the guard came to fetch him from his cell, he would go willingly now, eagerly anticipating the prick of the needle. It became a routine. He would be given the injection, then return immediately to his cell. This would happen several times a day. The doctor did not bother to observe him any more. Karl did not question the purpose of such treatment. He was seldom lucid enough to think rationally. Time meant nothing.

He woke one day to find himself in darkness. After the days – or weeks was it? – of constant light the blackness was threatening, unsettling. His anxiety grew during the day. No one came to fetch him for another injection. No food was brought. The door to his cell did not open, not even when he banged on it and shouted for the toilet. He kept shouting until he began to tremble so much he had to stay quiet. The trembling continued until he shook violently. Now he was sweating. He needed another injection to stop the shaking, to calm him down, return him to that blissful state he had enjoyed until today. Why had they not come for him?

He began to pace the cell in his agitation, feeling his way around the walls, then stood by the door listening for the sound of footsteps. Had they forgotten him? Irrational fears fought their way into his head. He banged on the cell door yet again, shouted for the guard, but got no response. He hated them for this! They weren't going to give him any more injections.

A guard eventually came, but Karl was only taken to the washroom and allowed water. When the guard began to walk back to the cell, Karl made a dash in the other direction to the locked doors, but there was no guard there to unlock them. He banged on the doors until the guards came and dragged him back into the cell. Darkness enveloped him once more.

He could not sleep. His mind had a single purpose. To get another injection. He felt really ill now. He would die if he did not have more of the drug. He begged the guard on his next visit. The guard grinned and told him he would have to beg harder than that.

"I will!" Karl cried out. "I'll do anything you want."

He had not meant it. Or rather he had, but he had not expected them to take him up.

He was taken back to the room with the chair. The doctor showed him the phial containing the drug he craved.

"I will give you some, if you will do one thing for me first."

"Anything," Karl said in his relief.

He was led out of the room, to the far end of the medical wing and into another room. Goslar was there!

Goslar gave a cruel smile. "I have been offered the chance to see you eat your words, Driesler. I've been assured you are ready to obey any order I give you now. Is that right?"

Karl could not speak. He suspected there was a terrible truth in Goslar's words.

At a nod from Goslar the door opened. A man of indeterminate age was brought in. His spindly legs would hardly bear his weight. He was held up by two guards.

"This man is a Jew who has exploited the Fatherland to his own ends. Now he is being punished for that offence." Goslar put a chair close to the man then lifted up one of the emaciated legs and rested the man's foot on the seat. "You will be rewarded if you obey my order," he reminded Karl, "and punished if you do not. Break his leg!"

How could he refuse? Karl was desperate to obey, to be taken back to the doctor, given release for a few more hours. But the voice of reason was not completely shut out. It would only be for a few more hours. What would happen then? Another Jew? Another order? What the hell! He had to obey now.

He faltered for a moment, but the image of the needle and the terrifying blackness of his cell were too strongly imprinted on his mind. With a sudden wild movement he stamped down hard on the leg, hearing it crack, trying to ignore the screams of the man to whom it belonged.

Goslar gave another thin smile. "You know, I didn't believe the doctor, but he's right! You're like a trained dog, waiting to be given the command. If only we could always be assured of such obedience! But I doubt that is possible. Perhaps we can find a use for you anyway, something you will want to do."

Despite the promises, Karl was returned to his cell without being given another injection. He spent the next two days in continual light once more, alternately flinging himself at the door, or lying in a shivering heap on the floor, crying with despair as the drug slowly worked out of his system. After a few more days he knew he still craved it desperately, but the worst effects were over. When food was brought, he found he could eat the gristly sausage and dry bread again at last. He had lost so much weight he had to hold up his trousers with one hand, but his hands were steadier now and his mind clearer.

He felt terribly ashamed. He should have been able to stop himself obeying the order. Why had he not done so? Was it more of the same weakness he had shown before? Guilt lay heavy on him. He wept for his cowardice.

The religion of his childhood came back to torment him. Was all this divine retribution? If he believed that, then he must pray for forgiveness. "Forgive me Father, for I have sinned." He could not continue. It had lost all meaning, if it ever had any. The words were as empty and futile as the promises of the Führer. He had to find some other comfort.

Ilse. He tried to recall her face. They had taken his wallet containing her photograph with his uniform. If only he could see her picture again. In her last letter, which he received just before his court-martial, she told him she was pregnant and said how pleased she was. She was longing for his next leave when they could marry.

He thought of the baby, a part of himself living free with Ilse. She would make a good mother. After all, looking after children in the Kindergarten was her job. She would have to give that up now, of course. Would she stay on in Medebach, or go back to her parents in Hamburg? His own parents would let her stay with them. It would be far too dangerous to go back to Hamburg.

The baby would surely have blond hair, like its parents. Would he ever see it? This new responsibility gave him a new angle to consider. If ever he did leave this place, which was more important to him? To survive for the sake of Ilse and the baby, or assist in the downfall of the Nazis? His determination to pursue the latter cause had weakened, not strengthened, over the days and weeks. He felt numbed by everything, powerless to resist. He perceived his own frailty and doubted his ability to live by his convictions. He had failed them twice now. His instincts for self-preservation proved to be the dominant factor in his life. How could they call him a hero of the Reich? His bravery in battle was only the same instinct for survival. The Russian machine-gun post needed taking out or else his unit would have been hemmed in and frozen to death. Physical bravery was one thing, moral courage quite another.

Footsteps came down the corridor. Karl wiped tears from his face and stood up, in an effort to regain some dignity.

"Out!" the guard bellowed.

He was taken to the doctor's room again, told once more to sit in the chair. As the straps were tied, Karl's heart sank. He would not be given the drug he had become addicted to. They did not need to restrain him for that.

Another man entered the room. Small. Weaselly. Civilian. Gestapo.

The man laid his hat on the doctor's table and sat down expectantly. "So, doctor. You're finally to demonstrate this latest drug of yours, I hear?"

"Yes indeed, Herr Breitner!" The doctor filled a hypodermic needle as he spoke. "I've tested it on a number of subjects already to ascertain the correct concentration and the period over which the antidote is effective." He paused, gave a little shrug. "I had some losses, of course, but I'm confident now I can control the proceedings with some precision."

"Excellent. I note your choice of subject today is appropriate!" The man watched closely as the doctor emptied the syringe into Karl's arm then started the clock. Breitner's eager stare took in every detail as Karl gasped at the first reaction to the drug.

He was gripped by intense shooting pains whose source he could not identify. He clenched the arms of the chair and bit his lips to keep control of himself. The searing pain piled on in relentless waves, building up in a crescendo which did not slacken. With the pain came terror, a loss of rational thought, so that he succumbed more readily to the pain. He writhed against the restraints, opened his mouth in a scream of agony. He longed for unconsciousness. His breathing became more and more ragged with every scream. He was dimly aware of the doctor checking his pulse. There was the prick of a needle once more. The pain quickly receded, leaving Karl gasping weakly, his eyes closed. He heard them discussing the results.

"What is the maximum time a subject has lasted out?"

"I've let them go to an hour before now, and brought them back, although the risk of heart failure at that point is quite high. Of course, we usually use new, fit prisoners, as your subjects would presumably be, Herr Breitner. This man has been with us a few weeks now, and is not in the best condition. This demonstrates the level of medical care needed, if the subject is to survive to give the information you want. The endurance time is often much shorter the second time. If necessary, that is. Once is quite often enough." The doctor demonstrated what he meant by approaching Karl with another needle.

Karl began to scream. "No! Not again, please! No more!" He fought as he had never fought before to escape the restraining straps, but as he felt the prick in his arm he slumped back in his seat. The ticking of the stop-clock was drowned by his cries of agony. He did not feel the antidote ten minutes later.

CHAPTER FOURTEEN

He was moved to a forced labour camp much further north, near a large city. Essen. He was put in a work party which went out under guard each day, dodging air raids to clear the roads of rubble, fill bomb craters and dig corpses from ruined houses, factories and hospitals. Occasionally they found someone still alive, missed by the search parties. Then their labours became worthwhile. Usually they were assigned the areas of greatest devastation. Sometimes they were moved on to another of the Ruhr cities which had suffered a recent raid, but it was difficult to tell one city from another when all you saw were piles of smouldering rubble and human limbs suspended from telegraph wires.

Frequently their work was interrupted by yet another air raid. Denied shelter, they huddled in the ruins and watched the rumbling crosses drop their glistening, death-dealing clusters. American aeroplanes these. Flying Fortresses. Sometimes one would hurtle earthwards, a plume of black smoke belching from its engines; always more came to replace it.

It took him a month to settle in. He was uncommunicative and withdrawn. As a result the others – political dissidents, communists or men whose neighbours had reported a careless word – left him alone. One man tried to be friendly. He nudged Karl out of his apathy, made him eat the meagre food, ensured he was in the right place for roll call and inspection. Karl grew accustomed to having a spaniel-eyed, curly-headed shadow. Thanks to Johannes Heiber, Karl slowly adjusted to the rigours of the labour camp, and found a new cameraderie amongst the inmates he had not enjoyed since leaving his unit in Yugoslavia. Until he discovered that the pink triangle on

274

Heiber's clothing designated him homosexual. Ordinarily the knowledge would not have bothered him, but his experience at the hands of the Partisans coloured his opinion, and he shunned Heiber's company, turning away without explanation, flinching at his touch. Now it was Heiber's turn to retreat into miserable silence. Karl ignored him, wanting to make his distaste clear. His rejection proved effective. Next day Heiber made a run at the gate and was shot dead.

Once more Karl drifted towards depression, burdened by guilt, until early in January an unexpected letter arrived from his parents. He was not allowed to write himself, had no idea they knew his whereabouts. He lay on his bunk to read the letter.

Our beloved son,

Imagine our horror when the authorities finally relented and told us where you are. We've all been distraught, not hearing from you for so many months. Not one word came from your unit to say what had happened to you. We can't even guess why you are in a labour camp, but we are praying daily for your prompt release.

You won't know that Ilse's parents were killed in a raid last August. She decided to leave here and go to her sister's in Mannheim. She keeps in touch with us, so we have enclosed her letters for you to read. As you will see from the last one ... you are a father! Ilse had a little boy on 20th December. All went well and she has called him Siegfried. Congratulations, Karl! We'll inform Ilse where you are so she can write and tell you all about Siegfried.

Little Uwe is growing rapidly and can just about crawl. Anna hears occasionally from Thomas, but Rudi is as bad about writing as ever. You are so close now; we long to see you and are doing all we can to make this possible. Hopefully our letters will be delivered to you now. In the meantime think of us all praying for you, and be comforted by news of your lovely baby son.

Our fondest love to you, from Mother and Father

Karl devoured Ilse's correspondence with his parents, reading each letter several times. The last he handled like a sacred object. She was a mother now.

The occupant of the adjacent bunk noticed his excitement. "Good news?"

Karl looked up from Ilse's world, glad to share his news. "Yes. I've a son. Siegfried."

"Congratulations, mate. I hope you get to meet him some day."

Karl's raised spirits were reflected in the glittering frost of the following morning. They were quickly dampened when he saw the extent of the last air raid. Another day's hard digging and gore lay ahead of them.

The streets were filled with people. Soldiers, and men from the National Labour Service were beginning the task of clearing up. Some citizens sat stunned and dejected, others scrabbled in the ruins of their homes, searching for scraps of property or food, or timber simply to keep warm in the windowless shells of their houses. Messages to loved ones were scribbled on walls, telling of a family's relocation. Red Cross workers and the National Socialist Women's Organisation doled out soup and clothing for those with nothing but memories.

The unmistakeable sweet, fatty smell of bodies still lying in the ruins reached the noses of Karl's party. Some firefighters were at work on a building opposite, but there was no hope for the occupants of the flats, which were now a collapsed dolls house, open fronted, wallpaper and pictures still hanging on the back walls, a bathtub suspended by its piping. The civil defence teams had long since moved on to where hope still existed.

Six bodies were laid out on the street, ready for disposal, by the time work was halted by the next air raid. One was a young woman clutching a tiny baby. Karl thought of Ilse. He knew that southern German cities were being targeted. Nowhere seemed safe now from attack. The Eastern Front was drawing closer. Rudi was embroiled somewhere out there. Was Rudi safer out East, than he was in the middle of Essen during an air raid, Karl wondered? At least Rudi could fight back.

The piercing whistle of high explosive bombs meant they were close by. Karl knew to keep his mouth open to protect his eardrums from the concussion blast. The fallen door, under which he and another man were sheltering, cracked as a large lump of loose masonry fell on top of it. Fortunately it did not collapse. The bomb had fallen at the end of the street onto a shoe shop, and brought down half a neighbouring house with it.

Rescue workers were quick to assemble. A boy was sent running to the guards of the labour force to request assistance. Cries could be heard from the cellar of the house, he said. A woman was trapped with her little girl.

They ran across the rubble, dodging round a previous bomb crater and a ruptured water main. Dust was still settling around the house. The anti-aircraft guns fell silent and the all clear sounded. The citizens of Essen once more emerged from their cellars and bunkers.

An elderly woman muttered to an onlooker. "It's Frau Vollmerk and little Anneliese. She's expecting her second, too, poor wretch." The onlooker muttered in sympathy as the elderly woman divulged more. "She was evacuated to Bavaria but hated it so much she came back. She said she would rather take her chances here, near her family. Much good it's done her."

The workers were quickly organised into a human chain to move bricks and broken furniture from the area where the cries could be heard. A boy in the uniform of the Hitler Youth, no more than twelve, lowered himself down into a natural tunnel in the debris to see how far he could get. He was pulled out, feet first a couple of minutes later, covered from head to foot in white dust, looking like a corpse himself.

"I saw her!" he cried excitedly. "She's not injured, but she's eight months gone. Her little girl's with her. There's another woman – grandmother. She's unconscious. I got right up to the cellar, but then there's a barred window and a two metre drop into the cellar. The bars on the window will have to be removed. It won't be easy getting through the window even so. It's quite small. The little girl could get through; not the mother."

Karl was impressed with the clarity and conciseness of the lad's report. No doubt he had made many similar.

"Would there be room for a man to get through the window once the bars are removed?"

The boy considered the question. "The shoulders would be the main problem of course, but I think so." He pointed directly at Karl. "He'd do. He has to be fairly tall. It's a long drop into the cellar."

The thickset air raid sentry sized up the men standing around him. His eyes confirmed that the tallest of the men under guard was the best choice. He looked agile enough to contort himself into the cellar, yet strong too.

"You! Come here!"

The guards waved Karl to step forward.

"You heard the boy's report? If you can remove the bars on the window, you're to go in and get the little girl and the grandmother out, while we carry on clearing." It was going to be a long job.

A length of rope was tied around Karl's waist. He tucked a torch, hammer and chisel into his overalls, knelt on the loose bricks and squeezed himself sideways into a gap between a water tank and a wall. He turned onto his stomach and wriggled forwards using toes and elbows, easing his shoulders awkwardly past a loose beam which seemed to be holding up another wall. He paused and called out.

"Frau Vollmerk! Can you hear me?"

A shrill voice came up to him from the blackness. "Yes! Thank God you're coming. The baby has started!"

Scheisse! thought Karl. But he called back: "We'll soon have you out. I'll just have to remove the bars on the windows."

He inched his way forward, set the torch by the window in front of him and, lying awkwardly and painfully on his side, began to chip away the mortar. Every so often he heard the woman's gasps of pain, and he hurried to remove the last bar. He peered over the edge and saw a woman's eyes searching for his. A little girl of about three, her hair still neatly braided, clung wide-eyed and silent to her mother. He looked for the grandmother. He could see what the younger woman could not. The older woman's body was crushed and half-buried by fallen rubble. For her he could do nothing. Frau Vollmerk groaned and held her extended belly. She panted through another contraction, then looked up again when it was over. There was no way she was going to be able to lift the child up to him, as he had hoped, or even tie a rope round her. He eased his shoulders through the window to check they would fit, then withdrew. The drop was too great to attempt head first.

"Frau Vollmerk. I am going back up the tunnel to turn around. I will come back down and bring Anneliese out. I'll tell the people out there that your labour has started."

The woman's piteous voice cried out at being left alone again. "Hurry, please. My mother is injured. This baby's coming quickly."

"I'll be as quick as I can." He wriggled backwards as fast as he dared to the water tank where the rescuers were waiting, and made his report. "The grandmother will have to be dug out, if she's still alive, which I doubt. Frau Vollmerk's gone into labour. The contractions seem to be quite close together. It may be you won't get to her in time. I'll pass the little girl out, then stay with the mother until you can dig another way."

The air raid sentry was taken aback by the prisoner's air of authority. "It would be better if a nurse or a woman could stay with her," he said brusquely.

Karl smiled grimly. "If you can find one with slim hips who is willing to go down, then of course, it would be better. I shall go back and stay there until she comes. Someone should follow me to take the girl."

Once more he picked his way down the tunnel, but feet first. Bits of mortar and showers of plaster dust fell as he went. The terrified child let out a scream of fear as he dropped into the cellar. He knew he too must look like a ghostly apparition. He brought the torch down with him and laid it carefully on a flat brick. Frau Vollmerk was trying to comfort the child, but broke off as another contraction began.

There was a slithering noise up by the window, followed by a voice. "Are you ready with the little girl?"

Anneliese clung tightly to her mother. There was no way she was going to let this strange white figure take her away. Frau Vollmerk, tried to reason with her daughter.

"Lisl, do as I say. The man will help you out of here. Just let him lift you up to the window there. The other man will take you out into the fresh air. I'll be with you soon, I promise, darling."

Karl bent down and combed pieces of mortar and dust out of his hair. It stuck up comically in spikes. He grinned at the little girl, and saw her fear lessen. Now he looked more like a white-faced clown than a ghost. Tentatively she relaxed her hold on her mother and Karl reached for her, held her under the arms and raised her high, having to shift his hold to boost her another few centimetres so that the man above could catch her arms. She was frightened again by this, and struggled as she was pulled through the window. Karl heard the child's wriggling continue up the tunnel, the man swearing at her to keep still. Suddenly there was a rumbling crash. A choking cloud of dust poured through the window into the cellar.

When the dust settled, Karl hoisted himself up to look at the tunnel. He could see nothing but rubble.

Frau Vollmerk called up to him. "What's happened? Is Anneliese safe?"

Karl had no idea. He let go of the window and dropped back into the cellar. "I'm sure she's out. She must have kicked something out. It would have fallen behind her. She'll be all right. Probably means it will take them a bit longer to reach us. If you don't mind, I'll turn off the torch. Save it for when we need it. Give me your hand, then you'll know where I am."

As they waited in the dark for sounds of rescue he felt her fingers grip his tightly as the contractions kept coming. Her hand was hot, despite the freezing temperature of the cellar. Karl shivered and he wished he could benefit more from the woman's body heat. She was lying on a loose pile of bricks, but he could feel a blanket poking out from underneath, brought down into the cellar for the night-time raids. He switched on the torch and dug out the blanket. He was about to put it round himself when he realised the baby would need it, when it was born. His overalls were too bloodstained and filthy from broken sewers to risk contaminating the blanket, even though it was already full of brick dust. He shone the torch at Frau Vollmerk's face. She was sweating and concentrating hard.

"Anneliese was easy. I hope this one is too." She gasped, swallowing hard, the dust caking her mouth. "It's nearly here I think. Can you help me?"

Karl looked at his hands. He had been touching corpses all morning. The military were issued with rubber gloves, but the prisoners were not granted this benefit. This baby's first contact with life would be the smell of death. He rubbed his hands with brick dust to scour as much grime from them as he could, then helped Frau Vollmerk with her underclothes. He was thankful it was her second child and she knew what to do. She held her breath and pushed down hard.

"Look. Can you see it yet?" she panted. "I can feel it there."

He shone the torch. Sure enough a glistening bulge had appeared. He wedged the torch between the bricks and stayed ready with the blanket. On the next push, the head emerged and Karl supported it, waiting for Frau Vollmerk to push again. As she did so the shoulders, then the whole body slipped out.

"It's a girl!" cried Karl. The tiny form began to cry almost immediately, and he wrapped the blanket around it.

"What do I do with the cord?" he asked.

Frau Vollmerk propped herself up on her elbows to take a look at her new daughter. "I think you have to tie it tightly before cutting it."

Karl pulled two long threads from her petticoat, tied them three centimetres apart and found a piece of broken glass nearby to cut the cord. He handed the baby up to its mother, who tucked it inside her coat with her.

"It's not finished yet," she told her strange midwife. "There's the after-birth to come yet. It's a good thing you're not squeamish. Then I don't suppose anyone is these days."

The baby was still crying so she put it to her breast and the crying stopped.

"If it had been a boy I would have named it after you," Frau Vollmerk said out of the gloom. "What is your name, anyway?"

Karl told her.

"I suppose my mother is dead, isn't she?" she asked with a fatalistic certainty.

He crawled over to the back of the cellar to the lifeless figure. "Yes, I'm sorry. Perhaps you should call the baby after her," Karl suggested.

"Yes, I will. She'll be little Frieda."

"My little boy is called Siegfried," Karl told her. Now the excitement of the birth was over, he did not want Frau Vollmerk to begin to fret. She was still elated with the birth; he hoped to keep her that way as long as possible.

"What's he like? Your boy?" she asked him.

"I've never seen him. But his mother is beautiful." He began to tell her about Ilse, to keep his own spirits up as much as hers. He turned out the torch again.

She heard his teeth chattering. "You're cold, Karl. Lie here next to me. My coat can go round all three of us."

"No. I will call up the tunnel to see if I can find out what is happening. You rest. You must be tired."

Taking the torch with him he hauled himself once again up to the window and through it this time. The tunnel seemed to be blocked about a metre along, but he could see chinks of daylight now and hear the sound of rubble being shifted. He called out and heard his call answered.

"The baby is born," he yelled to them. "What's taking you so long?"

"When the tunnel collapsed it left a dangerous wall. We had to shore that up first. We're nearly through now."

"Is the little girl all right?" Karl shouted.

"Yes. She's with the Red Cross here."

"Tell her she's got a baby sister called Frieda."

Karl heard the cheer go up as the news was passed on to the other rescuers. "I'm going back down to Frau Vollmerk now."

The torch grew dim as he felt his way to where Frau Vollmerk lay. He could hear the baby's whistling breath in the stillness. Anxiously he groped ahead of him and his hand came in contact with Frau Vollmerk's skirt. It was sodden with blood. He shone the failing torch beam over her. She seemed to be asleep and yet there was no sound of breath from her. On the bricks beneath her blood trickled stickily, picking up dust as it flowed.

Karl shook her urgently. "Frau Vollmerk!" There was no response. His fingers went to her neck. The pulse there could hardly be felt. Dropping the torch he scrambled up the wall and through the window to alert the diggers to the new emergency. As he reached the blockage a brick was removed from above his head. He blinked as daylight poured in.

"Hurry!" he yelled to the face he saw there. "She's bleeding heavily!"

The diggers redoubled their efforts. He moved back down the tunnel, out of the way of falling rubble. He reasoned it was possible Frau Vollmerk might fit through the cellar window, without the baby inside her. She was not a big woman. It would save the time it would take to enlarge the window or dig an alternative way in. The rope which had been tied around his waist still hung from the window. He lifted out the baby from underneath its mother's coat, which he then removed to reduce her bulk. He tied the rope under her arms then felt her pulse. It was very weak. Her hands were cold now, colder than his own. He laid her coat back over her and held the sleeping baby close to his chest, waiting for the first face to appear at the window.

More clouds of dust trickled in amidst a clamour of voices. They were here at last.

"Take the baby," Karl said, handing it up.

The baby disappeared from view. The face reappeared.

"I've tied the rope round her, if you can pull her up."

He carried Frau Vollmerk to the window, supporting her body as it was lifted. He knew she was already dead.

Her blood had soaked his overalls, chilling him further. Only now did he realise how exhausted he was. He sank onto the cellar floor, waiting to be told that the way was clear to leave the cellar. The torch battery gave out, but now there was just enough light to see. A pale face stared at him from the back of the cellar. For one heart-stopping moment the faces of the dead Partisans filled the gloom, like in his dreams. Crying out in fear, Karl shot up the wall and through the window space.

Helping hands pulled him out into twilight and falling snow. He was greeted by brief, muted applause, the sight of Frau Vollmerk's blanket-draped body, and a guard waiting to take him back to work.

His nightmares took on a new intensity after that. The faces of the dead would loom out of the darkness, disembodied arms would grab at him, trying to drag him down into a bottomless pit. Occasionally the dream was different. He would be choking in dust or water, fighting off the Partisan named Vjeko who was wielding a hypodermic needle. Even when he knew he was awake, the faces would linger in front of him, bringing his nightmare into reality, so that he could not fall back into sleep. The other occupants of his hut cursed him for repeatedly disturbing their sleep, although some managed to sleep through the commotion. Tiredness overwhelmed him at work. He would stumble and drop his spade, so that the guards kicked and butted him back to alertness.

As the air raids continued relentlessly, and the long winter nights grew shorter, they worked later into the evenings; always more bodies, until the stench of death was so normal they ceased to notice it, despite the arrival of warmer weather.

He longed to hear how Ilse and Siegfried were faring, whether they were still in Mannheim or had been evacuated east or further south, but his parents could give him no news of her in their letters. He could not forget the two girls he helped, now cared for by relatives, until such day as their father might return to claim them. What if Ilse were killed and Siegfried disappeared into care? Would he ever be able to find his son in the chaos, let alone prove his right to him?

In late June the rumours started. A new arrival told them the Allies had landed in Normandy. Thousands of German soldiers had been captured or killed. They heard the news with mixed feelings. Some welcomed it. Others wanted to defend the Fatherland. A few feared for their own safety. Their guards might find an easy way to relieve themselves of their burden of dissident prisoners. Their informant told them anyone caught spreading defeatist talk now was summarily executed.

One hot summer's evening Karl was standing in the queue for the evening rations when a guard called out his number. With great reluctance Karl left the queue and reported to the guard, knowing that latecomers to the queue would find little food. The guard told him to report to the gate, where a sentry checked his identity before allowing him through. Another guard led him to the administration block.

Karl had difficulty keeping up. The guard butted him with his gun to get a move on. Halting outside an office, the guard knocked before entering.

Karl stood before a desk, swaying with fatigue. He looked up as the guard was dismissed by the SS officer seated at the desk. For a moment he thought he was hallucinating again. Surely the officer was Paul Zopf!

The Zopf family owned a large construction business in Dortmund. Before the war they were regular weekend visitors to the Driesler home. Paul was only a year older than Karl and they became firm friends. When Paul joined the SS he tried to persuade Karl to do the same. He was bitterly disappointed when Karl preferred the Wehrmacht. Paul's progress was swift, aided by his zeal and his ability to impress the right people. After losing his right arm in Russia, Paul was given a useful desk job.

"Karl! You look even worse than I thought you would." Paul waved to him with his remaining arm to sit down.

Karl's reply was cautious. "You should have seen me before I had a wash." He was unsure how familiar to be with his old friend. The uniform Paul wore demanded respect.

Sensing this Paul smiled. "For God's sake Karl, how did you manage to get yourself in a place like this? I couldn't believe it when your parents told me where you were. They asked me to try to help, but there are limits."

Karl's hopes sank. "You mean you aren't here to get me out?"

Paul laughed. "Did I say that? Thanks to the present er ... setback, your prospects have improved dramatically. The Reich is desperate for experienced soldiers like yourself. We can't afford to have you wasted in here, not with the dregs we're having to recruit."

"That sounds like defeatist talk to me. If we're so short of soldiers, why are our own men shooting so many who dare to speak as you have done?"

The smile left Paul's face. "You've changed, Karl. Everyone has to some extent, I know. But you more than most. You've turned against everything you valued in the past – even me it seems."

"Paul, I'm here because I refused to obey the orders of an SS officer. You are an SS officer, a Sturmbannführer I see. As such you represent everything bad that has happened in the name of our Fatherland."

Paul thumped the desk. "Come on, Karl! Be realistic! We do our duty to the Führer. What makes the Wehrmacht so blameless, eh? You're not the innocent you make yourself out to be. You volunteered." He stood up and walked round the desk to confront Karl. "You still call Germany your Fatherland. Surely you don't want to see it overrun by our enemies? If you listen to what I have for you, you could find yourself out of here today. Otherwise you're going to die in here, of dysentery, typhus, whatever. You're so run down now even a touch of 'flu could kill you." He drew closer. "Karl, you want to survive, don't you?"

A spark of interest glowed. Paul pressed on. "I hear you have a son, by Ilse. You could find them, marry Ilse, and fight for their future, not waste your life rotting in here."

Survive. The word was precious. He considered what Paul was offering. Death or survival in battle; death or survival here. What were the odds in either situation? Impossible to say. The survival of his country was at stake also. That was still important, regardless of the way he had been treated. His decision was really made by the thought of finding Ilse. He could not do that here.

"What have you arranged then, Paul?"

Paul beamed. "Enlistment in the SS." Karl's face registered dismay. "I couldn't pull any strings in the Wehrmacht. Not that I really tried. I always said you should have joined with me."

Karl felt too tired to protest. Survival was all that counted. Paul was right. He would die here. If joining the SS assured him of a decent meal, he was willing to risk dying in battle, even being captured by the Russians, if he could see Ilse and Siegfried first. He still had a query.

"Why is the SS willing to have me after my record? Surely I'm the last person they would want?"

"Call it a measure of our desperation. We're having to recruit anyone we can find – Rumanians, sixteen-year-olds straight from the Hitler Youth, veterans, anyone able to hold a gun. I managed to persuade certain people to overlook your little misdemeanour – for the time being. Unusually you're being given a second chance. Don't waste it, and don't let me down. I've staked my own reputation speaking up for you."

Karl spotted a flaw in the argument. "But I'm not fit to hold a gun, am I?"

Paul dismissed the remark. "A temporary condition. You'll be given time to recuperate, before you report for light duties. You never know, the war might be won before you have to fight."

"Won by whom?"

"By us of course! Or were you joking? We'll beat our enemies back. A German soldier is far superior to anything the Americans or Russians have."

"And the British?"

"We've beaten them at Dunkirk, and the Canadians at Dieppe. We'll beat them again. Besides, a new secret weapon has just been launched on the British; a rocket-propelled flying bomb which needs no aeroplane to deliver it. It's devastating London right now. Paying them back for Hamburg! And all the rest. London will be begging for mercy soon, you watch."

Paul picked up a pile of papers from the desk. "I have all the documentation for your release and enlistment. I need your signature on two of them, then you can leave here for a convalescence hospital near Mannheim. I'm told Ilse is living there now. You see, I've done everything I can to help you."

Karl glanced through the papers. "I see I'll be back in the ranks."

Paul snorted. "What do you expect, Karl? Not even I can persuade them to take you as an officer."

"Just as well. I don't want that kind of responsibility."

Paul cast a warning glance. "Between you and me, Karl, you'd better learn to control remarks like that, or you'll end up in front of a *Feldjäger* firing squad." He handed Karl a pen. "As from now you're a serving member of the Waffen SS. You are expected to behave as such. We have a reputation to maintain. You're going to help train new recruits, which is why you're taken on as sergeant. They will be young lads, fanatically loyal to the Führer. The slightest sign of treachery and they'll report you, without thinking twice. Do you understand me, Karl?"

"Perfectly. You want me to train mere boys to fight to save your skin. If the Allies win, the likes of you are going to be in deep trouble, aren't they, Paul?"

Sturmbannführer Zopf scowled. "On your feet, Driesler! You are talking to an officer. Be grateful I recommended you as an instructor, rather than send you to one of the punishment divisions in the East. I could easily reverse that decision!"

As Karl jumped to attention, the hot office began to sway. Paul's voice turned into a buzzing noise. A golden haze surrounded his angry face. Karl's breath came in short gasps and he keeled over onto the floor.

A hand slapped his face. Opening his eyes he saw Paul's dark eyes peering anxiously at him. "Fainting on parade now, Karl?"

It was a while before Karl realised that Paul was caressing his cheek. He turned his head abruptly aside, appalled.

Paul laughed. "Don't worry, Karl. I like women as well as you. Even so, I've always had a soft spot for you. We were like brothers once. That must explain why I still want to help you, despite everything you've said. Can you sit up?"

Karl brushed aside the hand offered in help, and slowly stood up. "Just get me to Mannheim."

On day passes from the convalescence hospital, SS Oberscharführer Driesler scoured Mannheim for signs of Ilse. She was registered with the police at her sister's address in the northern suburbs. When he got there he found only a wasteland; no forwarding messages scrawled on the walls; no neighbours to ask her whereabouts. He went back to the police, the Red Cross, all the hospitals. No one could tell him what had become of Ilse and Siegfried.

On his last visit to Mannheim, Karl left his own message on the blackened walls where Ilse had lived, asking anyone who knew of her to contact him.

He wrote to his parents asking if they had any news of Ilse. His mother's reply caught up with him in September at his training barracks in the Hunsrück hills.

Darling Karl,

I'm so glad you're feeling much better. I've already written to Hildegard Zopf to thank her for Paul's help.

We have heard nothing at all from Ilse since we told her your circumstances. Her disappearance is most worrying. If we do hear from her, you can be sure we'll let you know immediately. It's possible she's been sent further east to escape the bombing, although she should have come here. She knows our home is hers and Siegfried's, even though we're overflowing with evacuees. We have a

wretch of a mother with six children. They are little monsters!
Father is constantly having to turf them out of the sawmill. At least
Anna is busy, keeping an eye on them all, and is starting to get over
her grief for poor Thomas.

Wherever you find yourself now, darling, take great care. I know
you will write when you can, and make up for Rudi's slackness. My
prayers go with you.

Your ever-loving Mother.

Karl thought of his father's reaction to the household
invasion. A stern disciplinarian, but with a soft heart, it was
surprising he did not feature more in the letter. Usually his
signature appeared alongside his wife's. Perhaps he was too
busy trying to run the business without either son to help. Karl
knew his father would disapprove of him joining the SS. He
was the main reason Karl had not originally done so.
Volunteering for the Wehrmacht was bad enough; Rudi
waited to be drafted. Recently his father was called up into the
Volkssturm to join the defence of his country. Karl wondered
how his family could possibly cope with the business and with
all those evacuees. This war would destroy them all.

Karl's trainees turned out to be as fanatical as Paul
predicted. Their whole childhood had been spent under the
Nazi regime; they had neither experience nor maturity to see
through its evil teachings. He remembered only too well how
easily he had been taken in. He was careful now to keep his
own doubts quiet. Executions were all too frequent.

The boys passed through training in a matter of weeks.
Most were already competent with machine-guns. They knew
little about the world, except how to fight. Karl felt alone at
the barracks, not daring to make a friend lest he report him for
a careless remark. He began to fear more and more that Ilse
and Sigi were dead. Why else had she not been in touch?

Early in November he was assigned to an infantry unit of
the 2nd SS Panzer Division based in the Eifel, close to the
Belgian border. Now he was given the chance to fight again.
On 13th December all units took up their positions in the
greatest secrecy, opposite the Ardennes. The Americans were

taken completely by surprise in an attack on 16th December; Karl enjoyed once more the sweet taste of victory. He soon notched up twenty kills and was awarded his sniper's badge, third class – a blackbird's head amongst oak leaves.

American prisoners taken now were fearful of their SS captors. Karl commented on this to a fellow sergeant.

"You know why?" the sergeant asked bitterly. "The Sixth SS Panzers shot some American POWs, as well as Belgian civilians. Bloody fools! We'll all be tarred with the same brush, if things turn against us."

Later Karl realised neither of them had spared a thought for the murdered American prisoners.

Their victories could not last. The cloud lifted, allowing Allied air support to strafe the ravine in which Karl huddled, camouflaged by a white snow suit which barely kept the freezing air at bay. Leaving the wounded to die or be captured, he joined the retreat on 8th January. Struggling through snowdrifts, ravines and icy streams, Karl and the remaining members of his unit were eventually picked up by a passing troop lorry, already laden with stragglers, and returned briefly to the barracks in the Eifel.

Talk now was of being sent east. As Hitler lost faith more and more in the ability of the Wehrmacht to stem the Soviet advance, most SS divisions were diverted there. Karl could not believe his luck when he was moved to the southern Netherlands to block Anglo-Canadian forces surging towards the Rhine. At least they might adhere to the Geneva Convention.

In early February the weather was atrocious. Visibility was poor for Karl and his small band of fifteen and sixteen-year-old snipers. They hid in the shelled ruins, fending for themselves as best they could: picking out targets, moving on swiftly, all the while trying to keep contact with their own lines, as the Allies advanced ever closer towards Germany.

With their Fatherland under direct threat, the boys showed a matchless determination not to surrender an inch of soil. They fought against impossible odds. Karl knew it would not be long before they were cut off from their own lines and surrounded. What was to be done then? Fight to the death as ordered? He did not doubt the boys would do so.

They took cover in a farmhouse overlooking the River Maas. A low-flying Hurricane swooped and strafed their position. Artillery fire opened up, with a direct hit on one end of the house. Their rifles were useless against such weapons. Karl ordered the boys out of the farmhouse into the pinewoods. Retreat was impossible with the waters of the Maas at their backs. There was heavy shelling around Roermond to the south. They would have to go north, where enemy troops were moving up, and find a location where they could pin down a convoy with a few well-aimed shots, before being routed or killed.

Despite the cold they were sweating as they darted through the pinewoods towards a clump of bushes which commanded a good view of the road. The lack of undergrowth within the woods aided their progress but made them conspicuous to an armoured car hidden in a gulley. A stutter of machine-gunfire sent Karl sprawling to the ground. He sought cover in a muddy ditch, leaving two boys wounded in the open. The machine-gun raked the ground over the ditch, making their rescue impossible. The remaining four and Karl wriggled on their bellies until the ditch petered out. They had no more cover. They were trapped. Karl decided it would be futile to resist further. The war was lost already. Surrender was their only hope. He did not want to see another patrol die around him.

"Throw out your rifles," Karl told the disbelieving boys. "There is nothing more we can do."

Two boys followed Karl's example, ducking instantly as bullets raced over to their new position. Shouted orders came from the forest, then silence. Karl assumed the enemy was waiting for further evidence of their surrender. He signalled the two remaining lads to throw out their weapons. The boys glanced at each other, confirming their decision not to accept defeat.

One pointed his rifle at Karl. "Traitor!" he snarled.

Karl determined to stay in command of the situation by giving orders. "Throw them out!" he yelled at them. "You'll gain nothing by staying here." He made a sudden grab for the rifle and hurled it over the top of the ditch to land with the others. The machine-gun was silent. Their surrender was acknowledged. The fourth boy seemed taken aback. Karl ignored him, waved a handkerchief overhead then cautiously poked his unhelmeted head up to assess whether it was safe to emerge from the ditch. As he did so, a number of infantrymen joined the armoured car, which was American. They scurried from tree to tree towards the wounded boys, and checked them for weapons.

At the sight of the Germans leaving the ditch, the Americans bristled, alert for treachery. As the fourth boy's head appeared above the edge of the ditch, his rifle barrel came with it, aimed ahead. A volley of shots rang out, sending the Germans sprawling into the mud once more. The boy died a hero's death, as he had been ordered, his fifteen-year-old face blown away.

Karl lifted his head again. The Americans were standing well back. Karl slowly got up, hands raised. "Stand up!" he snapped at the boys.

Cautiously the soldiers approached, guns at the ready, and removed their backpacks, belt of hand grenades, ammunition and knives. Karl heard anger in one man's voice as he spotted their collar patches. Amongst the flood of English words, Karl heard the letters "SS".

They had surrendered for nothing. The soldiers facing them were increasingly hostile, although the youth of the boys seemed to temper their desire to kill their prisoners outright. They were in a hurry to press on. Would they bother taking SS prisoners? If only Schwab had not decided to play the hero.

A shout reached them from the road. An officer wanted to know the cause of the delay. Karl never discovered what was in the minds of the soldiers. The officer despatched two men to accompany the prisoners to a collecting point, the remainder pressed on towards the Maas.

Running at the double down the road, their hands raised, the prisoners passed lines of trucks filled with soldiers on their way to the river. For Karl, despite all the propaganda about the fate of SS captives, the relief at surviving capture was overwhelming. The future of Germany was out of his hands.

In a meadow by the road, a huddle of prisoners waited under guard to be transported away from the front lines. Karl and the three boys were dumped there too. Even though they were prisoners, Karl's little troop was acutely aware of their insecure status in their tell-tale uniforms. Ripping off insignia would not help. It would still leave the outline of the eagle on the left sleeve rather than over the right breast. They were even eyed with suspicion by Wehrmacht in the group, as though their presence put them all in jeopardy. Karl sat on the wet grass next to another small group of SS captives. Their guards seemed to watch them particularly zealously, as though they were still capable of infinite depravity.

Putting on his forage cap for warmth, Karl felt he ought to try to keep up the boys' spirits. Surely the Allies would treat their prisoners properly, no matter what German rumour made out? He glanced sideways at the three of them. They showed varying degrees of bitterness towards the position they were in. Ettlinger, the one whose rifle Karl had snatched from him, was still fuming at the indignity of it all. The other two had given in to lethargy, and were smoking quietly, trying to blot out the scene of defeat around them. Karl felt curiously empty. He dared not contemplate the future. Living each day for itself had become his habit, now he felt sure Ilse and Sigi were dead.

Transport never came. The column of marching men was faced with the hostile abuse of the villagers whose homes had been wrecked and livelihoods destroyed. In a makeshift barbed wire enclosure, Karl had all his personal belongings and money taken, his details noted. Finally he was given a cup of water and some biscuits. They had no cover in the pouring rain that night. The following day they were marched on again to yet another collecting ground. This one was far larger, but just as disorganised, with little shelter or food, and no sanitation. They were there two days, interrogated, given a medical inspection, and transported by goods train to Belgium. On the journey German prisoners discovered that Russian, Polish and other foreign members of the Wehrmacht had been allowed to keep their money in order to buy water from their now Canadian guards. The German prisoners went without water. In Belgium there were tents as shelter, but not enough for the number of prisoners confined. There were not even enough blankets. Karl spent the cold nights wandering around the quagmire in an effort to keep warm until he was too exhausted to remain awake. Food and water rations continued meagre, supplemented by rainwater they collected themselves. The drumming of rain on canvas was almost drowned by the incessant coughing from within.

Amongst the SS contingent the fear remained that they would be shot. The hunt for SS hiding amidst Wehrmacht soldiers was made obvious to one and all by the "arms-up" parade. The men had to display the left bicep to reveal if there was the SS blood group tattoo there. As a newcomer to the SS, Karl was without such a tattoo. The availability of blood plasma at field medical stations in recent months had obviated the need. Despite this, Karl felt branded with the SS stigma. Not only defeated, but disgraced. To prove the point, the Canadians were free and easy with sticks and rifle butts when they wanted the prisoners to move. They relished picking on the SS men.

Karl hoped he would be able to mingle with the Wehrmacht, with whom he felt a greater affiliation, but after ten days in the camp, all the SS were rounded up and put into trucks. Many were convinced that execution was just around the corner, Karl amongst them, his hopes of fair treatment dashed.

They travelled to Ostend, thence by boat to Tilbury. On the other side of the Channel, conditions improved dramatically, so much that some prisoners thought it was a softener for condemned men. Railway coaches with upholstered seats took them to the interrogation centre on Kempton Park racecourse, where they were promptly deloused and screened for political ideology. As a member of the SS, Karl was automatically designated "C", or "black", with no chance to speak for himself. Too many Germans were renouncing Nazi beliefs for the sake of a whiter grading, for the voice of one SS man to be heard.

He was first sent to Lancashire. There were many members of the Waffen SS in the camp, but he gradually realised there were a few others like himself, who seemed not to be ardent Nazis. At first they would not trust him, fearing he was only a spy for the Nazi element, the vocal majority. Hitler's birthday on 20th April provided him with a chance to demonstrate his antipathy to Nazism. The occasion was to be celebrated with due ceremony, despite the increasingly dismal news from home. Taking an enormous risk, Karl joined the small protest group who refused to take part in the Hitler salute at roll-call. It was his last attempt to stick by his principles. If he failed this time he would completely lose that scrap of self-respect he retained.

The protest was noted, but under the eyes of their guards the Nazi element could do nothing until later that evening. Karl was leaving the mess tent when he was jumped by several men. His mouth firmly gagged to prevent him alerting the guards, his hands bound, he was spirited away to a tent where a secret court-martial was convened. The other protesters also stood bound, awaiting their punishment. They were to be hanged on the spot.

Karl's anger overrode his fear: anger at the Nazi mob; anger at their British captors for allowing such a thing to happen; anger at himself for his foolhardy gesture. He watched in silent rage as five nooses were strung from the ridge-pole. As the last was secured, the watch outside whistled the alarm.

His warning came too late for the self-appointed hangmen. Before they could disperse, ten Tommies burst into the tent, hustling the watchman in with them. Released from their bonds, Karl and his fellow protestors were escorted to safety for the night. The following morning they were moved to a different camp, where there was a larger proportion of "grey" and "white" prisoners. The death of Hitler ten days later released these prisoners from their oath of loyalty to the Führer, and made life simpler for those who believed the news.

The end of the war brought a sombre mood to the camp and no hopes of release, since no peace treaty had been signed. As a category "C" prisoner, Karl believed he would be held indefinitely, so it came as a pleasant surprise when, at the next screening later in the summer of 1945, he was re-classified "B" or "grey" and allowed out to work in the fields.

The shadow of Nazism was finally lifting, and Karl could begin to put the past behind him.

CHAPTER FIFTEEN

Goldberg made notes throughout Robert's narrative. After adding a few last thoughts, he slowly put down his pencil.

"That is certainly enlightening, Mr Murdoch." Goldberg referred briefly to his notes. "What it boils down to is that Karl can't handle his guilt; his initial acceptance of Nazism, the ease with which he could kill people – the sniper's badge you mentioned is a good example. But it is probably the SS association which troubles him most. Miss Carter wielded a most potent weapon when she accosted him with that." With lips pursed he gazed over Robert's shoulder in contemplation. His eyes returned to Robert. "What do *you* feel is Karl's main problem? You've not given me your own impressions. Bear in mind I've never spoken to Karl."

Robert folded his arms and sat back to consider the question. "Well ... Complete loss of self-respect, I think. Miss Carter has rejected him, so he's rejected himself. That's my theory, anyway.

Goldberg smiled encouragingly. "Not bad, Mr Murdoch. We do of course have to consider the drugs he was given. They might have some part to play."

"Neurological damage, you mean?"

Goldberg shrugged. "Not necessarily, although it's possible. Since I have no idea which drugs were used, I can't really speculate. We shall have to concentrate on the psychological factors. Find something he still believes in." He looked at his watch. "I shall have to leave it there for today. Other patients to attend to. If I think of any points I haven't raised today, may I telephone you?"

"Of course."

During his ride home, Robert mulled over what he had told Goldberg. Karl had lost everything he valued, except for his own family. Robert had never heard what happened to Siegfried, whether he survived or not. All Karl had told him was that Ilse severed her connections with Karl and his family. Now Katherine had done the same thing.

The day was hot, the leafy lanes a stark contrast to the oppressive confines of the hospital camp. Karl would not be allowed unaccompanied into the grounds. Watching him sitting quietly reading his book, Robert had seen beneath the apparently calm exterior. Karl was deeply depressed, alone and unable to communicate. What would he think about, with no recollection of where he was or what had happened to him? Goldberg and his staff all seemed very caring and devoted, but Karl had no conscious contact with them. Surely he needed someone he knew well and could recognise?

Katherine must be the key. If it meant telling her Karl's past in order to win back her sympathy for him, then that was what he must do.

"Blast them!" Katherine hurried over to the chicken run to right a toppled container of insecticide. A dark pool of liquid had already seeped under the wire netting. "Those two are more trouble than they're worth."

She shooed away a couple of inquisitive hens from the mess then hurried to the toolshed for a shovel. Here too was disorder. Les and Dick had left all the tools in an untidy heap, instead of hanging them on their appropriate hooks. As she searched for a shovel, Katherine nicked her ankle on a scythe. She stooped to inspect the wound. Nothing serious. Only the latest in a series of mishaps since Andrew's men came to work for her. If only Karl were ... No! After what he did to Andrew ... She dragged the shovel out from under the pile and strode angrily back to the chicken run.

The telephone rang. Katherine dropped the shovel and ran into the house. It was Robert asking if he might come up.

"Please do! I need someone reliable around here. Les and Dick are useless. Must dash. See you soon."

She was selecting lambs for market when she heard his motorbike. She headed back to the house.

"Good morning Katherine!" he greeted her breezily. "It's another glorious day, is it not?"

Katherine smiled briefly. She had too much to do to waste time. "You feel like doing some work today then? My vegetable patch needs a jolly good hoeing."

"I really came to talk to you."

Immediately her suspicions were aroused. "What about?"

"Karl." He saw her turn away, and held her arm. "Wait! You've *got* to listen!"

"Why? Why should I waste my time listening to you try to excuse him? I've got the lambs to sort, the sheepshearer to contact, the ..."

"I'll help you with all that. Just give *me* an hour now. I promise you won't regret it!"

His sincerity was plain. Katherine wavered enough for Robert to press home his advantage.

"I won't try to excuse him, Katherine. You'll hear everything he did."

Karl's hidden past had always intrigued her. "So you're finally prepared to reveal all." She gave a rueful smile of relent. "I don't suppose you'll leave me in peace until I agree to listen." She nodded towards the garden. "Let's go and sit in the shade. Then you can tell me all there is to know."

"So how do you judge him now?" Robert asked at last. "Is he worthy of your help or not?"

She looked upwards for guidance. Through the tears in her eyes the leaves of the pear tree shimmered against the clear blue sky. High overhead a lark sang lustily, like a voice from heaven. She listened to its clear song as she weighed up what she had heard.

She gave a long, drawn-out sigh, her voice husky and subdued when she at last spoke. "Poor Karl. I can't imagine what it must have been like for him. Now I understand why he never told me. He didn't lie, did he? Except by omission."

Her head drooped sorrowfully. Robert held her hand.

300

"The important question is, Katherine, will you help him? No one can reach him. You meant more to him than anyone. Perhaps you are the only one who can penetrate the barrier round him. You did it before, I saw it happen. Yes, he opened up to me, but he blossomed under your care. Perhaps he will respond to you again."

"Or Ilse."

"Ilse is his past, like Andrew is yours."

"You said Karl can remember only the past. It would be Ilse who means most to him."

"Maybe. But it's the present he's lost. You are the key to the present."

The lark continued its intricate song. Life was not simple. Katherine realised that now.

"How can I help him then?"

Robert squeezed her hands hard in triumph. "By going to see him."

Karl remembered his hand had been bandaged. That was several weeks ago, he guessed. The weather grew hotter all the while. Unbearably hot, and stuffy. He gazed longingly out of his barred window. His scarred hand told him why they could not let him out alone. Alone was too risky. He might find a sharp stone, a piece of string. It was clear he had tried and failed. Why had he not made a better job of it? Next time he would succeed – before he died of loneliness.

Out on the lawn he could see people – patients – with nurses in charge. But he never saw anyone close enough to speak to. He only knew he was a POW in an English hospital because a doctor, named Goldberg, left explanatory messages. Goldberg asked him to leave messages in return, saying what he knew about himself, why he was here, how he felt. Karl always tore up the notes. How dare they try to trick him into revealing information! Even if he could have remembered anything since early 1943, he wasn't going to tell the English!

A new message magically appeared on the table. It simply said: *Robert Murdoch came to see you.*

He shouted at the door: "Who the hell is Robert Murdoch?"

If only Ilse would appear at the door, smiling, her long blonde hair loose around her shoulders. "Ilse!" He called her name out loud to conjure up the images so vivid in his dreams, her laughter as he chased her through the forest, carving their names on the lion-shaped rock, lying on a blanket of pine needles ...

He sat silently on the bed, staring at the floor. He could not survive on daydreams. Ilse was far away, or even dead. She could not come to him.

He had no appetite for supper, pushed away breakfast. Starvation was as effective a way as any of dying.

His full stomach told him they force-fed him lunch. His infuriating lapses meant they could do anything they liked. His body was at their mercy. He had no way of stopping them.

He sat by the window. Another beautiful day. He thumped his scarred hand in frustration against the bars. "There *must* be a way! Another day of this and I'll go mad." He snorted at his stupidity. "You're mad already."

His hand fell to his lap. Slowly he raised it again, fingertips touching the window pane. Glass. "This time!"

He leaped to his feet, grabbed the chair by a leg and rammed it through the bars against the window. Shards of glass fell free. He flung down the chair and swooped on a large fragment.

The door burst open.

He lay still, his limbs too heavy to move. Slowly he turned his head and inspected his surroundings without any great interest. A different room. No window. They must have been watching.

He felt defeated. Why had they stopped him? What did it matter whether he lived or died? He studied the ceiling for an hour but it gave him no answer.

He rolled over. Another message lay on the small table beside him. He picked it up. *Don't despair. Help is on its way.* What help could they possibly offer, unless ... Ilse? He grasped at the straw. Surely he would not shut himself off from Ilse?

He grabbed the message pad and wrote: *Is Ilse coming?*

They were still watching. The reply appeared within minutes. *Yes. She is coming tomorrow.*

At last! Something was being done to give him hope. Was it really four years since he had seen Ilse? He had to believe the dates on the magazines he had read. It seemed only a few months. Would she have changed? Did she still love him?

There was no need to force-feed him now; his renewed will to live was too strong. He tossed and turned with excitement half the night and still woke at dawn. Later that morning he found himself in a sunny room, with two chairs and open windows. Ilse would be there any moment!

Katherine was glad of Robert's company. She was apprehensive about meeting Karl again, even though he might not know her. Were they all expecting a miracle? If Karl did not acknowledge Robert, why should he be any different with her?

Dr Goldberg did his best to set Katherine at her ease, offered them tea, chatted about the weather, then came to the matter in hand.

"Well now, Miss Carter. Shortly after you telephoned yesterday, Karl reached a crisis point. It may have had something to do with being told of your visit, Mr Murdoch. We're not exactly sure. Anyway, it was plain watching him he was about to try to kill himself."

There was a gasp from Katherine. Robert leaned forward anxiously.

"Don't worry. He's all right. We sedated him the rest of the day, then I left him another message: "Help is on it's way". By that I meant you of course, Miss Carter. I wanted to give him some hope. It seems to have done the trick."

Katherine was appalled. "Thank God Robert made me agree to come."

Goldberg held up his hands. "It's not quite as simple as that, I'm afraid, Miss Carter. I didn't specify you. I only said "Help is coming". His next message asked if it was Ilse who was coming. I thought it best to encourage that belief. I hope you understand."

She smiled at the doctor. "I'll try to remember who I'm supposed to be. I don't speak much German though. Only a few words I've picked up from Karl."

"That's the least of our worries, I suspect. First we have to make contact. I'm afraid we're relying on you for that. We've tried everything else."

"That's a heavy responsibility," she said sombrely.

"Indeed it is." He stood up. "Well, if you're ready, I'll take you along to see him. He's in high spirits at the moment, so it may be our best opportunity."

Robert crossed his fingers and wished her good luck. "Do whatever you have to, Katherine, for Karl's sake."

They followed Goldberg down the corridor. Katherine felt a rush of adrenalin. Karl knew Ilse was coming. What would his reaction to *her* be?

"We'll be nearby, in case you want us," Goldberg told her. "I won't come in now, of course."

He unlocked a door. Katherine uttered a quick prayer and stepped through.

Karl was looking at the space she occupied. She could tell by his vacant expression he was not seeing her. She stepped nearer, saw how pale, how wasted he was. His eyes remained fixed on the doorway. He did not know she was there.

She sat down on the chair opposite and studied him, getting to grips with her own senses. This was a different Karl from the one she thought she knew. This was the real Karl. The one hidden from her.

She understood him at last. She knew what his scars were, physical and mental, his fears, his self-doubt, his guilt. He had not trusted her enough to tell her the truth. She must try to show him he could trust her. She would not fail him again.

Katherine pulled her chair closer to his and gently turned his head so that he faced her.

"Karl?" No response. She reached for his limp hands and held them, stroking them. Physical contact was not resisted. He must feel her touch. She lifted his hand and put it to her own face, making him feel her skin, her hair, her lips. He could be made to eat and drink in this state, she knew. What would happen if she kissed him?

Putting thoughts of observers to the back of her mind, she remembered Robert's words. "Do what you have to". She stood up, moved forward and sat herself on his lap, wrapping his arms around her. She clung to him, making sure his hands stayed where she had put them, on her breast. Resting her head on his chest she could hear his heart beat. It was slow and steady.

She ran her fingers firmly over his face and down his neck, massaging the muscles of his neck and shoulders. How well she knew this body, if not his mind. She pulled his mouth towards hers. His lips were dry, unresponsive. If she expected a role reversal of the Sleeping Beauty, she was mistaken. Karl remained obstinately oblivious.

She moved her mouth close to his ear. "Oh, Schatz! Why can't you hear me?" she moaned.

Under her hand his heart started to thud. At the same moment Karl tensed. She leaned outwards to see his face. His astonished eyes met hers, but to her dismay they held only bewilderment.

He pushed her abruptly off his lap. "*Wo ist Ilse?*"

He realised his mistake when he saw her anguish. Whoever she was, she was the first person he had spoken to in weeks.

"*Entschuldigung!*" he apologised, trying to control the turmoil of his emotions. He was expecting Ilse, but another woman was here, offering herself to him. Confusion and anguish overwhelmed him. He buried his head in his hands to cover the tears of frustration.

Katherine knelt beside him and held him tight, just as he held her on the day her father died. She tried to hide her disappointment, but it hurt. His awareness had returned but not his memory. He wanted Ilse. She was a poor substitute.

Gradually his sobs died down. She lessened her hold on him. "Better now, Karl?"

He raised his head from her breast. "*Englisch?*" he asked uncertainly, hearing the foreign language.

"Yes. English," she replied. She saw him draw back. "I'm a friend," she said quickly, before he could retreat further. "I want to help you."

He looked blankly at her. He had not understood. His eyes narrowed. The blankness became suspicion. He was alert now, distrustful. He stood up, arms folded. In control. She began to feel uneasy at being alone with him.

His aggressive silence unnerved her. Katherine gave up. She would have to leave it to Dr Goldberg now to sort him out. She went to the door, feeling Karl's steely eyes boring into her back. She called out for Dr Goldberg who appeared promptly with Robert.

Robert was completely taken aback by the unexpectedly hostile situation. He thought Karl would regain his memory, but that was clearly not the case. Katherine seemed distressed, but was managing to keep calm.

Goldberg was deliberately casual. "*Wunderschön, dass wir uns endlich unterhalten können, Karl!*" he proclaimed cheerily, shaking him heartily by the hand. "*Setze dich zu uns. Du wirst viele Fragen haben, nicht wahr?*"

It took Karl a moment to react. He was thrown off balance by the man's informality. When he did react it was with restrained acquiescence. He decided cooperation was his best tactic at the moment. He sat down, feeling calmer at last, more self-assured, as he got over the shock of seeing people again.

Goldberg asked Robert to fetch two more chairs.

"*Wer sind sie?*" Karl asked first, with a nod at Robert and Katherine.

"*Deine guten Freunde, Herr Robert Murdoch und Fraülein Katherine Carter.*"

Karl remembered "Robert Murdoch" from the message left for him, but the look he flashed at Katherine made her blush. "*Wieso?*"

Goldberg turned to the two Britons. "He wants to know why you're his friends. I don't want to tell him too much at this stage. I'd rather he remembered for himself. If you want to stay here while I get him accustomed to talking to me, you're welcome. It will show him you're interested in him, even if you don't understand a word of it."

Goldberg spoke to Karl for a while, explaining the course his illness had taken, making sure he understood his POW status. Watching Karl's changing expression, Katherine and Robert tried to glean some idea of what he was being told. At length Goldberg and Karl both stood up.

"I'm going to take Karl along to the day-room to talk to some of his compatriots, hear their side of things. I'll meet you back in my office in a few minutes."

Karl gave a brief bow of farewell to his English acquaintances. Once he had gone, Katherine let out a sigh of anguish, although Robert was smiling at the overtly German mannerism.

"He's so different, isn't he?" Katherine commented as they walked back down the echoing corridor. "In some ways I can see him as he was when he first came to work for us, the formality and all that. But I'm afraid I don't trust him now."

They settled down in Goldberg's office. Robert had a burning question to ask of Katherine. "Tell me, how did you get through to him?"

Despite herself Katherine blushed again. "He didn't respond to any caresses, nor even a kiss. I think it was when I called him "Schatz". Perhaps Ilse used to call him that too."

"What happened then?"

Katherine bit her lip. "I suddenly knew he could see me, that I wasn't Ilse. He pushed me away. I think he apologised straightaway, but then it was awful. He began to cry really hard. I thought he would never stop. After that he became rather cold and distant, perhaps to cover his embarassment."

"I was interested in his reaction to Dr Goldberg."

"Why?"

"It's fairly obvious from his name, Goldberg's a Jew. Remember, Karl was in the Hitler Youth. Was no doubt indoctrinated with all that anti-Semitic nonsense."

Katherine frowned. "I'm not quite sure what you're driving at. Did you expect Karl to attack him, or something?"

"No. Just be less polite than he was, perhaps. He probably realised it was politic to keep Goldberg on his side, being his doctor and all."

Goldberg rejoined them, smiling broadly. "That was a triumph, Miss Carter! You must tell me the secret of your success."

"She kissed him and called him "Schatz"!" Robert answered for her.

"It's only because he was expecting Ilse that he responded, I'm sure."

"Well we had planned that, hadn't we?" Goldberg consoled her. "I caught what you said as I came in just now, Mr Murdoch. He has adapted remarkably quickly to his changing situation, but he's got an awful lot to learn yet about the post-war world. Most of it will not be very pleasant for him. Sometimes unpleasant memories are best left forgotten."

Robert nodded. "I wish I could forget mine."

Goldberg smiled in sympathy. "Don't we all, Mr Murdoch. Don't we all. However, we can't leave Karl with any Nazi ideas. He must remember what he went through to make him the pleasant character you say he became. There's a certain – dare I say it? – arrogance about him at the moment. I believe we will end up with a more complete and worthwhile person if we try to make him remember. Do you agree?"

"Yes," said Katherine decisively. "I'm not sure I'm too keen on him now."

GREY

CHAPTER SIXTEEN

When he woke up Karl feared that the events of the previous day had never happened. He had dreamed it all, or else it had only been a temporary recovery and he would find himself alone and isolated as before.

He quickly tried the handle of his door. That Jewish doctor had promised it would not be locked. Sure enough it was not. He glanced along the corridor which had been both a barrier and the way to freedom. There was no sign of life. Too early still? He checked the time on his watch. It was six-fifteen. He had plenty of time to wash, dress. And shave. They had actually given him a razor.

Looking at his reflection, Karl was painfully aware of the march of time. The youthful looks he remembered had gone; beaten out of him. He looked much older now, older even than his supposed twenty-six. It was his face which persuaded him this was not all just an elaborate British hoax designed to make him give information.

Depression had left its mark on him. Optimism was rapidly replacing it. If the future held any hope, he wanted a part in it, a part in Germany's renewal. A future with Ilse.

A face sprang to mind, but it was not Ilse's. What was her name? Katherine Carter. She reminded him of Ilse. Nothing to do with her looks. No, it was something she said. What it was he could not recall. She had spoken only in English, expecting him to understand. Why?

He remembered the English magazines given to him weeks ago. Had he learned English since his capture? No doubt it would all come back to him in due course.

After a rather sobering breakfast with the other patients, during which he heard of the devastation of Germany, Karl was taken to see Goldberg.

"I've been thinking a lot about my family," Karl said as soon as he was seated. "I need to know whether they, and my fiancée, survived the war."

"If it will set your mind at rest, I can tell you they did survive," Goldberg replied cautiously. The loss of Ilse to another man was a blow he did not yet want Karl to have to experience, so soon after his first stage of recovery. "I wrote to your parents informing them of your ... illness. I'm sure they'll be thrilled to hear from you."

"I'll write today."

"Good." Goldberg arranged Karl's notes neatly on the desk. "So. To work. You told me that one of the last things you remember is being home on leave, after you were wounded in Russia."

"Yes. It was the first time I'd been home since I was promoted to Lieutenant. Ilse was very impressed. I should have married her there and then." He broke off. "Perhaps we did get married, and I don't remember. Can you tell me?" he asked suddenly.

Goldberg's brown eyes did not waver as he replied. "I told you yesterday, Karl. I don't want to tell you what you have forgotten. We must work to make you remember it for yourself."

Karl looked wistful. "Then you won't tell me what that English woman has to do with it."

"You're right. I won't ... for the moment."

The hardest part of writing to his parents was the date. It was still unbelievable. He read over what he had written.

Dear Mother and Father,   *27.5.47*

I gather from my doctor you know I've been ill. It seems I'm over the worst now. I just have to regain my memory of events from the summer of 1943. Dr Goldberg won't tell me what happened to make me ill, or any details of the time I've forgotten. I'm tempted to ask you to fill me in, but that would apparently be cheating! I've got to do it for myself, so Goldberg says. He seems confident he can help me. I'm certainly feeling far happier than I did recently. Just imagine – I didn't even know the war was over! The other patients here have told me much about what happened during the war, and it's pretty hard to stomach.

Enough of politics! I would dearly love to hear all your news. Don't forget – I can't recall anything from July 1943. It's only my own experiences I have to remember for myself. I'll keep you informed of my progress.

All my love,
Karl

By the end of the week he had not recalled any of his lost memories. Dr Goldberg suggested a new approach, and the following Monday they set off with a driver for Herefordshire. During the journey Goldberg filled Karl in on the details he needed to know; that he had been living with Robert Murdoch's family, and working for Miss Carter on her farm.

"That's hardly likely!" Karl interrupted. "The Geneva Convention states that officers don't have to work."

Goldberg avoided telling Karl he had not been an officer when captured. "Even officers get bored staying in camp all the time. Many volunteered to work. Anyway, the Geneva Convention no longer applied once hostilities ceased. The Red Cross looks after your interests now."

They sat in silence for a while, watching the sun-baked fields and meadows pass by.

"It will be difficult for you now, not speaking the language," Goldberg said at last, "but I'm sure you'll cope. The Murdochs have been well briefed. I'm coming with you in case they have any further questions or you want to say something important to them. Something may jog your memory during your week's stay. If you have any problems or want to discuss anything with me, you can always telephone me at the hospital. The Murdochs have the number."

A distant ridge of high ground came into view, drawing Karl's eyes irresistibly towards it. A hint of home, like the black-and-white houses he had seen along the way. He smiled. He supposed he could have been happy here. He studied the landscape. Luxuriant hedges divided colourful meadows from fields of wilting root crops.

"A good shower of rain would be welcome once the hay's in," he commented.

Goldberg forgot for one moment not to give away details of recent history. "Indeed. Such a contrast to the diabolical winter." He caught a glimpse of a signpost. "I believe we're almost there now."

The enclosing valley hid the distant range of hills. Karl concentrated on his immediate surroundings.

"Do you recognise any of this?"

Karl shook his head. He suspected his stay here would be a complete waste of time, but at least it had him out of the hospital for a while. Weeks of inactivity there had left him lethargic and bored. He could have done with Ilse's company. He smiled at the memory of their most recent reunion.

Goldberg misunderstood the smile. "It's not all going to be pleasant here, Karl," he warned. "By no means all the British will be as friendly as the Murdochs."

Karl laughed. "You think I can't look after myself?"

The car slowed as it approached another village. A string of terraced cottages flanked the river; opposite them several side roads led off up the hillside. They came to the centre of the village, and drew up outside the bow-fronted window of Penchurch Post Office and Village Stores.

While the driver went inside to ask for directions to Yew Tree Lodge, Karl watched the children in the playground of the village school across the road. He did not see the elderly storekeeper, a portly, keen-eyed woman, leave her shop to point out Cutbush Lane.

Mrs Tucker's eye was caught by the blond head in the back of the car. She ducked slightly to see inside. Her suspicions were confirmed.

She banged on the door. "Karl!" she cried loudly through the open window.

Karl turned his head at the sound of his name, to see a woman waving and smiling broadly at him. It would seem that he had been a popular chap amongst the English, despite what Goldberg made out. He waved back.

The driver got back into the car and turned it round by the memorial cross. They drove back a couple of hundred yards to one of the side roads leading up the hill, and soon found the house they were looking for.

Karl studied the large red-bricked house he was supposed to have lived in. No memories stirred, not even when the front door opened and a tiny woman came out, accompanied by someone he did recognise – Robert Murdoch.

Gertie rushed forward when she saw Karl. She could not help giving him a warm hug, hanging onto his arm as she chirped: "I know you can't understand me, Karl, but I've simply got to welcome you back properly." Without a pause she then addressed the pleasant-looking man who accompanied Karl. "Dr Goldberg, I presume!" she said, offering her hand.

"Mrs Murdoch!" he replied, equally jovially. "It's a pleasure to meet you at last."

"Come on in, won't you. Have a drink. You must be parched after that long hot drive." Gertie herded them all in out of the fierce sunshine. She directed the driver to the kitchen and Megan. The others filed into the living room where Robert showed Karl to a chair by an open window. Megan soon appeared with a tray of glasses and a jug of lemonade, before disappearing back to the kitchen.

Karl sat back and drank the lemonade, letting the conversation pass him by, watching his new hosts carefully. Mrs Murdoch was charming, and clearly intended making a fuss of her guest. Karl smiled in amusement until he realised Robert was watching him. Their eyes met briefly. Karl saw mild rebuke and realised he could not take Robert's apparent friendship for granted.

After a lull in the conversation, Goldberg turned to him, reverting to German. "Have you anything you want to say to or ask the Murdochs before I go, Karl?"

Karl reckoned some form of polite acknowledgement of their hospitality was in order. After Goldberg had translated Karl's words he gave Karl his POW identity documents and also a small book, which Karl saw was a German-English dictionary.

"This is yours. You may need it again now. If there's nothing else you want to say, I'll leave you to these kind people for a week. Don't forget, you can always telephone me if you want anything." He switched back to English. "That goes for you too Mr Murdoch, Mrs Murdoch. Don't hesitate to call me if you need to."

Once Dr Goldberg had gone there was an embarrassing silence, until Robert said to his mother: "I think we'd better just talk to Karl like we used to, as if he could understand, otherwise life will be a bit of a strain. I'm sure he'll know what we mean if we mime as well. We could show him round the house for a start. See if he knows which was his old room."

Robert beckoned to Karl to follow him. He led him upstairs, then paused on the landing.

"Which is your room then, Karl?" he asked, sweeping his arm around to take in all the doors.

Karl heard Robert's interrogative tone and guessed what he had been asked. His recent optimism suddenly deserted him. He stared at the doors, then gave a forlorn shrug.

Robert's sympathetic hand fell lightly on his shoulder. He led Karl to a room which overlooked the front garden. To Karl's surprise he saw that his kit-bag had been brought up and the contents unpacked. He had hardly expected to be waited upon.

"You charmed Megan like you charmed the rest of us," Robert explained to deaf ears. He showed Karl the rest of the house, then outside.

Gertie called to them from the middle of her herb garden. "Lunch is on the kitchen table."

"Thanks, Mum. We'll go straight on up to Katherine's afterwards. She's behind with the hay."

Gertie stepped onto the lawn, clutching a bundle of mint stems. "Don't let Karl work too hard, dear. Remember, he's not done any work at all for two months."

"True. But I think we'll walk up there, rather than go on my bike. It'll give him the chance to see if he can find his own way."

"Are you hopeful of that?" she asked.

"Becoming less so, but you never know. Something may prompt his memory." He turned to Karl. "Let's eat." He mimed using a knife and fork.

On their walk through the village after lunch, a number of people spotted Karl and greeted him. Karl ignored them. He realised he ought not to seem arrogant but it was difficult to produce a smile. His self-assurance was wavering, confusion was setting in. He was beginning to suffer from culture shock. In the hospital he could easily have been in Germany. Now he was bombarded by new sights and sounds, new expectations of behaviour. He found it wearying, even after such a short time, especially trying to concentrate on catching the odd word whose meaning should be obvious.

When Robert stopped by the memorial cross to light a cigarette, Karl expected to be offered one too. He had asked for cigarettes in the hospital, but was refused them, even after they were sure he would not try to set fire to his room.

"*Darf ich?*" he asked Robert, pointing to the packet.

"What? Oh ... yes, of course. I suppose you've forgotten your dread of addiction." He offered him the packet and a box of matches. "Keep them. I'll buy some more at the shop if it's still open."

Mrs Tucker was not yet closed for lunch. She beamed when she saw her customers. Karl recognised her from earlier that morning and glanced awkwardly at Robert. He would have to handle this.

"It's good to see you again, Karl," Mrs Tucker said. "I've missed you popping in on your way back from Lane Head. I'm glad they've allowed you back at last. There's one or two round here quite envious of you having a go at Mr Kellett. Strictly between you and me of course," she said with a wink.

"That's all water under the bridge, Mrs Tucker," Robert put in quickly. "We were just on our way up to Katherine's, when I realised I was out of cigarettes."

Mrs Tucker was diverted and fetched him a packet of Players. Karl hung back in the shadows while the transaction was made.

"Cheerio," Robert said, before Mrs Tucker could speak to Karl again.

"Goodbye," Karl managed in English.

They were out of the village before Robert spoke again. "They'll all know about your amnesia soon enough, once Megan lets loose her tongue. I wonder what they'll make of it."

Karl lit a cigarette. He was beginning to feel more at ease amongst the English. Goldberg was wrong about people holding grudges.

Although the day was hot, the walk along the valley road was pleasant. Both men discarded their jackets, and walked in step in companionable silence. After they passed a small lane leading diagonally off to the right, Robert suddenly stopped and turned around.

"I wanted to see if you noticed the turning, but you didn't," he said to an uncomprehending Karl. "It's this way." He set off up the lane with Karl in his wake. As they climbed higher, Karl could once more see the distant range of hills which he had found so compelling from the car. He paused at a gateway to admire the view.

Robert was aware of Karl's interest. "That's Hay Bluff," he said clearly. He waited for some sign of recognition. Karl only nodded and moved on.

At the next gateway Robert paused, giving Karl a chance to look across the paddock towards the huddle of farm buildings. In the middle of the paddock was the stump of a great tree, felled not so long ago. Its hollow centre showed clearly why the tree had come down. Karl could hear sheep nearby, could smell their distinct odour above the scent of new-mown hay. He spotted them in a meadow beyond the

317

paddock, newly shorn and happier for it in the intense heat. The slope of the hillside obscured the rest of the farm.

Robert stepped on up the lane. "Still nothing coming back? I expect Katherine will be out in one of the meadows with the hay, but we'll try the house first, just in case."

At the top of the lane, where it came to a dead.end, Robert opened the gate into the yard and headed for the back door of the house, which stood wide open. He stuck his head through the doorway and called Katherine's name loudly, but there was no reply.

"As I thought. She's down there somewhere, in one of the meadows."

The scent of hay told them where to look. In the meadow beyond the sheepsheds they saw Katherine, sitting behind a horse-drawn mowing-machine. She was only just in time. Another few days and the grass would have gone to seed. Karl supposed a shortage of labour prevented faster progress. Two farmhands did not seem intent on tiring themselves, raking together scythed hay on a steeper slope.

Robert shouted down to Katherine. Joss barked an immediate welcome and came running up. Katherine waved, halted Beth and followed at a more leisurely pace.

Ignoring Robert, Joss bounded up to Karl, fawning over him and whining in his delight at seeing his old friend again. Karl was amazed at this reception, but returned the affection in kind.

"*Wie heisst er?*" he asked Robert. Robert looked blank, so Karl rephrased his question. "*Seiner Name ist ...?*"

Robert understood that time. "Joss."

"*Hallo, Joss. Erinnerst du dich noch an mich?*" Karl had no doubts that the dog remembered him. Such a greeting was reserved for special friends. It gave him a contented feeling of belonging at last.

Katherine had arrived by this time, looking hot, weary and sticky. She smiled uncertainly at Karl, but saw only a self-assured, arrogant young man. The look he gave her was disconcertingly penetrating. She knew what was on *his* mind. Her words of welcome froze on her lips.

"Well, here we are, Katherine," Robert said brightly, to ease the tension. "I thought I might as well bring Karl here straight away. Have you any work for us to do?"

Katherine found Karl's attitude disturbing, stirring up a strange cocktail of emotions: revulsion mixed with compassion, anger, love and desire. She was so confused she decided she would feel better if he worked away from her, until she could compose herself.

"You can roll up the fleeces. I haven't had the chance yet. I'll come and show you what to do."

The fleeces were all lying in an untidy heap to one side of the barn. Katherine was grateful for the shade, even though it was dusty and stuffy. She was acutely aware of Karl's eyes on her all the while she demonstrated how to roll a fleece.

"Pick any straw or thorns out first, fold the sides to the middle, roll the tail to the head, tie in a bundle with the twisted neck piece as a rope. There!"

She held up the bundle, which looked like a blanket roll, then put it in a sack. "Let's see you do it."

When she was happy with their efforts she left them to it.

As he worked, Karl revised his opinion of Miss Katherine Carter. She was not the flighty, flirtatious creature he had thought from his brief encounter with her at the hospital. She was a serious, hard-working young lady, who appeared to be running this farm by herself. Competently too, he thought. How many German women were having to do the same now?

They had worked their way halfway through the pile of fleeces when Katherine returned with glasses of cider for them to quench their thirst. She sat with them, drinking too, trying to accustom herself to a man who looked like Karl, but was not.

"Does he still not understand any English?" she asked Robert, avoiding Karl's eyes.

"A few words. And the guessable ones. The ones which sound the same in both languages." He flashed a grin at her.

"Listen to this." He pointed to one of the as yet unrolled fleeces and said to Karl: "What is that?"

Karl grinned too, appreciating the reason for the question. *"Ein Vlies,"* he replied, pronouncing it in exactly the same way as the English word.

"Good heavens!" she uttered politely. Her eyes were on him now and she felt more comfortable under his gaze. He had lost that glint in his eyes. Yet he was still a total stranger. She had not found it at all difficult to kiss him in the hospital. Then it had been as if he were merely asleep. If she kissed this man, handsome as he was, it would be out of pure desire, not love; that was not the way she lived her life. She had given in to desire before with Karl. She would never manage to free herself entirely from his attraction. She had become Karl's woman, willingly at first. She was less willing now.

Karl noticed she was flushed. It was too hot for her to be working outside in the full heat of the day. Her complexion was fair, tending to burn, despite her outdoor life. She ought to finish the fleeces while he and Robert worked in the meadow. He raised his hands as if to gain attention in a public meeting. Seeing he had their attention he launched his trial run of English.

"You are too hot. You work here," he said, pointing to Katherine. Then, indicating himself and Robert, he added: "We work out there."

They both spontaneously applauded his heavily accented effort and he bowed in acknowledgement. Robert, however, had other plans. He spoke to Katherine.

"He's right. You've been working out there too long. You stay in here and cool off a bit while I take my turn with the hay rake. But I think Karl should stay here too; my mother reckons he oughtn't do too much at first."

She shot him a sly glance. "Do I detect an ulterior motive there?"

Robert smirked. "Take it how you like, but it's a good opportunity to work another miracle, don't you think?"

She stuck her tongue out at him playfully, leaving Karl to wonder what on earth was going on. "I'm not so sure I want to be left alone with him, actually," she continued more seriously. "I can't seem to reconcile this one," she was deliberately mentioning no names, "with the old one. Bearing in mind they are one and the same, it makes me wonder whether I properly assessed the old one."

She felt awful talking in front of Karl like this, but she had to make Robert understand.

Robert tried to persuade her. "You must do something, for Karl's sake. You did it before. Admirably, if I may say. They're not the same person, I assure you. Dr Goldberg was at pains this morning to tell us we might not like Karl's attitude. We've got to get him back to the Karl you knew, not this one, don't you see?"

Put like that, Katherine could hardly refuse, but she hoped she would not find herself in over her head again. "Having met this one, I'm not so sure I want the old one back either. If I'd never met this one, I could readily have welcomed him back, but there's something I definitely don't like here. He puts my back up just looking at me with those calculating eyes of his. He'll be friendly if he thinks it's advantageous, but not otherwise."

"Come off it Katherine! How on earth can you tell that?"

Karl watched in amazement. His simple statement had resulted in a full scale dispute, obviously about himself.

"Let's just leave what I feel out of it, for the moment," she declared. "Can't you see we're embarrassing him, talking like this? I'll do what I can for him, I promise."

Robert left the barn, instructing Karl to stay with Katherine. Karl sensed Katherine's reluctance to be left alone with him. Why?

They bundled fleeces in silence, maintaining a respectful distance. There was so much he wanted to know about her, yet could not ask her. Had she meant something to him? Had he abandoned Ilse? Most probably she had not waited for him. Was Katherine her replacement? Or merely a passing fancy? Or nothing of the kind whatever?

The memory of finding her on his lap was too clear for the last possibility to be true. She had meant something to him, and he to her. So why was she holding back now? Because he was?

He put down the fleece he was holding and touched her arm lightly. She watched him warily, wondering what his intentions were.

"*Wir waren einmal gute Freunde. War das wirklich alles?*" he asked as gently as he dared.

Removing his hand from her arm she tried to think about what to say. She could not bring herself to encourage his advances – not yet. Not while his Nazi mentality was still so evident. She had to give him some explanation, even if he would not understand it.

"Once there was something between us, but not now. Now there's nothing. *Nichts.*"

She felt herself starting to cry, blatantly refuting her last statement.

"*Nichts? Wirklich?*" He could not believe her, when the tears were running down her cheeks like that. She was lying or else deceiving herself.

"Leave me alone please, Karl. I should have known it would be hopeless. You are German, I am English. There can be nothing between us."

He understood better now. Whatever there was, it was finished. It made no difference. He was content to leave her alone as she seemed to ask. He turned back to the fleeces. Neither of them spoke again until all the fleeces were bundled and put into woolsacks.

Katherine was aware Karl was ignoring her now. As far as he was concerned, she was simply the farm owner. As they walked together back down to the haymakers, a deep pang of regret touched her heart. She almost reached out to hold Karl's hand, but she stopped herself.

"How's it going?" she asked Robert.

"Give us another hour." He held out his palms for inspection. "I think I've got blisters on my blisters. Perhaps Karl can take over now."

Katherine guessed he wanted time to discuss Karl with her alone. They left Karl in the company of the two farmhands, strolled along to the river bank, and sat in the shade of a pollarded willow.

"That water looks inviting," Robert said. He took off his shoes and socks to bathe his feet.

"Bring your trunks tomorrow. We can have a swim before lunch," Katherine suggested. "I often pop down here in the evenings when Les and Dick have gone home."

Robert imagined the lonely figure in the cool, silent water. "You're cutting yourself off from the world, Katherine. I know you never were a great one for going out in the evenings, except when Andrew was here, but we miss you down in the village. You ought to come to the Penchurch Players, join in with life more. You're behaving like I did when I first came home.

"I would say, knowing you as well as I do, that you're in mourning for Karl. You're fooling yourself when you think you don't want him anymore. I can see that you do. Why can't you forgive him his past?"

She was vexed by his question. "I did forgive him! That's why I went with you to Gloucester. But since I've seen this other Karl, I've been terribly confused. I can't feel such sympathy for him now as I did when you told me his past. His attitude puts me off. I start to back away. Suddenly he's a German, not Karl."

Robert picked up a pebble from between his toes and cast it out into the river. "Trust your heart, not your head. You loved him well enough for what he was before you knew about his past. Why do you think he can't remember all that? It's because he doesn't want to, and you're not giving him any encouragement to try to get back to you. As things stand, unless you have a more positive attitude, he's better off not remembering everything he went through to become a decent human being."

Joss, who was lying in some long grass nearby, sat up and snapped at a passing fly, then slid down the bank for a drink of water.

"Karl is still Karl as far as Joss is concerned, so why not for me too?" Katherine rubbed her eyes wearily as she felt defeated by what was being asked of her. "You're right, of course. I would give anything to have Karl back as he was."

"Just encourage Karl to want to remember. It may help, it may not. There can't be any harm in trying."

She looked at him. "It seems a bit of a long shot, doesn't it? He's not going to remember now, if he hasn't already, is he?"

Robert pulled his feet out of the water and let them dry in the sun. "Let's give him a bit more time before we give up hope."

Robert and Karl were both in low spirits as they walked back to the village that evening. Karl was lost in thought and Robert left him to it. As they passed the church they met John and Olive Thornton coming out, accompanied by Mrs Collins, who scowled and walked quickly away.

"I heard you were back, Karl," Thornton said, a shade more cool than formerly. "You've certainly given the village something to talk about you know, being in the SS and all. Still, we like to think we're a charitable bunch, and don't hold it against you."

The scowl on the face of the woman who had walked off, coupled with something he thought he heard the parson say, made Karl decide enough was enough. Ignoring the parson, he spoke to Robert.

"Warum glaubt er, dass ich SS bin?"

Robert sensed trouble brewing in Karl. The last thing they needed now was for Karl to cause a scene in the middle of the street. "I'm sorry, Reverend, but we're in a bit of a hurry. I'll explain later." He grabbed Karl's arm and pulled him up the street.

More trouble was lurking at the corner of Cutbush Lane. Mrs Collins was waiting for them. Robert groaned as he saw her, but it was too late to avoid her.

"I've held my tongue until now," she hissed, her eyes like those of a cobra about to strike. "When I heard you always knew he was in the SS, Mr Murdoch, and never let the rest of us know, it convinced me you were a Nazi sympathiser. Now you've proved it! Your father should be ashamed of you. And as for you," she said directly to the man who personified her hatred of the world, "you ought to be hanged along with the rest of them. God will punish you for your sins, and if He doesn't, I'll do it for Him!"

Karl was not worried in the least by her attitude. Giving her a scornful glance he walked away, followed quickly by Robert, who was far more disconcerted by Mrs Collins' outburst.

Determined to forget the unpleasant incident, Robert suggested playing croquet with his parents that evening. He played badly, blaming it on his blistered hands, but in reality still troubled by Mrs Collins' accusation. Karl, on the other hand, rapidly picked up the rules and aggressive tactics of the game, so that as a team they were not too far behind when Donald and Gertie hit the final post and won the game. As Dr Goldberg had predicted, Karl settled in well, but they were all keenly aware of his change for the worse.

"He needs bringing down a peg or two," Robert heard his father comment to his mother as they were preparing to shut the house for the night.

Gertie tried to stand up for Karl. "He's lost some maturity, that's all."

"Well he'd better hurry up and find it again, is all I can say. He's lapping up all the attention you're paying him, Gertie. Don't fuss over him so much. He'll be even more insufferably arrogant. Did you hear him ask if Megan was Jewish? I'd have thought twice about having him here this week, if I'd known he was going to be like this!"

"I don't think he meant to sound insulting, dear. We don't know exactly what it was he said, after all."

"Well I didn't like his tone of voice. I never thought I'd speak of Karl like this, but if I catch him doing anything to upset her again he'll have to go back to hospital, and no arguments. Let Goldberg sort him out. I can't see anything coming of this week anyway."

Robert slunk upstairs out of earshot. His previously tolerant father was overreacting to what could have been a straightforward question by Karl. He only wanted to know whether Megan was friend or foe, after their experience with Mrs Collins. Megan's dark, Celtic looks could be taken for Jewish. Lack of communication was proving to be a major problem.

Karl came out of the bathroom as Robert reached the top of the stairs. "*Gute Nacht, Robert. Schlaf gut!*"

"Sleep well yourself, Karl," he replied. "No nightmares, eh?" As he said this, it struck Robert that Karl could not have nightmares, at least not the same ones as before. It might almost be worth having amnesia to be rid of his own nightmares.

First thing the following morning, Robert sorted out towels and swimming trunks for Karl and himself. His old pair would have to do for Karl. They ought to fit, he decided, despite the disparity in their heights. All his mother's efforts had failed to put much weight on either of them. Karl seemed to have lost weight while in hospital.

Robert decided to drive to Lane Head from now on, and thus avoid unpleasant or awkward meetings in the village. Karl rode pillion, their lunch and swimming things in a rucksack on his back. Katherine was waiting in the kitchen, catching up on housework while she had the chance. Dipping the sheep was next on the agenda, once the hay was in, but Karl would be gone by then.

The morning was spent turning the hay. As they paused for a breather, Robert mentioned the problems of the previous evening, out of earshot of Karl. As they spoke, Katherine noticed Karl smoking.

"If it had been up to me, I wouldn't have given him any cigarettes, he's so against them." They were walking back up to the house to change into swimming costumes.

326

"You don't smoke," he replied. "You don't know what it's like to want a cigarette so much that you'd rather starve than go without one. I saw men of skin and bone in the camp who traded their food for cigarettes."

"All the more reason why you shouldn't have started him smoking again."

Robert shrugged. "Try explaining that to him."

"*Ihr redet wieder über mich,*" Karl complained. He did not like them talking about him in front of him, as though he were deaf or an idiot. He knew they were discussing whether he should smoke or not. It seemed an important issue for some obscure reason.

Katherine and Robert changed the subject to Sarah's forthcoming graduation. When they were all changed and walking down to the river bank, with their lunch in the rucksack, Katherine told Sarah's latest news.

"She's been offered a post with the planning department in Reading. She'll be starting in August, so she has time to sort out lodgings and suchlike. It'll be a great relief not to have to support her any more, I can tell you. Les and Dick's wages are crippling me at the moment. I could scarcely afford to buy in the lambs we usually fatten off."

"You need a husband to work for you for nothing," Robert laughed.

Involuntarily Katherine's eyes turned to Karl, who was walking ahead of them.

"You're probably right, but I'm having trouble finding him," she said mournfully. "I had him once, then I threw him away. He's not come back yet."

"He will, Katherine, I'm sure he will. It's just a question of time."

Karl turned round with a scowl on his face. They persisted in talking about him behind his back. He knew now when Katherine spoke about him, because she always sounded tearful. He could not make her out at all.

Leaving the rucksack in the shade of a willow tree, Karl strode straight into the river. It was only just deep enough to swim in. There were gravelly patches where his hands struck the bottom, but he swam across and back again before Katherine had eased herself carefully into the cold water. Robert needed some coaxing before he finally had the courage to immerse himself. Neither Robert nor Katherine proved to be very expert swimmers, content to potter near the bank, leaving Karl to show off until Robert retaliated and gave Karl a ducking.

When Karl resurfaced he sat stock still in the water, a look of fear and bewilderment on his dripping face. He stood up abruptly and hurried out of the water, sitting on the grass to dry in the sun, his thoughts elsewhere, searching for the significance behind his sudden fear. Whatever it was, he knew he did not want to go back under the water.

Robert and Katherine joined him, aware of a possible breakthrough.

"What's the matter Karl? Did you remember something?" Robert had a good idea what it might have been.

Karl looked helplessly at him, a flick of his hands signifying his inability to understand his fear. A deep sense of insecurity had invaded his life in that instant under the water. Fear must have been a part of his past; intense fear. But he felt it was not merely the fear engendered by battle. It held an even deeper significance than that.

Katherine felt her heart lurch. A faint spark of vulnerability and humility had surfaced. At last she could allow her own compassion and love for him to return with it. She knelt beside him, ready to put her arm round him to give him strength.

Karl drew back, feeling no desire for the intrusive presence of this English girl. He searched in the rucksack for cigarettes and lit one, keeping silent about what he had felt in the water.

Katherine felt the rebuff and left him alone. She knew now she must not push him. "He definitely remembered something," she remarked excitedly. "Perhaps we can find other ways to jog his memory."

Robert was dubious. "It seems they will have to be unpleasant, similar to what he experienced. I'm not prepared to do anything like that, are you? I'll telephone Goldberg and tell him what happened. He may be able to suggest what to do."

Karl was subdued for the remainder of the day. The arrogant superiority was gone. He sensed he was somehow vulnerable. The two Britons knew why; he did not. It gave them a power over him which he did not like. Robert went to telephone straight after their lunch by the river. He asked Karl if he wanted a word with the doctor too, but Karl declined. There was nothing to say. The doctor would not answer any of his questions, so what would be the point of asking? Judging by Robert's brief conversation with Katherine when he came back from the telephone, Goldberg was not able to suggest much.

During the long afternoon Karl worked steadily alongside the two farmhands, turning the long rows of drying hay with his fork, his mood gradually brightening as he enjoyed the rhythm of the work and the tranquillity of the surroundings. He paused for a moment to look across the valley towards Hay Bluff, which held such magical attraction for him. His pagan instincts warmed to its domineering relief, like a vast altar awaiting some sacrificial offering. The pause was brief, however. Hard work helped him concentrate on the chasms which were begining to open in his mind. His attitude towards these people who were trying to help him swung rapidly between resentment and gratitude, like a magic lantern switching from one picture to another. First he trusted them, then he suspected their motives. If suspicion were his former nature, then trust must be the new. He knew his ambivalent attitude was confusing them as much as it did himself. He just wished they did not expect so much of him.

Les and Dick called at the Walnut Tree on their way home that evening. They complained loudly to the other regulars that the German tried to make them look lazy. Their comments reached Andrew Kellett. He was incensed to hear Katherine's German lover was back, and disturbed by the jealousy he still felt. It made him realise that it was still Katherine he wanted for his wife, despite his present relationship with Audrey. He had to find a way of making Katherine vulnerable, show her she could not manage without him. If it meant blasting her reputation sky-high, so that no other man would look at her, he would look all the more noble when he came to pick up the pieces and offer her respectability by marriage into the Kellett family.

Andrew Kellett grinned to himself as he formulated his plan. He would kill two birds with one stone. He would have Katherine as his wife, and the German would be properly punished at last for daring to seek the love of an English girl.

CHAPTER SEVENTEEN

He was drowning. Hands held him immobile in the swirling water. Above he could see the light of air, impossible to reach. He could feel the water in his nose, his throat, pouring into his lungs. He couldn't breathe ... until a voice called his name.

Karl woke up gasping, clutching onto a pair of arms as though they were a life raft. It was light already, the faint greyness of early morning in midsummer. Robert's concerned, enquiring face showed dimly in the gloom.

"Karl! What did you dream about? Tell me!" Robert urged him.

Karl lifted a shaking hand to a level over his head. *"Wasser. Bis hier."*

His experience in the river yesterday was repeating itself; being underwater had woken some memory struggling now to be released. Karl cleared everything else from his mind, willing whatever it was to emerge from the murky depths. He grappled with his memory, concentrating fiercely on those thin threads of recollection which, like streaks of wispy cloud, rapidly expanded into towering cumulo-nimbus, pouring down a flood of intense images. *"Es war in Jugoslawien – die Partisanen!"* Karl exclaimed suddenly.

Robert gripped his arm. "Any more?"

Karl's head was swamped with images of the events leading him to the water trough. He tried to pass beyond that to what came next, but could come up with nothing.

Wondering exactly how much Karl had remembered, Robert tapped Karl's back. "Your back. Do you remember how you got the scars on your back?"

There was no sign that Karl understood. Robert pulled him out of bed and over to the dressing table mirror. He turned

331

Karl round, so his back was to the mirror. Robert repeated his question.

Peering over his shoulder, Karl saw his scars for the first time; long grooves of paler skin. His memory was prompted. He could feel the nail-studded sticks of the Partisans. The women first, then everyone. They tied him to a fence to hold him up, then ...

Karl let out a gasp of horror. He screwed up his eyes to block out the scenes of carnage which came next. He staggered back to the bed, put his head in his hands.

"The children?" Robert asked him, rocking his arms as though cradling a baby.

Karl looked at him through his fingers and nodded. He succeeded in dispelling the scene. He felt angry with himself for his sympathy for the Partisans. They had been trying to kill him. Why did he feel such horror? He needed to think.

"*Bitte, lass mich in Ruhe!*" he told Robert, pointing to the door.

Reluctantly, Robert went out.

At breakfast, which, to Gertie's concern, Karl hardly touched, he asked to be allowed to speak to Dr Goldberg. It was too early in the day to contact him. Robert suggested they should wait until they reached Lane Head.

Katherine noticed Karl's forlorn air as they arrived. Robert explained what had happened, then took Karl in to telephone Goldberg. Their conversation lasted some time, with Karl doing most of the talking, until he indicated the doctor wished to speak to Robert.

Goldberg soon confirmed Robert's hopes that they would see a change in Karl. "He says he suddenly understands how wrong Germany was. He's unsure of himself now, feels even more in the dark than before. It's left him wondering what he did to ease his conscience, if anything." Goldberg paused to emphasise his next comment. "Most interesting was that he asked about the Holocaust, as though he wanted to listen this time."

Robert promised to keep Goldberg abreast of events then reported back to Katherine. "Let's hope he remembers some more soon," she said, as Karl slunk out of the kitchen.

Karl's mind was not on his work that day. Les and Dick nudged each other when they noticed his lack of progress down the meadow. After their mid-morning break, Karl wandered off up to the woods without a word of explanation, accompanied as in the past by Joss. Katherine watched him go, head down, dejected and lost, in stark contrast to his confident, soldierly bearing of yesterday. At this stage in his original history, he had been too ill to think about the consequences of his rescue. Events had moved on for Karl then, carrying him with them. Here he was stuck in limbo until his next revelation came.

Katherine was not the only person to observe him. Andrew Kellett was watching too. He had ridden over on Trojan to see for himself what the German was up to now. Leaving Trojan tethered at a safe distance, he saw Karl heading towards him. Slipping from his hideout behind a dense bush, Kellett followed his quarry up a sheltered, grassy track to the woods, the scene of their previous confrontation. The German had no axe this time. Kellett had come prepared with a sheath knife, although he hoped he would not need it. He remembered only too clearly how well the German fought.

To Kellett's satisfaction, Karl crossed the summit of the hill, out of sight of the farmhouse, and sat down on a log in the shade of a large ash tree. Joss flopped beside him, but lifted his head and gave a quick beat of his tail when he saw Kellett approach.

Karl, aware of Joss's friendly greeting, assumed the stranger was an acquaintance of Katherine. Possibly he ought to know who the man was. His confident approach showed he expected to be recognised.

Not a friend, Karl quickly decided, as the man glowered down at him. Karl stood to redress the balance. Even though the man's belligerent posture prompted a stirring of aggression in Karl, he fought to control his instincts, and kept his face placid as the man began to speak.

"So you're back, Driesler. You've got a nerve coming here again after last time!" His opponent's silence was disconcerting, but Kellett continued his tirade, gritting his teeth to restrain the violence he wanted to inflict.

"I kept quiet about you and Katherine for her benefit, but seeing you here has made me think twice about that. You'd better warn her the whole world is going to hear about your disgusting goings on. She'll be the one who suffers most." He leaned closer, pointing a warning finger. "Everyone's too soft on you lot these days, especially SS scum like you. Katherine's going to be the centre of gossip of the whole county because of you – understand?"

Karl heard Katherine's name mentioned and again "SS". The man was threatening him with something, but what?

"No! Not understand," he said quickly. "I speak no English."

Disbelief and rage flew across Kellett's face. "What are you playing at? Of course you speak English!" he shouted. "You tell Katherine what I said! She's in for a rough ride. I hope they lock you up good and proper this time, you bastard!"

Satisfied he had made his point, Kellett took his hand from under his jacket where it had been ready to whip out the knife, turned on his heel and strode off to where he had left Trojan.

Karl watched him go. Yesterday he would not have let the man speak to him like that. Yesterday he had been proud of his nationality; today he was not so sure. And again, mention of the SS. What was it all about? He felt more disturbed than ever by the encounter.

Alone in the wood, Karl had to admit that he could not say what he had or had not done. He feared the worst. What terrible crimes had he committed he wished now to forget? War had certainly brutalised him. He had recognised that early in the war. It was an advantage not to have any qualms about killing when your own life was at stake. He knew he could be brutal if necessary.

Katherine found him still sitting on the log at lunch time, his head between his hands. She sat beside him and laid a hand on his back. She was pleased, and sorry also, to see some of the sadness had returned to his eyes. It was with some difficulty she stopped herself from hugging him. He was not ready for that yet.

"Are you all right, Karl?" she asked, gently.

She saw him pull himself together, straighten his back in an effort to regain some dignity. A vestige of self-esteem remained because his worst memories were still hidden. She pitied him having to learn them again. She gave his shoulder a light squeeze as a promise of support for the future.

"Come on. Let's have some food," she said, standing up. Karl and Joss followed her back to the house, Joss remaining outside, Karl taking his customary place at the kitchen table, facing the back door. Some things about him had not changed, she noticed.

While they were eating Robert had an idea. "I wonder what would happen if Karl saw a photograph of himself, taken recently? Have you got one, Katherine?"

"No. I kept meaning to take one, but never got around to buying any film. You took some, didn't you, of him on skis?"

"Yes. There's one of you and him together, and a secret one I took later on of you both looking suitably lovey-dovey."

"Oh don't show him that!"

"Why ever not? Might be the very thing he needs. We've got to try anything and everything to make him remember. Don't you think it would be better for it to all come back to him here?"

"I just find it embarrassing. It was the way he looked at me when you first came on Monday. I don't want him looking at me like that again, as though I were ... another Audrey."

Audrey's name was an unpleasant reminder of another episode in Karl's past. "If you say we ought to try everything, by rights we ought to bring her here, but I don't think I could stand that."

"Not forgetting Andrew," Robert said. "After all, he was the last person Karl saw before he disappeared off to Hay Bluff."

Katherine rolled her eyes at the thought of arranging a meeting between those two, but she had to concede that it could be traumatic enough to stir Karl's memory. "Karl's not going back until Monday; he can watch the cricket with us on Sunday and see Andrew there. Hopefully the setting will prevent anything too disastrous."

"Last resort?"

"I suppose so, if all else fails."

Karl was tucking into his lunch, dwelling on the strange reference to the SS from the man by the woods.

He suddenly groaned in despair. *"Ach, mein Gott!"*

"What is it, Karl?" Robert asked.

Karl slapped his hands down on the table, rattling the crockery in his frustration. *"Ich muss es wissen! Was habe ich getan? War es so schrecklich, dass ihr es mir nicht sagen könnt?"* he cried.

"Try in English. Please, Karl," Katherine begged.

He looked annoyed at her request. It was impossible! He only knew a few words. He did his best.

"You know what I in the ... er ... *Krieg* do. Say me."

Robert looked apologetic. "You must remember for yourself, Karl. The doctor said it was best we told you nothing."

His words were lost on Karl. "I ... not good?"

Robert exchanged a look of dismay with Katherine. How could they cast judgement? Karl desperately needed an answer.

"Yes and no."

Relief appeared on Karl's face. It seemed he had not been all bad.

He worked alongside them again that afternoon, as the last of the hay was finally stacked or brought into the stable loft. Robert and Karl were able to leave the farm earlier than on previous evenings. Katherine followed a little later on her bicycle. She wanted to see Karl's reaction to the photographs. She heard their voices in the garden as she leaned her bicycle against the garage, next to Robert's motorbike which reeked of hot oil. It was another sultry evening. Katherine was grateful for the shandy Donald poured for her. She strolled round to join Karl and the Murdochs in their deckchairs on the lawn. The croquet hoops were ready for a game, but there was no sign of Robert.

"He's inside finding the photographs," Donald said. He lowered his voice. "What a difference there is in Karl today. Have you noticed?"

She nodded. Robert had mentioned his father's new intolerance of Karl. Seeing Gertie busy chatting to Karl, Katherine posed a question to Donald. "Do you think he can take remembering it all? Learning about it the second time around seems harder for him than experiencing it in the first place. He has to adjust his reactions and thoughts too quickly to catch up with what he learns about himself. I think he's still finding it difficult to change his Nazi attitudes, despite what we tell him."

"You mean the younger Karl, resurrected by amnesia, is refusing to be buried by the Karl we know."

"Something like that. There's still an awful lot of the young Karl in him, although I can see the older one starting to emerge. It's a weird experience. I just hope the Karl we end up with manages to shake off all the remnants of his old views."

Robert arrived on the lawn, clutching a photograph album. "Karl, come and look at these," he said, sitting down on the low wall enclosing the rose garden. Karl excused himself from Gertie and went over to join Robert. Katherine sat on the other side of Robert, so that she too could see the photos.

"Here you are!" Robert said, opening the pages near the end of the album.

Karl looked, and stared in amazement at the photograph of a man on skis in thick snow in this very garden. The man's face was not too clear, but the hat was his own skiing hat, which he had found with his belongings at the hospital. He looked at the next picture, clearly Robert on skis, then the next. This was a picture of Lane Head Farm in the snow, himself about to help Katherine up onto her feet. The next photograph was very revealing. It was taken from a distance. A man standing with his arms around a woman, both looking deeply into each other's eyes. There was no doubt who the man and woman were.

He loved her. It was clear from the photo. He felt Katherine's eyes on him now, and he leaned forward to look past Robert, to read in her eyes what they had to tell him. What he saw confirmed the photograph. She was prepared to love him still.

Hurriedly he turned the page. This was an emotional entanglement he could do without. He felt nothing for her. It was best left that way.

Katherine's aura of disappointment was tangible as he flicked through the remaining photographs. He wished he could tell her how confused he felt, how nothing meant what it might have before. She stood and walked away. She seemed a sensible girl, taking it all so calmly. So like Ilse.

Robert took the album indoors, as disappointed as Katherine at Karl's response. When he returned he handed out the croquet mallets to jolly everyone up. His father chose to sit the game out, preferring to read his latest journal. Gertie teamed up with Katherine in a match of the women versus the men.

Half-way through the game, Katherine felt she was being picked upon by Karl. He continually chose to send her ball hurtling into the flower bed when he finished making a croquet. Gertie's would have done just as well. It seemed to show he had some interest in her still, even if only as a means to winning the game. She caught him giving her a few sidelong glances, not lewd at all, but she was sure what was on his mind. He wanted to know whether they had slept together.

As she cycled back in the late evening twilight, Katherine began to fantasise about reawakening Karl as before, not just by a kiss, but by actually making love to him. Her body pined for his, and now that his arrogance had gone, the thought was pleasurable once more. He would expect her advances now he had seen Robert's photograph, might even welcome them, flattered by her interest. He would not love her yet, but at least she would be loving him, she was sure of that now. Desire might reawaken his love. It was not the Sleeping Beauty this time, more the Frog Prince, who had to share the Princess's pillow before he would turn back into a Prince.

Could she do it? Could she seduce him like that, make all the running, totally out of character? How far would she have to go before he would take over? If only she were like Audrey, able to approach a man and make her intentions clear.

There was no guarantee such a plan would work. She could not bear the thought of flaunting herself to no avail. What would he think of her afterwards? That she was cheap, not worth having? She would hate him to think that, even temporarily. No, if he made the overtures, she would respond. She could not do it the other way around. It had been a pleasant daydream, that was all.

She was putting away her bicycle in the shed when Audrey returned to mind. Audrey had seduced Karl once already. What if she were to again? There would be nothing lost if it had no effect on Karl's memory, and Robert said they must try anything and everything for Karl. If it included sharing him briefly with Audrey, then so be it. The trouble was, Audrey was in close collusion with Andrew now. She might object to such a request, now that she was in with a chance of becoming the Mistress of Froxley Grange. Katherine just hoped her old habits might persist. She would approach her tomorrow.

The men were all busy: Les and Dick erecting the hurdles around the sheep dip, Robert and Karl overhauling the car's engine. Katherine had time to call Audrey at the solicitor's office where she worked, and arrange a meeting with her.

Audrey was very surprised, but agreed to come up to the farm that evening. She suspected it was to do with Andrew and their mutual claim to him, but Audrey trusted Katherine to be amicable and not cause trouble. She rode up on horseback at eight o'clock, to find Katherine waiting expectantly.

They sat out in the garden in a soothing aroma of night-scented stock. Audrey had not been to the farm since her secret visits when Karl was there. She was greatly surprised when Katherine began by mentioning these.

"It's a rather delicate subject, Audrey," Katherine said diffidently. "I hope you won't be offended by my talking about what went on between you and Karl here." She hurried on. "I expect you know Karl is back here in the village. I don't know if you are aware of what has happened to him."

Audrey looked at her curiously. "Well, I've heard he's lost his memory."

Katherine nodded and explained briefly about Karl's mental breakdown and subsequent amnesia. "He's here now to try to jog his memory. Accidentally we got him to remember one incident from four years ago, but nothing else." She stopped, too embarrassed to continue.

Audrey was quick to spot the direction Katherine's thoughts had taken. "Do you, by any chance, want me to remind him of our little escapade by a repeat performance?"

Katherine smiled her relief, but was taken aback by Audrey's next comment. "Why don't you do it yourself, Katherine? Surely it would mean more. I was nothing to him, nothing at all."

"What makes you think I ..."

Audrey gave her a derisory look. "Come off it, Katherine! Of course you did." Her expression changed from incredulity to suspicion. "Why do you want me to do your dirty work, anyway? What if Andrew found out, eh? Bang would go my hopes of marrying him, same as yours. Tempting as your suggestion is, I've found a cosy nest, and I want to stay in it! Andrew's going to be disgusted with you when I tell him about this."

"You wouldn't do a thing like that, Audrey, would you?"

Audrey smirked. "He's pretty annoyed with you for having Karl back here. He doesn't know about Karl's amnesia, though. But I don't suppose that'll make any difference. Andrew says he can't forgive you for betraying your own countrymen and everything they fought so hard for."

340

Katherine wished she had never asked Audrey to call. "I'm sorry to have dragged you up here for nothing, Audrey. I quite understand your wish not to become involved."

Audrey was easily mollified. "Don't worry, Katherine," she reassured her. "I'm flattered you asked me to do such a thing with someone who means so much to you. But I still don't understand why you won't do it yourself."

Katherine could not tell the truth. "I don't know how," she excused herself lamely.

Audrey stifled a giggle. "It's true, I suppose. I can't see you giving anyone the eye!" Her mind went back to those two nights in January. The thrill of the chase, the final capture then ... his long limbs entwined with hers. She could have that all over again! She shivered with excitement and made her decision. "Look. I'll do it for you, no strings. We'll both keep our mouths shut about each other. If Andrew finds out, I'm done for."

"Of course." Katherine felt an intense reluctance to hand Karl over to Audrey now. "Just remember, he's not the same as he was. He doesn't even speak English. You'll have to make your intentions perfectly clear."

"Don't worry, Katherine. I'll look after him."

On Friday morning Robert was approached by a coy-looking Katherine.

"I'd like the whole afternoon alone with Karl tomorrow," she said, hoping he would understand without explanation.

"I wondered when you would get around to it. Lucky old Karl. Doesn't know what he's in for!"

Katherine blushed. "There's no need to be like that about it, Robert Murdoch!" she said, rebuking his twinkling eyes. "We've only got tomorrow and Sunday left. I've got to do something, haven't I?"

Karl wished he knew what they were plotting now. When Katherine and Robert got in a huddle like that, they were inevitably discussing him. There was nothing he could do about it from up this ladder. He turned back to scrape more flaking paint off the upstairs window. This side of the house

341

felt the direct force of the sun, as well as the worst weather. It was a sun-trap against the glaring white wall.

The sun had burnt him terribly in Yugoslavia. Burnt. That was what they did to the villages. Why had he been made to burn? And the other things they had done to him. Retribution. Revenge. It was a powerful force to be reckoned with.

"I don't want to remember," he told himself. "I have to live with myself. So what if I'm a stinking Nazi and shut my eyes to what was happening to the Jews because it didn't concern me!" He stabbed the paint scraper into the corner of the window frame, gouging out a lump of wood. His resentment boiled up inside him. "Robert and Katherine seem to think they can save me from my sins with their understanding and forgiveness. I don't want any of that. I want to return to my old life and Ilse, and forget the whole damned war!"

And another thing. As far as he knew, he was not being paid. They were using him, an officer of the Wehrmacht, as free labour. It was not right. He had played along with them for long enough. They would get nothing more from him.

He climbed down the ladder, left the sandpaper and paint scraper at the bottom and without a backward glance at the astonished Britons, began to wander off up to the woods, where he felt more at home.

"What's the matter, Karl?" Robert called, running after him. He was surprised at the mutinous cast to Karl's features.

"Ich bin Offizier des deutschen Wehrmachts, und kein Sklave. Ich arbeite nicht mehr."

"He doesn't want to work any more," Robert told Katherine as she caught them up.

Katherine put her hand on Karl's arm, sensing the tension in him. "You don't have to work, Karl. Come and sit in the garden," she pleaded, wondering what had brought on this latest mood.

Reluctantly he allowed himself to be led back towards the garden, annoyed with himself for once more giving in to these people. They left him to sit there alone, but he knew they were keeping a watchful eye on him – Robert from the yard where he returned to his paint-scraping, Katherine from the kitchen garden. It was not long before he returned up the ladder. Idleness did not suit him.

When they stopped work for lunch, Robert asked if he wanted to speak to Goldberg again.

"Nein. Es geht. Ich warte bis Montag."

There was nothing more they could do or say. Katherine cleared away the dirty plates then served out fresh raspberries. "I think he'll be glad to get back to the hospital," she said as she handed Robert his portion. "I wonder what made him suddenly behave like that. He's definitely less friendly than he was this morning. He seems to be up one day and down the next."

The scraping of Karl's chair on the floor interrupted Robert's reply. Karl picked up his bowl of raspberries and took it into the garden. He felt very depressed. He wanted to be alone. He was not sure why he felt depressed, which depressed him even more. He had felt fine this morning, amenable to the world, content to wait and see what his memories would tell him. Now it was all different. Thinking about Yugoslavia seemed to have changed his perspective again. The gap between then and now was too great to bridge. He could stand one side or the other, a soldier in battle or a mad prisoner of the English. Without a transitional bridge he was lost.

His depression carried into Saturday. Painting Katherine's house was tedious, hindered by rotted and crumbling woodwork. He could not make a good job of it, which annoyed him. Do the work thoroughly or not at all.

Surprisingly, Robert left him after lunch. Katherine seemed tense too, as though something were planned. Les and Dick were nowhere around. It looked as if they had been given the afternoon off. He was left completely on his own with Katherine. His suspicions were aroused.

At about two o'clock Katherine came to the foot of his ladder, changed out of her usual dungarees into a cool frock. Karl was now working on the guttering and she had to strain her neck back to call to him.

"Karl!" She beckoned to him. "Would you come down, please?"

He stood the paintbrush in the pot of green paint and carried it with him to ground level.

"I'm going out. To visit a friend." She pointed to her bicycle which stood against the wall of the house.

Karl noticed that she was not looking him in the eye. She seemed anxious, eager to be away.

"I'll be back at five o'clock." She pointed to the five on her watch. He nodded in comprehension. "Another friend has come up to keep you company."

Her words meant nothing. Karl followed the direction of her eyes towards the garden. He saw a female figure seated decorously on the garden bench.

"Leave the painting. Come and meet Audrey."

There was reluctance in her voice. She was unhappy at leaving him with this other young woman. As Katherine and Karl approached she turned to face them. This woman was dazzlingly beautiful, and both she and Katherine knew it.

"Karl, this is Audrey Patterson."

Katherine saw the interest in his face. Few men were immune from Audrey's smile. Karl had succumbed to it before, probably would again. Just in case he had any inhibitions, Katherine was leaving them a jug of cider to smooth the way. She felt awful setting him up like this. After spending a sleepless night, she had been ready to call the whole thing off.

Audrey gave Katherine a meaningful glance. "You'd better be off, Katherine. I don't know how much time I'm going to need. I'll expect you back at five."

Katherine reluctantly took her leave. "Good luck, Audrey. I hope this works. I won't promise I'll be thinking of you, because I can't bear to."

"No. I know you can't. I'm doing this in the spirit of European unity. I'll try not to enjoy it!"

Katherine collected her bicycle and sped off down the lane. She had no real plans for the afternoon. She would probably cycle aimlessly around, trying to avoid people she knew. There were numerous little lanes she could take, but the weather was still so hot cycling held little pleasure. Before long she stopped, found a shady tree in a meadow already mown, and began reading a novel she had brought in her saddlebag.

The words on the page danced in front of her eyes, not penetrating her thoughts. She ought to be with him now. She really ought! She felt furious with herself giving Karl to Audrey. She looked at her watch. They'd had half an hour. How far would Audrey have got? It was agonising to imagine them together. She had failed him once again.

The time passed desperately slowly. An hour, an hour and a half, two hours. She could not possibly go back yet. Five o'clock she had said, and five o'clock it would have to be.

She sat quietly for so long that half a dozen rabbits came out of the hedgerow to graze the mown grass. Saturday was the traditional day in winter for locals to shoot rabbits. These were safe for the moment, but she had become quite numb and had to move. With a flash of white tails, the rabbits were gone. She walked her bicycle, trying to kill time.

Audrey raised her glass. "Cheers!"

Karl followed suit. "*Zum Wohl!*"

As he put down the drained glass, he noticed his fingers had left a smudge of green paint. He pulled a rag from his pocket and wiped the glass then his fingers. As he did so, Audrey shuffled closer along the bench to him. She reached for the rag and used a corner to dab at a splash of green on his forehead. Karl tilted his head down. His eyes were confronted by her gaping blouse. So that was why she was here!

"*Robert! Du kluger Kerl!*" he muttered with a grin. Very considerate of Robert, providing for his every need. No wonder Katherine was ill at ease, entertaining a prostitute. If the woman was here specially, he'd better not delay her. No doubt she had other customers waiting.

He reached for her hand and rose to his feet, deciding the stable was as good a place as any. He had often rolled in the hay with Ilse. He fingered a lock of Audrey's blonde hair. She might almost be Ilse! Almost.

He led her to the privacy of the stable. Without a word, Audrey followed, too astonished by his behaviour to intervene. Once up in the hayloft he wasted no time or affection. He lowered her to the floor, opened her blouse, raised her skirt and enjoyed her.

Afterwards, while Audrey briskly tidied herself up, Karl helped by picking hay out of her hair. She seemed peeved for some reason. "*Danke, Fraülein,*" he said, thinking she expected thanks. He certainly could not pay her.

"Thank you! Is that all I get? I was looking forward to this afternoon, but it was a waste of time!" Audrey flounced over to the ladder and disappeared from view.

.Had he done something wrong? Karl scrambled down the ladder after her, but she only scowled at him then turned her back and headed for the garden. Karl expected her to leave now her job was done. Instead she lit a cigarette, picked up her book and steadfastly ignored him.

Karl felt uneasy. What was all this about? Had he misunderstood? If so, he had made a grave mistake. But he was sure that was why she had come. He shook his head in bewilderment and went back to his painting.

At five o'clock exactly Katherine entered the yard of Lane Head Farm, impatient but fearful of hearing Audrey's report. To her surprise she saw Karl back up the ladder. He noticed her return, but did not acknowledge her. Katherine hurried to find Audrey, who was sitting where she had left her, reading a book, looking thoroughly bored, the pile of cigarette stubs on the ground evidence of her vigil.

Audrey put down the book as Katherine sat on the bench beside her and looked at her in anticipation.

Audrey was all righteous indignation. "Well, I did my job. It did nothing for me. You're right, he is different. I felt like second-best, which I didn't before. This time he made no attempt to show any interest in me as a person. He knew why I was there; that was enough. Charming, I thought to myself! That's the last time I'll do a favour like that."

Katherine repressed the smile which was desperately trying to reach her lips. So Karl spotted Audrey for what she was. It would be funny if Audrey was not so hurt. "At least you made the effort, that's the main thing. As I promised, I won't breathe a word of this to anyone, if you won't."

"Don't worry, Katherine. I wouldn't mind forgetting this occasion completely, let alone brag about it. Good luck to you is all I can say."

Audrey made a prompt exit. Katherine delayed going to speak to Karl. Audrey felt second-best. To whom? Me or Ilse?

She saw Karl watching her from the top of the ladder, but he did not come down. He almost seemed to be sulking up there. She wondered whether to leave him. But if he had a grievance then she ought to make him tell her.

She called him. He looked down at her, scowling. She had to call him again. He came down with painful slowness, an indication of his displeasure.

Katherine found herself at a loss. She had not expected him to be resentful. Inspiration struck her. "I expect it was Ilse you really wanted."

He frowned. So she knew about Ilse. Perhaps she knew more. How to ask her? "Ilse ..." he began, then stopped. The English words would not come. He shook his head in his frustration and grasped Katherine by the shoulders, as if he could wring the information out of her.

Katherine faltered. Should she tell him about Ilse? And his son, Siegfried? While he still clung onto hope about Ilse, he was not going to be interested in any English girl. His agony of ignorance was heartbreaking, and she relented.

"I'll tell you about her, Karl. Come and sit in the garden."

She felt the pressure on her shoulders release, saw the distress in his features diminish. She had a moment's anxiety as to what he might have done if she had not told him. She did not know what to expect from him. He had been capable of extreme violence with Andrew. There was a violence in him still.

Sitting herself on the bench Audrey had recently vacated, she invited Karl next to her. He seemed wary now, and kept the length of the bench between them.

Smoothing the skirt of her frock demurely over her knees, Katherine broke the news to Karl about Ilse. "Ilse is married to someone else."

Karl only looked blank. He had not understood. She described a ring around her fourth finger. "Ilse is married," she repeated. "She is a Frau not a Fräulein."

It was apparent he had suspected as much. Her words came as no great shock. "*Nicht meine Frau?*" he asked in clarification.

"No. I'm sorry." She knew she could not possibly tell him about Siegfried as she did not know what had happened to him.

He was silent. He contemplated the significance of what she had told him, then he turned his head abruptly, catching her watching him. To her astonishment she saw him smile.

"*Was hat es mit Audrey zu tun?*" He shifted along the bench towards her. His face became more serious. "*Warum nicht du?*"

She felt sure he had asked her why it had been Audrey and not herself today.

"*Wir liebten uns, nicht wahr?*" he persisted.

It was the closest he had come to acknowledging their relationship. Katherine reached for his hand. "Yes, we loved each other. I denied it before when you asked me, because I felt you were not what I wanted, but you're starting to change, Schatz. I can see it at last."

It was as though a thunderbolt struck him. "*Schatz! Du hast mich eben Schatz genannt! Genau wie im Krankenhaus.*"

He remembered now. It was what she had called him in the hospital; what had reminded him of Ilse and enabled him to accept people again. This English girl sitting beside him meant as much to him as Ilse once had. Why could he not feel the same again? He felt the grasp of her work-roughened hand on his. The contact brought no feeling of intimacy. He withdrew his hand from hers.

"I am sorry, Katherine. *Jetzt ist es anders.*"

She decided to make light of it. "That's all right, Karl. I haven't given up hope, yet. I just wish now I had the courage to do what Audrey did. Perhaps it would have made all the difference – you never know."

Had she sounded convincingly calm? Sitting here alone with him like this, she felt bold enough to try. Yet Karl had spurned her attentions already, withdrawing his hand from hers, and she had only herself to blame for her shyness. On an impulse, she leaned forwards and kissed him lightly but very tenderly on the lips.

To her dismay, he made no response. Just like in the hospital he remained impassive, until her lips left his, whereupon he stood up and turned his back on her, so that she could not see the consternation on his face. She deserved some explanation for his reluctance. He turned to face her again.

"Ich will nur nach Deutschland wiederkehren, verstehst du? Mein eigenes Land ruft mich, meine Familie braucht mich. Du hast nichts damit zu tun."

His voice sounded harsh to her now. He was rejecting her totally.

"You don't remember enough to know what you want, Karl," she said. "It will be different once you do, you'll see." There was no point in further discussion. The language barrier was too rigid, his views inflexible. Katherine left the garden.

Karl watched her go. He had been deliberately hard on her, because of their communication difficulties. He *had* to make her understand she had no claim on him.

It was with relief that he heard the throb of Robert's motorbike. Katherine came back out of the house, no doubt to make her report on the day's events to Robert. Karl gave the pair a minute to confer before he joined them.

"It looks like Andrew must come up trumps tomorrow, then," Robert was saying to Katherine. "Otherwise we'll have to report almost complete failure to Dr Goldberg." He noticed Karl and greeted him. "No joy, eh, Karl? I really thought Katherine's charms would work a second time, but they say lightning never strikes in the same place twice."

Robert was surprised at the nonchalance of Karl's farewell to Katherine, considering what they were supposed to have done that afternoon. Had Katherine lost her nerve after all?

He did not discover the truth until the following day, when, at his mother's insistence, Karl came with them to the Morning Service at the church. Gertie had been perturbed by Karl's changed personality and thought a little Christian influence might do some good. Karl's reluctance to attend only confirmed her belief that he ought to go. Robert backed up his mother's request. It was with ill grace that Karl presented himself once more to the scrutiny of the village, although his scowl lifted slightly when he caught sight of his partner of the previous day walking up the churchyard on the arm of the pugnacious man from the woods.

In that look of conquest Karl directed at Audrey, Robert saw what he had expected to see between Karl and Katherine. So Katherine had asked Audrey to do the deed after all! He found it difficult to understand why.

Audrey studiously ignored Karl. He gave her no further sign of recognition. He wanted to avoid a meeting with Audrey's friend, as well as that woman who accosted him and Robert in the street. She was entering the church too.

Karl felt ill at ease during the whole service. The only German amongst a crowd of his country's former enemies, all of whom seemed to be gawping at him. He was also worried about the connection between Audrey and the man in the woods. The man had threatened him with something. Was it to do with Audrey or Katherine? The man gave no hint he knew Karl, or wanted to speak to him. Of course the church was not a proper place for confrontation.

The Murdochs dallied in the churchyard afterwards, unaware of Karl's agitation. Katherine had gone over to a corner of the churchyard to stand alone by a grave for a moment.

Robert noticed Kellett steer a very unwilling Audrey towards them, as Katherine picked her way back through the headstones. The closer Andrew and Audrey approached, the more nervous Audrey looked. Robert feared Andrew had primed Audrey to do some dirty work for him. He tried to get his family to move on, but his parents waited for Katherine, who arrived at the same time as Audrey.

After a nudge from Andrew, Audrey spoke in a loud voice which carried across the entire churchyard; even Mrs Collins chatting to the Rev. Thornton by the church door could hear.

"We all know why you're so keen to have your German lover back, Katherine. Was your bed getting too cold without him?"

Katherine reeled at the sudden and wholly unexpected attack. The silence around her was total. Only yesterday Audrey had promised to say nothing. Why had she gone against her word so soon, and so devastatingly publicly? Now the whole village knew.

"You're a fine one to talk, Audrey Patterson!" she began, then caught sight of Andrew's smug face. This was his doing! His desire for revenge against her and Karl had finally come out. Somehow he had forced Audrey to do this. She bit back her next words, concentrating instead on keeping calm, as though there were no truth in Audrey's words. If Audrey wanted Andrew that much, she was sorry for her. Andrew was not worth the effort.

"I'm sorry, Audrey. I would have thought, now you have Andrew for yourself, you wouldn't need to play tricks like this."

Before any more could be said, Katherine turned to her companions. "Shall we go?"

As they left the churchyard, Katherine did not dare to look at the faces of the villagers. Robert took her arm as proof of his public disbelief, whatever he knew in private. Donald and Gertie held their tongues. They knew the truth as well as Robert did. It would be awkward to have to lie in Katherine's defence.

Only Karl was reluctant to depart the scene and leave Audrey's friend to his apparent victory. He had seen Katherine and Audrey part on friendly terms only yesterday; whatever Audrey had said was done under pressure from her partner. Was this the threat he had detected in the man's tone of voice that day in the woods?

He stood a moment directly in front of Kellett, as a warning not to try anything else against Katherine. His intention was misconstrued by those around as well as by Kellett himself.

"You're in trouble now, you filthy Kraut," Kellett said loudly, so all could hear. "You'll learn to leave our women alone, once your commandant hears about this."

Karl sensed there was more to this than he understood and decided enough was enough. With a scornful glance at Audrey, he turned on his heel and followed the retreating Murdochs.

It was only when she reached the safety of the house that Katherine allowed her emotions to come out. "The swine! How dare he make Audrey do that. I could see poor Audrey was terrified I would retaliate. He must have promised her something very special to get her to do that."

"Probably a condition of marriage," Robert suggested. "Wouldn't marry her otherwise. But how cowardly, not to do the deed himself!"

Katherine flinched. His comment applied equally to herself. She noticed Karl scrutinising them intently, perplexed by the whole business. "If this is reported to the camp, and I can't see how that can be avoided, I won't be able to deny it. What will happen to Karl? How can they punish him for something he doesn't know he's done."

She saw Robert's grimace and realised that Karl could be punished for what he had knowingly done yesterday at her own connivance.

Donald sighed heavily. "It seems to me, you're just going to have to accept whatever comes of this. It will be doubly hard on Karl, of course, having to sort this out as well as his other problems, but as he is at the moment, I don't think he'll find being punished as hard as the old Karl would have. I think he's surprised at the leniency of his treatment so far. He's not suffered internment yet. The Karl we knew was mighty fed up with it."

Robert was amazed at his father's astuteness. "Even so, we'd better steer Karl clear of the cricket match."

"If we don't go, it will look as though I'm ashamed," Katherine said. "I'm not going into hiding. My best course is to continue as though there were nothing in what she said."

Gertie clapped her hands. "Hear, hear! I think Karl ought to go too, to back you up and show he still has our approval. What do you think, dear?"

"We might as well all go," Donald agreed.

Robert laughed. "It's high time the government showed more sense over this. If they're going to let POWs outside the camps, this is bound to happen. Perhaps we can even make a test case."

"That would mean a lot of publicity, wouldn't it?" Katherine asked.

"Would be in a good cause, though, if you won."

Katherine shuddered at the thought.

After an early light lunch, they all set out, Robert carrying a bag of sports clothes, the others deckchairs. Karl was intrigued. They did not have far to walk before they arrived at a large, open grassy area, already occupied by a number of spectators and players. They set up their deckchairs in a shady spot under some trees. Robert disappeared into the pavilion.

Katherine's arrival caused a slight stir and a few surreptitious nods. Karl wanted to protect Katherine from gossip, despite his determination not to become involved, and swore softly when Kellett's two-seater sports car pulled onto the grass nearby.

Kellett jauntily approached. "Katherine! You may be interested to know that a certain person has already taken it upon herself to report your lover to his camp commandant. No doubt you will be hearing from that quarter very shortly."

"Who was it?" Gertie demanded.

Kellett smiled darkly. "Your old friend and mine, Mrs Collins. She asked whether I had done anything about it. When I said I hadn't she seemed pleased to have the chance to be the one to turn him in. Enjoy the cricket!" His cocksure grin faded as he caught the scowl on the German's face.

There was no way Katherine could enjoy the match after that, especially when Penchurch were all out for seventy-four by tea. She did not really care about herself. It was all true anyway; she had prepared herself long ago for this

353

eventuality. Karl was another matter. How would he cope? He was watching the cricket, trying to understand the game, oblivious to what lay ahead.

At tea, Karl went to join Robert by the pavilion, while Gertie did her bit serving. Katherine was cornered by a supportive group of village women who maintained they refused to believe Audrey's scurrilous accusation. It was clear to Katherine they hoped it was true, hence their interest to hear her denial so they could examine it minutely afterwards to detect a shred of a lie. Now that Karl had been reported to the camp, it seemed pointless to deny it. She was about to come clean when a disturbance erupted over by the pavilion.

CHAPTER EIGHTEEN

Robert stood on the boundary line by the cricket pavilion, gesticulating wildly, trying to explain to Karl how it was that the Penchurch team had fallen so swiftly.

Standing nonchalantly, hands in his pockets, Karl nodded every so often, to pretend that he had understood. In truth, the game had baffled him. To start with he could not tell which team was which. The players all wore white, or a hotch-potch assortment of working clothes. When he worked out that only two of the Penchurch team were on the field at any one time, batting, he then had to fathom out the scoring. Katherine had helped him with that, but she could not explain why two of the batsmen had been "out", when nothing appeared to have happened. Robert tried to explain the LBW rule as if his life depended it. He himself had chalked up a measly twelve runs, before being caught, but Kellett saved the team from total ignominy by a respectable thirty-seven, not-out.

"I see you don't know what I'm getting at," Robert sighed. "Why don't we go and get some tea."

A sudden cry halted Robert's advance to the already besieged refreshment table. "Mr Murdoch!"

Les Whitelock and Dick Davies, also on the Penchurch side, had a message from Kellett, the team captain. Fielding and bowling tactics were to be discussed before tea. Robert began to move towards the far side of the pavilion, where half the team had already gathered. Karl too found himself shepherded along.

The only team members so far summoned, apart from Robert, were two other Froxley Grange estate workers, Eric Bateman and Jimmy Prescott. The remainder were already taking tea and chatting to the opposition.

"Go and round up the rest of them, would you, Robert," Kellett drawled.

Robert obligingly left. Immediately Karl felt the mood of the men around him change. They closed in around him, until he had his back to the pavilion wall. Kellett took the centre of the semicircle, and spoke basic German in a low voice.

"We meet again, Driesler. Now you will learn what we do to Germans who sleep with English women!"

Kellett stepped back, allowing his men to move in. The two older men, Whitelock and Bateman, seized Karl's arms and pinnioned him against the wooden boards of the pavilion. Prescott and Davies began laying into Karl. Using the two older men as supports, Karl arched his back and kicked out with both feet, catching Dick Davies full in the midriff. Davies fell to the ground as the two supporters struggled to hold their captive. Prescott dodged and delivered a hefty blow to Karl's jaw, sending his head crashing into the wall behind. Prescott managed another couple of blows before his legs were kicked from under him. With both assailants down, Karl turned on the men holding him, lunging forwards to set them off balance before leaning backwards and swinging his arms together with a satisfying smack of heads.

Karl was free and Kellett could no longer keep out of the fray. At the risk of suffering again at the German's hands, he dived at the legs of the fleeing man and brought him down in a flying tackle. Kellett was the first to recover from the impact. He hauled up his winded enemy by the shoulders to deliver him back into the hands of his men, who were more ready for him now that they had his measure.

Karl saw the danger. His hands went for Kellett's throat and his knee swiftly came up and drove home.

Robert had gone off wondering why Whitelock and Davies were not sent instead, since it was they who fetched him. He got as far as the tea table and located Frank Pierce, when he heard a thud from behind the pavilion. Above the noise and clattering tea cups it was difficult to be sure, but Robert's suspicions were aroused. He told Pierce to find the others and hurried round the pavilion.

Already he could hear the sound of scuffles. As he rounded the corner he saw the four estate workers hauling a furious Karl off a beleaguered and battered Kellett.

At the sight of Robert the four men tightened their grip on Karl, who suddenly stopped struggling and stood shaking his head, as if to clear it.

Robert hurried forward to support Kellett, who was doubled over in pain. Others had heard the commotion, Katherine and Audrey among them, and joined Robert.

"You saw that?" Kellett wheezed, pleased, despite his pain, at the way his plans had worked out. "That Kraut of yours suddenly took it into his head to attack me. If my men hadn't been here to stave him off he would have killed me, like he tried before!"

"That's a lie!"

The shout had come from Karl. It took a moment for both Robert and Katherine to fully realise that Karl had spoken in English. Karl started to struggle with the four men again, trying to shake them off, but they had a firm grip on him now.

"That's a lie," he repeated, speaking directly now to Robert. "He tries to make more trouble for me. His men attacked me first."

Karl was well aware of Robert's astonishment at his fluent use of English. During his close-quarters fight with Kellett, Karl had suddenly frozen, bewildered by a sudden jumble of memories which he experienced at that moment. Like a door opening in his mind, English was a learned language once more. What had been a babble was now comprehensible, catching Karl so much by surprise that he had allowed himself to be restrained by the other four men.

He had no time to explain. Two policemen rounded the corner of the pavilion, pushing their way through the crowd. They took one look at Karl's POW clothing, at the dishevelled state of the men around him, and took control.

"This looks like who we came for," one of them said.

Robert saw his father behind the policemen. "Karl's memory's back!" he called over their heads. "He can tell you himself what's been going on here!"

A constable laid his hand on Robert's shoulder. "Just a minute, sir, if you don't mind. Let's hear from Mr Kellett first."

Kellett had recovered enough to speak for himself. "This German tried to kill me, constable. It's well known around here he's tried it once before. I suggest you apprehend him immediately before he hurts anyone else. These men are having trouble holding him."

This was clearly not the case. Karl stood stock still, his mind back on that day in April when Katherine turned against him so completely. Nevertheless, the bigger of the two policemen, not wanting to take any chances, produced a pair of handcuffs.

Katherine desperately tried to catch Karl's eye all the while. She longed to see recognition there at last. When she did see him look at her she was horrified by the fury in his eyes.

"Judas!" he cursed her, as the handcuffs were snapped around his own and the policeman's wrists.

Katherine turned to see who else he could have been talking to, but Audrey had gone to comfort Andrew, and Robert was with his father, talking to the second policeman.

"That's enough, you!" the constable warned Karl, leading him away from the scene. The murmuring crowd parted to allow them through to their car in the lane. Their first priority was to take the German to Kingshill.

Katherine watched Karl's departure in total dismay. All three Murdochs were nearby, the cricket match forgotten. "What are they going to do with Karl now?" she asked fearfully. "They can't put him in solitary confinement again, surely? Not if he remembers everything that happened before. And he seems to think I've betrayed him somehow. He called me "Judas"!"

"Goodness only knows what Andrew Kellett might have said to him to start the fight," Donald said.

Robert reappeared with his sports bag. The cricket match was rapidly restarted without him, but the spectators were as keen to watch the departing group as the play. Katherine felt their eyes upon her yet again.

"What on earth does he think I've done?"

358

Robert could give no easy answer. "We'll have to wait now until Goldberg speaks to him. Trouble seems to follow Karl wherever he goes."

"It's almost as though he's being punished by God, isn't it?" said Katherine, as they crossed the valley road.

Robert snorted in derision, but Gertie backed Katherine.

"I have no idea what it is he's supposed to have done, but it does seem that way. He really didn't want to come to church this morning. We almost had to force him. Such a rejection of God can only spell unhappiness."

"Mum, you don't know what you're talking about, so please don't try to understand him."

Donald did not like his family squabbling. "We'll leave it there, if you don't mind, everyone. I shall telephone the camp as soon as we're home."

"I hardly think it was Karl's fault, Dad."

"That's for the law to decide, Robert."

Major Alderton waited in his office for the police to arrive with Driesler. He re-read the report he had written back in April. Driesler had only himself to blame for everything. He had abused the trust placed in him when billeted on the farm. Liaisons between local girls and prisoners were not unheard of, but they were usually Saturday night affairs, a mere letting off of steam. Driesler's case was a different kettle of fish.

He heard a car draw up outside his office. The police brought in their captive, handcuffed and with several abrasions and bruises to his face.

"Did he give you trouble?"

The less burly of the two police constables made his report. "The prisoner was in a fight when we arrived to collect him, sir. If you've no objections we'd like to take a statement from him."

"Certainly." He remembered the doctor's report. Driesler spoke no English now. "I'll have to get hold of one of my interpreters and the German camp leader before we start. They like to know what's going on, you know."

Karl had stood silently so far, still trying to control his anger at what had happened, but he felt he had to appraise the commandant of the changed circumstances. "I have remembered how to speak English, sir," he said flatly but respectfully.

"Have you now?" commented the commandant. "And what else have you remembered all of a sudden? I suppose you know why you've been brought back here like this, instead of staying with your friends in Penchurch?"

"No, sir, not exactly. All I know is that it is not because of what happened this afternoon."

Major Alderton frowned. He might as well charge the man now, since he could understand English after all. "It has come to my attention, that you have had an illegal association with a woman of the local community. Is that right, Sergeant Driesler?"

"Yes, sir. But you seem to have my rank wrong. I am a lieutenant, not a sergeant." How could they have got that wrong?

By way of answer, the commandant held up Karl's POW index card for him to see. There was his photograph, with his POW number on it, as well as his personal details: date and place of birth, religion, marital status and SS rank.

It came as a shock to see it boldly written there like that, but at least it explained all the references to the SS which he had been hearing recently. In those few seconds in which he looked at the card, Karl dredged up the events of the end of the war and remembered that he had indeed been fighting with the Waffen SS, not the Wehrmacht, when he had been captured. There was no time to dwell upon it. He had to explain himself to the commandant.

"You are right, sir. I remember now. I had forgotten certain details."

"Perhaps there are other details you ought to remember, Driesler? Your case strikes me as warranting further investigation. A sergeant who thought he was a lieutenant indeed!"

The office became quite crowded by the time the two Germans arrived, vexed at being called from band rehearsal. Chairs were found for all, but the policemen preferred to stand. Karl was given no choice, handcuffed as he was to the heavyweight constable beside him.

The camp leader's first action was to request the removal of the handcuffs, which was done. Karl was then asked to make a statement.

"Different from what we heard," the smaller policeman said, once Karl had finished.

"Of course it would be!" Karl stormed, his temper finally getting the better of him. "It is the word of one German against that of five Englishmen. I do not expect you to believe me. You English are nothing but liars and hypocrites – with your belief in your wonderful justice. I wanted to stay in your country once. But not now. I know what sort of people you really are!"

"That's enough, Driesler!" warned Alderton. He turned to the policemen. "Presumably the complaint goes that Driesler began the fight?"

"Yes, sir."

Alderton consulted a moment with the camp leader, acquainting him with the charge of fraternisation, before making his decision.

"I feel bound to put you under lock and key tonight, Driesler. You have caused too many problems for the police already to risk having to call them out again. You'll spend the night in solitary confinement before being returned to Gloucester under guard. Dr Goldberg will need to discharge you from his care before we can proceed with the charges against you. Do you understand?"

"Yes, sir, but I do not know what will happen if I am in solitary again. I ..."

"It will only be for one night, Driesler! You can manage that, surely?"

"Yes, sir," he answered sullenly.

The cell was horribly familiar, now that he could remember all that had happened before. Karl lay on the bed and stared up at the ceiling, running back in his mind and making sense at last of everything he had forgotten since he had first come to England.

He felt like two people now; simultaneously the man he had been only that morning, who spoke no English and viewed the English with deep mistrust, but also the man willing to love the English and live among them. He felt more affiliation with the first man. Everything that the Murdochs tried to do for him was overshadowed by what Katherine had done.

"She never forgave me for being in the SS," he told himself. "She only pretended to help me so she could thrust the knife in deeper. She asked Audrey to come to the farm yesterday so she could report me for it today! That's what the scene in the churchyard was all about. They were all three in on it together. Audrey did the deed – she wouldn't mind the scandal – to keep Katherine's reputation clean for Kellett."

Katherine. He could remember his love for her, remember the times they made love. How could she do such a thing to him now? He only had to remember her hateful rejection. Her subsequent actions were logical enough. Ilse, Katherine, Audrey; all the women in his life had turned against him. Ilse had cut all connections with him for betraying the Nazis. His reunion with the Nazis as a soldier of the Waffen SS had resulted in Katherine's rejection. He could not win. Who knows what Audrey's motive was?

Then there was his son. Where was he? Would Siegfried ever see his father?

A niggling worry made him cast his mind further. He remembered Yugoslavia, the labour camp, joining the SS. What had happened to send him to a labour camp? It was the one shaft of sunshine, the one ray of hope in his life, that he must have stood against the Nazi regime at some point and been punished for it. Why could he not remember what he had done?

Karl's return to Gloucester was more formal than his departure. He had an armed escort now, and was searched

362

thoroughly. He was considered a criminal by the commandant and treated accordingly. The commandant spoke of the fraternisation as though it were equal to rape. It occurred to him that he did not know for certain who was the named female. He had assumed it to be Audrey, because at the time recent events were uppermost in his mind. What if his assumption were wrong? Could his relationship with Katherine have been reported?

When he was eventually shown into Goldberg's room later that day, Karl's burning question froze on his lips.

"You don't seem pleased to see me, Karl." Goldberg's patient had changed dramatically since their last meeting. He sensed that their rapport was broken.

Karl sat down uneasily. He felt himself break out in a cold sweat, his heart was pounding and his hands started to shake. What was happening? He began to speak to gain control over himself.

"I can remember most of it now, doctor. Did Major Alderton tell you that?"

Samuel Goldberg stiffened in surprise. "No! I was only told to keep you confined to the hospital because of two new serious charges. Was it as a result of those that your memory returned?"

"Things came back to me when I found my hands on Kellett's throat, almost the same as I attacked him before. The only thing I still can't remember is what happened over the summer of '43. Everything else is there, except that. And now, when I see you, I feel frightened. Very frightened. It is very difficult for me to talk to you now."

Goldberg thought he might know why this was. "Is it because I am a Jew? Because I am a doctor? Or both?"

The question was inexplicable to Karl and his face showed it, but he instinctively answered: "Both."

"In other words you know what you fear, but not why. That's very interesting." He decided to leave that and probe the new personality which had emerged. He had never known the older Karl, so a proper comparison could only be made by

363

Miss Carter or Mr Murdoch. He would have to arrange for them to come down as soon as possible. In the meantime he could at least study the current Karl.

"This other charge – "Fraternisation". You obviously remember all about that. How do you feel about Miss Carter now?"

Now was Karl's chance to hear exactly what the charge was. Although his nerves were still very much on edge, he kept himself talking. "Major Alderton did not say who the lady in question was. Are you sure he knows about Miss Carter and me?"

There was a slow smile from Goldberg. "Why? Could someone else be involved?"

Karl grimaced. "Yes. On Saturday afternoon Katherine arranged for a ... friend to keep me company. Katherine deliberately left us alone. This friend made her intentions clear. I thought it was to this friend Major Alderton referred."

"The charge specifies Miss Carter. Does that make a big difference?" he asked.

Karl swore in despair and hung his head by way of answer. His deductions seemed to have been totally false. After a while he looked up at Goldberg. "I blamed Katherine for what happened yesterday and on Saturday. I thought she hated me still and wanted to have me punished. My mind is so confused. What I thought yesterday is never what I think today. It all changes so fast. I don't know what to think now," he moaned. "Please, set me right. Tell me what Katherine was trying to do when she left me with Audrey."

As Goldberg explained Katherine's tactics, based upon the initial events in the river, Karl deeply regretted his misplaced anger.

"What must she think? I called her a Judas!"

"She knows what you've been through. I'm sure she will understand," Goldberg said consolingly.

His words had the opposite effect. "I don't want her to understand," Karl exploded. "I never did. I can't face her now she knows ..."

"Now she knows what?" Goldberg prompted him.

"Oh God! I wish I knew!" It was a cry from the heart. One which the doctor could not ignore.

"Are you absolutely certain you *want* to know, Karl? Perhaps you should content yourself with what memory you have regained. What is lost is best forgotten."

"Not if everybody else knows it and I don't!" Karl shouted. "I remember you saying before I left here, you had something else you could try to make me remember. I demand you try it now!"

"The sooner I discharge you, Karl, the sooner you have to face those charges and be punished for them."

The assumption of guilt was too much. Karl jumped up in anger. "You're as bad as all the rest of them! You think I attacked Kellett, when really it was the other way around."

"Calm down, Karl! I don't know what happened yesterday, but you and I both know that you're guilty of the other charge. I want you to stay here as long as possible, so you are in a fit state to defend yourself properly. If you keep losing your temper like this, it will look bad for you."

"I'm sorry. I think I am angry because I don't know why I'm afraid of you." He sat down again and composed himself, consciously breathing slowly and deeply to calm his nerves.

Goldberg watched him. "It's good that you can do that. Relax like that and hypnosis will be easy."

Instantly Karl was unsettled again. "Hypnosis? Is that what you have in mind?"

"Does the prospect disturb you?"

"Yes," Karl said emphatically. "I am frightened of you, and yet you are asking me to let you have control over me."

"Then first you must learn not to fear me. As you said yourself, everything is happening too quickly. Tomorrow you will fear me less, the next day even less, who knows, the day after that not at all."

The suggestion had been made. Now it had to take root and grow in the patient's mind. Meanwhile another diversion was necessary. Goldberg switched to English.

"I'm told you speak quite good English. Mr Murdoch and Miss Carter will appreciate being able to talk to you again."

There was silence. Goldberg wondered whether Karl had indeed understood until he finally spoke, still in German. "When can I see them?"

There was no great enthusiasm in his voice, which was disturbing, backed by his refusal to speak English.

"Theoretically, you are not allowed to see Miss Carter but I'm willing to overrule that on medical grounds," he replied in German. "You can see her just as soon as she's free to come here. No doubt Mr Murdoch will come at the same time."

As he spoke, Goldberg reached for the box of cigarettes on his desk and offered one to Karl.

Karl began to take one then hesitated. He could not decide whether he wanted to smoke. His hand crept nearer to the box, but there was a strange reluctance in him to actually take one, something as hidden as his fear of the doctor. Karl reasoned overcoming the reluctance to take a cigarette might help overcome his fear of the doctor, and immediately helped himself.

"You were watching to see if I would take one," Karl observed, as Goldberg handed him a lighter. "Why?"

"The interaction of memories. You've just demonstrated that the effects of your lost time are starting to manifest themselves in your consciousness, even though you are not aware of the reason for them. It indicates there is too much of a problem lurking just beneath the surface of your consciousness to ignore. It could break through again as it did when you were in solitary confinement. If I had any doubts about whether to proceed with hypnosis, then they are gone now. You still need help."

His sympathetic voice touched Karl, made him want to trust this doctor whom he inexplicably feared. But his willingness to accept the doctor's help was hindered by a deep-seated terror. "You're saying I'm likely to go mad again, is that it?"

"As I said, unless we can confront the source of your fear, it will remain a threat. Madness is not a word we use. It implies an illogical state of affairs. *Your* condition is entirely reasonable. Your mind is simply trying to control something it would rather had never happened. In some respects it has succeeded, but not entirely."

"To control my fear I must let you control me," Karl said bleakly, feeling sweat break out once more on his brow.

"We'll begin slowly to give you time to get used to me. I can give you something to calm you, to make you more relaxed if you like."

"No!" The reaction from Karl was instantaneous.

Goldberg sighed and leaned back on his chair. "Take it easy, Karl. I won't ask you to do anything you don't want to. I want you to feel as much in control of what we do as I am. Only when you're entirely happy about it will we try hypnosis. In the meantime I'll get in touch with your friends at Penchurch and ask them to come down to see you, now you know who they are!" He finished with a warm smile. "I gather you want to apologise to Miss Carter for something you said to her."

Karl stubbed out his cigarette. "I think I must speak to her," was all he said.

Katherine put down the letter from Sarah and felt disappointment creep up on her. She had looked forward to having Sarah home from Bristol for a month. Now Sarah had been asked by a friend to stay at his family's country house in Norfolk for two weeks. She would be going there straight from Bristol. If this were the start of a great romance, Katherine could hardly complain, but it meant another two weeks of loneliness.

Last week the shifting sands of her emotions stirred and resettled into their former pattern. Since April she had loved him, hated him, been frightened of him and frightened for him. Last week she learned to love him again, accepting his past for what it was. She had felt nothing could come between them, ever again. Then came the events at the cricket match. His bitter accusation that she was a Judas wounded her deeply, but Karl was probably totally confused about what was going on. She hoped he had managed to sort himself out by now. She knew he had been taken back to Kingshill Camp. She had telephoned the next day only to be told she must have nothing more to do with him.

The lonely future stretched like an empty road in front of her. The way to Karl was barred, and she did not know how to get round it. She returned Sarah's letter to its envelope. She already had Sarah's room ready. It was certainly a last minute arrangement. Typical really of Sarah's impetuous nature. The boyfriend must be equally impulsive. They should make an ideal couple.

That was what the Murdochs had said of her and Karl. An ideal couple.

The grandfather clock in the hall struck the half hour. Katherine shook herself out of her reverie and prepared to face the kitchen floor, which needed a jolly good scrub. Housewives' Choice was in full swing on the wireless and it helped her buckle down to the task.

The telephone rang as soon as she had wet her hands. She grabbed a towel as she hurried into the hall, turning down the wireless as she went.

After hearing Goldberg's summons to Gloucester, she rushed to the woodshed, where Robert was chopping logs.

"I told him we'd be there in the morning," she said in a fluster of excitement. "Is that all right?"

He beamed in delight. "Of course. I'm as anxious as you are to talk to Karl. I just hope he doesn't mind that I told you all about him. He must realise that by now."

His words put a damper on her exuberance. "I'd forgotten about that. Still," she continued more brightly, "we'll see tomorrow. Won't we?"

The rest of Tuesday passed as slowly as any day when the next day is longed for. Katherine washed her hair, then laid out the dress she had chosen to wear to meet a Karl she had not seen since early April.

Next morning Robert arrived promptly at nine o'clock. She wrapped a headscarf tightly round her head, left Joss to keep an eye on Les and Dick, then sat behind Robert to enjoy the ride to Gloucester.

An hour later they were shown into Goldberg's office. He shook their hands warmly.

"Welcome! Strictly speaking, Miss Carter, you should not be here, so I'd be grateful if you did not broadcast your visit too widely. Karl is fully aware now of all the problems concerning your relationship, and also understands what occurred on Saturday and Sunday last. He said he wanted to talk to you about that."

Katherine smiled. "Robert said it was only because Karl was in such a muddle that he called me what he did."

Goldberg returned her smile. "You're going to find life hard, the pair of you. You must accept that, Miss Carter."

"I know. But as long as I know that Karl will still want me whenever he's free, I don't mind how long I have to wait."

Goldberg looked grave for a moment. "I've been finding out some facts on cases like yours. About fifty written requests have been received so far from girls wanting to marry German POWs. Their hopes seem slim, since I just heard that a young man who got his girlfriend pregnant is going to be prosecuted. We should hear in the next few days what the result of that is. No doubt it will be reported in the newspapers."

Katherine was not to be made downhearted so easily. "Well, I'm not pregnant, so they'll have nothing to gloat over. Perhaps I ought to get my written request in now. I wish I'd known such a thing was possible. It rather gives the game away, doesn't it? At least we'll be reasonably near the head of the queue when things do change; I'm sure they must eventually."

"You'd better have a word with Karl first. Do you want to see him now?"

"Please," she eagerly replied.

Two minutes later Goldberg returned to his office, where Robert waited. "Miss Carter will find us again when she's ready. I wanted to speak to you alone, because I want to explain to you what I hope to achieve. The thing is, it's not going to be as straightforward as I hoped. His experiences at the hands of those Nazi doctors have left him with a deep fear of men in my profession. This was not evident when he first came here. His partial return of memory has re-awakened it."

"*Partial* return? What do you mean? I thought it had all come back."

"No. Not his time at Dachau. Because of his fear of doctors and of losing control over himself, it may well be hard to hypnotise him, although I hope to succeed eventually."

"What can hypnosis do?"

Goldberg beamed. "Now you're asking about my pet subject." He cleared his throat to deliver his lecture. "Basically, hypnosis is a state of deep relaxation. The conscious part of the brain rests, and the sub-conscious is allowed to dominate. The subject is not asleep. He can respond to stimuli, if appropriate, can answer questions, but, except in certain highly suggestible subjects, can't be made to do anything he would not normally allow himself to do." Goldberg leaned on his elbows, fixing Robert with a wide-eyed stare. Robert was taken aback and hurriedly looked away. Goldberg laughed. "I was only joking. I can't hypnotise you without your consent. You've got to *want* to be hypnotised. That's the problem I have with Karl at the moment.

"But you asked, "what can hypnosis do?" and I haven't answered your question. It's a means of bypassing the conscious mind, of gaining access to memories which lie deeply buried, memories which may have been considered forgotten. I've treated men beset by nightmares, who have lost the power of speech, control of a limb, or like Karl, whole chunks of memory. Sometimes regaining the memory is not the best solution. Amnesia is a protective mechanism. If we make Karl remember his time at Dachau, it's possible it may cause more problems than it solves. I'm going to have to work very carefully with him to enable him to deal with those memories when they return."

370

Robert was intrigued. "You mentioned nightmares. I wonder if my own could be – "

Footsteps running up the corridor heralded the return of Katherine.

CHAPTER NINETEEN

Happy and confident of a successful reunion, Katherine stepped through the doorway Goldberg indicated.

Karl was leaning against the window, not seated as she expected. He looked at her. She searched for the recognition she now expected to see, and to her joy found it. She forgot about the anger in him, so horribly evident the Sunday before. Throwing down her handbag, she ran to him, flung her arms around him, and clung to him in the longed-for embrace.

He let her stay like that for a moment, his arms by his sides, then took hold of her and pushed her gently away.

"Sit down, Katherine. I have to talk to you."

Katherine blanched at his unexpected coldness. Nervously she did as he told her. "What's wrong, Liebling? I thought everything would be all right now between us. You remember what we meant to each other, don't you?"

Karl hated what he was about to do. He had thought hard about it, ever since his talk with Goldberg. Avoiding her eyes, he moved to the window, distancing himself from her.

"Last week you said to me, that I was German and you were English, therefore there could be nothing between us."

Katherine groaned inwardly. So he had understood that much English at least. "Yes, but that was when I was still afraid of who you seemed to be," she protested. "You're different now. I saw you change throughout your week with us. Now you're back as you were."

"You're wrong, Katherine." He faced her at last. "I'm not the same. You're not the same. You know all about me now. That is something I never wanted. In fact, now you know more about me than I know myself. What I do know is that I was a sergeant in the SS, when before I had been a lieutenant in the Wehrmacht. That change seems to have blackened my name. Can you really marry a man whose name will become yours, whose past will always be like a dark cloud over you and our children? I think it will take a very long time before the world forgives what my country did. I was in the Waffen SS and no one will let me forget that. You were shocked when you heard that. Now as well as that shame, I have also the shame that I was mad. I still am. Goldberg says it is not madness, but I know I do not think right sometimes. I know too that the madness is close." He tapped his skull. "It is here still, in my head. One day it may come again. I do not ask you to live with that."

Katherine began to protest; he waved her abruptly to silence. "Let me finish what I must say. I think you are here today because you feel sympathy for me, because your God tells you that you must love and help people like me. You are a very good woman, Katherine; I know that, but I do not want only your sympathy. Last Saturday you made Audrey do what you could not. I know now why you brought her that day. But surely, if you really loved me, you would have done it yourself?"

"I *do* love you, Karl! You don't understand how difficult it was for me when you were so different, when I couldn't talk to you, or anything. You were a stranger. I couldn't sleep with a stranger. You know how much better Audrey is at that."

"So I was different. I still am. I think before that I was trying to be English, to forget that I was German. Now I don't feel like that. Perhaps it is because of what Goldberg has done for me. Also my past has come closer. I have thought much about my home, my family ... and my son."

It was the first time Karl had ever mentioned his son. Her lack of reaction told him she knew about Siegfried. "I need to go home, to a place where I am no different from anyone else; where my guilt is their guilt; where I will not have to make difficult explanations. I must thank you for your help and kindness, but you must not feel you have to give me any more than that. Please forget this mad German. Go home and marry an Englishman."

It seemed he had finished his speech. She had waited impatiently for him to disclose what was on his mind. Having heard him out, she could not believe he wanted to abandon all that they had meant to each other.

"There's no need to run away from me. You *know* I love you. It won't be nearly as bad as you think. People will forget, you'll see. Besides, we're not the only ones. There are other girls wanting to marry Germans. If they have hope, so can we!"

She saw him hesitate. "Give yourself more time, Karl. Dr Goldberg says you've still got some adjustments to make. Don't condemn me to a life of loneliness and regret. Think of my feelings as well as your own."

Those words decided him. "I am. That is why I think it would be best if we forget each other. I can only offer you worry and uncertainty."

"What happened to love and comfort? Have courage, Schatz. I need you."

"You need a man who is worthy. I am not that man."

His stubborn resistance was infuriating. "I'm telling you that you are! Don't you think I ought to know what I want? I want *you*, Karl. No one else, and I'm willing to wait until you can see sense! I don't understand you now."

"I don't understand myself either. I don't know why I hated my country so much, why I wanted to leave it for you. My choice is different now. This country holds bitter memories for me; too much is said against me, even by you. You have not shown me a reason to stay. I will be glad to go."

Katherine was incensed. In her frustration she sprang to her feet and grabbed him by the elbows. "Is that all you wanted me for? To give you a respectability, which you've now lost?" She tightened her grip. "You think you can cast me aside? What do I have to do to convince you that I love you still, that I'm truly sorry for the way I behaved?"

"Please don't argue with me, Katherine," he said coldly, releasing himself from her grasp. "I do not trust your love if you think all I wanted was your respectability."

He returned his gaze to the window. "Tell Sarah I am sorry I won't see her again."

"Tell her yourself!" Grabbing her handbag, she ran from the room.

In early July Katherine read with anguish of the POW sentenced to twelve months detention for getting his English girlfriend pregnant. This latest news seemed to confirm that Karl had been right after all, that a future together was impossible, even though Dr Goldberg continued to offer her hope that Karl would understand himself better soon.

The Murdochs looked out for further correspondence in the newspapers and informed her daily of the growing support for the POWs. If British servicemen could marry German girls, the people asked, why could not British girls marry Germans?

On 8th July the Minister of War announced that such marriages would now be permissible, and that sentences already pronounced would be examined and possibly remitted, if appropriate. Suddenly the future looked less bleak.

As if in demonstration of this, Sarah finally came home, full of her fortnight in Norfolk with Perry. On the evening after her arrival, the sisters sat in the garden with the sewing box in front of them, sorting through and mending Sarah's outfits. As they worked, Katherine told Sarah of her problems with farm suppliers.

"Even though Karl's not going to be prosecuted, word's got about the county, and some firms won't supply me any more – usually with the most feeble excuses. Only one firm referred directly to Karl as the reason."

"That's crazy, though!" Sarah burst out. "They're doing themselves out of a valuable customer." Angrily she pulled a blouse from the pile and snipped off a dangling button.

Katherine had other suspicions on the matter. "Something that was said makes me think it isn't quite as simple as that. The feed merchant said that given the choice between a big or a little customer he had to choose the big. I read it that

Andrew has put pressure on them not to supply me. If they supply Lane Head Farm, they can forget about supplying Froxley Grange. What do you think? Would Andrew do something like that?"

"Goodness knows! You know Andrew better than I do. I wouldn't put it past him. What are you going to do about it? Confront him and demand an explanation?"

"There's no point. I know the explanation. He wants to put me out of business. Prove I can't manage the farm on my own."

"How childish!" exclaimed Sarah indignantly. "He's got Audrey now. Surely he can leave you alone?"

"You would have thought so, wouldn't you?"

Sarah finished sewing on the button, folded the blouse, and added it to the pile on the ground. "You look as though you could do with a good holiday, instead of worrying yourself sick. At least you've got me off your back at last. There's me going on about what a super time I had with Perry, and you're left to cope with all this. Perhaps I ought to forget my career and help you with the farm."

"Don't be daft! You've never wanted to stay here. You'd be miserable, then I'd have you to worry about as well. Things will sort themselves out eventually. Perhaps someone will come along who wants to share the farm and my life with me."

"Now you're the one who's being daft. You know very well Karl is your choice. Don't give up on him yet!"

"You weren't there when he told me to forget him. He meant it, Sarah. All he wants to do is go home and find out what happened to his son. Which will probably mean finding Ilse. I certainly don't fit into his plans anymore."

"His son? His and Ilse's you mean?" Sarah asked incredulously. Certainly there was much about Karl she had never known.

"Yes. I found out when Robert told me about Karl's past. Karl thinks his son may have been killed in an air raid, but he's not sure."

"And there was I hating him for Mummy's death, when his own son may have been killed the same way. How awful for him! I'm surprised he never mentioned it."

"It was all part of his plan not to talk about himself. He was trying to forget."

"And now he wants to forget you."

Katherine gazed bleakly across the garden towards Hay Bluff, and slowly nodded.

It took time, but gradually Karl allowed his trust in Dr Goldberg to grow, until hypnosis was possible. The sessions were going well, but proving traumatic. At the end of August Karl revealed more than Goldberg ever expected.

Karl lay on the couch in a deep hypnotic trance. He had just experienced being made to break the Jew's leg. He was shuddering with horror. Gradually the shuddering ceased. He relaxed totally.

Goldberg did not expect this. "How do you feel, Karl?"

"Good."

"Why?"

"Another injection."

Goldberg was puzzled. There should have been no more injections of the narcotic. He had a horrible suspicion something else had occurred which not even Robert knew about. Cautiously he probed further. "The effects are wearing off now. You're irritable again, you want some more. What happens now?"

Karl gave an anguished cry. "Nooooo!" The cry faded away, his body relaxed.

Goldberg frowned. Karl was still blocking the memory. He would have to go even deeper into hypnosis. "You're feeling calm and safe. Perfectly safe. You're back in our tunnel. You're walking down it, deeper and deeper, feeling calmer with every step. Do you feel calm?"

"Yes."

"There's a door. Open it and go in the room you were in just now. You feel perfectly calm. Tell me what you see."

"Goslar, the doctor, a ... child."

"Is Goslar telling you to do something to this child?"

Karl winced.

377

"You still feel quite calm and detached from what is happening," Goldberg reassured him. "What is it you have to do?"

"Kill her."

Goldberg's voice remained steady. "Do you want to?"

"No."

"Are you going to?"

Karl's reply was barely audible. "Yes."

"Why?"

"I have to."

"Why do you have to?"

"The injection. I can see it. I need it. I must have it."

Goldberg decided to circumvent the actual killing. "She's dead now. Did you kill her?"

"Yes." His voice was flat, devoid of the emotion he suffered at the time.

"Do you think it's your fault she's dead, Karl?"

"Yes."

"Don't you think it's Goslar's fault? Tell yourself it's Goslar's fault."

"It's Goslar's fault."

"Goslar's to blame, not you. Repeat that, Karl."

Karl repeated it.

"Do you blame yourself now?"

"No."

Goldberg paused and wiped his brow. He often found his work harrowing, but the rewarding part was the reconstruction and repair he would attempt next. He cleared his throat in readiness.

"When I wake you, you won't remember what you've just told me. The little girl is gone. She is Goslar's history, not yours. You need not feel any blame for her death, or for injuring the other man. Only Goslar is to blame. You will remember the rest of your time at Dachau, how the SS doctor experimented on you, made you addicted to a drug. That you

378

can cope with. It was unpleasant, but it will not be any problem to you in future. You can think about it without fear. Do you understand?"

"Yes."

"In a moment I'm going to wake you. When you wake you will feel calm and relaxed, able to remember your experiences without fear, just as I told you."

Goldberg woke him. "How do you feel?"

Karl lay quietly. He was reasonably composed as usual, despite the trauma he had recently been made to relive, but he felt something new this time.

"I feel angry. Very angry. That bastard, Goslar." Goldberg gave a grim smile. "Is that what you intended, doctor?"

"Yes. Goslar is your scapegoat. It would be foolish of me to leave you with nothing against which to direct your anger."

"What about injections?" Karl asked. "Will I be able to have them now?"

"We'll need at least another session, I think, and it will have to be tomorrow. I must discharge you on Friday."

The doctor's words came as a shock. "Why so soon?"

Goldberg tried to look modest. "My successes here have been noticed. I'm being transferred to another hospital, to help British service-men cope with their experiences."

Karl felt a moment's panic. "What if I'm not ready to be discharged?"

"You're doing fine, Karl. I would say you've made as good a recovery as I could have hoped for. You can always see me again, but I really don't think that will be necessary. All you need now is to go home in due course and start to re-build your life. You're to be sent to a different camp. They won't have you back at Kingshill."

Karl accepted this statement stoically. "All right. I can wait another six or seven months. But what about all this business with Kellett? And Katherine?"

"Under the circumstances the six months detention has been waived, and the charges concerning you and Miss Carter have been dropped. You're being given a clean slate as a result of your illness. Try to keep it that way. In the meantime, prepare yourself for your return home by learning to stand on your own two feet again."

"Without Katherine to prop me up, you mean?"

"I didn't mean that exactly, but it's a valid enough point. No, I meant freedom brings with it responsibilities and choices of behaviour. You must make sure that you're equipped to make the right choices for you and your country."

"In other words, re-education. Don't you think I've rid myself of Nazism, then?"

"It's not so simple, Karl. You've got to learn about what's replacing it, to fill the void. You need to develop political awareness. Have instruction in democracy. They'll give you that at your new camp. You were too isolated from the world in Penchurch. You must catch up with your compatriots."

Karl wrote to Robert the day before he was sent to a camp in Oxfordshire. He had decided he needed to sever all links with Herefordshire. He told Robert that he wanted to put the past and all that it entailed behind him, so he could have a completely fresh start in Germany. He thanked Robert for his help and friendship but requested him not to reply.

Karl sat and read the letter through. It was hard to write, not only because of its finality, but also because he was unused to writing in English. Words he had spoken so easily were impossible to spell. At least Robert would have something to laugh about.

Sarah sipped at her coffee in her new office in Reading, a letter from Katherine in front of her.

I can't believe it's all over; that Karl can just turn his back on us like that. Until now I lived in hope that after the hypnosis all would be well, but my hopes have been dashed. Robert says he'll try to write to Karl and influence him, but Dr Goldberg seems to be encouraging Karl to look towards Germany for his future. Maybe it's the best thing for Karl, but it's certainly not best for me.

I can't be bothered with the farm now. I suppose I must feel pretty much like Daddy did when Mummy died. I've lost interest. Without

Karl to share it with there's no point in wearing myself out. If you agree, I'm going to advertise for tenants. I'll find myself a job and live in Hereford.

I'm sorry to lose you your home, but I can't take the strain any more. I'm sure you understand. Please let me know what you think as soon as possible.

The coffee in her cup grew cold as Sarah pondered what to do. If Karl was hell bent on going back to Germany, and Katherine on leaving the farm, she might as well go with Karl, if he could be persuaded to marry her.

Today was Friday. She could spend the weekend on a last bid to make Karl see sense. She spent her lunch hour finding out where Karl had been sent. It needed some persuasion on her part, and the feminine touch to convince the clerk in the hospital records office, but at last she had an address. It turned out to be barely twenty miles from Reading.

Sarah decided to make a weekend of it, to stay overnight in an inn near the camp. On Saturday morning she took her bicycle on the train and arrived at the camp in the early afternoon. It did not look a particularly large camp. It was possible that some of the inmates would know Karl. Standing her bicycle against a wall, she approached a couple of men emerging from the gates.

"Excuse me. Do you speak English?" she asked them, hoping they did not take her for an amorous "camp follower".

"Yes, I do," said one, his young face heavily scarred by acne.

"Oh good. I wonder if you can help me." Sarah realised she was gabbling and made herself slow down. "I am trying to find a man who came here a few weeks ago. His name is Karl Driesler. Do you know him?"

The young German conferred with his companion and by the shaking of heads, Sarah gathered they were not acquainted with Karl. "What does he look like?" She gave him a brief description. Again he shook his head. "I'm sorry. We can't help you. Perhaps someone else knows. I will go and ask."

Sarah had not expected such helpfulness. She followed them towards the gate, but did not go too near, feeling awkward in such an environment. The helpful POW returned to her with a smile.

"Your friend works on a farm near here, but always he stays in the village until evening. You can leave a message for him here, if you want. It is not certain that he will get it."

Sarah thanked the young man profusely, then hunted in her bag for something to write on, but could find nothing suitable. She decided to cycle down to the village where, no doubt, she would be able to buy some notepaper.

As she entered the thatched village shop she was astonished to find Germans in there. Then she remembered that since July they were allowed part of their pay in cash and could now buy things for themselves or to send to their families. She waited her turn patiently, as negotiations were rather slow. Not all the prisoners spoke such good English as Karl, or the one near the camp.

The shopkeeper was used to having a large proportion of her customers from the camp. She spoke to them in a friendly way, even seemed to know some of their names. This gave Sarah an idea.

Once the Germans vacated the shop, Sarah got into conversation with the shopkeeper about the prisoners having money.

"Oh yes," the woman replied. "They earn quite a lot on the quiet. They're not supposed to have more than thirty shillings on them, but I know for a fact that they have more, some of them. They do all sorts of odd jobs round here, as well as working overtime in the fields. The amount of stuff they send back to their poor families in Germany is incredible."

The conversation was leading on nicely. "I suppose it's only the ones who can speak reasonable English who do jobs for people, is it?" she asked innocently.

The shopkeeper was only too pleased to chat to this stranger. "Good heavens, no! You only need to wave a rake at them, and they know what you want. There are one or two who come in here who speak English really well, and there's even one who seems to have a bit of a Welsh accent. He's only been here a short time. I expect he was transferred from a camp in Wales."

Sarah could not have asked for more luck than this. Her own local accent had been modified by her time in Bristol. When she had first gone there, other students assumed she was Welsh, not from the Marches. "Where does he work, do you know?"

"Well, when he's finished in the fields for the day, he tidies up the vicarage garden. He's a strange one is Karl. You never see him off out with the others. Now the evenings are drawing in it's too dark to be working outside. I reckon the vicar's got him working on some secret project or other. He can't be gardening all the time." She suddenly seemed to remember that Sarah was a customer. "What can I do for you, then, dear?"

Sarah bought her notepaper, but hoped she would not need it now. The vicarage was easy to locate. It was a large, Cotswold stone house right next to the church. From what the shopkeeper said, it was unlikely Karl would be there.

Leaving her bicycle by the front gate, Sarah boldly went up the path and rang the door-bell.

The door was opened by a tall, dapper man in his thirties, in a dog collar; hardly Sarah's idea of a village vicar. Perhaps the proximity to Oxford had something to do with it.

"Good afternoon. My name is Sarah Carter." She watched to see if the name meant anything to him. He only blinked at her through his glasses.

"Good afternoon, Miss Carter. What can I do for you?"

Now what was she to say? She might as well come straight to the point. "I've heard you have a German by the name of Karl who tidies your garden for you."

The vicar was looking a trifle suspicious now. "Ye-es," he said, with an upward inflection.

She was still on the doorstep, feeling awkward now. "Well, if it's the same Karl, he used to live on our farm in Herefordshire. We're rather keen to keep in touch. We haven't heard from him, you see."

The vicar's expression softened. "Ah, yes, I see. Won't you come in, Miss Carter? I think we may have a lot to talk about before Karl gets here."

Sarah followed the vicar down the dark hallway into a room overlooking the back garden. No wonder he needed help in controlling it. The garden seemed to stretch for miles and to either side of the house.

"May I introduce you to my wife, Miss Carter? This is Amelia. Oh, and my name is Peter Wilcox," he added.

Sarah smiled at an attractive woman seated near the window. Amelia Wilcox put down the heavy book she was reading and took Sarah's proffered hand.

"Miss Carter has come to see Karl," Peter Wilcox told his wife. "I think she may be able to shed some light on our unfortunate friend."

"Unfortunate? In what way?" Sarah asked.

Wilcox gestured to a comfortable chintz covered chair. "Perhaps I'd better explain how we got to know Karl. That may answer your question."

Amelia decided refreshments were in order and hurried out to make tea. Her haste made it clear she too wanted to hear whatever it was Sarah had to say.

There was a sudden crash from the garden and a squadron of young boys hurtled past the window, flying imaginary aeroplanes.

Wilcox gave an apologetic smile. "Excuse the noise, Miss Carter. Those are my sons and a couple of friends."

Sarah smiled too. What a lovely, homely atmosphere Karl had found, Battle of Britain excepted. Perhaps it had been a deliberate policy on Karl's part to find another sanctuary. She switched her attention back to her host as he began to talk.

"It can only have been a short time after Karl first arrived, that I found him sitting alone in church one evening. Not praying or anything, just sitting there, looking lost. I wondered whether to leave him alone or speak to him. When he saw me watching him, he stood up as if to leave. I didn't want to frighten him away from the church, so I told him to stay if he wanted to. I realised he was very unhappy and possibly had no one to talk to, so I asked him if he would like to come into the house. He declined at first, although I could see the invitation was tempting. When I pressed him he agreed. Immediately he pointed out to me that he had been in the SS. It seemed to be vitally important to him I knew that. I learned later a local farmer had refused to employ him for that very reason. I told Karl it made no difference to me. He seemed happier after that. I've found that with a lot of these SS chaps. The ones we have here are no different from any of the other prisoners on the whole. One or two can be a bit shirty, but there's no trouble with them."

"No, I don't suppose there would be, now."

"Anyway," Wilcox continued, "Amelia made him feel at home and we got him talking a bit about himself. He said he had been billeted on a farm – yours I take it? – and then with a local doctor, but had been moved here. He was finding it difficult adjusting to being in a large camp again. Amelia suggested that he might like to help us out with our jungle of a garden, to give him somewhere other than the camp to spend his time. He jumped at the offer. But he has never expanded on his life in Herefordshire. It led us to wonder whether he was made to change camps for any particular reason. Now it seems you're here to provide the answers."

Amelia came in with tea, setting the tray on a small table where her book lay.

Sarah accepted a teacake. The squadron sped by again, shooting down an enemy plane as they went.

"What does Karl think of all that?" she asked, tossing her head towards the squadron.

Amelia laughed. "Oh, he joins in, sometimes. They love having a real enemy to attack. He doesn't mind in the least. He's superb at playing hide and seek with them too. They lose him for ages and call in my help to track him down. He camouflages himself so well amongst the bushes, I've looked straight at him and not known he was there. I suppose he learned that in the war."

Sarah had to laugh too. "You still call him "unfortunate", even though he seems so much happier with you. Why is that?"

Amelia answered. "It's because underneath the fun and games he's still unhappy, and we don't know why."

It was her cue to reveal all, but Sarah was reluctant to disclose details of such a personal nature to strangers, no matter how nice. But they deserved to know something.

"I'd better explain what happened. He and my sister were in love. They had a misunderstanding and Karl was sent away. But my sister is desperate to see him again and patch it all up. Do you think she stands a chance?"

Peter Wilcox cast a glance in his wife's direction, as though relying on her intuition. Again it was Amelia who answered. "He's never mentioned any of this. All he talks about is going home." She looked awkward for a moment. "He's mentioned trying to find out what happened to his son. Do you know about him?"

"Very little. The mother married someone else." Mrs Wilcox had not answered her directly, but the subject of her reply was probably answer enough. "You think my visit here will be a waste of time?"

Peter Wilcox shrugged. "Who can say until you ask him yourself? He usually arrives in time for tea at six o'clock. I'm sure Miss Carter can stay and eat with us, can't she, darling?" he asked his wife.

"Of course. Unless you have any other plans, Miss Carter? If you've come all the way from Hereford you've probably booked into an hotel or something."

"Call me Sarah, please," she replied. "No, I was going to find an inn or something nearby. I can do that between now and six o'clock, save me taking up any more of your time."

"Oh, but you can't stay in an inn when we have a room here."

How like the Murdochs they were. So friendly and hospitable. "That's really very kind of you, but I don't want to be any trouble to you. I haven't actually come from Hereford today. I've recently started work in Reading."

By the time she had told them about her new job, she realised that the assumption had been made that she would be staying the night at the vicarage. Peter Wilcox suggested she brought her bicycle in off the road. She had left her rucksack of belongings in the hall, and Amelia had already taken it up to the spare room by the time Sarah's bicycle was safely stowed away.

To allow Peter and Amelia time to get on with their work, Sarah went out into the garden to have a look around. The boys, aged between six and nine, had landed their Spitfires and were swinging from a rope suspended from an enormous horse chestnut tree. They looked curiously at her, but soon ignored her as she followed the gravel paths of a sunken garden. Eventually at the farthermost limit, she looked over a tumbledown fence across a watermeadow, to gently rolling hills, brown where the tractors had ploughed in the corn stubble.

She remembered the vicar's words about the farmer who had refused to employ Karl. She had been such a person once. Worse in fact, as her hatred had extended to all Germans, not just those in the SS. It brought home to her Karl's new unwillingness to stay in England. How much did that have to do with his dismissive attitude to Katherine? With only a fraction of the truth at her disposal, Sarah simply could not reconcile Karl's behaviour with the person she had last seen at Easter, even accounting for his breakdown.

She looked at her watch just as the church clock struck five. Another hour. It was growing chilly already. She turned back towards the house to offer her services in preparing tea.

Karl said farewell to his fellow field workers, who intended visiting a local dance that evening, and strode off towards the village. His step quickened in anticipation of tea at the vicarage. He knew he was incredibly lucky to find such good replacements for the Murdochs, whom he missed very much. He ought to have gone with the others to the dance, but had no heart for such things, despite Dr Goldberg's efforts. Robert would understand.

Stedwick Vicarage offered a new haven, a place where he could learn to live with himself all over again. This time he

387

would have to achieve it without Katherine's help. Smoke drifting from the tall, ornate brick chimney gave evidence of a warm welcome. Tony and Pip, the Wilcox boys, had taken an instant liking to him, accepting him with unquestioning grace. Likewise their parents seemed to know full well he was troubled by his past, but never pushed him to reveal more than he was willing. In offering a refuge they were helping him more than enough. A few more months and he would be on his way home.

As he entered by the back door, he heard a whoop of greeting from the boys, whose friends had already gone home. He had been told not to bother knocking as he was always expected. Little Pip jumped onto Karl's back, in his usual boisterous assault, and Karl had to playfully wrestle him off.

"There's someone to see you!" Pip shrieked from his upside-down position. Karl lowered him carefully to the floor.

"A lady!" Tony added mischievously, on seeing his mother's brow furrow in a silent warning to be quiet.

Amelia chivvied along her brood before they could say anything else. "Run along. Make sure you wash those hands!"

"Is it true?" he asked, over the clatter of running feet. The boys were renowned for playing pranks; this could just be one more.

"Yes. She's waiting for you in the living room." Amelia paused just long enough to assess Karl's reaction. Her impression was of hurriedly concealed alarm. She thought she had better reveal the visitor's identity, before Karl said anything which might be heard up the corridor. "It's Sarah Carter. She arrived in the village this afternoon and found you quite by chance. Come along and see her, once you've washed your hands."

Karl picked up the piece of soap left dirty by the two boys. He was grateful to Mrs Wilcox for allowing him time to digest this turn of events. The immediate alarm he felt turned slowly to resentment. The Carters would not allow him any peace. They were bringing his past here, where nobody except himself and the authorities knew it. He was almost tempted to walk out of the house without a word, and not have to face Sarah. But that would be cowardly and churlish. He braced himself and walked to the lounge.

The Wilcoxes were sitting there, with Tony and Pip, giving a reassuring air of normality to the room. Sarah was helping Pip tie his shoelaces. She looked up as Karl came in and beamed at him in a smile which reflected their long separation.

Karl could not return her smile. He sat down hardly giving her a glance. Her visit was not welcome.

"It's good to see you again, Karl" Sarah said, determined to make Karl communicate with her. His lack of greeting hardly surprised her, but she was not going to let her efforts to find him go to waste. "I'm working in Reading now. I thought it would be nice to look you up and see how you were getting on. You seem to have settled down well here."

Karl could not be bothered with formalities, but the presence of the Wilcoxes kept his tongue civil. "Does Katherine know you are here?"

Sarah took the abrupt question in her stride. "No. It was my idea completely." She leaned forward. "You don't know how much she misses you, Karl."

Her words alarmed Karl, who glanced anxiously at the Wilcoxes.

"Sarah has told us a little of your life in Herefordshire," Peter said. "If you would rather we left the room so you can talk in private ..."

Karl shook his head. "Please stay. We shall not talk about the past. Sarah can tell me about her job and her life in Reading. Any news of Robert will be welcome, but I will not talk about anything else."

Pip wailed suddenly. "Mummy, I'm hungry."

It seemed an opportune interruption. The conversation had become too serious. They all rose to troop into the dining room where the table was set with sandwiches, cakes and tea.

The atmosphere lightened considerably in the hubbub of the meal table. Tony and Pip regaled Sarah with tales of tricks they had played on Karl: stealing his spade, lying in ambush for him, dropping worms down his shirt. With the boys as a distraction, Karl found he could relax and speak more openly to Sarah and made no objection when Sarah began, solely for Karl's benefit, to tell Amelia Wilcox how difficult Katherine was finding life at the moment, and how much she was missing Karl.

Karl listened in growing anger as he heard Sarah expand on the trouble Andrew Kellett was causing.

"What about Audrey?" Karl asked, despite himself.

Sarah suppressed a grin which wanted to break out on her lips now that she had Karl's interest. "Audrey is hanging onto Andrew by her fingernails. She's decided he's a catch and wants to keep him. We all reckon that he's just dallying with her until he has Katherine back."

"Then Katherine should go back to him. She will grow to love him. She loves everyone. Then she will have no problems."

"I will tell her what you said," Sarah replied coldly. "Would you pass the jam please, Tony?"

Even the two boys could not help being aware that Karl's visitor was not welcome to him, but Pip was not yet practised in the art of tact. He was a bit confused as to who loved whom and he wanted a point clarified. "Karl, do you love Sarah or Katherine?"

Tony kicked his younger brother under the table. He could see that such a question was out of order by the furious look on his mother's face.

Karl's answer was given to a hushed room. "I love Katherine."

Pleased to have got an answer, despite the glares from everyone else, Pip persisted with his questions. "Why don't you marry her then? Daddy's always marrying people who love each other."

"Philip! You mustn't ask such personal questions." Amelia tried to smile an apology at Karl.

He was not looking at her, nor indeed at anyone. It was as though his statement had come as a surprise to himself, as though he had only just acknowledged how much he still loved her.

Sarah saw her chance. "Shall I tell that to Katherine too?"

Karl realised how much he wanted to say yes. He clenched his fist on the crisp, white tablecloth. "No," he replied with a finality which put an end to discussion.

Sarah was not too downhearted. There was always tomorrow.

At a quarter to ten Karl returned to the camp. The Wilcoxes were free to ask Sarah, slumped in an armchair by the fire, some questions of their own.

"If he's free to marry her, and he loves her, why on earth won't he?" Amelia asked.

"I don't know. When he admitted he loved her still, I thought he was prepared to change his mind about everything. I'm sure if he just saw Katherine he would realise what he's missing."

Peter Wilcox butted in. "I can tell you what it is he's missing. It's self-respect. How can a man offer himself to a woman when he feels what he has to offer is worthless? Maybe you know more about him than we do, Sarah, but I've seen him sitting in my church all alone, searching for himself and finding nothing. He needs to find his roots again, and they are in Germany, not here with your sister."

Sarah ran her fingers agitatedly through her hair. "I hate to admit it, but I think that is what Karl has been told and believes."

"Told? By whom?" Amelia asked quickly.

Sarah felt sure the Wilcoxes ought to be told more. It seemed to her all Karl's problems stemmed from his secrecy. Wasn't a vicar as used to sharing confidences as a doctor, after all? "By his psychiatrist," she replied. "Karl tried to kill himself after the ... misunderstanding with Katherine. He spent some months in hospital and left there to come here." It was the truth as she had been told it, although she omitted to mention his amnesia as an unnecessary detail.

Peter Wilcox commented on his earlier choice of word. "Unfortunate indeed."

Sarah continued her explanation. "I think he and Katherine need each other to survive. She gave him back his self-respect originally. When she withdrew her support, he collapsed, just

391

as she is doing now without his. She's in a mess and has finally admitted it. She's coping with the farm well enough, but to the exclusion of herself. She never goes out, works all the hours God gives her. For what purpose? At the rate she's going she'll never have any heirs to pass the farm to."

Amelia listened intently. The enigma was being revealed; the solution was an obvious one. "It sounds like your sister needs a break. Would she like to pay us a visit sometime soon?" she asked, with a twinkle in her eye.

There was a steady stream of men walking back through the village in time for the ten o'clock curfew, strictly enforced as one of the few restrictions on their liberty. As usual Karl walked alone, still unable to reestablish the cameraderie of bygone days. Tonight in particular he needed to be alone. Seeing Sarah had been a shock. Her account of Katherine's troubles touched him as deeply as she had intended. No doubt tomorrow she would continue her pressure on him to make him reconsider his attitude.

He knew only too well what it was like to be abandoned. Katherine herself had of course done it to him, but Ilse too had abandoned him, to protect herself and Siegfried from suspicion, retribution and the shame of his disgrace. His name meant shame from everyone's point of view. Katherine must not continue to live in hope that he would ever return to her. She would do best to accept Kellett as her suitor again. He decided he would avoid meeting Sarah again and would, for once, spend Sunday in camp. He would send his apologies to the Wilcoxes through one of the prisoners who attended church. No doubt the Wilcoxes would side with Sarah in their ignorance of the truth. It would be a great pity if Sarah's intervention destroyed his temporary sanctuary.

Six months was a long time to wait until he was repatriated, but once he got home and could begin his search for Siegfried he would be all right. The Wilcox boys had revealed to him how much he yearned for his own son. He had managed to convince himself that Siegfried must have survived the air raids along with his mother. That part of himself in Germany

392

was a piece of his life surviving from before the destruction set in. He had thought much about Ilse over the last few months. He hoped she might be persuaded to leave that baker husband of hers, whom she had no doubt only married out of necessity. In the new regime, his former disgrace would be seen by Ilse as a positive advantage. She would accept him with open arms and he could settle down with a ready-made family, amongst his own kind. The question of Ilse having more children by now was the only flaw he could see in his idyll.

Karl's failure to turn up the following day did not deter Sarah and the Wilcoxes in the slightest from going ahead with their plans. Sarah was all for arranging a surprise meeting, but the Wilcoxes advised that it would be best if Katherine at least knew what to expect. She must also be fully aware of Karl's attitude. The surprise must be for Karl alone. If he suspected Katherine was at the vicarage, he would surely stay away.

Sarah could not bear the thought of missing out on the excitement and wanted to come too, but with the apple harvest imminent Katherine would be reluctant to leave it at such a crucial time.

"We can't wait until after the apple-picking," Sarah moaned. "Or at least, I can't wait. I want to see this settled one way or the other as soon as possible, for Katherine's sake. Can I suggest she comes here with me next weekend, assuming she can find someone to look after the animals?"

Amelia consulted their engagement diary. "You've got a wedding on the Saturday, Peter, and you were going to visit the Cooks in the afternoon, but I seem to be free all weekend. If you can arrange it we'll be delighted to have you both for the weekend. We'll try to make sure Karl turns up at six o'clock on Saturday, without giving the game away."

Peter was dubious. "It's all very well having these romantic notions. What if Karl is offended by our skulduggery and refuses to come back after that? Where will that have got him? He'll have lost the only friends he seems to have, and in view of what Sarah said about his previous mental state, I wouldn't like to think myself responsible for a relapse."

There was silence. Tony and Pip had already been excused from the meal table and were playing outside.

The two women looked at each other. The plan was fine if it worked, but had the potential for catastrophic failure. "A little optimism in the face of uncertainty is needed, I think," Amelia declared authoritatively, sensing a stalemate. "We can keep an eye on Karl if necessary afterwards, if things don't work out."

On her return to Reading that afternoon, Sarah telephoned home.

Katherine took a while to grasp the details. "You went and found Karl? You actually saw him?" she asked, dumbfounded. "How was he?"

"Unhappy. He won't accept that he needs you, even though he says he loves you. He asked me not to repeat that to you."

"So of course you do," Katherine teased, thankful for her sister's inability to obey.

"Don't get your hopes up too high," Sarah warned. "Karl seems like a sheep in front of a pen at the moment. He could walk meekly in, or break away at the last moment and be lost. He'll need very careful handling."

"If there's any hope at all I'm willing to try. I'll make arrangements this end, and hopefully see you in Reading on Friday evening. It will be good to get away for a break – whatever happens," Katherine added bravely.

As Katherine put down the receiver her heart was thumping with excitement. It was impossible not to allow her hopes to rise. Karl had said he loved her.

The following Friday, on her way to Hereford to catch the train, Katherine stopped by her father's grave for a few minutes to say a quiet prayer for success in her mission. The peace of the churchyard on a damp, misty day steadied her nerves. It was almost the anniversary of her first meeting with Karl on just such a day last October. A grey day, but a momentous one. A day which marked a turning point in her life, changing her outlook and experience of the world completely. If it had not been for that day she would be Mrs Andrew Kellett by now. Now she never could be, no matter what hopes Andrew might still hold.

CHAPTER TWENTY

Karl opened the back door of the vicarage, wiped his feet on the mat and waited for the whoop of greeting from Tony and Pip. The warm kitchen was filled with the smell of baking, but empty of boys. Amelia was by the oven, taking out a tray of scones.

"Hello. Those smell good!" Karl looked up the deserted corridor. "Where are the boys?"

"Oh. Hello, Karl. They've gone out to tea," she explained, her back to him. She took out a sponge cake and put it next to the scones on a cooling rack. "Peter's out visiting some parishioners. It's rather quiet here at the moment. Would you like to go on through to the living room?" She turned to the pile of mixing bowls and utensils by the sink. "I'll join you in a few minutes, once I've tackled this lot."

Karl strolled along the corridor to the cloakroom and found clean soap for a change. The house had a completely different feel without its younger occupants. They had scolded him severely for not turning up last Sunday, and on Monday evening demanded an extra long game of ludo as a penance. He scrubbed his nails and found himself thinking of Siegfried. The boy would be almost four by now; old enough to enjoy a bit of rough and tumble with Ilse's husband. He ground his teeth at the thought. He *must* find Ilse!

Moving into the living room he stopped abruptly. He stared in disbelief at the lone figure by the fireplace. Her tired, anxious face cut through all thoughts of Ilse. His resolve crumbled. "Schatz!" Involuntarily his arms spread wide.

Katherine took her cue and ran into them.

No words were needed. They were content simply to hold each other close again, to relish the other's presence and to know that this time the pieces of their love fitted perfectly, with no rough edges left to snag. Karl surrendered readily to emotions which could no longer be denied.

"I should have listened to my heart," he murmured into her hair. "I told myself you would be much better off without me, that you would easily learn to live without me. I forgot that I could not live without you. When I saw you just then I felt so good, I could not fool myself any longer."

She looked up at him. "Don't try to explain, Liebling. I've been through the same doubts and questions myself, and ended up listening to my heart, with Robert's help. There must be no more looking back now. Only forward."

She could smell the fresh soap on his hands as his fingers brushed her lips. His head bent down to hers. His first kiss was reverent, a slow and mystical joining, his lips only lightly pressing on hers. To Katherine it evoked all the tenderness he had ever shown, the love and care he promised for the future. Their lips parted briefly before joining again. This time he did not hold back his passion. She responded in kind, relishing the familiar taste of him, jubilant she had won him back so easily.

He broke away at last, breathing hard. He stepped back so he could look at her, his arms resting lightly on her shoulders, fingers entwined in her soft hair. He pulled at a strand. "How soon can we marry?"

Katherine could not help uttering a gasp of delight at the swiftness of his decision. "As soon as possible!" She thought for a moment. "I know! How about your birthday? That's the week after Princess Elizabeth's wedding. We can hardly upstage her, can we?"

"Almost two months! So long?" He would have married her there and then if Peter Wilcox could oblige. "Of course we will need time to make arrangements and get permission." He leaned forwards and kissed her again, setting a seal on the exorcism of Ilse.

"I really didn't think it would be so easy," Katherine laughed as their lips parted. "Sarah was under the impression you would need more persuasion than that!"

Karl shrugged. "I tried to put you out of my mind. At first I was cross because she woke the memories and made me think about you all week. The more I thought, the more I missed you and the more I tried to comfort myself by thinking about Ilse. You came here at the right time. I was a fish waiting to be hooked."

"Or a sheep waiting to be penned!" Katherine laughed, remembering Sarah's observation. She blushed as a more intimate interpretation sprang to mind. "You are a bad influence on me, Liebling," she said to explain her red cheeks. "We'd better go and tell the others the good news before we get too carried away."

"Others? There is only Amelia here."

Katherine looked sheepish. "Sarah is waiting upstairs. She couldn't bear not to come too."

"I see. And I suppose Tony and Pip are out so that they could not tell me you were here. It's all a big ..."

"Conspiracy?" she laughed. "You're right. No one seems to be able to let us get on with things by ourselves!"

"Well, you must admit, Schatz, I seem to need help. I must learn to trust people. But first, as you said, we must tell Sarah and Amelia there will be a wedding soon."

Hand in hand they stepped into the hall. Katherine called up the stairs to Sarah. As they saw the radiant faces of Katherine and Karl, it was obvious to both women that the plan had been successful.

When Peter Wilcox came back a short time later, the house was already ringing to the sounds of merrymaking and Tony and Pip's squeals of enthusiastic delight.

"And may all their troubles be little ones," he whispered solemnly to his wife as he accepted a celebratory glass of sherry.

The day before his twenty-seventh birthday, Karl returned to Penchurch on a weekend pass, accompanied by Amelia, Pip and Tony. To his deep regret, Peter had parish commitments, but his heartiest good wishes and blessing for a long and happy marriage went with them.

The bus dropped them off at Cutbush Lane. The Murdochs had insisted on the Wilcox family being their guests for the weekend. Karl was given his old room at the front of the house for his last night as a batchelor. His Best Man, Robert, arrived later from London, in time to take Karl for a drink at the Walnut Tree.

Next morning at Lane Head Farm, Katherine and Sarah put the final touches to their parents' old bedroom. While Katherine hung her bluebell-wood picture over the bed, Sarah placed a vase of purple Michaelmas daisies on the dresser. She would be staying with the Murdochs tonight.

Donald and Gertie arrived at ten o'clock to help the girls with their last minute preparations and accompany them down to the church. Promptly at eleven Katherine processed proudly up the aisle on Donald's arm, with Sarah a few steps behind. They had chosen complementing dresses and hats of powder blue for Katherine, royal blue for Sarah. Princess Elizabeth wore white for her wedding, but Katherine had to be able to wear her dress again. She carried a simple bouquet of winter jasmine and the very last yellow rosebuds from Gertie's garden.

As she passed by she smiled at the guests who were distributed equally either side of the aisle. Her own relatives naturally sat on the left, but villagers made up the numbers on the right. Karl's only invited guests were the Wilcoxes, and Dr and Mrs Goldberg.

As she reached the chancel steps, where Karl waited in a borrowed navy suit, Katherine's heart finally began to flutter. She had remained reasonably calm all morning, but now the sight of Karl jolted her into realising that her wedding was actually taking place. She had not seen him since the weekend of their reunion in October, but here he was, looking handsomer than ever, in a colour which suited him so well, even though the cuffs and turn-ups fell a little short. The glance they shared told them the wait had been worth it.

As he spoke his marriage vows, Katherine listened for the conviction in his voice. She knew he was making no promises to a God he did not believe in. He looked directly into her eyes, his voice earnest and sincere. The ring he slipped onto her finger was the first he had given her, paid for from his own earnings. She treasured its gold simplicity far more than the glittering gems Andrew had given for their engagement.

The bells of St Michael and All Angels pealed their message across the valley as the couple stood in dim sunshine outside the church to receive the greetings and congratulations of the villagers. Mrs Tucker made a point of kissing the groom on the cheek, before doing the same to Katherine and murmuring: "Well done, "Mrs Driesler". You got him in the end!"

The reporter from the local newspaper was impressed by the general goodwill. Those who did not approve of the wedding stayed away. The Kelletts were invited out of diplomacy, but declined to attend. Audrey, soon herself to become Mrs Andrew Kellett, wanted to accept but thought better of it.

With no daughter of their own to provide a wedding for, the Murdochs volunteered their home for the reception. Katherine moved from one group to the next, sherry in hand, introducing her husband to his new relatives. Most of her mother's family lived around London and she was pleasantly surprised at how many had come all the way to Hereford. She suspected that their overwhelming curiosity to see Karl was the most plausible reason.

Gertie and Katherine had been cooking and baking for the past week. Cold cuts of beef, pies, even a dressed salmon adorned the dining table. On a side table stood the two-tiered cake.

One of Katherine's cousins, Edith Bagnold, dragged her eyes off the groom long enough to examine the cake. "Is that real icing?" she asked Katherine.

"Yes," Katherine laughed. "But I can't believe today is real!"

Later, as she and Karl formally cut the cake, Katherine's rapture was apparent to all. She continued cutting as Karl handed round plates of cake. Tony and Pip Wilcox were first in line. His obvious care for the two boys made Katherine determined the top layer of the cake would be eaten at a Christening within a year.

The Best Man's speech made brief allusion to this likelihood, along with his own message to the happy couple.

"Those of you here who know me will appreciate the thanks I want to express to Karl for the help he gave me at a time when I had forgotten what life was all about. The small part I was able to play in helping to bring him and Katherine together is something I shall always be grateful for. Although these two were made for each other, this was not always obvious to them!"

Karl winced and reached for Katherine's hand. Robert had told him the format of an English wedding, that the groom usually made a speech of thanks, while the Best Man could say whatever he wanted, but Karl was unprepared for Robert's finale.

"There are four telegrams from people who could not make it here today," Robert continued, holding up the forms. He read out the first from an elderly uncle and aunt of Katherine's who were too frail to travel. The second was from a cousin who had just had a baby. "Now these next two might have given me some trouble, but I managed to find someone to help me with them," Robert announced, displaying the two remaining telegrams. "According to our good friend, Samuel Goldberg ..." He waved to the corner where the doctor sat. "... this one reads: Heartiest congratulations to Karl and Katherine on the occasion of their marriage, from the inmates of Stedwick Camp."

There was a murmur of approval around the room from the assembled guests. Katherine squeezed Karl's hand to show how pleased she was. He seemed surprised at the telegram's origin.

With a grin at Karl, Robert held up the fourth telegram. "And last, but certainly not least, this one translates thus: On this day we may not see you, but our love can reach you both. Congratulations, Karl and Katherine, from all your family in Germany."

All eyes were on Karl as he digested the words. He dropped his head for a moment, eyes closed, and cast his thoughts to Medebach. It was only for a few seconds, but in that time he travelled there and back, sure in the knowledge that his family was thinking of him.

Katherine blinked away a tear. Her new family had reached out and embraced her as surely as if they had been right here in the room. She had known of the telegram's arrival, since it was delivered to the farm that morning, but deliberately had not mentioned it to Karl. Earlier during the afternoon she had wished she had, especially since during his speech he had made reference to the fact that neither bride's nor groom's parents were there. Now she was glad she had not. Its impact on him was remarkable to watch.

Karl allowed his emotions to settle down before he looked with brightened eyes around the room. Everywhere he saw beaming smiles.

"One day soon we'll be able to go there," Katherine promised.

Night had fallen by the time Robert loaded Karl's kitbag into the Austin and tied a bundle of tin cans to the rear bumper. The guests pulled on coats and hats to wave off the newly-weds on their short drive back to Lane Head.

With hugs, kisses, handshakes and thanks finally completed, the Austin pulled out of the drive with Katherine at the wheel. They drove in contented silence up to the farm, where Joss barked his welcome and came running to offer his own affectionate greeting.

Karl rekindled his acquaintance with Joss then took a deep breath of sheep-scented air. "Mmmm. It's good to be back! It seems so long since I was here." He unloaded his bag from the car, whisked Katherine up into his arms and carried his bride over the threshold of Lane Head Farm.

But there were chores to be done before they could settle down for the evening. Karl went upstairs to change out of his suit while Katherine filled the kettle. She waited impatiently for him to return from tending to the animals. It was odd seeing Karl in a suit, almost like seeing a stranger again. Suddenly it occurred to her that she did not know whether her own husband smoked now, or not. She asked him, as they sat down to tea in the familiar cosiness of the kitchen.

"No," he replied to her question. "I stopped smoking as soon as I remembered why I gave it up before. I've never spoken of those times to you, Schatz. I never will. You know enough about me to explain my sometimes strange behaviour. Please, never ask me about it."

Katherine nodded, annoyed at herself for spoiling the festive mood of the day. She was beginning to feel impatient for the delights she knew were to come. "It's only eight o'clock but I feel tired after all the excitement," she hinted.

"Are you trying to tell me something, Mrs Driesler?" Karl asked. With a smile she rose from the table. He followed her up the stairs and into what had, until that day, been her parents' room.

"Only that I love you," she replied, as he unbuttoned her dress and let it fall to the floor.

As they lay cradled together in the darkness, watching clouds scudding across the starry sky, Katherine asked: "Do you know what I wish, Liebling?"

"That I didn't have to go back tomorrow?" he guessed.

"Well, yes, of course," she agreed, "but I wish too our parents could have been there to see us married."

"But your parents were there, weren't they?" he asked in surprise. "Don't you believe that they watch over you?"

"Yes, of course I do, you oaf!" she said, digging him lightheartedly in the ribs. "You know what I meant. In person." She cuddled closer to him again under the bedclothes. "At least my father met you. Your parents have never even seen their new daughter-in-law."

"One day they will. Perhaps we should have another wedding celebration in Medebach, for my family to enjoy?"

"That sounds like a lovely idea," Katherine sighed happily, running her fingers over the lump on his collar bone. "I'd better start learning some German."

"*Wenn du willst,*" he grinned.

ABOUT THE AUTHOR

Caron Harrison was born and raised in Epsom, Surrey. She was educated at Rosebery Grammar School and the University of Durham before commencing a short period of work with British Telecom. Marriage to an RAF doctor brought numerous house moves and overseas postings to Cyprus and Germany whilst trying to write *Shades of Grey* and its sequel, *Divided Loyalties*. She is now settled on the Isle of Man with her husband and two daughters.